PRAISE FOR *TACKLE!*

'The perfect antidote to the real world, full of warmth,
wit and Rupert Campbell-Black'
Sunday Express

'A breathless plot that . . . sizzles with all
the scandal, scheming and saucy shenanigans
a reader could hope for'
Mail on Sunday

'I felt my mood perceptibly improve over the few days
of reading . . . The only problem with *Tackle!* is that you
have to ration yourself or you'll gobble it up in one go'
Telegraph

'Cooper's appeal is her ability to guide you into a
dazzling world you might otherwise never see'
The Times

'The queen of British bonkbusters'
The Economist

'Clever and enormous fun to read'
i newspaper

'A total treat'
Daily Mail

www.penguin.co.uk

Jilly Cooper is a journalist, author and media superstar. The author of many number one bestselling books, she lives in Gloucestershire.

She has been awarded honorary doctorates by the Universities of Gloucestershire and Anglia Ruskin, and won the inaugural Comedy Women in Print lifetime achievement award in 2019. She was also appointed DBE in 2024 for services to literature and charity.

Also by Jilly Cooper

FICTION	Riders
	Rivals
	Polo
	The Man Who Made Husbands
	Jealous
	Appassionata
	Score!
	Pandora
	Wicked!
	Jump!
	Mount!
NON-FICTION	How to Stay Married
	How to Survive from Nine to Five
	Jolly Super
	Men and Supermen
	Jolly Super Too
	Women and Superwomen
	Work and Wedlock
	Jolly Superlative
	Super Men and Super Women
	Super Jilly
	Class
	Super Cooper
	Intelligent and Loyal
	Jolly Marsupial
	Animals in War
	The Common Years
	Hotfoot to Zabriskie Point (with
	Patrick Lichfield)
	How to Survive Christmas
	Turn Right at the Spotted Dog
	Angels Rush In
	Araminta's Wedding
	Between the Covers
CHILDREN'S BOOKS	Little Mabel
	Little Mabel's Great Escape
	Little Mabel Wins
	Little Mabel Saves the Day
ROMANCE	Emily
	Bella
	Harriet
	Octavia
	Prudence
	Imogen
	Lisa & Co
ANTHOLOGIES	The British in Love
	Violets and Vinegar

TACKLE!

JILLY COOPER

PENGUIN BOOKS

TRANSWORLD PUBLISHERS
Penguin Random House, One Embassy Gardens,
8 Viaduct Gardens, London SW11 7BW
www.penguin.co.uk

Transworld is part of the Penguin Random House group of companies
whose addresses can be found at global.penguinrandomhouse.com

First published in Great Britain in 2023 by Bantam
an imprint of Transworld Publishers
Penguin paperback edition published 2024

A CIP catalogue record for this book
is available from the British Library.

ISBN
9780552177849

Typeset in 11/13.5pt New Baskerville by Jouve (UK), Milton Keynes.
Printed and bound in Great Britain by Clays Ltd, Elcograf S.p.A.

The authorized representative in the EEA is Penguin Random House Ireland,
Morrison Chambers, 32 Nassau Street, Dublin D02 YH68.

Penguin Random House is committed to a sustainable future
for our business, our readers and our planet. This book is made
from Forest Stewardship Council® certified paper.

To my grandsons, Jago, Lysander and Acer Tarrant,
and my granddaughters, Scarlett and Sienna Cooper,
with huge love and pride

CAST OF CHARACTERS

JAMIE ABELARD   Gay journalist at the *Cotchester Times*, likes laying out pages.

EDDIE ALDERTON   Rupert Campbell-Black's grandson, gilded brat, poster boy and flat-racing jockey.

PARIS ALVASTON   Dora Belvedon's boyfriend. Ice-cool Adonis, recent first in Classics at Cambridge, very good writer, also forging highly successful acting career.

MARTIN BANCROFT   Appalling fundraising creep and Etta Edwards's son.

HARMONY BATES   Rupert's very good but rather large Assistant Head Lass.

Dora Belvedon

Twenty-two-year-old smart cookie, besotted with horses, dogs and Paris Alvaston. Also Rupert's ghostwriter and press officer.

Jupiter Belvedon

Dora's much older brother. Art dealer and Tory MP for Cotchester.

James Benson

Rupert's very expensive private doctor, later enlisted to administer to Searston football players.

Alan Bordesco

Vermelho's golden-haired goalkeeper.

Wilfie Bradford

Very small, whippet-quick Searston Rovers forward who's absolutely crazy about horse racing.

Mary Bradford

Wilfie's sweet mother, who has single-handedly raised her children and works all hours as a cleaner to make ends meet.

DOUGIE BRADFORD	Wilfie's vile bully of a father who only returns home to plunder Wilfie's wages and beat him up if he plays badly.
ADRIAN CAMPBELL-BLACK	Rupert's younger brother, owner of Chelsea Art Gallery.
RUPERT CAMPBELL-BLACK	Ex-world showjumping champion. Hugely successful owner/trainer/breeder. Tory Minister for Sport in the eighties. Despite reaching sixty and being as bloody-minded as he is beautiful, he's still Nirvana for most women.
TAGGIE CAMPBELL-BLACK	His second wife, an angel. Recently suffered an operation for breast cancer.
BIANCA CAMPBELL-BLACK	Rupert and Taggie's ravishing adopted Colombian daughter. Lives with Feral Jackson, a rising football star. Party animal and shopaholic, Bianca is not intellectually endowed.

MARCUS CAMPBELL-BLACK	Rupert's son from his first marriage and a world-famous concert pianist.
RUBEN CARLOS	Sneaky Vermelho midfielder known as the Weasel.
JACKIE CARSLAKE	Editor of the *Cotchester Times*.
DOLPHY CARTER	Incredibly talented, very young and shy member of Deansgate Football Academy. Formerly in horrendous children's home. Longs above all for a family.
MIDAS CHANNING	Older, rather chubby but smiling Searston striker. Once of great promise, everything he touched turned to goals. Keen gambler, struggling to keep up a huge mortgage.
CHARMAINE CHANNING	Known as Charm. Attempts a more upper-class accent, calling her husband 'Maydus'.

CHARLIE	Searston Rovers masseur, very good at applying man-tan.
CHEFFIE	Chief cook at Searston Rovers.
BASTIAN CLARK-ROGERS	Uppity young Searston Rovers and ex-England Under-Eighteen forward, already writing his autobiography.
DAFFODIL CLARK-ROGERS	Deeply daffy Wag, who later in the story marries Bastian. Daffy gets wildly excited by a sign saying 'POSH CAR BOOT SALE', expecting David Beckham to be manning a stall.
GEMINI COATES	Pretty counsellor at Searston Rovers, employed to sort out players' mental health problems.
ABNER COHEN	Very rich and powerful rabbi.
RUTH COHEN	His loving wife.

ELIJAH COHEN	Their son, who, much to their disapproval, became a football player, and later a manager when a horrific injury put him out of the game. Now manages Deansgate Academy, which caters for players under eighteen.
MADISON COHEN	Elijah's wife and token leftie.
ISAIAH AND NAOMI COHEN	Elijah and Madison's children.
TOMMY DOWNING	Potentially dazzling Searston forward, whose ethos is, 'If you're drowning, swim out to sea.' Given to punching other players and telling the manager and ref they've made a cock-up.
JOSEF DROZA	Brilliant Searston midfielder from the Czech Republic, whom manager Ryan Edwards keeps endlessly on the bench, punishing him for making a pass at Ryan's teenage daughter, Princess Kayley.

LLOYD DUDSBRIDGE	Chief Constable of Rutshire.
LYALL DUDSBRIDGE	His son, who has far-fetched ambitions to be a professional footballer – nicknamed Lout.
VALENT EDWARDS	Yorkshireman of the people, ex-Premier League and England megastar. His hawk-like goalkeeper eyes have since found gaps in every money market, making him a major player on the financial world stage. Later, ace at coaching goalkeepers.
ETTA EDWARDS	His adored second wife, a brilliant gardener. She and Valent are co-owners with Rupert Campbell-Black of flat racing's World Cup winner Master Quickly.
RYAN EDWARDS	Valent's son. Intransigent and very socially ambitious manager of Searston Rovers.

DINAH JEPSON-EDWARDS	Ryan's very bossy, redheaded wife, who refers to herself as Dinah-mite and imposes her will on other Wags.
OTLEY JEPSON-EDWARDS	Dinah and Ryan's teenage son, now at Bagley Hall, a local public school, and shaping up as a moderate footballer.
KAYLEY JEPSON-EDWARDS	Ryan's 'Little Princess'. Also at Bagley Hall.
SIR CRAIG EYNSHAM	Chairman and owner of Deansgate Football Club and hugely successful inventor of different products. Highly ambitious, he is determined Deansgate will go up to the Premier League, playground of the world's billionaires.
LADY GRACE EYNSHAM	Almost more up herself than Sir Craig. Keen tennis player, bossy-boots and social mountaineer.
ALAN GARCIA	Highly successful but dodgy footballers' agent. Very bung-ho.

FACUNDO GONZALES	Brilliant Argentinian footballer who later joins Searston Rovers on a massive salary and expects other players to provide both goal and girl opportunities.
BOWEN GRIFFITHS (GRIFFY)	Lovely older Searston player, henpecked and utterly exhausted by his model wife, Inez, who expects him to do all the housework and the shopping, look after their children and iron all her expensive clothes.
INEZ GRIFFITHS	A model who is not a model wife.
LADDY HEYWOOD	Brilliant, handsome and priapic Deansgate forward.
BARNEY HUGHES	Ace sports reporter on the *Cotchester Times*.
FERAL JACKSON	Star striker and playmaker, living with Bianca Campbell-Black. Brave and beautiful but insecure about dyslexia and very troubled background.

NANCY JACKSON	Feral Jackson's mother, fighting drug addiction.
LUDOVIC KING	Older Searston defender. Not prepared to sacrifice his social life, so often takes hangovers on to the field. Adoring fans sing: 'Ludovictorious, happy and glorious.' King of banter. If the manager tells him: 'You were shit today,' Ludovic will crack back: 'That's not what your wife said last night.'
KITSY	Searston kit man.
GAVIN LATTON	Rupert Campbell-Black's assistant trainer. Mutually in love with Gala Millburn, Rupert's leading work rider.
COLONEL TERENCE LIGHTFOOT	Pompous chairman of Drobenham Football Club.

JANEY LLOYD-FOXE	Billy Lloyd-Foxe's widow. A sexy, totally unprincipled journalist, on the hunt for a rich new husband, and hell-bent on bringing down Rupert Campbell-Black.
LOUISA MALONE	Very pretty Penscombe stable lass, known as Lou-Easy because she's so free with her favours.
BRUISER BEN MARTIN	Drobenham's centre forward, massive 6 ft 6 in. brute, known as Big Ben.
ZEUS MARTINEZ	Megastar manager of Portuguese team Vermelho.
EZRA MATTA	Adorable Searston Rovers defender from Nigeria. Great player but scatty and always losing things. Also having had his pin number tattooed on his arm so he can remember it, he cannot understand why he never seems to have any money in the bank.

ANGUS MCLEAN	Searston full back and bully. Known as Anger Management.
MIMI MCLEAN	His lovely wife, who unaccountably adores him. Teaches GCSE English at nearby Larkminster Comp and permanently takes work home, even marking essays during football matches.
MARKETA MELNIK	Gorgeous, volatile, voluptuous Penscombe stable lass from the Czech Republic who dotes on the opposite sex. She and Louisa Malone are inseparable, specialising in threesomes, giggling over escapades: 'What was he like in bed?' 'Can't remember, I was too busy reading his tattoos. I love reading in bed.'
GALA MILLBURN	Rupert's leading work rider.
SUSAN MORECAMBE	Executive Chair of the Integrity Committee of the General Football Council.

JARRED MORELAND	Ruthless, crooked, sadistic Director of Football at Deansgate.
AHMED NELSON	Heroic Searston midfielder from Sierra Leone.
MILES NEWALL	Senior Searston defender. Frightful bore, known as Know-All because he's always banging on about past achievements.
EAMONN O'CONNOR	Horse and football-mad Irish charmer who moves into Penscombe as bouncer, chauffeur and general factotum.
SHELAGH O'CONNOR	Eamonn's adored and adoring wife, ex-cancer nurse at Cotchester hospital, who joins her husband at Penscombe Court to look after Taggie and help run the house.
ORION ONSLOW	Very gifted Searston forward. Own clothes range with a million followers. Hates training, prefers to rely on natural talent. Outlandish behaviour redeemed by a sense of humour.

ALPHONSO PACHINO	Freelance South American pilot.
PETER PARKINSON	Known as Parks. Searston Rovers captain and one-time great defender but slowing up. Warrior on the pitch, nicest person off it.
ROSALIE PARKINSON	Parks's incredibly tactless wife. Always tells Wags their husbands are about to be sacked or are being unfaithful. Rosalie, who runs a boutique in Cotchester High Street, gets asked to parties because everyone loves her husband. When she and Dinah-mite Edwards arrive at a party at the same time, it's known as a 'bitch invasion'.
WILSON PHIPPS	Known as Tipsy Phipsy. Manager of Deansgate, who drinks heavily to relieve the stress of the job.

BARRY PITT	Known as Pitt Bully. Searston goalkeeper. Very vocal, famous for his distribution skills as well as his goal-stopping abilities.
SANDRA PITT	His cuddly, blonde wife, known as Sand Pitt, who doesn't work but has had a lot of work done on her.
TIMON AND SAPPHIRE RANNALDINI	Rupert's eight- and six-year-old grandchildren.
GALGO RODRIGUES	Lightning-fast Spanish forward playing for Searston Rovers, who's very slow at learning English.
NARCISCO ROMANO	Vainest player. Deansgate forward, known as Moan of the Match because he's always grumbling.
MITCHELL SIMPSON	'Groundsy', brilliant groundsman, keeps Deansgate pitch like a billiard table. So attractive he's also known as Grounds for Divorce Man, but loves his wife and children.

HARRY STANTON-HARCOURT	Very promising member of the football team at Bagley Hall. Winner of numerous 'Fastest Boy' medals. Quiet and gentle manner conceals burning ambition. Nicknamed Hooray Harry.
LADY EMMA STANTON-HARCOURT	Harry's beautiful, divorced mother who lives in a crumbling stately home. Reluctant to marry again as it would mean relinquishing her title.
ERIC STEVAS	Hugely rich initial chairman of Searston Rovers. Refuses to invest in the club. Trousers any takings.
BYRON STOCKWELL	A glamorous and accomplished Deansgate goalkeeper known as Stopwell.
LARK TOLLAND	Very pretty and loving Penscombe stable lass, blissfully betrothed to Eddie Alderton.
GHENGIS TONG	Hong Kong aeroplane trillionaire, creator of the Green Galloper, a little plane that can carry one horse and several humans.

JAN VAN DAVENTER	A handsome South African who helped Taggie Campbell-Black at Penscombe Court. Now in prison for many years for trying to murder Rupert and fatally sabotaging so many of his horses.
JEAN JACQUES VOLTAIRE	Vermelho's star striker.
PETER WAINWRIGHT	Very successful, recently retired football manager of Larkminster Rovers, gave Feral Jackson his first break.
SEPTEMBER WEST	Nicknamed Tember, adorable secretary to the chairman of Searston Rovers. Possessor of lovely long red hair and a tawny-gold complexion, reminiscent of autumn. Cherishes any unhappy player.
CADENZA WESTERHAM	Glamorous, talented and opportunistic photographer on the *Cotchester Times*.

1

Rupert Campbell-Black, despite being one of the most successful owner/trainers and one of the handsomest men in the world, was in the darkest of places. His adored wife, Taggie, had just endured a gruelling operation for breast cancer and would shortly undergo chemotherapy.

He had also recently discovered that Jan Van Daventer, his dotty father's South African carer, who'd helped run Rupert's very large Penscombe Court, had only ingratiated himself into the household because he was convinced one of Rupert's ancestors in the eighteenth century had robbed him of his birthright, consisting of a vast estate and fortune.

As a result of Jan's clandestine sabotage, the stud psychopath, a stallion called Titus Andronicus, had been let out of his pen and savaged to death Rupert's beloved leading sire, Love Rat. Jan had also orchestrated the kidnapping of Rupert's other favourite horse, the yard mascot, Safety Car, sending Safety on a nightmare journey across Europe before he was rescued in the nick of time from a slaughterhouse in Italy.

Finally, Rupert's equally beloved black Labrador, Banquo, was suffering from a broken leg, having been chucked down a ravine in a nearby wood. This had happened when Jan had tried to murder Rupert because he was madly in love with – and determined to marry – Rupert's wife, Taggie. Luckily, Jan had only succeeded in cracking Rupert's ribs and puncturing his lungs, before a tipped-off local CID stormed in and arrested him.

Rupert, an accomplished gambler, had some years ago had a successful bet that, as a very mature student, he could pass a GCSE in English Literature. Having acquired a B grade as well as a fondness for Shakespeare, he now recalled Scene Five, Act IV of *Hamlet*:

'When sorrows come, they come not single spies, but in battalions.'

It was a measure of Taggie's extreme unselfishness that she had been so desperate not to distract Rupert when one of Love Rat's last colts, Master Quickly, was competing in the World Cup in Dubai, that she had not revealed to him that she'd been diagnosed with cancer, not even that she was undergoing a lumpectomy operation. But, wised up to this in Dubai by one of his work riders, an utterly devastated Rupert had jetted straight home to Taggie in hospital. The only redeeming feature being that although Rupert had missed the World Cup, Master Quickly had won the race.

As so many of Rupert's other horses had come first in earlier races in Dubai, he had been reluctantly persuaded to attend a parade of Master Quickly and other victorious horses and riders through the nearby Cotswold villages, ending up with a big party at Rupert's local, the Dog and Trumpet, which was attended by a mass of media.

Escaping from the revels to get back to Taggie, Rupert drove through the little village of Penscombe, with its church spire and ash-blonde cottages, and swung into his long drive, which was lit on either side by the white candles of an avenue of horse chestnut trees. Below on the left, a lake glittered azure in the late April sunshine.

Ahead, dominating the valley, was Penscombe Court, his beautiful gold Queen Anne house, sheltered from behind by a great green halo of beech woods, which were carpeted by bluebells fighting for space against a Milky Way of white wild garlic flowers.

Beyond the house and garden, stretching down the valley, lay a huge yard for horses in training and half a dozen royal-blue-and-emerald-green lorries bearing the words 'Rupert Campbell-Black Racing'. Further on was a stud where his stallions lived and strutted their stuff; barns for visiting mares, mares in foal or with foals; cottages for staff and tenants; and a helicopter pad and hangar. Beyond stretched a tangle of flat and downhill gallops for all weathers and distances, and all around were lush paddocks with plenty of shade for every kind of racehorse.

Penscombe Court had been in the Campbell-Black family for more than 250 years but it had been Rupert, with his vision and unceasing and stupendous labours, who had created this empire. But what was the point of an empire, Rupert thought with a shiver, without its empress. *Oh, please God, keep Taggie safe.*

Reaching home, however, Rupert found his wife, who'd only just returned from hospital, sitting out on the terrace in a pale-blue poncho, her mane of black hair lifting in the breeze, her huge silver eyes sparkling, looking happier than she had in weeks.

'Look, Rupert, look at the old boy,' Taggie called out as she pointed to the field below, where a miraculously recovered favourite horse, Safety Car, dark brown with one ear and a straggly tail, was gingerly playing football with Rupert's yapping Jack Russells, Cuthbert and Gilchrist.

An equally delighted Rupert was just asking Taggie whether she was warm enough and had she had any lunch, when the telephone rang in the kitchen.

'I'll answer it,' cried Taggie.

'I'll just check the yard. Don't let Safety Car overdo it,' said Rupert. 'Then I'll be in.'

The call was from their twenty-one-year-old daughter, Bianca, who lived in Australia with a Black English footballer called Feral Jackson. Bianca was ecstatic that Ryan Edwards, the son of World Cup-winning Master Quickly's co-owner, Valent Edwards, and the manager of nearby football club Searston Rovers, wanted to buy Feral to help Searston – nicknamed the Gallopers – go up to the Premier League next season.

'Several other Premier League teams are putting out feelers for Feral,' crowed Bianca, 'and he and I can come back and live in Gloucestershire and look after you and Daddy.

'Also,' Bianca added, 'I know Daddy's heartbroken over Love Rat dying, but it would give him a huge new interest to take shares in Searston Rovers, co-manage the club with Valent and Ryan and help them buy some really good players.'

'Only if he can sign up Safety Car,' said Taggie.

*

Visits to the yard always took longer than intended. Rupert returned to the kitchen, which had low beams, windows overlooking the valley and yard, and every surface weighed down by 'Get well soon, Taggie' cards and even yellow buckets from the yard filled with flowers. Here, he found his wife sharing a dilapidated rust-brown sofa with Forester, her brindle greyhound; Purrpuss, a fluffy black cat who was Master Quickly's stable companion; and poor Labrador Banquo, with his leg in plaster, who thumped his tail as Rupert approached.

'Isn't it brilliant, darling,' cried Taggie, putting down the telephone, then, in her deep voice with its soft Irish accent, relaying the conversation she'd had with Bianca.

'Everyone wants Feral, he and Bianca would come home again, and you'd have fun running a football club.'

Although pleased to see Taggie looking even happier, with a flush of colour in her pale, wasted cheeks, Rupert was less keen on the idea. Now bloody Jan Van Daventer was inside, he'd have to find someone to run their very large house, because the most important thing was to keep the pressure off Taggie, particularly as she was soon to go through chemo. Bianca was a sex-and-shopping party animal who'd fill the place with chaos and A-lister friends. And his daughter Tabitha and Taggie's sister Caitlin would use this as an excuse to dump their children as well.

Rupert, whose cracked ribs were killing him, topped up the dogs' bowls and his own large glass of whiskey with water, and said he was extremely fond of Bianca's boyfriend, Feral, 'but not of football – all those players skipping around like ballerinas and having group sex every time someone scores a goal'.

And with Feral having been brought up in a nearby slum area, the Shakespeare Estate, with a mother who was a temporarily reformed heroin addict, and her lover, a pernicious drug pusher who was currently inside, Rupert felt Feral and Bianca were much safer in Perth. Whereupon Taggie brimmed up: 'I know it sounds awful, but once I found out I had cancer, I panicked that I might die and never again see Bianca or Xav' – Bianca's brother, who lived in Pakistan.

Disentangling her from the menagerie on the sofa, taking her sobbing into his arms, Rupert was appalled by the corrugated sharpness of her ribs. How could he be so fucking selfish? As soon as Ryan Edwards's father, Valent, was back from China, where he had been investigating the bloodstock market, he'd go and see him about Searston Rovers buying Feral.

2

Valent Edwards, now in his seventies, was a football legend, still remembered for his last-minute save which enabled his team, West Riding, to win the FA Cup. Having retired from the sport, he now lived in Badger's Court, a beautiful eighteenth-century house, whose garden his wife, Etta, had transformed, and which was now a rainbow riot of spring flowers.

Valent was a modest man, so the extent of his football glories was confined to an extended cockpit at the bottom of the garden, which was where he welcomed Rupert two days later. Here, every cabinet was filled with glittering trophies, dominated by a replica of the FA Cup trailing blue and white West Riding ribbons, signed footballs, Player of the Year accolades and Golden Glove awards for goalkeeping, and shirts swapped with Bobby Moore, Rodney Marsh and Bobby Charlton. The walls were covered in medals and photographs of victories, including one of the triumphant West Riding team on an open-topped bus tour through Wharfedale, all wearing dark glasses.

'We'd been partying all the night before,' explained Valent, 'so we were bluddy hoong-over.'

Having kept more 'clean sheets', football slang for matches where he hadn't let in any goals, than any other England keeper, Valent, on retirement, had found niches in markets all over the financial world and become exceptionally rich.

Rupert was very fond of Valent, who for some years had kept horses with him, including co-owning Master Quickly and a grey stallion, Master Quickly's brother, called New Year's Dave. Black-browed, square-jawed, handsome in a strong-featured, friendly bulldog way, Valent made no attempt to hide his Yorkshire accent, but had disguised the fact he had put on weight since his marriage by wearing his red-checked shirt out-side his trousers. Madly in love with Etta, his newish wife, he displayed her photograph on his desk, beside a vase of red roses. Rupert thought Etta was a drip but hid the fact from Valent. Also on the desk was a picture of Ryan, Valent's son from his first marriage.

'I gather your son wants to buy my future son-in-law, for Searston Rovers,' said Rupert, accepting a cup of black coffee.

'Correction,' countered Valent, 'Ryan wants to buy *back* your future son-in-law. Feral, as you know, played for Ryan before he went to Perth. Ryan thinks the world of Feral – he's just the striker Searston need, and when Stevie Gerrard and Alan Hansen were playing in some testimonial there recently, they made a special journey to watch the lad. Ryan needs to nail him before the Premier League do.'

'He'd do better in the Premier League; he'd get more money. Bianca's wildly expensive, although she claimed to Taggie that Searston would soon be up in the top rung anyway.'

Valent shook his head. Bianca, who never listened, had got everything wrong. Searston were actually bottom of the third rung, League One, with only four games to go in the season ending on 22 May, and therefore the bookies' favourite for relegation.

'Even more reasons for Feral to go to some club miles away,' said Rupert. 'He's a lovely boy, but he's got some very unsavoury connections – mother a drug addict, in and out of rehab, went on the game to support Feral and his brothers and sisters. They're all grown up now, but Feral sends them all money.'

'He's a local boy,' said Valent, 'the fans like that.'

'Not coming from the Shakespeare Estate, where they can hardly afford tickets, and the place is so rough – needles and chewing gum all over the pavements – that none of the fast-food firms will deliver there. Feral also has a police record,' Rupert added. 'He was in a young offenders' unit for several months for mugging passers-by and pulling knives on other pupils, and we don't want the press digging all that up.'

Valent, however, was not to be deflected.

'Let's go and have a spot of lunch at Searston and watch the match,' he said, donning a blazer and threading a red rose from the vase into the buttonhole.

'Etta created this rose for me,' he added proudly. 'It's called Valent Edwards and it's in all the catalogues.'

'"My love is like a red, red rose,"' observed Rupert. 'Should be white, as you're from Yorkshire. Who owns Searston Rovers?'

'Chap called Eric Stevas. English football's the world's leading playground for billionaires. Stevas made a bomb in hedge funds, got a jet, five houses and several companies. But he longs to be a celeb, like a lot of businessmen, and get asked to charity balls, mix with A-listers on the red carpet and have fans singing his name.'

When Rupert had been Tory Minister for Sport back in the eighties, he had dramatically reduced football hooliganism, which had consisted of riots after both semi-finals in the FA Cup, petrol bombs being thrown at the police, two policemen stabbed, cars overturned and endless people rushed to hospital. But, coming out of politics, he had lost interest in the game. Now he asked:

'What sort of money would Feral get in the Premier League?'

'If he's any good – which he is – a hundred thousand, perhaps two hundred thousand pounds.'

'A year?'

'No, a week.'

'Christ, he can keep me! It's more than Titus Andronicus gets for a shag. Mind you, Bianca could spend that in a day.' He grinned at Valent. 'I could sell the more successful players some horses and introduce them to failure. No wonder you're so rich.'

'Different in my day,' said Valent, waving at Etta in the kitchen window as he and Rupert climbed into his dark-blue Bentley. 'Lucky if you got two hundred pounds a week when I started. Stevas assumed Searston would go up to the Championship in his first season and the Premier League in the next, and he'd make a fortune. Now he's paying himself five million a year, and refusing to let Ryan refurbish the squad and buy Feral. Sponsors have all dropped out. Merchandise sales are non-existent. He's just sold a player for ten million and trousered the lot. He's already halved the players' wages and hasn't paid for the two lads bought in January. Even had the fooking cheek to suggest I put in twenty million so he could trouser that too. The fans detest him. He's got his own song but not one he wants.

'"Oh, Mr Stevas,"' Valent sang in a deep baritone, '"we think you're grievous, why don't you leave us." Morale's rock bottom and if they go down, my Ryan's bound to get the sack, and he's a first-rate manager. On the other hand, the club's favourite for relegation so we might pick it up very cheap in a couple of days and, gal-vanised by new owners, they might win or draw the next three games and stay up.'

As they drove out of Valent's village of Willowood, with its thousand willows rippling in the late-April sun-shine, celandines and primroses were starring the verges, but a bitter east wind was stripping the cherry trees, so their white petals snowed down on the car.

'The only other footy club round here is Deansgate, four from the top in League One and very likely to go up to the Championship. It's owned by Craig Eynsham.'

'That prat,' snapped Rupert.

'Done well,' said Valent. 'Three hundred and some-thing in the *Sunday Times* Rich List. Copies all over his house, opened at his name.'

'Bastard wants to slap des res on everything,' said Rupert.

Valent, whose hugely successful housing company, Attractive and Affordable, had cleaned up with first-time buyers, didn't respond.

'Bastard's always claiming great chunks of our adjoin-ing land are his and wants to divert a motorway through mine,' went on Rupert.

'He can have a prat race with Searston's Stevas, then.'

As they drove through the lovely town of Cotchester, the assault on the High Street was noticeable: shops shut or closing down, even charity shops and cafes empty.

'That hotel's going belly up,' said Valent. 'University's very undersubscribed. *Cotchester Times* is losing circulation. Needs a good football team to pull in the punters. When Brighton and Hove were promoted the year before last, the contribution to the city's economy was two hundred and twelve million. This would be a bluddy miracle for Cotchester.'

Searston itself, two miles on, had pretty Cotswold gold houses round a village green, a post office, an antiques shop and a pub called the Running Fox. Searston's ground, named Deep Woods, lay half a mile away, in a wooded valley with tall trees lining the rickety East Stand, which looked across to a green hillock on which a flock of sheep were grazing above another row of larches lining the back of an even more rickety West Stand. The pitch itself looked almost as much brown mud as green.

As they left Valent's Bentley in the players' car park, however, Rupert expressed surprise at the number of Ferraris and Porsches.

'Looks more like a Formula One rally.'

'Footballers can always afford cars,' said Valent.

Inside, the dilapidated club had paint peeling everywhere, doors loose on their hinges, scuffed carpets and dark and cramped dressing rooms.

An hour before kick-off, Searston, in ruby and purple colours, and opposition Crowfield, in dark green, were gently limbering up, rolling on their backs on the grass, stretching different muscles and dancing back and forth across the pitch. With their streaked blond curls, flying dreadlocks and white partings across dark hair like aeroplane trails, Rupert again thought how poncy they looked, particularly as so many of them had necks and arms so heavily tattooed that they appeared to be wearing women's paisley dresses beneath their short-sleeved shirts.

Three match officials in black shirts were jogging round the pitch – keeping fit so they could scarper if things got nasty, thought Rupert.

Quite a crowd had already gathered. Valent always felt upstaged, both mentally and physically, when he went to the races with the outstandingly handsome and famous Rupert. Now he enjoyed being the star of the show as onlookers nudged each other and nodded in his direction, and rushed forward for selfies. Even the players looked over in excitement.

Second sets of goalposts had been temporarily added at each end, to enable the players to practise shooting into them and not further rough up the ground between the main goalposts. And when Valent went down to chat to the Searston team and stood in goal, idly stopping every ball with his lace-up leather shoes, everyone laughed and cheered.

As Rupert waited on the touchline, a player with a shaved head called out:

'Didn't you used to play for Wolves?'

'No, but I was one,' shouted back Rupert.

The laughter that greeted this died as Ryan Edwards came out of the tunnel and barked at his players that they'd better get kitted out. He then turned to greet his father and Rupert, handing them programmes and a team sheet and telling them that their pre-match lunch was ready in the Directors' Lounge.

Ryan was indeed good-looking, with glossy dark-brown hair, a high smooth forehead and features less pugnacious than Valent's. There were also black circles under his slightly-too-close-together dark-brown eyes, and a muscle flickered in his clenched jaw. *Not someone who sleeps well at night*, reckoned Rupert.

'Rupert'd luv to talk about Feral,' murmured Valent.

'Not now,' snapped Ryan. 'Later in the week – that's if I'm still here.'

All around the ground, spectators were reading reports on their iPhones, predicting Ryan's demise.

Valent put a hand on his son's arm.

'Won't coom to that. Is Stevas cooming?'

'No, he's in the States. Doesn't bother to attend matches any more.'

Ryan had a very put-on voice, decided Rupert.

In the Directors' Lounge, which had an entire window looking over the pitch, directors from both Searston and Crowfield stood around, forking up food, but not mixing with each other. The home-side top brass, however, immediately drew Valent aside.

Rupert was starving, having had only two cups of black coffee for breakfast. Seeing him standing alone, a tall girl with long gold-red hair, large hazel eyes, tawny freckled skin and a full, sweetly smiling mouth, came over and introduced herself.

'I'm September West; everyone calls me Tember. I work for the chairman. Would you like a drink?'

'I could murder a triple whiskey,' admitted Rupert.

'I'm afraid we don't offer alcohol. Ryan doesn't like the players drinking, but hang on a sec.'

She returned a couple of minutes later, saying, 'Black tea,' and handing him a mug full of whiskey.

Almost worse, on offer for lunch were only quinoa and avocados, with totally bland chicken and pasta. After a couple of mouthfuls, Rupert put down his plate, vowing that if he and Valent bought the club, they would provide booze and decent grub.

'Ryan's passionate about diet,' confided Tember, 'particularly for the players.' Then she whispered, 'I bought some salmon and cream cheese sandwiches on the way in. Would you like some?' And she handed him a plate covered with a napkin.

'Thanks, angel,' said Rupert, vowing Tember would certainly stay on if they bought the club.

When it was time for kick-off, Valent sidled up, saying he wanted to go on networking with the non-playing staff and other directors.

'I don't want you to appear too involved, or Stevas will jack up the price, so I'll leave you with luvly Tember.'

'That's no hardship,' said Rupert.

3

In the quarter-full stand, Rupert and Tember took up seats at the end of a row, out of earshot of most of the spectators.

'Now you can give me the gossip about the players.'

'Oh dear,' sighed Tember. 'The sheep in the field opposite have gone behind the trees. We only tend to win when they're visible.'

'Perhaps they don't like watching boring games,' said Rupert. 'He's useless,' he added, five minutes later, as a Searston striker clouted the ball above the crossbar for the second time, 'and that midfielder . . . but that boy's bloody good,' as a little redhead hurtled through the pack, smiting the ball into the Crowfield goal so the leaping goalkeeper only just managed to stop it with wildly outstretched fingers. 'Looks like one of those children players lead on at kick-off.'

'Wilfie Bradford – he's adorable,' whispered Tember. 'Mother's a sweet single parent, horrible drunken father returns intermittently and beats Wilfie up if we don't win, which is most of the time, sadly. Wilfie's mad about racing, always sidling towards the touchline to ask who won the three forty-five. He'd adore to meet you.'

Listening to Rupert's comments, Tember realised he was as instinctive about football as he was about racing.

'Crowds want goals so you've always got to attack; it's the same with racing. You wait for the gaps and power through them to finish first. Footballers have got to get the ball between the posts, end of.'

Rupert also noticed a very good-looking but very pale Searston defender, with dark straight-back-and-sides hair, who seemed to have difficulty keeping up with the Crowfield forward he was marking, because he kept glancing up in their direction. Rupert surmised that Searston created chances but struggled to convert them. They desperately needed a decent striker like Feral.

'Who's the geriatric?'

'Miles Newall, known as Know-All because he's always saying, "That reminds me . . ." and going into a flurry of memories.'

'And who's he? The pale, dark and handsome one without any tattoos?'

'Bowen Griffiths, known as Griffy. He's a darling, a real gent, with a lazy tart for a wife. She makes him do all the housework,' said Tember, angrily, 'and get up in the night if the children are crying so she can get her beauty sleep, because she's a model. He's exhausted, poor man. And what's so cruel is the players have nick-named him Iron Man, because they were on a run past his home and, looking in at the kitchen window, found him ironing one of his wife's dresses. It's not funny.'

'And who's he, the shaggy one with long fair hair and a beard?'

'Ludovic King, another darling, brilliant defender, but not prepared to sacrifice his social life, so sometimes he brings his hangovers on to the pitch. Terribly kind to newcomers and very funny, but he's getting to the stage where his body won't go where his brain tells him. And Stevas has outlawed long-term contracts for veteran players. Fans adore him, though. Just listen.'

'Ludovictorious, happy and glorious, long to reign over us, God save our king,' sang the Searston Rovers supporters, as Ludovic belted the ball miles up the field to a blond Searston striker, who promptly gave it away to a Crowfield defender.

'That striker's useless,' said Rupert. 'He'll have to go too.'

'Bastian Clark-Rogers,' laughed Tember. 'Rather up himself. Captained England's Under-Eighteens last year. Yesterday he asked me to type out his autobiography, which he calls *The Hauteur Biography*.'

'At seventeen?'

'He's eighteen now but says he'll be too old to write it at twenty-three,' Tember giggled. 'He's not polite enough to the older players like Griffy and Parkinson, the captain. Calls them Grandpa.' Tember's tummy gave a thunderous rumble.

'Who's the red-haired midfielder who never stops shouting?' asked Rupert.

'Angus McLean, known as Anger Management. He's a thug, a bully and a letch. Avoid him in training if you don't want to get injured. Comes out first thing smothered in scarves and balaclavas, so young players don't know it's him. Clouts the ball into the nettles for them to retrieve.'

'Absolute sweetheart, then.' Rupert consulted the team sheet again. 'And Midas Channing?'

Tember giggled and lowered her voice even further:

'Known as Chubby Hubby because he tends to put on weight. He's got a shopaholic wife called Charmaine, known as Charm, who'll tell you, "May husband Maydus is a strayker. We met on-layne." Poor Maydus, who loves betting, is also fretting about his huge mortgage. Charm would like him to score more goals, so she can be Queen Wag and her children can stay at pray-vate school. God, I'm a bitch . . .'

'Is Charm here?' asked Rupert.

Tember shook her head. 'None of them are. Wags don't like losing.'

Then, as a player scorched past: 'That's Galgo Rodrigues, Spanish, even faster than Wilfie, but desperately homesick. I must find him some nice digs. And the handsome one on the bench is Josef Droza from the Czech Republic. Ryan insists he wears an Alice band to keep his long curls out of his eyes. Ryan won't play him, punishing him for making a pass at Ryan's teenage daughter, Princess Kayley, who wears so much make-up she looks about twenty-five. Poor Josef – he's known as the Pouncing Czech. And the fans keep singing: "If you pounce on Princess Kayley, you're off to the Old Bailey." '

As Rupert started to laugh, he noticed the pale older player with no tattoos – Griffy, was it? – still glancing in their direction, and missing several balls. He was obviously very interested in Tember, whose tummy gave another loud rumble. Those salmon sandwiches had been her lunch, Rupert realised. Her long hair lifting in the breeze was the same red as his beech woods in autumn. She was well named September: she was like a lovely gentle autumn, not quite in her first youth; in her early thirties, he thought.

Watching Ryan pacing up and down the oblong section halfway down the touchline, known as the technical area, barking louder and louder instructions to his players, Rupert wondered how many of them took in what he was saying. They were not playing as a team.

Demoralised by the prospect of relegation, Searston lost 3–0 to a chorus of boos. 'You'll lose your crown, you're going down,' sang the Crowfield fans, mockingly.

'Poor boys,' sighed Tember. 'I'm afraid I've been horribly indiscreet. But you're so lovely to talk to.'

'Where do you live?'

'In Searston; I've got a cottage next to the antiques shop, so I can keep an eye on goings-on at the club.'

'How long have you worked here?'

'About ten years. Before awful Stevas arrived, I worked for the previous chairman, who was another darling. He died horribly of cancer and begged me to stay on to look after the players. He was so brave. Oh God.' Her eyes widened. 'I'm so sorry. How's Taggie?'

'She's sort of OK. You must come and have supper with us to pay you back for giving me your lunch. I think your boys might perk up if they had a less anaemic diet.'

He was amused, however, as he and Valent reached the car park, to see three of the young Searston players, Galgo, Bastian and Josef, behind the raised boot of a car, stuffing themselves with pizza.

Next moment, little Wilfie, the redhead, had raced up.

'Oh, Mr Campbell-Black, can I have a selfie with you?

I'm so pleased Master Quickly won the World Cup. I had fifty pounds on him.'

Rupert's arms were much longer, so he held out Wilfie's iPhone to capture them both.

'Fanks so much,' cried Wilfie, 'and give Quickly a pat.'

'That was a fooking awful game,' said Valent as he drove Rupert back to Badger's Court, 'but at least Stevas should drop his price. Let's go and have a proper drink in the Cockpit.'

'OK,' said Rupert, 'I'll just ring Taggie and say I'll be back for supper.'

After a second large whiskey, Valent became more reflective.

'Football was all I thought of. Playing in the back streets of Brudford from dawn till long after dark when I was a lad. When I retired, I missed the buzz of playing in front of sixty thousand people each week. Missed the daily training, the banter in the dressing room. I missed my West Riding teammates, the ecstasy of winning, even the agony of defeat. So, when it all ended, I cried my eyes out, then sooblimated by channelling all my energies into pulling off business deals, to try and forget.'

'Very successfully,' said Rupert. 'I felt exactly the same when I gave up showjumping.'

'Like to get back into football. And Searston's near enough for me to get back to Etta. Nor would you have to leave Taggie.'

'I do have a yard and stud to run.'

'Won't be too much work. We can sort out the

business side, there's some good blokes there we can keep on, and Ryan can organise the players.'

Hmmm, thought Rupert.

'We'd better get moving,' said Valent. 'Roman Abramovich bought Chelsea in four days.'

4

Rupert, as he had pointed out, had a yard and a stud to run, four hundred employees dependent on him for their livelihood, and the flat-racing season hotting up with the first classic races for three-year-olds at Newmarket on the first weekend in May.

The 2000 Guineas had always been open to fillies as well as colts. But as fillies had scarcely ever won, they were seldom entered. This year, however, a lone filly, one of his beloved late leading sire Love Rat's last foals, the aptly named Delectable, who'd achieved glory scorching home in the Dubai World Cup Sprint in March, had been boldly entered by Rupert. He also had another last Love Rat foal called Fast Piece running in the fillies-only 1000 Guineas the following day.

He was very loath to leave Taggie, who was still very weak and dreading the onset of chemo in June, but she tearfully insisted he went on both days.

'Just think how wonderful it would be if Delectable beat the boys. She so adores you and would be heartbroken if you weren't there. And you must be there to cheer on Fast Piece. Love Rat will be looking down on you from heaven.'

'OK, I'll go,' said Rupert, hugging her and getting out a blue-spotted silk handkerchief to wipe her eyes, 'but I'll fly home tonight between the two races, and I promise you, my darling, once your treatment starts, I won't leave your side for a second.'

'But you've got so much to do,' sobbed Taggie.

'Nothing remotely as important and precious as you.'

Rupert's lawyer, Marti Gluckstein, and Valent were still wrestling with the endless complications of trying to buy Searston Rovers, and although aware that Taggie was praying for this to happen so Ryan could buy Feral and he and Bianca would come home, Rupert couldn't work up any real enthusiasm, particularly when he landed his dark-blue helicopter at Newmarket, which on cold days was the bleakest, most wind-savaged place on earth, a vast open grassland punctuated only by a few trees.

Today, however, blessed by an unexpected May heat-wave, it had been transformed into a green and pleasant paradise, stretching to infinity beneath a vast blue sky. Huge crowds were enhanced by women out for the first time in their prettiest summer dresses.

Guineas runners were being led round the parade ring, luxuriating in the hot sun on their backs. None gleamed glossier than little chestnut Delectable, who'd inherited her sire's blond mane, and who, as the only filly in the race, was being eyed up by all the colts.

Wearing a dark suit and a trilby pulled down over his nose, Rupert tried to slide into the packed parade ring unnoticed, to avoid the inevitable frenzy of flashing cameras that invariably greeted him and which would unsettle Delectable before the race.

But the first to spy her master was Delectable, who gave a great whicker of joy and tugged Lark, Rupert's pretty stable lass, through the throng of press, owners and trainers to reach him, and started to nuzzle his pockets for Polos.

The crowd roared with laughter and gave a great cheer as Rupert petted his filly, checked her tack and straightened her blonde forelock. As the jockeys came out in their coloured silks, punters as well as press were soon pestering him about her chances.

Rupert shrugged. 'She's forty to one and might be in the frame.'

'Any chance of a double?' asked the *Racing Post.*

'I hope so. Delectable is much more biddable than Quickly.'

This was a reference to last year's 2000 Guineas, when Rupert and Valent's World Cup winner, Master Quickly, yet another Love Rat foal, had held up the race, bolting two furlongs back round the course before being coaxed back into the starting stalls and trouncing all the other runners, establishing a course record of one minute and thirty-four seconds.

Quickly had been ridden by Rupert's grandson Eddie Alderton, who was also riding Delectable today, but who hadn't appeared, even though the other jockeys were already mounting their horses.

'Where the hell is he?' snapped Rupert.

'I'm here,' laughed Eddie, who was almost as beautiful and wicked as his grandfather had been in his youth, and who proceeded to seize pretty Lark and kiss her long and passionately on the mouth before jumping on to Delectable.

'Stop fucking about,' snarled Rupert, who'd had a dangerously large bet.

'Delectable will be a piece of gateau after Quickly,'

said Eddie, wiping Lark's pale-pink lipstick off with the back of his hand, 'and I should be allowed to kiss my future wife.'

'Let her make her own pace,' Rupert ordered him, 'and don't use that whip or I'll use it on you.' Then, turning to a blushing Lark as she led Eddie and Delectable off to the course:

'Are you sure you want to marry him?'

As he retreated to the owners' and trainers' stand to watch the race, Rupert was touched that so many people commiserated with him on Love Rat's death and sent special love to Taggie, hoping she was OK.

And, happily, unlike her refractory half-brother Master Quickly, Delectable went straight into the starting stalls and flew out down the course. Being so little, she could weave through the gaps, gradually gaining ground.

Rupert was ecstatic. 'Look at her! Come on, little girl, come on,' he yelled, and he had to forgive Eddie for the boy was riding like an angel, keeping his weight off the filly as much as possible but helping her forward with the thrusts of his body. Despite the flailing whips of the other jockeys, Delectable held off every colt and flashed past the post, two lengths ahead. The crowd went berserk as Lark, sobbing with delight, ran down the course to meet them, and Eddie gave her another passionate kiss.

Half the photographers were concentrating on them; others, hearing his shout of joy, captured the euphoria transforming Rupert's normally deadpan face, and he hardly noticed the pain as congratulatory fellow owners and trainers clouted him on his cracked ribs.

Immediately, Rupert's mobile rang and it was Taggie.

'Oh darling, congratulations, wasn't she wonderful? Brave little girl, and didn't Eddie ride her beautifully, and all the dogs barked and wagged to see you on telly. Oh, well done.'

'It's brilliant. You OK, darling? I'll ring you back,' replied Rupert as he ran downstairs to welcome Delectable, being led into the winner's enclosure to a fanfare of trumpets.

As he was posing for photographs with Lark, a weighed-in Eddie and Delectable, his mobile rang again. It was Dora Belvedon, his press officer. 'Wasn't she brilliant, beating all the boys? What a victory for feminism.'

'I'll ring you back.' And Rupert returned to telling the reporters what a great team he had.

Finally, as he went up to accept the most beautiful silver plate, which would later be engraved, and the cheers rang round Newmarket, raising the sky-blue roof, Rupert was wondering if he could ever fall in love with any other sport, when his mobile rang yet again.

'Just going up to the Royal Box to see the race,' he said. 'I'll ring you back.'

'We've got it,' said a jubilant voice.

'Got what?'

'Searston Rovers,' crowed Valent. 'Marti done fantastic. Beat the buggers down to twenty million.'

Thank God I had a big bet on Delectable, thought Rupert.

'Talk to Marti,' went on Valent.

'Well done,' said Rupert, trying to work up some enthusiasm.

'This is still subject to approval from the FA and the Football League that you're fit and proper persons,' explained Marti Gluckstein, 'but with Valent's financial track record and legendary football status, and your massive success as an owner/trainer, no one can doubt you've got sufficient funds to invest further in the club and are fit for purpose.'

'Fit for Purrpuss,' said Rupert, thinking of Master Quickly's cat stable companion. Then he said he'd brief press officer Dora to wait a couple of days before releasing the info.

He wished he could stay in Newmarket at his favourite hotel, the Bedford Lodge, and celebrate into the small hours with Eddie, Lark and the rest of the team, then get up late for tomorrow's three races, including Fast Piece in the Guineas.

Instead, he had to fly home and get up to return to Newmarket at the crack of dawn. Then he looked down at the Love Rat cufflinks, which Taggie had especially commissioned Theo Fennell to design for him, and knew he must get back to her.

Meanwhile, back in the Cotswolds, press officer Dora, despite being told by Rupert to hold off, was so excited by the news that she'd decided to strike while the iron was so hot. She'd nearly finished her press release about the most powerful combo of financial supremo and legendary goalkeeper Valent Edwards and the greatest owner/ trainer, Rupert Campbell-Black, joining forces to bring football glory back to the Cotswolds. How fitting that Rupert, known as 'the handsomest man in the world' – perhaps she'd better change that to England – should now be enhancing the beautiful game. And how the two charismatic chairs would be cheering on their new team, Searston Rovers, against Drobenham tomorrow.

*

Having left riotous celebrations at Newmarket, Rupert was ashamed to be irritated when he got home to find Taggie reeling with happiness. Valent's wife, Etta, had dropped in with a huge bunch of red roses.

'She stayed for drinks and she's so looking forward to coming to Searston Rovers with me and us watching matches – two chairmen's wives together. I love being the wife of a chair,' she giggled. 'Oh, darling, thank you for buying Searston. I'm so excited about Bianca coming home, and Feral. Where do you think would be the best place for them to live? Perhaps they could have a flat in the West Wing, or even a cottage, so we don't overcrowd them.'

'Or them us,' said Rupert, thinking of Etta and all Bianca's A-list friends invading their space. He was so exhausted, even after two large whiskeys, that he could not do justice to Taggie's boeuf stroganoff, one of his favourites.

'Anyway, you should not be cooking; we must get someone to run the house.'

'Darling Etta said she could drop in whenever we need her.'

' "Unbidden guests are often welcomest when they are gone",' reflected Rupert. How did Shakespeare always get things right?

Even when he fell into their huge red-curtained four-poster bed and switched off his mobile, Rupert's cracked ribs were giving him such hell that he only slept fitfully. Getting up, he found the whole world seemed to have retweeted Dora's press release, along with a vitriolic tweet from his detested near neighbour, Sir Craig Eynsham, which had also gone viral.

'How could Rupert Campbell-Black, the rudest, most

ungentlemanly bully in the world, possibly bring foot-balling glory to the Cotswolds? Talk about Prince Charmless – particularly appropriate when Searston play-ers, like Cinderella, are invariably late for the ball.'

The media, although praising Delectable's victory in the Guineas, had weighed in on the football front with horror and amazement.

'We all know Rupert loves dogs, but do he and Valent Edwards really have to buy a pup?' wrote Martin Samuel in the *Daily Mail*, describing Searston as the worst team in the league and red-hot favourites for relegation.

The left-wing papers were even ruder. They'd had enough flak from Rupert over the years, and were delighted to have a chance to put the boot in.

Rupert switched off his iPhone and was leaving the house for the helicopter pad, when the landline rang.

It was the *Mirror*: 'Hi, Prince Charmless.'

'Fuck off,' snarled Rupert, hanging up.

5

Climbing into his helicopter, Rupert turned his phone back on and switched it to silent, but increasingly throughout the flight he could see messages piling up and calls, particularly from Valent, pouring in. Landing at Newmarket, he thought, *Sod it*, and rang Valent back.

'Dora ought to be shot.'

'She's *your* press officer,' accused Valent.

'Not for any longer.'

Valent wasn't entirely displeased. There were too many pictures of Rupert with his arm round the Guineas winner, captioned 'Who's the most delectable?', and not enough of himself. He was also excited to be back in football and desperate to save Searston and Ryan's job.

'Who are Searston playing today?' asked Rupert.

'Drobenham, from Surrey. Bluddy good team, joint top of League One, and determined to go up to the Championship. Directors a lot of pompous arses in blazers and old school ties. They beat us five–one at their place.'

Rupert had reached the Newmarket stables and a whickering dark brown, Fast Piece.

'I've got to go, Valent.'

'See you at Searston later.'

'Can't bloody make it. I've got three runners, including the Guineas.'

'You've got to bluddy well get back for the game. The lads will be totally demoralised by the media coverage. They've only got three games to go and need seven points, at least, for safety. Unless we get a point tonight, we've had it. We've got to be there to rally the troops. Guineas is at three forty-five; you'll easily get back. Game doesn't start till seven forty-five. Do you honestly want to blow twenty million pounds?'

'I'll have to have a bloody large bet.'

'I'm about to spend several hours sharpening up our goalie, Barry Pitt, at the training ground, so you can fookin' get back.'

But Rupert had rung off. He was not going to be bossed around by Valent.

Waiting for the first race to start, however, he looked at his mobile again to check things at the yard. Instantly, it rang. Rupert recognised the soft, sweet voice of Searston's club secretary, Tember West.

'Congratulations on yesterday, Rupert. Little Delectable did so well – what a darling – and good luck with Fast Piece. And I'm over the moon you and Valent have bought Searston. I know it's a huge gamble, but we do have some great players; everyone's so excited. Particularly the Wags – they can't believe it. Charm is particularly delayted.'

'Good.'

There was a long pause.

'But the players are so demoralised by the press and worried about the future. Please come this evening; it would be such a boost to our morale. Please, please, Rupert. We're fighting for survival.'

There was an even longer pause.

'OK, I'll be there, but on one condition. I need you and I to have twenty minutes beforehand on the telephone, for another briefing about the players. And I want you with me when I meet them so I can distinguish Iron Man from Anger Management. And rustle up a couple of bottles of Moët and two dozen paper cups, or I won't come.'

'Ryan will go ballistic, but anything for you, Rupert.'

'And you're the only person who could persuade me to go to Searston.'

After the vast blue-sky roof and endless green open space of Newmarket, Searston, with its high surrounding woods, seemed depressingly claustrophobic. Having spent an hour checking on Taggie and being briefed by Tember, Rupert drove into the club only forty-five minutes before kick-off on another mild and lovely evening. He was pleased to see the huge if adverse publicity had brought a vastly increased crowd. The place swarmed with media as well as Wags from Searston and Drobenham, and wives and girlfriends of fans, who usually had no interest in football but had come to gawp at Rupert, who'd taken off his tie and was wearing a dark-blue jersey over his lucky blue-and-emerald-striped shirt.

He was greeted by Tember, who was looking lovely in a clinging dress the colour of marigolds, and who was accompanied by Luigi, a member of the kitchen staff.

'Ryan will have a fit,' she murmured, brandishing a carrier bag containing the paper cups and Moët. 'Luigi here,' she said, 'is going to open them.'

'I'll take the blame,' said Rupert, taking the bag from her, as they went into the dressing room. Here, kitted out, nervous-looking players were being revved up by Valent. Drobenham evidently had a lethal box-to-box player called Bruiser Martin, who could defend one moment, then hurtle up the pitch to score the next, on whom Valent was advocating putting three defenders to mark him. Both he and Ryan looked at their watches, boot-faced at Rupert's last-minute arrival.

'I'd like to introduce our new fellow chairman, Rupert Campbell-Black,' announced Valent.

Rupert, having dumped the carrier bag on a nearby table, slowly looked round at the players, then smiled, and it was as though the midday sun had invaded the dark room.

'Good evening, gentlemen. I'm sorry about the absolutely appalling press, which I'm sure you've all read.'

'Galgo can't read,' piped up little Wilfie, 'nor Josef – English, I mean.'

The team tittered nervously.

'Appalling press,' went on Rupert, 'but I hope it will fire you up to fight for your lives tonight. Martin Samuel in the *Mail* accused me of buying a pup. I love puppies, but they don't win football matches. This evening you've got to fight like a pack of fully grown Rottweilers, and guard your goal like Alsatians. One of the greatest pleasures in life is making the press look stupid, and that's what you're going to do tonight. To make a Rottie happy, you must give him a bone. To make a player happy, give him a bonus.' Then, as the players started to laugh: 'I gather your last chairman halved your salary, which will go back up if you win today, and if Searston avoid relegation, you'll get a decent bonus. And this is a pop talk, not a pep talk.' A resounding bang made them all jump as Luigi opened one of the bottles.

Aware of the outrage on Ryan's face, Tember was nervously handing out paper cups to the players. Rupert picked up the bottle and started filling them.

'What the hell do you think you're doing?' exploded Ryan. 'You can't give them bubbly!'

Rupert smiled. 'As your new chairman, I can do anything I like.' Hearing the centuries of disdain in his voice, and fed up with Ryan's constant carping, the players all grinned.

'They're only having one drink,' added Rupert to an equally outraged Valent, 'just to kick-start our first game together. Having a few drops to avoid the drop.' Handing the bottle to Luigi to carry on filling, he went around the dressing room, shaking very sweaty palms, starting with Peter Parkinson.

'Hi, Parks. Hell being a captain, so hard to score goals and concentrate on your own game when you've got to keep an eye on and worry about the rest of the team. I had the same problem with the British showjumping team. And you're Griffy, the great midfielder, and Midas, the star striker who turns everything to goals. I gather you've got a wife called Charm – wonder how she'll get on with Prince Charmless? And you're Angus McLean, who defends as ferociously as he attacks.'

Noting the surprise and delight on each player's face as he recognised them, Tember stayed close.

'Who's this?' he murmured as they reached an older player with a man bun and a middle parting like a maiden aunt.

'Miles Newall, known as Know-All,' whispered Tember.

'I remember we met at Elland Road,' announced

Miles, 'when you were Minister for Sport, sorting out hooliganism. There was a riot when I scored in injury time, and you congratulated me, and another time . . .'

'Tell me later.' Rupert took the bottle and emptied it into Ludovic King's cup, as Luigi opened the second bottle. 'Hello, Ludo, the great defender. Nothing gets past you and a good customer at Bar Sinister, I gather from my mate Bas Baddingham, who owns it. He'll be delighted when we start winning and fans pour into Cotchester.'

Then, turning to Barry Pitt, who had a shiny shaved head in contrast to a thick light-brown beard: 'Hi Barry, hope your workout with Valent wasn't too exhausting. He certainly knows his stuff. Goalkeepers have to be six foot and thick-skinned, because mistakes are so fatal. Found the same when I was showjumping – clear round's no good if you catch the last bar of the treble.'

Barry grinned. 'I'm a pitbull not a Rottie, hope that's OK.'

'As long as you frighten the opposition with growling.'

Then, turning to a young player who was checking his blond curls in the mirror: 'How's your *Hauteur Biography* going?'

'OK,' said Bastian in amazement. 'I'm not sure how to end it.'

'With us winning the Premier League.'

'You written yours yet, guv?'

'No, my past's longer than the Bible and far too outrageous.'

Then he turned to little Wilfie, who said, 'Congratulations, boss. Delectable and Fast Piece winning their Guineas races. I had them both. Two on the trot.'

'Win tonight and you'll make it a hat-trick.'

'Delectable's to die for.'

'I love them both. Foals you breed yourself are like grandchildren, and much less noisy. You must come and meet them.'

'This is Galgo,' said Wilfie. 'His English isn't great.'

Rupert broke into fluent Spanish, asking Galgo what part of Spain he came from and saying how much he was looking forward to seeing him play, and that Taggie had a greyhound at home but they'd always wanted the Spanish equivalent, a galgo.

'My country do terrible thing to them,' sighed Galgo.

Miles Newall had just moved in to tell Rupert something else that he'd remembered, when Rupert turned to the Pouncing Czech, Josef Droza, and, as the *coup de grâce*, introduced himself, producing a page of notes from his Czech stable lass, Marketa, enabling him to say in Czech how much he loved Prague and the Pardubice, the huge jump race he'd won in the nineties.

'That was with Penscombe Pride,' said Josef. 'He fell the year before.'

'Well done!' said Rupert in amazement.

And handsome Josef was in heaven.

'That's enough,' roared Ryan. 'Go and warm up before you all get plastered.'

So Rupert reached back for his own paper cup on the table and raised it to the players. 'Here's to you all, Gallopers – best of luck.' Then, before draining it, he added: 'If you win, you can drink some more later.'

Tember then put 'Nessun Dorma' on the loudspeaker.

'I know this tune,' said Rupert. 'If you stay up, you can have a double bonus.'

Having drained their cups, the players set off up the tunnel.

'What a great bloke, knew all our names and all about us, speaking all those languages.'

Having put up with an increasingly intransigent Ryan as they lost match after match all season, they had loved seeing Rupert stand up to him. Ryan, in turn, was incandescent, particularly hearing the roars of laughter. They must all be pissed already and would be slaughtered by Drobenham, and he stormed out of the dressing room.

'Well.' A furious Valent glared at Rupert, who shrugged and raised his palms to heaven.

'You see, I can do charm when it's needed.'

'You'd better see it works,' snapped Valent.

Just as they were leaving, a tall young player with dark-gold dreadlocks erupted into the dressing room, shoving them aside, tearing a dark-green sweatshirt off his lean, beautiful body, then reaching down to unlace his trainers so he could tug off his jeans.

'Where the hell have you been?' yelled Valent.

'Caught up in horrendous traffic; I left an hour and a half ago. You'd think this was Wembley. Never seen such a crowd.'

'Before you subject us to a complete striptease, Tommy,' said Valent, 'you haven't met your new chairman, Rupert Campbell-Black.'

'Oh, sorry, hi guv.' Pulling a towel over his cock with one hand, the boy waved the other in Rupert's direction. 'Got to get changed and warm up.'

'Who's he?' asked Rupert as he and Tember set out for the Directors' Lounge.

'Tommy Downing – always late, probably gambling or sleeping off a hangover. Potentially the best player in the team and a great striker, but his fuse is short. Tends to tell refs they've made a cock-up, not polite enough to Ryan, who leaves him on the bench like Josef.'

'My grandson Eddie is like that. Always rolls up the following day, although he's vindicated himself winning the World Cup and both Guineas this year, and he's calmed down now he's going to marry a sweet girl. Perhaps you should find Downing a steady girlfriend.'

'He's got millions of unsteady ones; girls adore him.'

With Josef and Downing on the bench, they need a good striker like Feral more than ever, thought Rupert.

As Valent went off to get a sandwich, and Tember to sort out things in the office, Rupert took refuge in the directors' box overlooking the pitch, making notes. He listed other collapsing stands struggling to cope with a vastly increased crowd, rusty railings, invasive undergrowth, the dark, depressing home dressing room. No sheep in the field: 'Better get a collie,' he wrote. He also noticed people edging away from the Searston horse mascot. Its purple-and-ruby costume was split down the back to reveal a large red-trousered bottom, whose tail had been tugged off. Also, several front teeth were missing. No wonder even children were refusing to accept sweets from it. 'New mascot,' wrote Rupert.

Opening the programme, he found endless pictures of Ryan and various spiels from him. 'New programme, new manager,' wrote Rupert.

In the crowded press box, journos were tapping away on their laptops, and down below, press and television were milling around in search of celebrities. Rupert could see Dora Belvedon, his blonde, very young and pretty so-called press officer, chatting them up, plying them with drink and snacks, giving each one her card, promising interviews with Rupert in the future. 'He's a bit busy at the moment giving his new team a first pep talk.' She didn't, however, come and say hello to Rupert, so he couldn't give her the sack.

The directors' box was filling up. A bossy redhead plonked herself down next to him.

'I'm Dinah, Ryan's wife. People call me Dinah-mite. Do you remember, we met some years ago, when Ryan was managing Feral?'

Rupert didn't. Next moment, a rather aggressive-looking brunette in a yellow trouser suit, with a square jaw and a lot of red lipstick disguising a rather small mouth, plonked herself down on his other side.

'I'm Rosalie Parkinson, the captain's lady. I'm so cross with the press being so horrid to you, Rupert. "Prince Charmless" is so unkind. I do so hope, as our new chair, you're not too upset.'

'I've had worse,' said Rupert.

'I see your child bride, Taggie, from time to time in Cotchester.' Rosalie slipped a card into Rupert's trouser pocket. 'These are the details of my boutique in the High Street. Tell her to pop in, she'll always be welcome.'

'Boutique sucks, new captain's lady,' scribbled Rupert, remembering Tember had described her and Dinah-mite as the 'bitch invasion'.

Saying he'd see them later, he got up to join Tember and Valent in the front row.

6

Kick-off time. A crackling burst of music and the names of the players read over the loudspeaker as the teams ran on to the pitch. Drobenham first in garish orange, with the loudest cheer from their fans for a black-bearded giant with a cruel clenched mouth which only softened fractionally as its owner nodded hello to the ref.

'That's Bruiser Martin,' confided Tember. 'Foul piece of work, literally. Always makes it appear opposition's fouled him. Hand in glove with the ref.'

Searston Rovers in their ruby and purple stripes, running on to the accompaniment of the *Black Beauty* music, followed Drobenham on to the pitch, Ludo getting the loudest cheer and snatches of 'God Save Our King'.

Drobenham won the toss, so, in the first half, Barry Pitt had to play into a setting sun so bright that all the Searston fans in the East Stand had to pull their cloth caps down or shield brows with their hands. A gaggle of Wags in the next-door stand were taking it in turns to borrow a pair of binoculars to gaze at Rupert.

'Isn't he macho, just layke a movie star,' said Charm.

'I didn't know it was *the* Rupert Campbell-Black. He lives in a 'uge house at Penscombe. He's lush.'

'He's well fit.'

'Fit for what?'

'Me, hopefully?' to hyena cackles of mirth.

'Very up himself,' said a dark-haired beauty in an emerald-green Stetson. 'A friend of mine who used to ride out for him said he's a dictator.'

'Dick's the operative word. Bring him on, and that Valent's a hot bloke.'

'Grite player,' said Barry Pitt's wife, Sandra, nick-named Sand Pitt. 'Barry had a session with him this morning, learnt a lot.'

'Your pupils are learning a lot,' said Charm to Anger Management's sweet schoolmistress wife, Mimi, who was marking a great pile of essays and only half watching the players.

Kick-off, and tall, blond and handsome Downing got the ball.

'Don't do anything silly, Downsy,' yelled a fan.

'Does he ever do anything else?' shouted another fan, as Downing dribbled it down the field, shaking off pursuers, whereupon he unleashed a 25-yard thunderbolt which just missed the goalposts.

Scooping it up, the Drobenham goalie booted it back up the pitch to a prowling Bruiser Martin, who, shaking off the three players ordered to mark him, powered through Searston's weak defence and fired an Exocet with his left foot, which Barry Pitt, blinded by the sun, let in.

'Oh, Barry,' wailed Sand Pitt.

1–0 to Drobenham.

From then on, the rattled Searston players were so desperate to score, they kept missing the goalposts.

'Shambles, because they're all pissed,' fumed Ryan.

'Prince Charmless's pep talk has not worked,' wrote the *Mirror*.

'Would you describe Rupert's eyes as Cambridge blue or Oxford blue?' enquired Camilla Long.

'Whatever team, he's lost the boat race,' mocked the *Sun*.

Five minutes later, Griffy rescued the ball from the melee outside Searston's goal, but mistakenly passed it to a young Drobenham striker, who promptly hoofed it in.

2–0 to Drobenham.

'Oh, Griffy,' wailed Tember in anguish.

'For God's sake, Griffy,' yelled the beautiful Wag in the emerald-green Stetson.

'Who's she?' asked Rupert.

'Griffy's model wife, Inez. Such a bitch,' muttered Tember – who was quite keen on Griffy, reflected Rupert.

Half-time. As the sun set behind the West Stand, floodlights were coming on and more lights round the valley could be glimpsed twinkling through the woods. Ryan, in the dressing room, was bawling out the players.

In the Directors' Lounge, the Drobenham chairman introduced himself to Rupert as Terence Lightfoot. 'Congrats on the Guineas, Campbell-Black. How much would one make for two classics like that?'

Rupert shrugged. 'Close to six hundred thousand.'

'Bloody good. Mind you, a decent footballer can earn that and more in a month. Although you can't breed from him. Championship, where we'll surely be next season, players can earn thirty-five grand a week. New ball game for you. Think you'll pull it off?'

'Early days,' said Rupert.

In the second half, Drobenham were getting smug and deliberately wasting time – subbing player after player, playing possession football, kicking the ball back and forth to each other – behaviour that so enraged Searston that they put in some ferocious tackles, for which the ref, clearly on Drobenham's side, red-carded both Downing and Midas Channing. Searston were down to nine men.

Then Anger Management, determined to remedy the situation, took the ball up the field, avoiding two defenders, then giving a great roar of pain as an old hip injury kicked in. Effing and blinding, he collapsed on the grass and two physios, clutching black medical bags, rushed out to minister to him while the players belted back to the technical area for water and, in Searston's case, another bollocking from Ryan.

Meanwhile, a Drobenham poet had been at work. As a Drobenham fan with a lovely bass voice began singing, the ground fell silent.

> You'd better go back
> To racing, Campbell-Black.
> Poor old Searston
> Will end in tears soon.
> They're going down,
> You'll lose your crown.
> Poor Prince Charmless,
> Your side's quite harmless.

44

This was greeted by howls of laughter and tumultuous cheering from Drobenham fans, and smirks from Terence Lightfoot and his fellow directors.

'Bastards,' spat Tember. Rupert's face was quite expressionless.

As Angus hobbled off, supported by the physios, and with his wife, Mimi, putting away her lesson plan and looking worried, Ryan was forced to send on his third and last sub, Josef, not even bothering to give him an encouraging pat on the back.

'Still hasn't forgiven him for making a pass at Princess Kayley,' said Tember, furiously.

But immediately Josef came on, he gathered up the ball and passed to little Wilfie, who passed to Galgo, who, like his canine namesake, galloped down the left side and passed to a waiting Parks, who kicked the perfect assist between the posts, where a hovering Bastian headed it in.

'There is some use for your blond curls, Bastie,' howled a fan over the thunder of cheering.

Two minutes later, Josef passed to Ludo, who clouted in a 50-yard wonder goal. 2–2.

Both sides then tussled without goals. Twenty minutes left, the floodlighting was getting brighter and the shadows more menacing. The moon came over the roof of the East Stand to have a look.

'Give her something to cheer about, Gallopers,' shouted a fan.

Predictably, raising two fingers to him, Drobenham scored again: 3–2.

Searston were feeling too exhausted even to respond.

All round the ground, fans were checking their mobiles for other clubs' results, to see how Searston's relegation rivals were doing. Much too well. With no points from their game, the Gallopers would definitely go down.

Ryan was pacing about, chewing gum, swigging water. 'It was all that bugger Campbell-Black's fault for giving them the bubbly.'

Ninety minutes gone and despairing Searston fans were leaving their seats. Jubilant Drobenham fans, feeling sure of promotion, were staying put, particularly when their star player, Bruiser Martin, was certain to be named Man of the Match.

'Four minutes' injury time,' yelled the fourth official, holding up his board, at which Rupert flipped and, leaping to his feet, yelled: 'Come on, Gallopers, get off your fucking arses!'

'Pack it in, Rupert,' roared Valent, 'and sit down.'

Terence Lightfoot and the Drobenham directors were looking appalled and about to appeal. Searston, however, were galvanised.

'All right, boss,' shouted little Wilfie, no longer feeling tired, while Josef dived between two Drobenham forwards, hooked out the ball and dribbled it down the field, then passed to Captain Parks who, seeing a hurtling-down Wilfie, kicked a beautiful assist landing high in front of the goalposts. Wilfie was about to bash it in with his left foot, then, remembering Ryan always told him his left foot was useless, instead ducked slightly and headed it in. 3–3.

The Searston players were all racing down to hug Wilfie, when Captain Parks roared, 'We've still got ninety seconds.'

The ball was then played by the opposition from the

centre spot. Intercepting it, Ludo howled at Griffy and all the other defenders to get forward, leaving their own goal perilously exposed. Then, making the break himself, Ludo dispatched the ball down the field 20 yards ahead of Wilfie, who again ran so fast he caught up with it and, with one touch, passed to tall Josef. He raced on towards the goal, passing to Griffy, who, confronted by a large Drobenham midfielder, passed back to Josef. Whereupon an even larger, smugger, more butch Man of the Match Bruiser Martin came pounding towards him. 'Don't you fucking dare.'

Josef dared, kicking the ball to the right, and, running to the left around the bellowing bully, he collected the flying ball. Then, weaving between unprepared Drobenham defenders before catching their goalkeeper off-guard, he exquisitely curled the ball into the net.

There was a stunned silence, then the whistle blew.

Searston 4, Drobenham 3.

As Josef disappeared under a mountain of overjoyed, yelling teammates, and ecstatic Searston fans erupted on to the pitch, a laughing Rupert turned to a beaming Valent.

'I told you I could do charm.'

'You bluddy can. Let's go and congratulate the blokes and have some more of that boobly.'

Ryan, now facing the media, was looking very pleased with himself.

'Good result. Let's say the lads rallied. Didn't want me to lose my job.'

'That Josef Droza was superb,' said the *Western Daily Press*. 'Why don't you play him more?'

'I'm bringing him on slowly, letting him find his feet. Don't want him to lose confidence,' lied Ryan.

Rupert and Valent went on to the pitch to congratulate the players, still being photographed and interviewed. Wilfie and Josef were talking to Sky Sports, with Wilfie translating: 'They're saying it's very special to score your first goals for Searston, Josef. Yes, he says it is very special. His mother will be very pleased.'

Downing, despite being red-carded, was taking the top off a bottle of champagne with his beautiful teeth.

'Dora's done very well to get so many press here,' said Valent. 'You're not going to fire her?'

'Not today,' said Rupert, then patting Ludo on the back. 'Bloody good first result. Well done.'

'Only if we win the next two for you.'

'We're not a pup, we're staying up,' chorused the overjoyed Searston fans.

'Rupert, Rupert,' cried a descending tsunami of Wags.

'Sorry, ladies. It's a great result; you must be very proud of your boys. I've got to get back to Taggie,' said Rupert, and bolted.

Galvanised by such a thrilling unexpected victory, Searston did win their last two games and stayed up. No one was more delighted than Taggie that this would mean Ryan Edwards buying Feral to help Searston go up to the next league, the Championship, next season, and he and Bianca would come home.

To Rupert's delight, local rival Deansgate lost their play-off final at Wembley and didn't go up, this despite the fact that their hubristic chairman, Sir Craig Eynsham, had built a new stadium to accommodate a vastly increased Championship attendance and was so sure of victory that he'd ordered an open-top bus for him and his players to tour the Cotswolds, which had to be cancelled when they didn't win. Sir Craig was so incensed that he fired Pete Wainwright, his excellent manager, and appointed his deputy, Wilson Phipps, a heavy drinker known as Tipsy Phipsy, as caretaker manager.

7

Jackie Carslake, editor of the *Cotchester Times*, had been so impressed after reading Dora Belvedon's recent reports on Searston staying up that he had asked her if she'd like to work on his newspaper and had invited her for an interview.

Always kept short of pocket money by her bitch of a mother, Anthea, who was jealous of Dora's charm and insouciance, Dora had supported herself, her pony and her dog, often by flogging scurrilous stories to the nationals.

Before the interview, she'd taken a look at the *Cotchester Times* and found it seriously boring, and filled with so many pieces about people going on walks to raise money for charity that there couldn't be a blade of Cotswold grass unflattened.

Deliberating on what to wear to look enterprising, questing and smartish, she'd abandoned her usual kit of baseball cap, jeans with torn knees and trainers. She had then settled for a pale-blue cashmere jersey that Paris, her boyfriend, had given her for her twenty-first birthday, a dark-blue on-the-knee skirt, ankle boots with little heels, and her blonde curls restrained in a pony-tail. Having sprayed on some of Paris's aftershave, Bleu de Chanel, she had covered her fingers with ink to look more literary.

Jackie Carslake's office was messy, packed with files, newspapers and magazines. Racing at York was on the television, which he turned down. A half-read Ian Rankin novel was face down on his desk and an empty bottle of whiskey in the wastepaper bin. In his late forties, Jackie had merry, bloodshot eyes and good teeth, and was wearing horn-rimmed spectacles, jeans, and the same aftershave as Paris. Dora resisted the temptation to say 'Snap!' A secretary in ripped jeans brought them a cup of tea.

'So, you're Rupert's press officer, although they call themselves "heads of communications" now,' said Jackie.

'Sort of. I ghost his column in the *Racing Post*, and I ghosted a column in the *Mirror* for his National winner Mrs Wilkinson's stable companion, a goat called Chisolm, but she's retired now.'

'How would you like to kick off by writing a big piece for us on Rupert?'

'I can't. He wants to keep Taggie's cancer as private as possible, and even if he's in a really dark place now, he'd never pitch his tent there.' Dora's voice dropped. 'But he and Valent Edwards are going to be brilliant at running a football club – he's so good at swearing and he won all the big matches when he was managing the England polo team.'

Jackie's bloodshot eyes lit up. He was tempted to switch on his tape recorder.

'That's a great story. You can see Searston Football Club from that window.'

51

'Convenient – you don't even have to leave the office to cover their games!'

Getting to her feet, looking over the town to a wooded valley, goalposts and a stretch of patchy green pitch, Dora then said:

'Why don't you have more weddings in the *Cotchester Times*? Gav, Rupert's assistant trainer, is going to marry Gala, Rupert's best work rider. They got together during a victory shag after the World Cup. Also, Rupert's grandson Eddie Alderton, a fantastic jockey, is going to marry Lark, Rupert's prettiest stable lass. And my brother Jupiter is Tory MP for Cotchester; he's a bit twitchy about the press, but he could be a great one for some local stories.

'I so worry about the newspapers; we're in the twilight of journalism,' continued Dora, still gazing out of the window. 'So many papers are being closed down and they are the guardians of our democracy, particularly locally, looking after the vulnerable. Who will right the wrongs, if they close? Crime will blossom.' Her shrill voice trembled slightly. 'I'd like to create a great paper, full of stories exposing wrongdoers that people are gagging to read. The Cotswolds are also teeming with celebs behaving badly. And as Rupert's taken over Searston, new fans will flood in from miles around to gawp at him – so good for the local shops and hotels, so good for Cotchester, put them on the front page. Rupert knows everyone. When my brother Dickie was being bullied at Bagley Hall, Rupert cheered him up by arranging for him to meet David Beckham.

'Rupert's daughter Bianca is my best friend. She lives in Perth with a brilliant footballer called Feral Jackson, who Rupert and Valent have bought to play for Searston.

She's terribly indiscreet so she'll be a fantastic source of football gossip and she might marry Feral soon, so that'll be another wedding for you.'

Shaking his head, Jackie Carslake got a bottle of Sancerre out of the fridge and filled up two glasses.

'How old are you?'

'Twenty-two.'

'And where do you live?'

'In a little house called Pear Tree Cottage on Rupert's estate with my boyfriend, Paris Alvaston. He's a fantastic actor. He's just got a first in Classics at Cambridge. And he writes like an angel too, so I'm sure he'll write for you.' Dora's curls were escaping from her ponytail.

'Cheers,' said Jackie, half emptying his glass. 'I know I shouldn't ask this, but you're not going to have a baby and push off on maternity leave?'

'No, no, Paris is going to play Bassanio in *The Merchant of Venice* at Stratford.' Then, seeing two springer spaniels racing across the Rovers pitch in the distance, she said: 'If I get the job with you, I'd like to run a Dog of the Week piece. Here's my dog, Cadbury; he's a chocolate Labrador.' Dora showed Jackie a picture on her mobile. 'He's fifteen now, and very grey, but he always wins Dog with the Waggiest Tail at shows.

'Oh my God!' Dora gave a scream. 'Why don't we run a weekly column featuring footballers' wives, called "The Wag with the Dodgiest Tale"?'

'Brilliant.' Jackie roared with laughter. 'Although I'm not sure they'd admit that. Wags all seem to have jobs now, even degrees.'

'Who else works here?' asked Dora.

'Three reporters. Each does about five stories a day. Only one photographer, the public send in so many pics. She's called Cadenza, dangerously provocative, gets in anywhere – you and she should do great stories together.

'Then there's a gay guy called Abelard, who designs the paper, claims he likes laying out pages. Writes a bit, too. Jenny, the secretary, types and makes coffee, and a girl called Tricia – we call her Tissues, because she's always got issues – handles the ads, and finally an ace sports reporter, Barney Hughes, covers all sports, takes pictures as well. If it's the twilight of journalism, nine pages of football keep it very much alive.'

At that moment, Barney, who was sandy-haired, freckled and weather-beaten, wandered in.

'This is Dora Belvedon, Rupert Campbell-Black's press officer, who's going to also write for us about football.'

'Hi Dora,' said Barney. 'Interesting to see how Valent Edwards and Rupert work out; they're both such strong characters. And how they handle their great rivals, Deansgate. Craig Eynsham's a dickhead and goes ballistic if we don't mention his knighthood, even bought a rugby player by mistake last season. But be careful what you write about him – he's in bed with both Lloyd Dudsbridge, the Chief Constable, and the local planners. I nearly sent him a packet of brown envelopes for Christmas.' Then, when Dora burst out laughing: 'I'm so glad you're joining us.'

After he'd gone, Jackie told Dora the circulation of the *Cotchester Times* was 67,000 online, and the maximum length of a piece was 250 words.

'But I like to write longer!'

'You can in the paper, which comes out weekly,

although the print run's only about six thousand five hundred.'

'What are you leading on this week?'

'Revolution in a children's care home, Oakridge Court.'

'Horrible, evil place.' Dora's sweet face was drained of colour. 'My boyfriend, Paris, was incarcerated there for several years.'

'The current inhabitants feel the same. Troubled teenagers have been trashing the place. There's talk of closing it down.'

'Thank God, and then kicking them out to join the homeless and jobless at sixteen. God knows how Paris survived.'

'He's got you,' said Jackie. 'We'll also be campaigning for tougher sentences for attacks on the police, because if we scratch their backs, they might give us better stories; and we're covering a hamster show in Willowood.'

'Heaven!' Dora perked up. 'I'd love to do that.'

'You're on. You can start next week. You can have a column and spread to yourself.'

'As long as I can still be Rupert's press officer as well.'

'Of course you can. What else would you like to write about?'

'The corruptness of charities producing bloody great shiny fifty-page brochures with huge photographs of the directors on three hundred thousand pounds a year, then asking the public for two-hundred-pound donations – only ten per cent of which goes to the poor victims. When you could put all the message you need on a piece of A4 and then most of the money could go to the animals or the children.

'I know one charity,' Dora continued, 'that has made hundreds of people spend a fortune sponsoring a donkey who doesn't exist, and another couple who spent a fortune sponsoring a greyhound, and when they moved to a lovely cottage with a garden so they could adopt him, the charity said the poor wretched dog had to spend the rest of his life in kennels because so many people were sponsoring him. It's dreadful.'

Only then did she realise Jackie was watching the 2.20 runners in the paddock at Windsor and having a bet.

'I'm sorry to bang on.'

'Great, great, go ahead and write it, make it as contentious as possible.'

Dora came in on Friday to find a grinning Jackie pouring a large glass of whiskey.

'I've got a great idea for a piece,' said Dora.

'You don't need to. Your charity piece has triggered off so many outraged letters, we can fill your entire next page with them. Let's go and have lunch at Bar Sinister.'

'That's owned by Rupert's great friend Bas Baddingham, a bloodstock agent. He's great on gossip, too.'

The next moment, Tissues had rushed in in hysterics.

'Jackie, how could you run that wicked piece? All the firms that sponsor charities are cancelling next week's ads!'

'They'll put them back in when they see we're printing their letters of outrage. I'm going to headline it "War and Piece".'

'I've got another idea for the sports page,' said Dora, unrelentingly, 'called "Hair Today", and each week we highlight – no pun intended – the most outlandish footballer's hairstyle.'

'Any news on Searston?' asked Jackie.

'Yes, they've bought Feral Jackson, so he and Bianca will be coming back from Perth soon, which should cheer up Taggie, who's about to start chemo, poor darling.'

8

It was a measure of Rupert's determination to protect and prove his love for his wife that when her first chemo-therapy session, at the beginning of June, coincided with Delectable running in the Oaks, he insisted on accompanying Taggie to Cotchester hospital and even on missing the Derby the following day, so he could look after her when she came home.

James Benson, the family doctor – who, like Marti Gluckstein, had steered the Campbell-Blacks through numerous crises – had warned Rupert what lay ahead, his smooth, handsome, raffish, red-veined face for once entirely serious.

'Taggie's got five hellish months of chemo ahead, which will utterly exhaust her and pull her down for at least a further eighteen months before she returns to her normal self. Chemo causes nausea, constipation, diarrhoea, headaches; she'll lose not only her lovely hair but probably her sense of taste and smell as well, and feel weaker than any kitten.'

'A piece of gateau, as my grandson Eddie would say.'

'Your Taggie's a workaholic, weighed down by dependants.'

'Tell me about it. I caught her creeping out to feed the badgers late last night. Everyone, including my first wife, uses this place like a hotel, particularly as it's free and the food's so much better. Does stress cause cancer?'

'Doesn't cause it, but it certainly exacerbates it.'

Oh Christ, thought Rupert. They hadn't been getting on last year. Not only had he forgotten Taggie's birthday, but he'd had a brief but rip-roaring affair with Gala, one of his work riders, and, having forbidden Taggie to give any surprise sixtieth birthday party for him, had flown back exhausted from the Melbourne Cup to find the entire Cotswolds and almost as many family swigging Bolly on the lawn. The ultimate party pooper, he had then ordered his pilot to turn around and fly him away.

'You need a decent couple to help out,' urged James Benson. 'Preferably a wife with nursing experience and a husband who's a bouncer to keep the ravening hordes at bay. At least you're rid of your father wandering in and out of bedrooms and loose boxes all the time.'

This was because Rupert's art dealer brother Adrian, in a rare act of altruism, had arranged for their increasingly senile father, Eddie, to be looked after in a very kind and cherishing care home near his own house in Chelsea.

Good-luck cards were still pouring in and once again Taggie was overwhelmed with shame that she couldn't read or write well enough to answer them. So, kind Tember had thank-you cards with a picture of Forester on them printed, so all Taggie had to do was scribble her name.

Neither Taggie nor Rupert could sleep the night before the chemo started. Aware that Taggie was absolutely terrified, Rupert held her trembling in his arms.

'It's going to be OK, darling. I'm going to be with you all the way.'

Nothing, however, had prepared him for the horror of the first session. Wearing his green-and-blue-striped lucky shirt, reeking of Galop d'Hermès aftershave because his shaking hand had poured on far too much, he had arrived at the oncology department of Cotchester hospital, oblivious to the excitement of all the nurses. He and Taggie were ushered into a large room with drawn dark-green curtains and a dozen tables and armchairs at which sat patients with drips going into their arms and companions sitting beside them.

On Taggie's table was a large box labelled 'Agatha Campbell-Black'.

As a smiling nurse with a soft Irish accent and down-turned blue eyes asked her name and date of birth, Taggie couldn't get her words out, so Rupert answered for her.

'As Agatha had her lumpectomy on the left,' explained the nurse, 'the chemo will go into her right arm, so it's best if you sit on her left.'

Then two more nurses, like angels of death, wearing masks, neck-to-ankle overalls and long gloves up to their armpits, came over to administer the first dose. They spent the next quarter of an hour tapping the inside of Taggie's impossibly slender arm, trying to find a vein to plunge a needle bearing the drip into, until Rupert lost it.

'For Christ's sake,' he yelled, then, as the needle shot off to the right again and more blood gushed out, 'you're supposed to be nurses – why can't you find the fucking vein?'

All around, patients and companions were looking at him in amazement, particularly when a bossy sister stormed in.

'Mr Campbell-Black, if you're going to use language like that, you can go outside.'

'Rupert, please,' pleaded Taggie, clutching his arm. Next moment, the needle slid in. The procedure for the next three hours was that a first and then second huge syringe of bright-scarlet liquid, known as the Red Devil, would drop into her little arm, followed by a drip of further meds also fed automatically, interrupted by constant beeping as machines finished drip-feeding her fellow patients.

And this has to go on every three weeks until November, thought Rupert, picking up a nearby paper and glancing at his horoscope: 'Scorpios tend to be outspoken, but sometimes it's better to stay silent than to say the wrong thing. Try to gain power over your future and turn negatives into positives.' He then turned to the one for Taggie, who'd ironically been born in Cancer: 'Cancers might not be pivotal to the survival of the planet, but would anyone be happy in a world deprived of its kindest, most generous, open-hearted inhabitants? It's important to remember how much you mean to everyone around you.'

You can say that again, thought Rupert. Glancing at his wife's sweet face with its cloud of dark hair and long, curling eyelashes, he noticed her eyes were closed. Taggie was too terrified to sleep, but, not wanting to worry Rupert, had shut her eyes, trying to relax. Assuming she'd dropped off, Rupert switched on his mobile to watch Delectable in the Oaks. *If she wins,* Rupert vowed, *Taggie will survive,* and he was relieved rather than ecstatic when the filly romped home by two lengths. Looking around the room, he noticed how ill or desperately pulled down the other occupants looked, but was amused when an old boy at the table opposite gave him a thumbs-up, muttering:

'Thanks, guv. I had Delectable, too.'

As Taggie's eyes were still closed, Rupert nipped out into the passage to ring and congratulate the team at Epsom.

'How's it going there?' asked Lark, Delectable's stable lass.

'Pretty ghastly. I'll tell you later.'

As he switched off his mobile, the lovely Irish nurse with the downturned blue eyes came over with a cup of tea and a slice of sponge cake.

'Taggie's OK, she's still asleep. The first time is always a shock – all that poison going in. Congratulations on the Oaks, by the way. Delectable's such a darling filly. My name's Shelagh.' Blushing slightly, she produced a piece of hospital writing paper. 'My husband's a huge fan of yours – could he possibly have your autograph? He's crazy about racing and football. He's so excited you've bought Searston Rovers.'

'What's his name?' asked Rupert, getting out his fountain pen.

'Eamonn O'Connor. He'll be so excited. Thank you so much.'

'To Eamonn O'Connor,' wrote Rupert. 'You have a Delectable and very kind wife.'

9

Taggie didn't feel too bad after the first session, except being alarmed on going to the loo in the night to find her pee blood-red. After the second, however, the horror kicked in; two of her nails turned black and fell off, her pee turned mauve and her crap was like gravel. She was feeling so sick that she completely lost her appetite and her sense of smell, and had to force herself to eat even a spoonful of porridge or half a yoghurt. Even water had a horrible metallic taste. Her teeth and gums were so sore that she had to use a baby's toothbrush. Strange that something that was to save you from death made you feel as though you'd died. The only thing she was forced to swallow was masses of antiemetics and steroids that made her face swell up.

Even worse was the beautiful summer morning when, running her hand through her thick dark hair, she felt a clump coming away. From then on, it kept coming, clogging plugholes, scattered over her pillow as though she were a polo pony having her mane hogged. And not just her hair, but thinning eyebrows, and her long curly eyelashes disappeared from her red, swollen eyes. She was constantly touched by Rupert's reassurance that he loved her and it would all grow back, but how could he love a hairless crone, particularly when, out in the yard, she could see the lovely stable lasses with their long, shiny, flowing locks. It seemed so unfair, too, that everyone fancied men with shaved heads. Barry Pitt, Searston's bald goalkeeper, got masses of fan mail. She'd been comforted most days by her father, Declan, making Zoom calls from Ireland, where he was researching a book, but now she couldn't bear him to see her without any hair.

The third session of chemo was even worse. She had so longed for Bianca and Feral to come home and had pestered Rupert into buying Searston Rovers to make it possible.

'But now,' she sobbed to Shelagh, the lovely Irish nurse, 'I'm not sure I'm up to their return. Bianca always turns everything into a party, and I'm scared I won't be able to bake Feral's favourite chicken pie and chocolate roulade to welcome them.'

'They'll understand,' said Shelagh.

'And I find myself getting so irritable because I'm feeling so helpless,' went on Taggie. 'I keep biting poor darling Rupert's head off. Oh Shelagh, why can't I be nice all the time, like you?'

Good things did come out of the third session, though. Taggie had fallen asleep at the hospital and Rupert had gone out to ring the yard when, hearing sobbing, he peered into a side room and found Shelagh, the Irish nurse, comforting a young man who was crying his eyes out.

'What's up with him?' Rupert asked, when Shelagh later brought him a cup of tea and some biscuits.

'Poor boy's got prostate cancer, can't make love to his

wife any more. He's a gym instructor and he longs to give her babies.'

'They'd better adopt, like we did.'

Shelagh thought that despite looking very tired, with black rings beneath his blue eyes and suntan fading from not going racing, Rupert was still so beautiful.

'How are you coping?' she asked. 'It's going to be tougher from now on. Just make sure she rests, and you too.'

'I've brought your husband a picture of Love Rat, and a book on Mrs Wilkinson, who won the National.'

'Oh, thank you, he'll be over the moon. May I have a word?'

'You can have several.'

'I hope you don't mind my asking, but I heard you were looking for a couple. I've done eight years here, I love the patients and their families, but I'd like to do something a bit more cheery.'

'Christ, I understand that.'

'Eamonn, my husband, and I adore the Cotswolds and love horses, and Eamonn, as I told you, is mad about football.'

'Can you cook?'

'Well, I'm a good plain cook, not Prue Leith, but I dote on your Taggie and I'd love to help her through chemo and radiotherapy and get her well again.'

'It's a pretty mad household. My daughter Bianca's coming home with her boyfriend, Feral, who's going to play for Searston.'

'Taggie told me. Eamonn remembers him playing for Larks Rovers.'

'Bianca will try and fill the house with friends. What's Eamonn's job?'

'Well, he's a bouncer in a nightclub.'

Rupert burst out laughing. 'You're on – he can keep the ravening hordes away. Tell your husband to call me.'

Eamonn O'Connor rolled up the following day. He had charcoal-grey eyes, a broken nose, high forehead, shaggy grey-and-black hair, a voice softer than an Irish mist, which could crescendo into a mighty roar, and a great bellowing laugh. He was also six foot four, with massive shoulders and a great sense of the ridiculous.

'Do you ride?' asked Rupert.

'Need a cart horse to carry me.'

'You look pretty fit – do you work out?'

'Only how to pay my bookmaker.'

Eamonn was clearly crazy about horses and went round Rupert's yard and stud in wonder, recognising and stopping to stroke the inhabitants and chat to the stable staff.

'You got a great team here.'

Out on the terrace, he gazed across the green valley.

'God, it's even more beautiful than Ireland. There's room for a football pitch down there. Searston's got a terrible training ground; you should get them to come up here.'

'What role would you like to play here?' asked Rupert. 'I gather you're a brilliant odd-job man. We always need an estate carpenter, and there's a mass of work to be done at Searston.'

'That'd be good. I can mend anything except my ways,' grinned Eamonn.

'But most of all, I want you to protect Taggie, my wife. We need someone to keep the paps and particularly the locals at bay while she's ill. It gives them an excuse to drop in, and she's so hospitable, she'll feel she has to stagger down to welcome them.'

For a moment, Eamonn looked serious. 'The thing I love most in the world is my Shelagh. We've seen so little of each other lately. Kids are both still in Ireland. It'd be great to be working together here, looking after you.'

'Where would you like to live? There's the lodge at the bottom of the drive, or there's a self-contained flat in the West Wing.'

'I think we'd prefer to live near you, while Mrs C-B's going through treatment. I'll try not to sing "Danny Boy" too loudly in the bath.'

'My father-in-law, Declan O'Hara, lives in that house across the valley.'

'I know, another hero. I miss his interviews on TV.'

'He's in Ireland at the moment, struggling to finish a book on Irish writers. He's a lovely bloke. Zooms Taggie most days. His wife, Maud, is out there too. When they come back home, you can protect us from her. She's always popping in to borrow things, usually other people's husbands.'

Eamonn laughed. 'Can't wait to meet them.'

He and Rupert then went and sat in the kitchen and, as it was half eleven, neither of them thought it was too early for a drink. Eamonn patted all the dogs. Next moment, a couple of pheasants wandered in.

'Probably starving,' said Rupert, opening a tin of nuts and chucking a handful on to the flagstones, which was promptly gobbled up.

'We must also try and stop my wife feeding every living creature on the planet. I caught her stealing out to fill up the bird baths last night. As if there wasn't a perfectly good lake for them to drink from.'

10

Each football season is preceded by a pre-season starting in early July and involving several weeks of drills, sprints, putting players through intense physical labour and enabling them to assimilate new signings into the team.

To Ryan's fury, Feral and Bianca didn't get back from Perth until late July, which left Feral little time to get match fit and for Team Searston to build combinations around their new star player. Rupert had sent his helicopter to pick them up from Heathrow. Determined to get maximum publicity, Ryan had tipped off the press that football's most glamorous couple would be landing on Penscombe's helipad on Thursday morning. Whereupon six-foot-four Eamonn the bouncer more than justified his new employment by dispatching the lot of them.

'I don't care if you're the Queen of Sheba. Out, sunshine!'

Bianca, who loved appearing in the press, was very disappointed. Ravishingly pretty, both she and her brother, Xav, had been adopted from Colombia. She had long dark curls, huge dark eyes peeping out from under the longest black eyelashes, a tiny turned-up nose and a big mouth, pouting then breaking into a smile, lit by the whitest teeth. Curvy but very slender, she danced rather than walked.

Clutching presents, she erupted into the house.

'Mum, Mum, Dad! We're home! Happy birthday, Mum!' Then, hurling herself into Rupert's arms: 'Where's Mum?'

'She's in bed, and not great,' admitted Rupert. 'Recovering from chemo on Monday, which makes her very tired. You must treat her gently, darling.' But as he tried to draw Bianca into the drawing room for a proper briefing, she wriggled out of his arms and scampered up the stairs.

'Mum, Mum, happy birthday, we've brought you some fantastic presents!'

Popping her head round the door of her parents' bedroom, she immediately retreated.

'She's not here!'

'Bianca,' whispered Taggie, from the depths of the huge Regency four-poster with its tattered red curtains.

Popping back in, Bianca discovered a balding ghost, far paler than her pillows, on which were strewn shed clumps of dark hair. Forester, lying beside her, thumped his long striped tail.

'Hello, darling,' gasped Taggie.

'Mum, what's happened to you?' shrieked Bianca. 'Where's your hair?'

'I'm so sorry, it's the chemo. It'll grow back.' Taggie held out arms so thin, Bianca was terrified of breaking them.

Rupert only left them for a minute. 'Leave Mum to rest, darling. You can talk to her later.'

As he half carried Bianca downstairs, she burst into a storm of weeping.

'She's dying, she's dying, her lovely hair's nearly gone and she's thinner than a skeleton.'

'It's the chemo, darling. She has to go through it. In a way, she's being systematically poisoned to kill off the cancer. She'll feel better in a few days, until the next session.'

He was feeling quite helpless, when there was a knock on the door, bringing Shelagh, who Rupert introduced.

'Shelagh and Eamonn, who so dramatically got rid of the paps, have come to look after us, particularly Mum. Shelagh was working on the cancer ward at Cotchester, so she knows the ropes. She'll explain things better than me.'

Leading Bianca into the kitchen, Shelagh took her in her arms.

'There, my lamb. I know it looks hideous. Chemo makes people so weak, they can hardly stagger out of bed.'

'I've got lots of lovely presents for her. She was always so beautiful.'

'And will be again.'

Having poured a couple of large whiskeys, Rupert went off to find Feral. He was ringing his mother, Nancy, who was back in a rehab clinic in Larkminster.

'I'll come and see you later in the day, Mum. Stay cool.'

'You need a rest,' chided Rupert, handing Feral a glass. 'That's a helluva long flight.'

The next moment, Feral's mobile rang. It was Ryan in a temper.

'Why can't you come in now? We've got to build the team around you.'

'I've got to sort out Mum, Ryan.'

'Well, mind you're in first thing tomorrow. You're getting good money, Feral. I'll drop in later in the afternoon and brief you.'

'I'll be sorting out Mum.'

Thinking Eamonn's bouncer skills might be needed again, Rupert grabbed Feral's mobile.

'Feral's exhausted, he needs time to settle in, so fuck off, Ryan.' Then he hung up.

Whereupon Valent rang five minutes later: what the fook was Rupert playing at, did he want to screw oop Searston before they''d even started? So, Rupert hung up again.

Feral went up to see Taggie. Having had an aunt, Dorothy, who'd survived cancer, he was less appalled by her appearance and, sitting down on the bed, he took her hand.

'Chemo's a fucker, Tag. But it'll make you be'er.'

'I hope so,' whispered Taggie. 'I'm so sorry not to be up to welcome you.'

Bianca then joined them and opened one of Taggie's birthday presents, a beautiful flower-patterned cashmere dressing gown, which was now much too large and long, but which she draped over her mother.

'And tomorrow I'm going to find you a lovely wig and a scarlet beanie to be going on with.'

Taggie half laughed. 'I don't think so. Daddy hates beanies even worse than beards.'

As Feral's Ferrari was on its way back from Perth, Rupert insisted Eamonn drove him to see his mother in

71

Larkminster, giving a delighted Eamonn a chance to exchange football gossip.

While Shelagh was coaxing a pile of pills down Taggie, Bianca wandered off to her old bedroom, in which Taggie had hung up photographs of Colombian beauty spots and Arsenal stars Arsène Wenger and Thierry Henry for Feral. No one, however, had put flowers by the bed, and the tin with the Jack Russell on the lid, which Taggie always filled for guests with newly baked shortbread, was empty. Rain was plummeting down outside. Fighting back more tears, Bianca found Shelagh in the kitchen peeling potatoes.

'Mum always cooks Feral's favourite chicken pie and chocolate roulade when we come home.'

'I'm afraid your poor mother's lost her sense of taste and smell, because of the chemo, so she can't cook at the moment. I know what a great cook she is. I'm afraid tonight you'll have to put up with my Irish stew and apple crumble.'

The Irish stew was in fact delicious, but when Shelagh popped upstairs with some crumble for Taggie, she caught her feeding the stew to a grateful Forester.

'Mam, you must try and eat something.'

As Feral was still out seeing his mother, Rupert dined with Bianca and tried to discuss the future – difficult, because every few minutes one of her friends rang up to welcome her back, then finally her best friend, Dora. 'Dore, how fantastic. Come over tomorrow. What's best for you, lunch or dinner?'

Whereupon Rupert lost it and grabbed Bianca's mobile.

'How many times do I have to tell you, Mummy's got

to be kept calm. The whole of the bloody Cotswolds is trying to drop in. I caught her staggering out to feed the badgers again last night. If you want to entertain your friends, you can move into one of the staff cottages.'

Bianca burst into tears. 'I thought Mum was desperate for us to come home.'

'She was, but she had no idea then how desperately wiped out she'd feel. Sorry, darling, I didn't mean to snap at you. We're all a bit uptight.' He patted Bianca's shoulder.

'You haven't opened my present to you yet,' sniffed Bianca, seizing a parcel, wrapped in a page of the *Perth Times* and welded together with Sellotape, which was waiting on the sideboard and thrusting it at Rupert. Inside was a wind-up koala bear singing 'Waltzing Matilda'.

'It's great, thanks so much,' said an enchanted Rupert, waltzing round the room with it. 'Talk about "bear with me".'

'I couldn't think of anything to get Feral's mum,' grumbled Bianca. 'The only thing she'd like is a ton of crack cocaine.'

'Shut up,' snapped Rupert, as car headlights appeared in the yard outside. 'Feral's back. Go to bed, darling, you're tired. I'll give him some supper.'

Ten minutes later, there was a piercing shriek from Bianca: 'No one's switched on my electric blanket!'

11

Next day, torrential rain was accompanied by a vicious east wind, and Feral came back from his first day's preseason absolutely shattered, collapsed into a bed littered with Bianca's clothes and slept until after dinner. He then couldn't get back to sleep, particularly when Bianca came to bed full of gossip after lunching with Dora.

Once Bianca had dropped off, Feral wandered downstairs to find Rupert in the kitchen writing instructions for tomorrow's runners at Ascot and York. Seeing Feral shivering, he turned up the central heating, and helped him to a large glass of red and the remains of yesterday's Irish stew.

'How was your mother yesterday?'

'Not great. Still in rehab trying to stay clean, not much incentive.'

'She can come and watch you.'

'I'd like that, but I don't think she's up to it. Can't think why I'm so fucking tired, man.'

'I can. You've just had a helluva long flight. No doubt Ryan's been at you all day and, although I'm devoted to my daughter, she's been so cossetted, indeed spoilt, by her sweet mother, she's incapable of putting a mug in the washing-up machine or hanging up a dress. Packing up all your stuff to move back to England must have been quite beyond her. You must feel as though you've carried a vast overloaded Pickfords lorry the whole ten thousand miles from Oz single-handed.'

'People adored Bianca in Oz,' protested Feral. 'There were lots of leaving parties for us. It was nice there. People didn't know she came from a posh family and I came from the gu'er. We was sort of equal.'

'You're going to be way above all of us soon,' observed Rupert. 'Top striker taking Searston up to the top of the Premier League.'

'That's the only way I can be wurvy of Bianca. I've got Mum and the family to support, feel I've got to get to the top and be earning serious dosh before I ask for her 'and.'

'You're worthy all right,' said Rupert. 'I'll never forget when I was in danger of losing my licence as a trainer and Bianca rang up from Perth, telling me not to worry, you were earning such a good whack, you'd love to help me out. God, I was touched. And I have to say, I'm incredibly proud Bianca's shacked up with such a brilliant footballer.'

'That's kind, not sure how brilliant.' Feral smiled at Rupert. 'Game's much tougher and more brutal over here. There's no relegation in Oz, so much less pressure.'

'Were any of your old mates training today?'

'Ludo and Midas haven't been allowed back – they've gotta lose weight at home, stop them playing too hard when they're unfit and triggering injury. Griffy was there – nice bloke, very welcoming, but he's aged a lot.' Feral gave a last bit of Irish stew to a drooling Banquo.

'Parks is a good bloke, good defender, plays it straight. If he goes down, you know he's really hurt. But every time he shouted at a player, Ryan shouted somefing different, and Parks is captain. Anger Management and Barry Pitt kept yelling somefing else, like sergeant majors, and a new cheeky sod called Bastian kept calling them Grandpa. Atmos isn't good; players don't seem to like each uvver very much. 'Spect Ryan's uptight about being nearly relegated. On the uvver 'and, you was a 'uge 'it, man, so many players fort you was grite for a posh bloke and asked after you – and little Wilfie, Josef and Galgo sent their best and asked when was you coming again.'

'That's nice.'

''Ope the wevver picks up soon. It was fuckin freezin' today.' Then, as Rupert topped up his glass: 'Ryan doesn't like players drinking. His dad was there today, coaching the goalies. 'E's tough.'

'Valent's a major player, got to the top in soccer and business, doesn't take prisoners.' Seeing Feral yawning again, Rupert urged him to go back to bed, but still Feral lingered.

'So sorry about Taggie, man, must be 'ell for you. She's such a lovely lady. My auntie Dolly had cancer. She got completely be'er. And, not being too personal, before Taggie loses all her eyebrows, you should ink some new ones over them to give some emphasis to the face. But you must do it in the right place now, or when they grow back, she'll have two sets of eyebrows.'

'Sweet of you. She'll be a highbrow.' Rupert laughed, then, noticing the forest of ink on Feral's arms: 'Can you recommend a good tattooist?'

12

Bianca had certainly endeared herself to Rupert by bringing him the wind-up koala bear singing 'Waltzing Matilda', which he absolutely adored and played all the time, and which reminded Feral and Bianca of Australia, making them wonder, after the sunlit barbeques and beach parties, how they'd cope with the colder English weather.

Not well, in Feral's case. Developing a chest infection and a hacking cough, he missed the first two games and had to be kept away from Taggie, whose immune system was at rock bottom. Leaving Shelagh and Eamonn to take care of them, Rupert, who felt he really ought to put in an appearance at Searston, took Bianca to the second game in late September. This was a local derby between Searston and Deansgate, who, having just missed going up to the Championship last season, were regarded as the vastly superior team.

Despite the rule that no one employed at a football club is allowed to bet on football matches, as Searston were rated only 100–1 to win, several Deansgate directors (including Jarred Moreland, the Director of

Football, and even chairman Sir Craig Eynsham himself) had large, secret and totally illicit bets on them. Byron Stockwell, normally Deansgate's ace goalkeeper, had consequently been secretly bunged £30,000, which could pay off some of his gambling debts, to let in every goal.

After days of cold, wet weather, Rupert and Bianca were cheered by hot sunshine and a warm westerly breeze as they drove to Searston, past gold harvested fields and cottage gardens glowing with hollyhocks, and hedgerows festooned with pale-yellow traveller's joy and blackened by sloes.

'Making sloe gin would be a gentle but rewarding pastime for Mummy,' said Rupert.

'That'd be good,' agreed Bianca. 'She keeps telling me how guilty she feels no longer cooking for all of us.'

Getting stuck in narrow lanes behind lorries weighed down by bales of straw, they didn't reach Deep Woods until after half-time, to find a euphoric Searston three-up and baying for Deansgate's blood.

Then Deansgate's goalkeeper, Byron Stockwell, caught sight of Bianca walking along the touchline with her glossy dark curls streaming down the shoulders of an incredibly seductive, tight-fitting red dress, and triggering a mass whistling which normally came from winning fans desperate for the ref to call time.

'That's bloody marvellous, three–nil,' said Rupert in surprise.

But Byron Stockwell thought Bianca looked so ravishing that, macho reasserting itself, he flew through the air to divert Midas Channing's Exocet, and proceeded to stop everything else.

Whereupon Deansgate rallied, with their star striker, Laddy Heywood, who also liked the look of Bianca, scoring two goals and the fans bursting into song: 'Our Laddy Heywood, he always plays good. Our fair Laddy, he's never a baddy.'

'I think someone's been bunged,' whispered Dora as she joined Bianca and Rupert in the stands. 'Byron Stockwell's known as Stopwell, because he usually does.'

'Who's the good-looking one who's just scored?' asked Bianca.

'Laddy Heywood. He's terribly naughty, screws so many women in the disabled loo because it's got a mirror and handrails to cling on to that it's known as the "Laddies" as opposed to the ladies.' Dora went off into fits of laughter.

'And who's the one with the red curls?'

'That's Narcisco Romano, known as Moan of the Match because he's always grumbling. And look at the way he smiles at the camera when he cuddles a goal-scoring player.'

'Why hasn't my ghastly neighbour, Sir Craig, rolled up to gloat?' asked Rupert.

'He's frightened the breeze might blow off his hat and show people how bald he is,' whispered Dora, who was thrilled by how many of her press contacts had arrived in the hope Feral might be playing.

Deansgate ended up winning 6–3, which enraged the Deansgate directors – who couldn't say anything – and later resulted in Byron Stockwell forfeiting his large bung. His wife, Maple, who had earmarked much of the

£30,000 for an indoor swimming pool and a 'harbore-tum', was absolutely livid.

'Don't worry,' Rupert reassured Bianca, 'Searston'll start winning once Feral's fit again.'

'There's Sir Craig's wife, Lady Grace, waving at you,' pointed out Dora.

Wags on both sides were irritated by the fans, players and photographers concentrating on Bianca.

'Who looks at the stars when the moon is in the sky?' wrote an already captivated Barney Hughes, sports editor of the *Cotchester Times*.

'Journalust,' giggled Dora.

As a furious Ryan was no doubt in the dressing room having a goalpost-mortem and bawling out his players, Rupert and Bianca popped into the Directors' Lounge, which had been newly decorated in ruby and purple. Previous chairman Stevas's portrait had been replaced by blow-ups of Rupert, Valent and Searston, full of jubilation after beating Drobenham last season. Something really had to be done about the indifferent wine and lack of whiskey, decided Rupert.

Bianca was having a lovely time being chatted up by Byron Stockwell, who, braving the wrath of his bosses, had invaded the Directors' Lounge and was as handsome as his namesake.

'Lovely dress,' he was telling Bianca, 'really suits you. I'd like it even better if it was lying on my bedroom floor.'

'That's naughty,' chided Bianca.

'Hope you'll come and have a catch-up when I'm in the area,' said Byron.

'And me too,' said Laddy Heywood, the Deansgate playmaker.

Bianca was also excited because the beautiful Narcisco had joined them, gazing at her with such admiration, until he adjusted his russet locks a second time and she realised he was merely checking his reflection in the mirror behind her.

Lady Grace, the chairman's wife, crossed the room to join them.

'Good evenin' to you, Rupert, so pleased you've stayed for a noggin, and I'm delighted to see your young wife, Taggie, has got over her cancer so well.'

'That's my daughter Bianca,' snapped Rupert. 'We must go,' he called to Bianca, who was very disappointed to be dragged away.

'Feral needs some looking after,' insisted Rupert.

Feral returned a fortnight later to a home game against Bideford, which brought the first chill of autumn. The Searston woods were still chiefly green, but the hazels were turning yellow, the sycamore keys browning, and the tops of the poplars were like paintbrushes dipped in gold.

'I'll have to run bloody fast or I'll freeze to death,' grumbled Feral.

The press were very excited about his return, the *Cotchester Times* describing him as a local boy returning to save the club and guide them to a higher division.

A large crowd had rolled up, including Valent and Etta, who had not only provided some of the last Valent Edwards roses for the boardroom, but also a large bunch of chrysanthemums to match Bideford's yellow colours.

'Prince Feral has finally showed up,' said Dora, joining Rupert and Bianca in the stands.

And certainly, as the players ran on to the pitch, despite having risen from his sickbed, none had longer legs, nor more muscular body and shoulders, making the rather tacky ruby-and-purple Searston strip look a billion dollars. Feral's face was again the most beautiful of all, tawny eyes curling up at the corner, thick black lashes forming a natural eyeliner, and an arrogant smile which said, 'I'm superior.' Which he was.

'Wow,' said Jamie Abelard from the *Cotchester Times.*

Bianca, ravishing but rather unsuitably dressed in her pale-pink cashmere minidress and high heels, was whipping through the programme, which had a lovely photograph of Feral on the front and several of Ryan inside, but none of herself.

'When's your Wag feature starting?' she asked Dora.

'Soon, but at least Banquo got Dog of the Week as the Labr-adore, so your dad'll be pleased.'

Bideford were a good young team – fourth in League One. But despite them putting half their defenders on Feral to nullify the threat, he kicked off, dribbling round each one of them before whisking the ball into the top right corner of the goal. Next, hurtling down the left side, he lashed the ball into the left corner, then, sauntering down the right touchline, he achieved the perfect cross, kicking the ball sweetly between two Bideford defenders just in front of the goal, so a lurking Downing headed it straight in.

Both Sky and BT Sport, who normally covered Premier League matches on Saturdays, had made an exception in reporting on a League One game. Feral's name, like that of a loved one, was constantly on the commentators' lips. They noticed how his eyes, like a feral cat's, swivelled the whole time, assessing danger, checking where everyone was going to be in five seconds, invariably passing directly.

Searston fans were yelling their heads off and singing:

'When you're in peril, send for Feral.'

They noticed also that Feral was as ready to defend as to attack. Galloping up the pitch, using his head to block a shot that was flying into Searston's goal, he let it slither down to his feet, then, scooping it up, thundered down the field to smite in a 30-yard wonder goal.

'Four–nil to Searston.'

'Like being overtaken by one of Rupert's racehorses,' grumbled a Bideford midfielder.

'Got enough practice in the past, running away from the police,' grumbled another.

The Wags were turning their binoculars on Feral even more than on Rupert.

'Well done!' cried Charm Channing. 'He's goin' through the Bideford defence like a knayfe through butter.'

New star players do give teams a lift. But although Searston were gathering round Feral and giving him hugs for the camera, they were edgy about his arrival. Winning is only orgasmic if you're the one scoring the goals.

'It's only because the sheep are in the field,' bitched an envious Anger Management.

'No, he's a bloody good player,' insisted Barry Pitt, and Downing, who liked winding Angus up, added: 'Left foot's as good as his right.'

Bastian was equally irritated at being supplanted as the team poster boy.

In the second half, Feral scored two more goals and

won a penalty. Bianca, who was cold, was wearing Rupert's coat and checking messages on her phone. Dora beckoned Cadenza, the ace *Cotchester Times* photographer, who'd been excitedly concentrating on Feral, and whispered for her to take some pictures of Bianca:

'She likes to be the centre of attention.'

Rupert, noticing that Feral was getting tired and seeing a crestfallen Josef, the Pouncing Czech, still confined to the bench, suggested Ryan subbed him for Feral in the last five minutes.

'Not worth it, don't want to lose the momentum,' snapped Ryan, as Feral was named Man of the Match and given the match ball for scoring four goals.

At full time, he was surrounded by press.

Having patted him on the back, and leaving everyone else to tell him he was marvellous, Rupert went into the club office to share his delight at the result with lovely Tember West.

Breathing in a sweet smell of lilies, he was intrigued to find her little office filled with boxes of chocolates and vases of dying flowers, whose petals were scattered over the carpet.

'She's away,' said a passing Ludo, who was off with another hangover euphemistically masquerading as a minor calf injury.

'What gives with her – is the whole team after her?'

'It was her birthday a week ago and she's the club secretary, takes the minutes of the meetings, so she knows exactly how much every player is earning, who's got raises, who's likely to be ousted by new signings or to be sold or sent out on loan, or which loanees might become permanent, which Academy graduates might be discarded or invited to join the senior squad. The permutations are endless. With new owners, there are bound to be changes. Tember has such a kind heart and, as you've probably discovered, is not great at keeping secrets. But she always comforts any player who's ousted, and gives away all the chocolates. Nice lady.'

'She got a bloke?' asked Rupert.

'Not sure. There are rumours, but she plays things close to her ravishing chest. Must get plenty of offers.'

Rupert then stopped to congratulate Valent on the improvements he'd made to the club. Valent's building company had clearly been at work mending rusty fences and collapsing stands round all four sides of the pitch, and cutting back any undergrowth to the edge of the woods.

'It's great,' he told Valent. 'Pity, though, you've painted out the graffiti in the gents – used to be such a good read.'

Valent laughed, and outlined other plans for the club: extending it on both sides into a series of suites which people could book for lunch before watching the match on a balcony outside.

'Beyond the right side, we should build on a big banqueting suite with a bar, tables and chairs, which could double up as a place where home and away Wags could bring their families.'

'Have to improve the food.'

'Such a pity your Taggie isn't oop and running to sort it, but perhaps next year.'

'I hope so.'

'Do give her our luv. And that Feral's a fooking star!'

'He's a good boy. And I think we should tart down the opposition dressing room, make it much darker and more cramped, reduce the heating and only leave the odd socket for them to plug in their mobiles and hairdryers.'

Rupert went back to collect Feral, who'd finished talking to the press and was now being pestered by a Bideford director to sign his programme:

'Could you just put "To Anastasia, Happy Anniversary, with best wishes".'

Knowing Feral hadn't a clue how to spell it, Rupert snapped:

''Fraid he hasn't got time to do anything other than sign his name. Come on, Feral.'

13

Even though Feral had transformed the team and Searston were beginning to win matches, discovering he was earning twice as much as any of them, the players started making snide remarks about him knocking off the chairman's daughter, and demanding parity.

Ryan Edwards was also edgy. People irritatingly assumed he was OK – money insulating one from sympathy – because he had a very rich father. But while he was well aware Rupert and Valent had saved Searston, he was wildly competitive and wanted to prove he was a greater manager than Valent had ever been a player: like Bambi and Bambi's father.

A fierce, demanding, hands-on coach, Ryan had very strong likes and dislikes. A control freak, he fined any player two weeks' pay if he arrived late for training or matches. He also put CCTV cameras in the hostel that housed several of the younger players, to see how many of them smuggled in girls.

With the party season approaching, he called a team meeting. 'I hope you're sticking to the diet I gave you, particularly with no ketchup, cutting right down on alcohol and not going out partying two nights before a game. It's the same with sex – I don't want you young lads smuggling girls into the hostel, and I think it would be best if those players with wives or partners didn't sleep with them the night before a game.'

'Why's Miles looking so happy?' hissed Downing.

'You obviously haven't seen his ugly cow of a wife,' hissed back Ludo.

Ryan was also very edgy about Rupert, who he feared wanted to have a say in recruitment. Rolling up at the training ground one hot October morning, Rupert found the players participating in a sprint, 320 metres in seventy seconds, round the edge of the field.

A loping Feral won easily, followed by Galgo, then Josef, Downing and little Wilfie, and lastly Bastian. The senior players – Angus, Parks, Griffy, chubby Midas and Ludo – however, were drenched in sweat as they tried to keep up, while Miles Newall was way behind, shambling along, stopping to eat blackberries, until Ryan was entranced to hear Rupert bawling him out:

'For Christ's sake, move your arse, you lazy sod.'

'You can't talk to players like that,' exploded Ryan. 'We have a duty of care.'

'I can talk to players any way I like. He's useless.' Then, pointing to handsome Josef, who had just joined a five-a-side game: 'But he's bloody good, very fast, and he was brilliant last season when we beat Drobenham. Feral needs a fellow striker. Why isn't he getting game time?'

'Never obeys instructions,' snapped Ryan. 'English is hopeless, complete waste of money.'

'Well, bloody get a translator to teach him. Well run, Wilfie,' Rupert added to the little redhead, who was also about to join the five-a-side game. 'I'm going to enter you for the greyhound derby.'

Wilfie smiled. 'Well done at Ascot, boss. Fast Piece ran great.' A nearby Angus, irritated by another player being singled out, promptly kicked the ball into some nettles and brambles and ordered Wilfie to go fetch it.

Whereupon Rupert shouted, 'I'll get it, I've got jeans on,' and when he retrieved the ball and kicked it back to them, all the players laughed and cheered, except Angus.

14

Taggie was drawing to the end of her chemo, and lovely Shelagh was so good at looking after her that Rupert, impressed by the improvements Valent had made, was now finding moments to put his stamp on the club. By November, receipts had rocketed, as fans and Wags with telescopes rolled up to gaze at both him and Feral, who was helping Searston win match after match.

Rupert still longed to replace the purple-and-ruby shirts with his own royal-blue and emerald-green colours but, for the time being, fans were spending a great deal in the club shop on replica purple-and-ruby kits for their entire families.

Rupert, because he had taken football off the back pages, was in addition a magnet to sponsors, and had started improving the catering, with decent booze in all the bars and Lemon Dribble cake proving to be a huge success. The theme from *Black Beauty*, which played when the players ran out on to the pitch, was already climbing up the charts, with the fans chanting 'Campbell-Black Beauty'. And everyone adored the new Galloper mascot, who was dark brown with huge eyes, a white blaze, one ear and a straggly tail like the real Safety Car, and who shook hooves with everyone.

Taggie, on the other hand, had never been more miserable. Having finished chemotherapy in November, four weeks later she had to endure radiotherapy. This involved a punishing five sessions a week for three weeks, ending in January, leaving her completely wiped out.

She was bitterly ashamed of feeling so ugly and often too weak to get up from a chair or out of bed, unless someone helped her.

Would her legendary cooking skills ever come back? And she so missed feeding the birds, foxes and badgers, walking the dogs and visiting the little foals.

Kind Shelagh constantly reassured her:

'Don't worry, little darling, chemo and radiotherapy make you weak as a kitten. In fact, a kitten'd feel like a prize fighter compared with you.'

Bianca was also trying hard to help, finding her pretty hats and luscious curly black wigs. Taggie's step-grandchildren were particularly sweet when they came to stay, eight-year-old Timon laying Master Quickly's red World Cup blanket over her and bringing her cups of tea, and, because she couldn't read well, six-year-old Sapphire insisting on reading her *The Tiger Who Came to Tea* and *The Cat in the Hat*.

But as Taggie got thinner and thinner, Rupert was desperate for her to eat properly and had endless discussions with Shelagh as to what might tempt her. One evening, he caught sight of a piece in the local paper about 'caring husbands who are ace cooks, freeing up their grateful wives to relax in the evenings'.

Fuck 'caring husbands', thought Rupert, he was jolly

well going to try to cook for Taggie himself. Having read that lemon juice, garlic, herbs, horseradish and pickles perk up the taste buds, he added a tablespoon of each to some chicken soup he'd found in the fridge, and which he'd already burnt on the Aga. He then proudly served this up for supper.

The result was so disgusting, Bianca raced to the nearest sink to throw hers up. Taggie, who was upstairs in bed, where even Forester rejected it, managed to empty her bowl down the loo, so as not to upset Rupert. But alas, he later found chicken scraps floating on the top and lost it, yelling, 'How the hell can you ever get better if you don't eat?' He then stormed out with the dogs to talk to Safety Car and have a drink with Eamonn and Shelagh. When he came back, rather drunk and mortified, Taggie pretended to be asleep.

15

Safety Car the horse was an applause junkie who'd do anything for attention. If he was ignored, he'd pick up the yard brush with his teeth and pretend to be sweeping up. He'd shake hooves with any visitor, gained a foot in height if ever he saw a camera and often invaded the kitchen in the hope of a bowl of red wine.

The morning in late January after Rupert and Taggie fell out, Safety Car popped in and found Taggie, who, coming downstairs, had caught sight of her glamorous portrait in the hall. Now she looked like one of those hairless old hags in the attic in horror films. Arriving home from shopping, Bianca found her mother in the kitchen, sobbing into Safety Car's dark-brown shoulder.

'Mu-um, what's the matter?'

'How can Dad love me any more when I look so hideous?'

Pushing Safety aside, Bianca hugged Taggie, then, pondering for a moment, said:

'Listen, Safety is honestly pretty ugly, particularly since Titus bit off one ear and most of his tail, but Daddy loves him more than any other horse, so why wouldn't

93

he still love you even if you've lost your looks and your hair?'

As Bianca got an apple out of the bowl on the kitchen table and gave it to Safety, Taggie started to laugh and said: 'But I haven't won as many races as Safety. Nor can I play football.'

'Hum,' said Dora, who'd been invited for tea, coming into the kitchen with a bunch of freesias, 'that is a very interesting thought.'

When Rupert came home that evening, mortified he'd been so vile to Taggie, he'd bought her a stunning grey jersey with a sequinned silver star on the front. 'Now I can follow you (like a not very wise man, admittedly) for ever.'

'It is so, so beautiful,' gasped Taggie. 'Oh, I'd so love to shine on you again. I'm sorry for being so bad-tempered.'

'And we only nag you because we love you and worry about you so much,' said Rupert, tucking her up in bed. 'Now, you look after your mistress properly,' he added to Forester.

Returning downstairs, he found Dora in his office.

'Rupert, I've got a great idea. You know Safety's such a success as a mascot – why don't he and the Jack Russells give a football demo at half-time, or even before kick-off? We could put AstroTurf down so they don't ruin the pitch. And now we've got this big room where people bring their kids, we could make it a Family Day once a month.'

'That's not bad.' Rupert looked up at a chart on the wall. 'We're playing Drobenham at home on February the fourteenth; this could really irritate them.'

So Family Day was born. Rupert arranged for his

sexiest stable lasses, Czech Marketa and golden-haired Lou-Easy, to bring Safety Car, in a ruby-and-purple muffler, and the Jack Russells, Cuthbert and Gilchrist, in red collars, along to matches.

Cuthbert would dribble the ball to Safety Car, who would kick it back and forth to both yapping dogs until one of them dribbled it up the field and nudged it into goal. Whichever dog scored would then be lifted on to Safety's back to give a flying Frankie Dettori jump off. There was only time for two or three goals, but the crowds were utterly ecstatic, particularly the children, who even all came off their phones to watch.

The opposition, however, were incandescent.

'Just like a zoo – how dare Campbell-Black trivialise the game?' Colonel Lightfoot had stormed on Valentine's Day, particularly when Searston went on to beat Drobenham 5–1. 'I'm going to report him to the FA.'

'Who'll do fuck all,' said a fellow director.

Victory apart, Ryan was even angrier.

'Fucking Rupert, ostentatious bastard, turning the place into a circus.'

The circus, however, really pulled in the crowds, even on the coldest winter day. And stable lasses Lou-Easy and Marketa loved every minute.

'So many fit men, it's like working in a sweetshop,' raved Lou-Easy.

Particularly as Marketa had been asked to help handsome Josef speak better English. 'So Josef will soon be able to say, "Fancy a fock?"' mocked Angus, who rather liked Marketa himself.

Marketa and Lou-Easy were also extremely eager to get to know the Searston players better.

'We've had all the decent blokes at Penscombe except Rupert,' claimed Lou-Easy, 'and he's out of bounds, so we've run out of bounders – ha ha.'

Lou-Easy was devoted to Rupert, who'd given her a dapple-grey newly retired racehorse called Bennet for her twenty-first birthday and let her keep him for free at the yard. She had also always been free with her favours, particularly with vets and farriers, who treated Bennet for nothing.

She and Marketa were the perfect contrast; Marketa, whom Lou-Easy called 'my bust friend', being big and full-breasted with dark slanting eyes, a huge scarlet mouth and the thickest black hair in a ponytail. Lou-Easy was more like a mermaid, sleek and slim with long silvery-blonde hair and blue-green come-to-seabed eyes.

'So ve don't appeal to the same guys,' said Marketa. 'But ven ve do, they can have us both at the same time.'

Out riding through Rupert's woods on Bennet and Safety Car in late February, they raved over the talent at Searston.

'That Downing's fit, and Galgo, and Bastian's cool. Feral's taken, sadly.'

'And that Josef's the best-looking. I'm hoping Rupert vants me to teach him more than English.'

'Ludo's nice, and Midas, and Griffy's handsome, but I think he's shy – he doesn't look you in the eyes when he talks to you. Ryan the manager's good-looking, but not as friendly as Valent, his dad, who gave me two grand after Quickly won the World Cup.'

Deep in the woods, out of the bitter east wind, rustling through fallen leaves, they moved on to the subject of Rupert and Taggie.

'Poor voman, looks so ill.'

'I cannot believe him missing out on the Arc, the Breeders' Cup and even Champions Day, and the Melbourne Cup. It's unprecedented; he must be crazy about her.'

'And even odder to leave Gav and Gala and Harmony to run the yard vithout interfering all the time.'

'Gala must be Olympic level in the sack. I reckon she's the only time Rupert's cheated on Taggie, not through want of every other woman in the world trying, but when he learnt Taggie had cancer, he was so devastated, jetting straight home from the World Cup and hardly leaving her side since.'

'And Gav and Gala celebrated vinning the Vorld Cup, falling into bed, and now ve're all being invited to their vedding.'

They had reached the little cottage at the heart of the woods in which Gav and Gala now lived.

'And they're always sloping off here for a shag after fourth lot,' giggled Lou-Easy.

'Hush, they'll hear you.'

'Do you think we ought to think about settling down?' mused Lou-Easy. 'I'm twenty-eight and it would be nice to have some kids. When I can't sleep at night, I try to count all the guys I've shagged, and I usually drop off by the time I get to thirty. Do you think that's terrible?'

'Not really. Sometimes I can't remember vether I've been to bed vith a guy or not.'

'And a footballer's a much better bet than a stable lad, and Valent and Rupert are bound to push those boys up to the Premier League, where evidently a lot of them earn more than two hundred thousand pounds a week.'

'Vonderful,' sighed Marketa. 'Vun vouldn't have to vork, and think of the clothes vun could buy.'

'But if I settled for one man, I'd have to be terribly in love or I might get bored with him. I'd never get bored with Bennet.' Lou-Easy patted his dapple-grey neck. 'I wish I could marry him. He can always get it – hup!' she cried as she jumped him over a small log.

'Those Searston boys are pretty exciting, though,' said Marketa. 'Next time ve take Safety and the Russells over there, let's fix a night to meet up. Ve can always settle down next year.'

16

Despite a succession of brilliant victories, putting Searston third in League One, Ryan Edwards was still fed up. He was finding himself increasingly irritated by his bossy wife, Dinah, with her Tabasco-red hair and her good figure – 'I never need to diet' – who saw herself as higher than Queen Wag and always made a beeline for Rupert whenever he came to games.

She had long been an imposer, asking some other Wag:

'What are you doing on Friday night?'

To which the other Wag would reply in excitement: 'Nothing!'

'Oh good, we can dump the kids on you.'

The kids, sixteen-year-old Otley and fourteen-year-old Kayley (Ryan's Little Princess) were now at Bagley Hall, a local public school which had recently introduced football into the curriculum.

Dinah-mite, wishing to impose her name on her children as well as Ryan's, had insisted they call themselves Otley and Kayley Jepson-Edwards with a hyphen, even if it did mean sewing on longer name-tapes. Ryan, feeling this was a bit common unless you were naturally double-barrelled, wanted to drop the Jepson. He was even more ashamed of Valent's broad Yorkshire accent, talking about 'droogs' and littering his conversation with 'bluddies' and 'fookings'.

'Please don't swear, Father, it'll encourage the kids.'

Ryan, on the other hand, loved Valent's wife, Etta, who came from a better background.

Bagley Hall itself was surrounded by exuberant forest sprawled over a vast green plain. The school was dominated by a big gold Georgian house called The Mansion, behind which were scattered numerous Cotswold stone buildings to accommodate 800 pupils and 150 staff. Perks included a vast library, a magnificent theatre, a swimming pool almost as long as Lake Windermere, and smooth green pitches stretching to infinity.

'If only I had a training ground like this,' sighed Ryan.

There were also stables where pupils could board their own horses, and school helicopters sent to pick up desirable pupils from faraway parts.

One afternoon in late February, Ryan went to watch sixteen-year-old Otley playing for the first team. Also in the side was Otley's classmate Harry Stanton-Harcourt, who turned out to be a natural, both scoring and feeding assists to other strikers.

His beautiful mother, Lady Emma Stanton-Harcourt, was at the match too, being wised up by another mum, Searston Wag Charm Channing – whose son Dixon, a new boy at Bagley Hall, was also playing – to the fact that Harry could make a fortune if he became a professional footballer.

'Mansion and Rolls-Royce for Mum and Dad, care home for Nan. Godsend to a working-class family.'

'Godsend to me,' sighed Lady Emma. 'I could afford a new roof. Do you work?' she asked Charm.

'I lost may-self as a stay-at-home mum, so now I'm wray-ting a kiddies' book about day-nosaurs.'

As it was a bitterly cold day, Ryan invited Lady Emma to join him and Princess Kayley in his very warm Volvo. Kayley – who, despite wearing too much make-up, was very pretty – fancied Harry, two forms above her, and would have adored living in a stately home, albeit with a crumbling roof.

Emma Stanton-Harcourt, who looked even more ravishing when she whipped off her beanie and her light-brown hair fell over her shoulders, said she found football desperately complicated.

'Harry has tried so hard to explain orf-side to me. As you're a frightfully grand manager, Ryan, you'll have to help me. Oh, well played, Harry. I know Rupert, your chairman, of course – he used to be so naughty before he married Taggie. Rupert's cousin Camilla and I came out the same year.'

Goodness, I didn't know Harry's mother was a lesbian, thought Kayley, looking up from her phone. She couldn't wait to tell her classmates, who also all fancied handsome blond Harry.

Ryan, meanwhile, thought Emma was absolutely gorgeous and was most impressed by her son.

'He seems rather a quiet, gentle boy,' confided Emma, 'but he's very ambitious and hungry underneath. He's won so many "fastest boy" medals and trophies, and the other night he left home because his father, my ex, beat him at ping-pong. My ex found him an hour later wandering the streets of Rutminster. It's a bit of a worry; he only scraped two GCSEs, he's not academic, spends all his time playing fantasy football.'

'I'll see if we can do something for him at Searston,' said Ryan.

A week later, Harry and Otley's class got a pep talk from the headmaster about taking A-levels in eighteen months' time.

'Only those pupils who have achieved eight A grades in their GCSEs and are of exemplary behaviour will be allowed to stay on.'

'That's me fucked,' came Harry's voice from the back of the hall.

Fortunately, while the debate was going on as to whether to expel such a dazzling athlete, Ryan proceeded to sign both Otley and Harry for the Searston Academy, which nurtured players from ten years old onwards, looking after their education and playing them in youth reserve teams before hopefully blooding them in the senior squad.

A desperately broke Lady Emma was thrilled to bits. 'It's not Eton, but hurrah – no more school fees! I shall take you out to dinner to say thank you,' she told Ryan.

Princess Kayley, however, was really sad that Harry had left Bagley, although she would still see him at Searston games. Wags like Charm and Rosalie Parkinson, on the other hand, were *de-layted* their children were now going to *pray-vate* school.

'Bagley is going to be flooded with nouves,' grumbled Ryan.

'Takes one to know one,' drawled Rupert.

A remark which Ryan's stepmother, Etta, overheard and did not forget.

17

Dora Belvedon's actor boyfriend, Paris Alvaston, the arctic Adonis with the white-blond hair, who was currently starring in *The Merchant of Venice* at Stratford, had been asked by Rupert to come down to the club to teach the young Searston players how to talk to the media.

'Hold your head up, smile, look your interviewer in the eye and speak slowly,' Paris told them. 'If you have to address a press conference, concentrate on one person, then move to another. If you can, call your interviewer by their name – media love to be recognised.'

In addition, Paris was giving elocution lessons to Harry Stanton-Harcourt, who was already making waves at the Searston Academy.

'Footballers resent public-school boys, so, for a start, you've got to lose your tee-haitches. "Parfway", "I fink" instead of "I think", "fick" not "thick", and say "pass" to rhyme with "gas".'

'I can't. They'll think I'm taking the piss – or the pass.'

'No, they won't. "Penal'y" instead of penalty. Drop your "t"s, too – "blood's ficker than wa'er". Drop your aitches: you're 'Arry, and your mum's Lidy Stan' on-'Arcour'. On the pitch, remember to spit on the ground, not at the opposition. Blow your nose on and wipe your sweat off with your shirt, and clap yourself when you're subbed.'

On the other hand, Paris was teaching all the players to dive, limp convincingly to fool the ref, and to crumple up and put on an anguished face to indicate they'd been fouled.

'And stay down – don't leap up immediately – until the ref clocks you. If you've fouled someone, sidle up to a nearby group of players, and if you're accused of a foul, look flabbergasted or outraged. "Really? Me? What are you talking about?" Find out the ref's name beforehand and call him by it, adding a "mister", and thank him after the game.

'Now, come on,' urged Paris, 'let's practise looking more anguished. If you can blub, even better.' Then, reverting to Mark Antony: ' "If you have tears, prepare to shed them now." '

A brilliant mimic, Paris also made them howl with laughter when he imitated Rupert's clipped, soft, very distinctive drawl and Ryan's attempts to shed any of Valent's Yorkshire accent.

Meanwhile, Dora was doing a great job boosting the circulation of the *Cotchester Times* with exclusive stories about Searston Rovers. When visiting Bianca at Penscombe, however, Dora sensed that Feral was very out of spirits, despite being Searston's star player, and suggested Paris should interview him for the paper.

Paris responded in February by writing a beautiful piece, starting off with the times when, known as the Wolf Pack, he and Feral had been pupils at a nearby sink school, Larkminster Comp. This reinforced Feral as a local boy who'd battled to make an incredible climb out of the roughest Shakespeare Estate.

There, Feral had been much better at passing balls than exams, and the much cleverer Paris had helped him with his homework. And, although he didn't mention it in the piece, Paris had also taken care of him after Feral's older brother, Joey, had dissed the head of a rival gang, who dragged him outside and shot him dead. Whereupon Feral's mother had retreated into drugs, leaving Feral to look after his younger brother and sisters.

The February interview had taken place over several drinks in Pear Tree Cottage, the lovely little house on the edge of Rupert's land where Paris and Dora lived rent-free. The walls inside were covered with books and paintings by Dora's family. Dora's ancient Labrador, Cadbury, snoozed on the sofa.

'Wish Bianca and I had a place like this,' sighed Feral. 'Rupert'd love us to move, but Bianca loves living in the house. Rupert's grite but he's so uptight about Taggie, she gets irritated too, and there are always Bianca's mates around the place. I just want to veg in the evening and watch the box. It was so much easier in Oz.'

Paris switched on his tape recorder.

'You started your career, Feral, kicking balls against the garage wall.'

Feral grinned. 'Didn't have no garage to kick against, man. And when I spent mumfs in a young offenders' unit, it was the first time I had a room to myself and a decent night's sleep. We built up our muscles lugging our folks home from the pub. God, it was rough. Teacher once asked me what I wanted to be when I grew up. I said, "Twenny-one." If you lived on the Shikespeare Estate, you was lucky to survive past the weekend. Teacher said if I didn't pull myself together, I'd be in prison for the rest of my life.'

Paris shook his head. 'That's ironic. As Montaigne said: "Fame and tranquillity can never be bedfellows." When you're a star footballer, fame becomes a prison. Wherever you go, the paps will be watching you. You've got to behave yourself, be a role model rather than a roll-in-the-hay model.' Paris was wondering how to work 'prison cell-ebrity' into the copy. 'And you have to put up with social media constantly putting the boot in.'

Feral grinned again. 'That's one good fing about not being able to read – can't take in all the shit written about me.'

Feral's honesty endeared him to players and fans alike, who, as Feral helped Searston to win match after match, were singing his song:

'If we're in peril, we count on Feral.'

Or even another version:

''E shoots with the left, he shoots with his right, our Feral Jackson makes Messi look shite.'

'It's Bianca who's Messi,' giggled Dora. 'You can't get into their bedroom for clothes on the floor.'

Paris's piece, which was picked up by all the nationals, had also captured Feral's beauty and how much he'd improved as a player since he'd come back from Perth, by quoting Keats:

'Then felt I like some watcher of the skies / When a new planet swims into his ken.'

'Who's Ken?' grumbled Bianca, the only unenthusiastic reader of the piece. 'Why didn't Paris mention me?'

Although she loved Feral, she was jealous that he was

becoming more and more of a star and needed a member of the publicity team at Searston to deal with media demands and cope with his ever-growing fan mail.

Bianca, who didn't have a job or even a house to run, like most of the other Wags, was very keen to have a baby and consequently wanted to be made love to night and morning.

Feral, because he was so good, was easily Searston's most fouled player, often in a lot of pain and exhausted by Ryan's relentless training regime. He was therefore less keen on sex, preferring to watch videos long into the night to improve his own game. He also found sex difficult in a bedroom only a few doors away from Rupert and Taggie, particularly as Bianca tended to make an unholy din, screaming her head off at the moment of orgasm.

18

Stable lasses Marketa and Lou-Easy's desire to have an erotic encounter with the Searston players, on the other hand, was frustrated by their having to load up Safety Car after his football demos and take him back to Penscombe, and the players having to return for the second half.

On a Family Day in March, however, Safety was enjoying the applause so much as he kicked the ball around the pitch that he refused to come off until Rupert went down to the touchline and, putting two fingers in his mouth, let out such a piercing whistle that Safety promptly trotted back to his beloved master, whickering and nudging him, followed by a wagging Gilchrist and Cuthbert.

The crowd was cheering and laughing and, crossing the pitch to collect Safety, Lou-Easy and Marketa had a chance to chat up the players waiting to go on.

'Let's have a drink one evening.' Lou-Easy thrust her mobile number into Downing's shorts pocket.

'Sure,' murmured back Downing, 'I'll call you. Have to avoid the boss. Hates us to party.'

That very week, Ryan watched the CCTV in the hostel where Bastian, Galgo, Josef, Wilfie and Downing lived, only to discover Miss Stroud and Miss Stonehouse, two local beauty queens, being smuggled out of a side door at four o'clock one morning. He was even more furious when a hungover Searston lost 3–0 later that day to a mediocre team in Sussex. On Monday morning, Ryan gave them a bollocking at the training ground.

'If you want to go up to the Championship, you've got to look after your bodies, eat properly, get plenty of sleep and don't drink alcohol or you'll be up several times a night having a pee. No wonder our fans booed you for losing. Just remember: booze leads to boos.'

With Marketa and Lou-Easy travelling with the horses to Newcastle, Doncaster or evening meetings at Wolverhampton and not getting home until very late, and Searston travelling round the country, it continued to be difficult for both sides to meet up. 'To synchronise our vatches,' as Marketa grumbled.

After the next Family Day game, Lou-Easy again managed to steal a few words with handsome Downing, who, now he'd replaced his blond dreadlocks with curls and grown a blond beard, was really gorgeous.

Encountering him when he returned a scrounging Jack Russell, Cuthbert, from the kitchens, Lou-Easy suggested: 'We must have that drink – how about next Friday? We're only going to Bath, and there's a party.'

'Friday's not great; boss hates us getting legless the night before a match and we've got to get up at the crack of dawn to go to Norfolk. Leave it this week, sweetheart, keep yourself on ice.'

'Ice'd melt in a trice, you're so gorgeous,' sighed Lou-Easy, giving him a lingering kiss on the lips.

Overhearing this exchange, a hovering Ryan, already insane with fury that Safety Car had crapped on the pitch, made some enquiries and summoned Captain Parks to his office the day before the Norfolk game.

'I don't know if you've noticed, but those two slappers from Rupert's yard who brought over those bloody animals have been trying to get off with our players. Evidently, they've had all the lads at Penscombe, three in a bed, bopping away to Abba till four in the morning, staggering out to the yard to load their horses and sleeping in the lorry all through to Newmarket. I want you to make sure you kill it dead. Clearly, they're complete tarts. Might easily give our lads some disease or get themselves up the duff. We simply can't afford to lose games. I'm relying on you, Parks, to keep Downsy and co. in particular on the straight and narrow – especially on Saturday, as I won't be on the coach with you. I'll be joining you in Norfolk.'

Looking at Parks's kind face, Ryan was reminded of a golden retriever. He'd always been jealous of Parks's popularity, and continued:

'Between ourselves, I'm going to town on Friday and staying overnight to suss out a few agents. We need to acquire some decent new players. Several of ours are getting past their sell-by date. Miles, of course. Ludo – you couldn't ever get past him in the old days. Now he's really slowed up. Griffy's slowed up too. Neither he nor Ludo has scored recently. Nor Midas much.'

Neither have I, thought Parks, and Rosalie was nagging him to take out a mortgage on one of the big houses in Rutshire's loveliest valley, known as the Golden Triangle.

'Young Feral's been scoring for all of us.'

'Not enough,' said Ryan. 'He might easily get injured. We need new young players too. Although Harry Stanton-Harcourt's a good lad. You can mentor him to take over your job. But you're still captain and your duty is to see the team behaves themselves, not drinking or screwing themselves insensible. I'm counting on you, Parks.'

Oh God, thought Parks, *I can't afford to antagonise Ryan.*

Later, he had a word with his friend Griffy.

'Ryan's on the warpath again.'

'I thought he was in a better mood.'

'He wants me to stop the juniors getting off with Rupert's stable lasses and exhausting themselves partying and fucking. Anyway, he's not coming on the coach with us to Norfolk because he's going to London to talk to agents about who he's going to buy, presumably because he's got more spending money from his dad and Rupert. He wants to replace several junior players, and retire a lot of senior players. He's got it in for Miles and Ludo.'

'That's crazy, the fans would go mad.'

'Says Ludo's slowed down and can't defend or score any more.'

Nor can I, thought Griffy. *That's me for the chop.*

His beautiful model wife, Inez, would go ballistic. She too had her eyes on a house in the Golden Triangle and Bagley Hall for the children. If he were retired without a job at thirty-four, would there be any other takers? What about his sweet children and his stepdaughters, who needed support? And what about the secret love of his life? Neither Griffy nor Parks slept a wink before the Norfolk game.

19

Searston were on the coach to Norfolk on another bitterly unfriendly March day. Torrential rain was chucking itself against the window, and a vicious east wind, like a cruel headmaster, was bending over and thrashing the bare trees.

'What a fucking awful day to play football,' moaned Angus.

'It'll be even colder and flatter in Norfolk,' grumbled Barry Pitt. 'Where's the gaffer?'

'Meeting us the other end. Gone to talk to agents in London. Now he's got more cash to splash, he's evidently planning to trim the squad and look for new strikers to replace both senior and junior players, so we'd better start looking for other clubs.'

'He won't like you bingeing on that,' accused Barry, as Angus got a massive cheeseburger out of his bag.

'He's not been in touch with my agent, I've just checked,' said Downing, switching off his mobile.

'Nor mine,' said Ludo.

'Nor mine,' said Midas.

'He's probably selling Miles Know-All for seventy mill

to Real Madrid,' mocked Angus. 'Or he's stayed back in Cotchester to put bugs in our houses, to check who we were shagging last night.'

Ryan, who had actually not left Rutshire, was complaining that it was so difficult working with Rupert.

'He keeps ordering the players to do something I've specifically ordered them not to do. I refuse to lose control of the dressing room.'

'My ex, Ralphie, felt the same,' giggled Emma Stanton-Harcourt. 'He always complained I hung all my ball dresses there, so he never had enough room.'

'You must be delighted about Harry,' said Ryan. 'The Academy are really excited about him, say he's already a lethal finisher.'

'Just like his father,' sighed Emma. 'He ended our marriage without a word – just walked out one morning, left me an electric blanket as a leaving present. At least I kept the house.'

Then, leaning over, she pressed her lips against Ryan's. 'That was so lovely.' Then, running her hands over his bare muscular chest and his flat taut stomach, down to his temporarily resting penis, she began to stroke it.

'Sensational,' breathed Ryan. 'You are the most beautiful woman' – ('and the best-bred one,' he nearly added) – 'I have ever been to bed with.'

On the dressing table, beside silver-backed brushes, lay her string of pearls and some little pearl earrings. Over the chair hung her jeans and striped prep-school shirt, with a name-tape saying 'Harry Stanton-Harcourt' inside. He was touched that she hadn't dolled up, having invited him to dinner last night. He'd been too

113

overexcited to make major inroads into the roast pheasant and apple pie.

The house had clearly seen better days. The curtains were coming away from their rails, there were cracks in the walls and the ceiling, moths had been dining on the carpet and on the walls; beside pictures of hunting scenes and ancestors were faded squares from where other pictures must have been sold.

After dinner and the most miraculous lovemaking, Ryan hadn't slept a wink, wanting to spend every second gazing at Emma, whose face wasn't smeared with mascara and eyeshadow because she wore no eye make-up. He found it endearing that she hadn't bothered to shave her soft brown bush or paint her toenails to show off her slender ankles.

Although he didn't like dogs, he didn't even mind Emma's yellow Labrador, Dasher, sleeping in his basket beside the bed.

'Such a kind dog,' Emma had sighed. 'Whenever someone turns up unexpectedly, Dasher always brings them a present, often a pair of my knickers or my bra – too embarrassing.'

'I can't imagine a more exciting present,' laughed Ryan.

Outside, his black Range Rover with the RE 1234 number awaited him. It was now nine o'clock and he ought to leave for Norfolk, but, reaching out, he cupped one of Emma's beautiful breasts and felt the nipple harden.

'I ought to go, Emma.'

'Oh, please no, we've got time for one, two or three more.'

'I should have brought the chopper, but I thought I

might get sussed. I'll have to drive like the wind to get there by kick-off and prevent Arsy-B antagonising the players and insulting the press.'

'Better than he used to be. In his showjumping days, the Golden Beast broke several photographers' jaws.' Wriggling down, she put her pretty unpainted lips round his cock, tickling it with her tongue and crying: 'Go on – per-lease – we've got time.'

As he slid back inside her and finally finished thrusting, Ryan shouted: 'I've reached the top of Everest. In fact, lovely Emma, I want to rest here for ever.'

Ryan didn't reach Norfolk until after half-time. Rupert, however, had flown in earlier, and, finding Searston a goal down, went straight into the dressing room at the break and ordered the players to switch off their mobiles so he could give them a bollocking.

When one rang, he went ballistic, then roared with laughter when it turned out to be his own, telling him Fast Piece had won at Southwell.

'Grite, grite,' cried Wilfie. 'I had her at twenty-five to one.'

And all the players laughed, relaxed and went out and won 2–1.

20

When Searston finally beat Deansgate in the Cotswold derby later in March and went to the top of the league, Rupert took the players to the Cheltenham Festival. Beforehand, he gave them a lunch of roast beef followed by bread-and-butter pudding and lots of red wine, and then took them down to the stables to meet his runners.

Later, Jerry Hatrick, a horse some chums had given him for his sixtieth birthday, came second, and Rupert took Wilfie down to lead him in, then told the excited players that if they went up to the Championship, he'd buy them a racehorse.

All this enraged Ryan, who had a shouting match with Rupert the following day:

'They've got a big game on Saturday, they were half asleep in training today, and hungover.'

Whereupon Rupert snapped back: 'They aren't laboratory animals, they deserve the odd reward.'

He then cited a local polo patron who, when his players won a big tournament at Cirencester, took them out to dinner and then on to a brothel in Bristol, which the Argentinian players particularly enjoyed.

'That's insane,' stormed Ryan. 'Think what diseases they might have picked up.'

Although he was adoring his affair with Emma and gratified to be managing a highly successful team, Ryan was irritated that Feral never bitched about Rupert, and that his wife rather fancied Rupert and was cross she hadn't been invited to the races. Ironically, Dinah was also excited by the idea of Lady Stanton-Harcourt and kept urging Ryan to ask her over to supper: 'She must be so lonely living alone in that huge house. We must find a super chap for her, and Kayley is so fond of Harry. Tell Lady Emma to bring him along too.'

It was debatable, however, who disapproved the most: Emma of Harry being pursued by Princess Kayley, or Harry of his mother being pursued by rough-trade bully Ryan.

Searston were well on their way to the league above, the Championship, when disaster struck. Feral was the victim of so many ferocious tackles that he had to drop out with a back injury. Without their star striker, Searston lost three games and ended the season in sixth place.

The form then, with three teams relegated from the Championship above, was for three League One teams to go up to replace them. The teams in first and second place went up automatically, these being Deansgate and Bideford, which resulted in nauseating gloating from Sir Craig Eynsham about hopeless Prince Charmless and Deansgate now being King of the Cotswolds.

However, there was still the third place to be filled, so the four teams below would undergo a mini post-season competition, the play-offs. In this, third place would play sixth, and fourth play fifth, both at home and away. The two winners on aggregate would then play each other at Wembley, with the winner joining first and second in the Championship. This was a huge challenge for teams exhausted at the end of a long season, but the incentive of a Wembley final created massive excitement.

For their first play-off game, on 11 May, Searston had to trail up to Lancashire and play a very tough Manchester Town, without Feral and Downing, who was also off with a dodgy knee. After an interminable journey and a vast yelling opposition crowd, Searston lost 4–0. Barry Pitt, having let in so many goals, got the most frightful press, everyone getting 'Absolute Pitts' into their headline. The coach drive home in utter desolation was not enhanced by the noisy and continued sobbing of Barry's wife, Sand Pitt.

A week later, on 18 May, Searston had to welcome Manchester Town back to Searston. An overconfident Man Town, with a 4–0 lead, regarded victory as a foregone conclusion and hadn't bothered to train much, even letting a couple of star players off for a few days' snorkelling in the Maldives.

Searston, on the other hand, had been fired up by Rupert, Ryan and Valent, and by the appalling press. This included Sir Craig, in an interview in the *Mail*, advising the Man Town goalie to take a deckchair and a good book to the match to pass the time.

Most important of all, Rupert had flown home his ace private doctor, James Benson, from a holiday in Portugal, who sorted out Downing's dodgy knee and rearranged the vertebrae in Feral's back.

Thus, when an overconfident Man Town arrived, having posted some silly song to their fans – 'We feel all trembly, because we're going to Wembley' – they found themselves swept away by a furious Searston and an incensed crowd making a helluva din.

Feral, Downing and Bastian proceeded to score in the first half, with an incandescent Barry Pitt stopping everything. Then, kissing the ball before clouting it upfield, he thundered after it, caught the Man Town defence off-guard and pounded it into a left-hand corner of the goal, yelling 'So much for a fucking deck-chair', and Sand Pitt's cries of delight echoed round the Cotswolds.

Then it was Ludo's turn. Dribbling the ball upfield, too slow to escape the Man Town pack, he flicked the ball to Wilfie running up beside him on the left, yelling: 'Run, you little bugger!'

Whereupon a giggling Wilfie, after one touch, can-tered down the field, his weak left foot forgotten, sliding a lovely goal diagonally into the right-hand corner.

5–0.

Finally, in stoppage time, a Man Town midfielder des-perate to get a goal, which would count as two and put them ahead on aggregate, mistimed a vicious tackle on a galloping-past Galgo, bringing him crashing to earth.

Free kick to Searston. Despite eight Man Town play-ers lining up in a wall, glued side to side and jumping collectively in the air to defend their goal, Angus sneak-ily blasted the ball under their feet, instead of over their heads, straight into the net.

6–0.

With sweet Mimi McLean leaping up and screaming with such joy that all the pupils' essays she was marking went flying, and the crowd making such a din, the final whistle could only just be heard.

Whereupon delirium took over. 'We're going to Wembley,' yelled the fans, a tidal wave of ruby and purple flooding the pitch, dancing, singing, shouting, embracing, with the *Black Beauty* music pouring out of the speakers, Bianca jiving with Dora, Safety Car the mascot neighing and dancing with the ground staff, and Wags taking the opportunity to embrace Rupert – 'Goodness, he's well fit.'

Ryan was talking to the press:

'We started four down, but I convinced my players to stay calm, and they showed character.'

As Wilfie was interviewed by Sky, his mother, Mary, was crying with happiness.

'Oh God,' sighed Tember, 'I hope his horrible drunken dad, Dougie, doesn't smell money and move back in.'

The only downside was that Drobenham won the other semi-final, so Searston would be facing Bruiser Ben Martin again.

'His other nickname's Big Ben,' giggled Dora. 'I hope he doesn't strike ten times.'

21

Yippee! Team Searston were ecstatic, pondering how to wow it at Wembley. As they were all pale from a long winter, Charlie the masseur was kept busy applying mantan. Downing had his shorts turned up three inches to show off his beautiful thighs and shaved off his beard. Midas dyed his black ponytail blond. Bastian dyed his blond ponytail black. Galgo had his hair shaved up the sides of his head, leaving a brushed-forward thatch on top – rather like a cottage in Somerset, said Rupert.

The Wags were going crazy, searching for new dresses, hoping the telly would seek them out in the banqueting suite and the paps would capture their arrival. The club shop was also making a fortune, selling replica purple-and-ruby kits for fans to wear to the match, and cuddly Safety Cars for them to brandish as they sang: 'Crack goes the whip, the wheels go round, giddy up, we're Wembley bound.'

Back at Penscombe, things were not so good. Taggie was recovering from radiotherapy but she was still feeling desperately weak and was distraught that her hair, slowly growing back, was not the former lustrous, rippling black cloud, but lank and grey. Consequently, she took refuge in the beautiful wigs Bianca had found her, but couldn't face a crowded Wembley seething with photographers and ravishing Wags. She felt awful because she lost it when Rupert tried to persuade her it would be a fun day out, snapping that she wasn't up to it and had no desire to go.

'Timon's wildly excited, he'll be much better company than me.'

So Rupert had stormed out, slamming the door, and Taggie had retired to bed in tears.

Five minutes later, Shelagh banged on the door.

'How are you, darling?'

'Fine,' sniffed Taggie, noticing Shelagh's hand was shaking as she put a cup of tea down on the bedside table.

'I hope you don't mind if I say something, Taggie, but it's a huge thing, this Wembley game. Eamonn's over the moon to be invited. I just think you should try and go!'

'I can't.' Taggie gave a sob. 'I look so hideous, with this awful hair sprouting out – so shaming for Rupert to be seen with me.'

'You never look awful, and with a wig and some make-up you'll look fantastic, and I hope you'll forgive me, but your handsome Rupert seems so sure of himself and confident, but I know how he misses you and needs your support. You've been so brave, but I think it would cheer you up if you experienced what fun and how exciting the outside world can be. I hope you'll forgive me. I'm know I'm putting my job on the line,' said Shelagh, taking Taggie's hand, 'and Eamonn and I love it so much here, but all the world are amazed how much

Rupert's stepped aside from racing, he's such a fantastically busy person, and' – Shelagh chose her words bravely – 'I know cancer's all-consuming, but I think it would mean the world to him if you put him first.'

'It's not that,' stammered Taggie, 'but he's so utterly gorgeous, I don't want him to be saddled with someone as awful-looking as me, and I'm scared of going back into the world.'

The next moment, they both jumped in terror as Forester's tail thwacked on the counterpane and Rupert walked in. But far from extending the earlier row, he was roaring with laughter.

'Sapphire said she'd finished reading you *The Tiger Who Came to Tea* and *The Cat in the Hat*, so she'd got this out of the shelves.' He brandished *The Joy of Sex.* 'But she says it's full of bare people who don't have names, except for one called Master Bate. "That's probably a bit grown-up for Granny," I told her, removing it, and that you'd find her some Enid Blyton, Shelagh.'

'I'll go and look,' said Shelagh, scuttling out.

'I've been thinking,' said Taggie, patting the bed. Then, as Rupert sat down, avoiding Forester's long brindle legs: 'Can I come to Wembley with you on Sunday? I'm so proud of you and Searston, and we haven't had a day out for ages, if that's OK?'

'OK? It's fucking marvellous,' said Rupert, and his tired, drawn face lit up so much that an enchanted Taggie stretched up and kissed him lingeringly on the mouth.

'That is so marvellous,' repeated Rupert. 'Everyone will be so pleased to see you, and Bianca and Timon will look after you if I have to pop down to the dressing room. And, best of all, I so need a bodyguard to protect me from ghastly Dinah-mite and Rosalie Parkinson. He'll be livid.' He scratched Forester between his front legs. 'He's so used to having you at home. I've got something for you.' He brought a bottle out of his pocket. 'Lou-Easy found it online. It's called Mane 'n Tail shampoo, and it fantastically transforms manes and tails, making them all thick and soft and glossy and full of bounce. It's worked like a charm on Safety – why don't you give it a try?'

'And then you can ride me,' giggled Taggie, pulling Rupert back into her arms. 'Can Shelagh come to Wembley too?'

22

Even so, as Sunday approached, Taggie grew more terrified. Apart from hospitals, she hadn't faced the outside world for well over a year. Happily, Shelagh, Dora and Bianca weighed in. The Mane 'n Tail shampoo worked like a dream, transforming Taggie's hair, leaving it bouncy and glossy, and although still short and grey, this enhanced her huge silver-grey eyes, no longer red-rimmed with tears after an enforced half-hour of eye pads in a darkened room.

Her slender body was then coaxed into black jeans and the grey jersey with a silver star on the front which Rupert had bought her, topped by a crimson satin jacket. And, as a result of heated rollers, Bianca daubing rouge on her blanched cheeks and Dora drenching her in half a bottle of Diorissimo and putting on the 'Post Horn Galop', Taggie was amazed and overjoyed as she came downstairs to be greeted by incredulous wolf-whistles, which were followed by:

'Wow!' from Eamonn; 'Goodness, Granny, you look like a film star!!' from Timon; and 'Christ, you look gorgeous – let's go straight back to bed,' from an enchanted Rupert. 'Thank God we've got Eamonn to keep the paps at bay.'

Fortunately, it was a lovely day, the first in June, as they drove past cows lying in the sun, kept cool by a light east wind; golf courses strewn with buttercups and dandelion clocks; and pale-pink wild roses festooning the hedges.

Ahead lay Wembley, soaring skyscrapers flanked by trees in their summer green, and the stadium itself like a vast round basket with its handle curling into the sky above. As endless security made the ladies empty their handbags on arrival, Dora remarked: 'It's a pity we can't empty Wembley of Bruiser Martin and all those other Drobenham bullies.'

On their way into the building, they passed a fine sculpture of Bobby Moore, who'd died of cancer, with his foot on a ball. Ahead lay a pack of supporters, smothered in orange or purple-and-ruby strips, scarves and jester hats, with their beards and moustaches dyed team colours and team flags painted on their cheeks.

'Rupert, Rupert,' shrieked a vast female fan, with half-purple and half-crimson hair and a cleavage like the Grand Canyon. 'We must have a selfie.'

'There's Taggie, too – isn't she stunning. 'Ullo, Taggie,' cried the other fans.

'Back off!' roared Eamonn, shoving them to one side.

'Christ,' said Rupert as they escaped into the Bobby Moore Suite. ''Strordinary the beautiful game could produce quite such hideous fans.'

'It's a fan-see dress party,' crowed Dora.

Also in the Bobby Moore Suite, having pre-drinks,

were directors and heads of ground staff from both Drobenham and Searston, as well as Wags and important guests. A lady mayor in trousers was talking to Drobenham chairman Terence Lightfoot, who was wearing an orange tie secured by a red squirrel pin, and to Dora's eldest brother and Cotchester's Tory MP, Jupiter Belvedon, a very successful art dealer, who kissed Taggie and expressed regret that Rupert wasn't buying pictures any more.

'I suppose all your money's going on players now.'

'A lot of it,' agreed Rupert. 'And if we go up today, they'll be even more expensive.'

'Not what the bookies say,' mocked Terence Lightfoot. 'You'd better go back to racing, Campbell-Black. I've got my own song now.' And he burst into a reedy tenor: '"Terence Lightfoot's team's on the right foot, they can use their left feet too, Lightfoot's lads are top of the queue." How about that, Prince Charmless?'

'Don't call Rupert that,' gasped Taggie. 'He's the most charming man in the world.'

Fortunately, the next moment, Valent's sweet wife, Etta, rushed up.

'Taggie, how heavenly to see you. Love your short hair; you're looking simply gorgeous.'

Taggie was not the only one. Expectation of Championship salaries, being targeted by the paps and meeting Rupert Campbell-Black face to face had sent the wildly excited Wags splurging on new outfits. There was hardly a plain woman in sight, all slim as blades, with skirts well above the knee and long rippling hair.

Bianca, in her favourite deep red and one of the prettiest, was talking to Bastian's girlfriend, Daffodil. Charm, in sleeveless crimson showing her 'Love Yourself' tattoo, was getting stuck into delicious Sauvignon. 'So nayce we don't have to drayve home.'

Irish Shelagh was getting on famously with Mimi, who, for once, hadn't brought any papers to mark. Timon, after a surreptitious second glass of wine, seized Taggie's hand: 'Come and see outside.' And it was breathtaking. A huge square of still mostly empty bright-red seats, surrounding a vast emerald-green pitch with two great big triangles on the grass – one containing Searston's shield of a galloping grey horse, the other Drobenham's red squirrel.

'Grandpa's team, isn't it great? I feel so scared for Uncle Feral. I hope that horrible Bruiser doesn't injure him. But I expect horses run faster than squirrels.'

'It really is exciting,' said Taggie, hugging him.

'Lunch,' called Tember from the doorway to the suite. 'Rupert's just popped down to the dressing room to check on the players. So lovely you're here, Taggie. Rupert's so, so delighted and you look so, so divine.'

'Oh, so do you.' Tember's gleaming Titian hair nearly reached the waist of her grey silk trouser suit.

'We've got a table, but I'm sure everyone's going to be too nervous to eat.'

'I'm really praying for Searston to win,' sighed Timon. 'But I bet all the Drobenham fans are praying for Drobenham to win. It must be really hard for God to decide which. Although Bruiser Martin is so evil, God might want to punish him.'

23

Drobenham supporters were situated on the right of the room, Searston supporters on the left, purple orchids wrapped in a crimson napkin on each table. Rupert and Taggie sat with Dora and Paris, Eamonn and Shelagh, Tember and Bianca, who was thrilled so many paps had taken her photograph.

Etta and Valent, who was still livid that Rupert wouldn't let him offload the thousand surplus cuddly Grand National-winning Mrs Wilkinsons in the club shop, sat two tables away with the lady mayor, who said it was such a relief that mayoresses were allowed to wear trousers now and that she didn't have to say 'a few words' today. Unlike the jokey speech organiser, who stopped at each table: 'Are you all right? I'm not going to do anything about it if you're not.'

During lunch, which was gentle and delicious – pâté followed by poached salmon and more buckets of white wine – the master of ceremonies made a speech.

'Whatever team goes up today, we'll be very sorry to lose you, but we'll be delighted for you.'

'You will tell me who the Wags are?' whispered Taggie to Tember. 'Who's that stunning blonde?'

'Bastian's girlfriend, Daffodil – well named, as she's completely daffy. If we win today, Bastian is going to propose. And that other blonde is one of Tommy Downing's harem.'

'And that beautiful brunette, in crimson?'

'That's Inez, the hen- or rather vulture-pecker,' said Tember, sourly. 'Griffy's wife. She must have spent a good six months of poor Griffy's salary on that dress, and I bet that new ruby necklace is real.'

'I think Griffy's rather gorgeous,' confessed Taggie, 'very good-looking. He reminds me of that sweet John Le Mesurier in *Dad's Army*.'

'He does,' agreed Tember. 'He's such a darling man and such a great player, and so kind to the younger players.' She'd better stop raving. 'That darker blonde is Midas's wife, Charm. She's downed so much "whayte wayne", she'll have to be carried out unanimously.' Then, as Taggie burst out laughing: 'God, I'm such a bitch!'

'And who's that sweet-faced older woman who just came in?'

'That's Wilfie's mother, Mary, a single parent whose brute of an ex-husband, wife- and child-beater Dougie, will try and move back home if we go up today. I know he's sitting somewhere in the stadium. Poor Mary's had to support three children and make ends meet by working as a cleaner for the ghastly captain's lady. Talk of the devils, here come the Bitch Invasion,' added Tember as Rosalie Parkinson swanned in with Dinah-mite, who was wearing a crimson-banded purple trilby over her red hair.

'Really, Tember,' cried Dinah-mite, 'you could have covered your orange hair with a Searston-colours headscarf. Everyone will think you're a Drobenham supporter.'

'You should have come to the Rosalie Parkinson Boutique,' chided Rosalie. 'I'd have found you more appropriate headwear.'

'Boo-tique,' scribbled Dora on her notebook and passed it to Tember.

'Oh, Mary,' shouted Rosalie, catching sight of Wilfie's mother at the next table, 'can you make it half an hour earlier tomorrow? With so many press dropping in, the place needs a good blitz.'

'Oh, Taggie,' said Dinah-mite, suddenly realising Rupert's wife was sitting next to Tember. 'Good of you to show up. Rupert around?'

'He'll be back in a minute.'

'Then perhaps we'll join you.'

'No, Mary's coming to sit here, aren't you, Mary?' said Tember with sudden and surprising firmness. 'Rupert's a huge fan of little Wilfie.'

'What a cow,' hissed Dora.

'That's very unkind to cows,' hissed back Tember.

Down in the dressing room, Ryan, in a very smart new dark suit, was giving his players a pre-match talk, ordering a posse of defenders to follow Bruiser Martin wherever he went.

'But be ultra-careful when tackling him; he's ace at fouling and diving, roaring his head off so the ref's convinced he's the one fouled. I want him hampered by purple-and-ruby players – particularly you, Parks and Ludo – until he loses it and punches someone in the face. But you must stay calm; Drobenham in turn will try to wind you up until you lose it and get red-carded down to nine or ten men, and they'll walk all over us.'

Feral was flexing his back and trying to sit comfortably. He was used to playing through pain as a matter of routine, but scared Bruiser would try to take him out. A loud snore made them all jump. Wilfie, far too nervous to sleep last night, had pinched two of Mary's sleeping pills, slept all the way up on the coach, and now dropped off again.

'For Christ's sake, Wilfie,' snarled Ryan.

Bastian, so excited about appearing at Wembley and on Sky, was scribbling his *Hauteur Biography* in between putting on a second layer of tinted moisturiser.

Guests in the Bobby Moore Suite toyed with strawberry mousse and were subjected to more speeches. One from the betting-company sponsors, who urged people to gamble responsibly – 'But a lot,' observed Paris – others from charities keen to bring on young players from disadvantaged homes or proud of helping clubs in financial trouble.

This was followed by a sad and chilling speech on prostate cancer. One in eight men would die of it, and by half-time today, another eight would have gone. Would everyone please put ten pounds for all types of cancer in the envelopes on the tables? Aware that everyone was glancing at Taggie, Rupert put a comforting arm around her shoulders and Tember took her hand.

With much rustling, Terence Lightfoot put a great wodge of £20 notes in his envelope, saying, 'Bobby Moore was a great friend of our family.'

'We have one of his match balls at home,' announced

Dinah-mite. 'Ah, here's my husband – doesn't he look smart in his new navy tailor-made outfit?'

Having been busy talking to the press and revving up his players, who were now warming up outside, Ryan had popped in for a drink and drew aside his father, Valent.

'Can you try and keep Rupert out of the dressing room, Dad? He'll only screw up the players. He's worried Feral's not a hundred per cent and wants him not to come on until after half-time, and he'll go ballistic if I leave bloody Josef on the bench. Just because Josef's mother's flown in from the Czech Republic.'

They were interrupted by the mighty Jonathan Northcroft, chief football correspondent from the *Sunday Times*: 'This must bring back great memories, Valent. I was here when you won the FA Cup for West Riding.' Then, turning to a delighted-to-be-recognised Ryan: 'Very good luck to you too, Ryan.'

On his way to the stands, Rupert passed a smirking Ryan on his mobile:

'I miss you too, dearest. Harry'll be playing here in a year or two.'

Out on the pitch, blue balloons drifted over the centre circle. The teams lined up to sing the National Anthem, with Galgo not knowing the words. Now that the red carpet and the huge triangles depicting the teams' crests had been rolled away, one could appreciate the vastness of the pitch: even Bruiser Martin and Ludo looked tiny.

Drobenham fans curling round to the right easily outnumbered little Searston on the left, but together both sets only totalled about 18,000 in a stadium that could accommodate 90,000. Not a huge crowd, but a wildly excited one, cheering, singing and drumming as though the gods were moving furniture around in heaven.

Taggie, in the stands outside the Bobby Moore Suite, was enjoying every moment. Everyone had been so lovely to her.

'I never dreamt it would be so exciting,' she told a desperately tense Rupert on one side and Timon on the other. 'And isn't Tember heaven? She's looked after me so well and told me who all the players were. That's Midas kicking off.'

It was, and the teams were away. Bruiser Martin thundering down, trailing Searston defenders and clouting the ball between the posts, and Barry Pitt in shocking pink flying through the air and stopping it with his fingertips, making Sand Pitt leap up in delight and Barry himself yell at his defence to keep the fuckers away.

'I'm programmed for defeat so I won't be too devastated,' said grey-haired smoothie Jupiter Belvedon. 'Or perhaps I'm not,' as Ludo sent a long pass to little Wilfie, who hurtled downfield, weaving in and out of Drobenham defenders, flicking the ball to Downing who, for once, paused to think before finding a space and lofting it into the net. 1–0. Whereupon Searston fans leapt yelling to their feet, arms flying upwards like ash tree branches, brandishing flags and programmes and cuddly Gallopers to the accompaniment of hunting horns and ecstatic drumming. And the television cameras panned on to the joy on Downing's face as he knelt and kissed the grass and his Searston teammates fell on top of him.

Another camera simultaneously picked up the dawning

despair of the Drobenham goalie, while another captured Ryan, who'd been frantically chewing gum and taking endless slugs of bottled water, but who now, most uncharacteristically, did a little jig, leapt three feet high and punched the air with his fists.

'I bet he's been practising that in the mirror,' observed Dora. 'Ryan doesn't do ecstasy.'

Ecstasy was short-lived: Bruiser Martin got to work as an old boy sitting behind, who turned out to be Bastian's grandfather, was giving a running commentary. 'Go on, Bastian, be a man, go on.'

'I hope he's not irritating you too much,' apologised his wife.

Not nearly as much as a Drobenham striker's goal at twenty-one minutes, followed by Bruiser penetrating a pack of Searston defenders like a police car through a traffic jam, until, tackled by Angus, he crashed to the ground, where he lay bellowing in pain until the ref gave Drobenham a penalty, which one of their top strikers belted in.

'Poor Prince Charmless, your side's quite harmless, but Terence Lightfoot's boys are on the right foot,' sang the Drobenham fans.

Ryan was wondering whether to bring on Feral when Searston rallied, passing to each other, causing huge excitement, until they realised Midas's shot from 20 yards had only shaken the outside of the net. Then, just before half-time, Griffy, clearing from the penalty area, passed the ball straight to a Drobenham striker, who powered it right back into goal. Griffy was promptly subbed. 3–1 to Drobenham.

However stunning one looks, it doesn't compensate for one's husband getting booed off, as Griffy was. So, over half-time, cups of tea and more glasses of wine, Griffy's wife, Inez, was just showing Charm, Mimi and Sand Pitt a lovely photograph of herself modelling a green jumpsuit in the *Daily Telegraph* colour mag, when the Bitch Invasion rolled up.

'You must be gutted, Inez,' cried Rosalie. 'Iron Man's had such a disappointing game. I suppose he is due for retirement. Mind you, you're lucky, Inez – Griffy is so domesticated, you'll be free to concentrate on your modelling career.'

Whereupon a passing Tember lost it.

'Griffy's brilliant,' she said furiously. 'He's the heart of our defence. All the players adore him and rely on his experience. Don't you dare bad-mouth him.'

'Hoity-toity,' mocked Dinah-mite as Tember stormed off. 'Tember was very quick at coming to hubby's defence, Inez. Is anything going on there?'

In the second half, tempers flared, with fans yelling insults at the opposition and players fighting on the field and flinging around four-letter words.

'Are you trying to undress me?' shouted Angus, as a Drobenham defender tugged at his shirt. Along the stand rails, policemen in orange jackets were sitting with their backs to the game, looking for signs of trouble in the crowd. Bruiser Martin had the ball and was roaring towards Wilfie, who next moment had keeled over.

'Oh my God,' gasped his mother, Mary, as her son lay motionless and concerned Searston medics rushed on.

'Christ, he's not breathing,' muttered James Benson.

The stadium fell silent. 'My little lad,' sobbed Mary.

My meal ticket, thought his vile father, Dougie. Then Wilfie opened his eyes and beamed up at the medics around him.

'Not dead, just tired; I needed a little siesta,' he giggled, leaping to his feet.

Bruiser had the ball again, Ludo and Parks leaping from left foot to right foot to stop him.

'God save our King,' sang the fans.

Taggie was amazed. What a thrilling time she was having!

'Are you warm enough, Granny?' Timon kept asking her, when he wasn't shouting his head off for Searston, particularly when Uncle Feral finally came on with twenty minutes to go.

'Bring on the cavalry,' said Rupert.

'I want goals at once, Feral,' ordered Ryan.

'Don't let Bruiser hurt you,' screamed Bianca.

Tall and beautiful, Feral carefully checked where every player was on the field.

'If we're in peril, send for Feral,' roared the fans.

Next moment, Bastian got the ball, passing to Parks, who sent a long pass to Feral, who, gathering up the ball, danced through the Drobenham defence, releasing a howitzer straight into goal.

3–2. Five minutes to go.

Officials in blue tracksuits, carrying ropes and platform equipment for the presentation, were now sitting in the gangway.

Only two players were left on the Searston bench: a despairing Josef and a junior Academy player making his debut. Ryan told them both to warm up. Josef's mother, over from the Czech Republic, was crossing herself.

Feral then produced another exquisite finish into the corner of the net, making it 3–3, but was brought down in the box, lying on the grass. As the players and medics

137

gathered round him in concern, James Benson sig-
nalled to Ryan to give him a minute, 'to see if Feral is
just winded, or if it's something more serious'.

Everyone was whistling for the final whistle, which
would lead to extra time. Rupert yelled at Ryan to send
Josef on for the last three minutes of injury time.
Instead, Ryan sent on the young Academy player, 'so he
can say he's played at Wembley'.

I must save Searston, thought Feral, struggling to his
feet, and, gathering up the ball, he staggered goalwards,
somehow flicking it to a hovering Wilfie, who flicked it
back, whereupon Feral powered it in.

4–3 to Searston and a hat-trick for Feral. For a second,
the camera captured the incredulous joy on his face as
he shouted, 'That's for you, Mum!' Then, as the whistle
blew, Wilfie jumped on top of him and, laughing and
clutching each other, they rolled over and over to the
delight of their fans.

The photographers advanced with an army of long
lenses to record ruby-and-purple players hugging each
other before tearing round the ground, clapping themselves and sliding on their knees to thank their fans.

On the pitch, a dais and big board went up, saying
'League One Play-off: Winners, Searston Rovers', which
Taggie couldn't read. But, hearing the thunderous
applause, the truth dawned, and, turning to Rupert and
flinging her arms around his neck, she screamed: 'We've
won, we've won, we're going up to the Championship!'

'You brought us luck,' said an overjoyed Rupert.

'Hold the whole paper!' cried Dora, scribbling away.

Valent tapped Rupert on the shoulder:

'We'd better go and congratulate the lads.'

The Drobenham stands were emptying fast, except

for security men checking for anything sinister, and sea-gulls searching for leftovers. Poor Drobenham players lay slumped on the grass like plants not watered in a heatwave. Then they struggled to their feet and climbed up the gangway of the main stand to collect their losers' medals, which sympathetic VIPs in suits hung round their necks.

They were followed by the Searston players, so hand-some by comparison because they were happy and being bellowed on by their fans as they, in turn, received their winners' medals. They then progressed along the top row to be presented with a gleaming gold cup, trail-ing gold ribbons, by the Duke of Kent. Passing it to each other, they brandished it for the photographers, Feral and Wilfie getting the loudest cheers.

Ludo, his hand over his mouth to stop the press lip-reading, was telling Downing:

'That bastard Ryan still wouldn't let Josef come on and he sacked Milesy this morning, told him not to come to the game. Poor sod left in tears.'

Holding up the cup, Ryan later told a media conference he was pleased with his squad. They'd shown resilience. Climbing from the relegation zone all the way up to the Championship. After their last defeat by Drobenham, he'd remotivated them.

'Overriding Campbell-Black and your father can't have been easy,' suggested the *Guardian*.

'They're my team. I manage them,' said Ryan, firmly.

A proud and joyous Mary, Wilfie's mother, was think-ing that now Wilfie was going to be on Championship money, she might not have to clean for the captain's lady any more. Wilfie's brutal father, Dougie, however,

139

was looking up estate agents on his phone to find desirable properties in the Searston area. The Golden Triangle looked very seductive. Charm Channing had passed out. Midas would have to carry her home.

Down on the pitch by the dais, Team Searston were drinking and spraying each other with champagne, scattering gold streamers and letting off gold and silver fireworks before going on to a party at the nearby Hilton.

'Are you sure you're up to it?' Rupert asked Taggie.

'Goodness, yes, I haven't enjoyed myself so much for years.'

'You've got to come to every game in future,' said Timon. 'You brought us luck.'

Taggie had just popped into the ladies to check she really did look OK. Perhaps her short grey curls weren't so dreadful. Then she heard sobbing in one of the cubicles and tapped on the door.

'Are you all right?'

A pretty woman in a Searston scarf came out, wiping her eyes and blowing her nose.

'What's the matter, you poor thing?' asked Taggie.

'I'm so sad for my son, Josef.' The pretty woman had a strong foreign accent. 'The manager not like him. He doesn't know many people in this country. He vas so excited to be in the team today and paid for me to come over from Czech Republic. Then the manager take him off the bench to varm up and never play him. He is so sad.'

'That's awful,' said Taggie, putting an arm around the woman's shaking shoulders. 'My husband, Rupert, thinks the world of Josef, and I know he wanted him to come on today. I'll have a word with him. Are you coming to the party?'

140

'No, Josef too sad. He taking me to the airport. It would be so kind, Mrs Rupert, if you could keep eye on him.'

'I will. We can't have lonely players at Searston.'

Later, at the party at the Hilton, Taggie bravely reproached Ryan for not playing Josef, saying both he and his mother had been very upset. To which Ryan replied sharply:

'Josef is a lousy loser. Today he stormed off in a huff and didn't even have the grace to pick up his winner's medal. It seemed far more appropriate to bring on a young English lad who was over the moon at making his Wembley debut. I like my players to be enthusiastic.'

'They're not enthusiastic about Ryan,' murmured Tember to Taggie.

Seeing Griffy standing alone, looking downcast because he'd played badly, Tember picked up a bottle and filled up his glass.

'I nearly lost us that game,' he said, despairingly.

'No, you didn't.' Tember gave him a quick hug. 'You're a brilliant player and you deserved that winner's medal,' she whispered, 'for all the games you've helped us win this season.'

24

Sir Craig Eynsham, chairman of Searston's deadly rivals, Deansgate, lived in a vast house on the edge of the Forest of Dean, with his football club half a mile away but visible from the terrace. Romantically conjuring up the bare trees of the forest against bright-blue sky, Deansgate's colours were light brown striped with azure.

Sir Craig, as he insisted on being called, was in his early sixties. He had invented many hugely successful products: No-Bese, which dramatically helped people to lose weight; Spot Kick, which got rid of acne; SpecFind, in which you pressed a button and your glasses told you where they were; Deertract, which kept deer off one's flower beds; and Poover, in which you placed a nozzle to the anus and – invaluable to geriatrics and young children – it gently sucked out the crap. This had considerably reduced the three billion disposable nappies thrown into the environment every year. His latest invention was Glittoris, a sweet-tasting silver liquid which a girl painted over her clitoris to enable her suitor to locate it.

Sir Craig was a networker, in bed with both the local

planners and the Chief Constable, Lloyd Dudsbridge. Adoring publicity, he also appeared in his own adverts, claiming No-Bese helped him maintain his excellent figure. He invariably attended important football funerals to be seen on television comforting the grieving lovelorn. With avarice masquerading as altruism, he'd built a new stadium to accommodate Championship and later Premier League audiences, so he could cover the land belonging to the old stadium with houses to 'enable poor homeless young people' to get a foot on the property ladder. He also supported boar culls, to prevent the wild boars digging up 'poor old ladies' gardens' as well as his own.

When he'd bought Deansgate football club, he'd changed their nickname from the Boars to the Kestrels, thinking kestrels sounded more aggressive and swoopingly predatory.

Eynsham was moderately good-looking with questing hazel eyes, but his rather large nose, curved over a receding chin, made him look a little like a camel searching for a better oasis. He worked out every day to keep his weight down. Above all, he hated his bald patch and receding light-brown hairline and, whenever possible, hid them under a dashing collection of hats.

Irritated that his wife had become a Lady when he was knighted and he only a Sir, he fretted that the House of Lords would be abolished before he got his peerage. He loathed and was insanely jealous of Rupert Campbell-Black, whose land bordered his.

Lady Grace was almost more up herself than Craig, the names droppin' like autumn leaves, and referred to herself as Savin' Grace because she helped so many people with her charity work. She also played lots of vigorous tennis. Smiling into the mirror, she would murmur, 'You look lovely, Lady Grace,' and always wore a black belt with floral dresses to show off her slim waist.

She also fancied Rupert and laughed naughtily when he called out: 'Toupee or not toupee, that is the question,' as he caught Sir Craig carefully combing his sandy hair over his bald patch in the mirror, before going into some football party. Clocking Craig's fury, Lady Grace tried to mollify her husband by crying: 'Isn't it thrilling, Rupert – Craig's gone up to number three hundred and ten in the *Sunday Times* Rich List.'

Whereupon Craig lost his gentlemanly poise and snarled:

'Shut up, you stupid bitch, or all the players will want raises.'

Owning a football team gives you status in a social world, and is the dream of countless businessmen eager to emerge from obscurity, enjoy the spotlight and mix with celebs. Like Stevas, who had previously owned Searston Rovers, Sir Craig had houses in tax havens all over the world, a jet, six companies and a couple of yachts in which he hung undeclared pictures, but still no one asked for selfies with him in the street.

Like Stevas, he was tight with money, as the rich so often are; he kept players and managers short, and wouldn't let them stay overnight in hotels if they were playing twice in the same area. At public dinners, he could be seen looking himself up in the programme, and during Rory Bremner's hilarious after-dinner speech would be checking his iPhone. He fired questions but didn't listen to the answers.

He also didn't know much about football. He'd sacked his excellent last manager, Pete Wainwright, when Deansgate failed to go up to the Championship the season before last but, although they'd gone up next season, like Searston, they hadn't started this first season well.

Poor Wilson Phipps, known as Tipsy Phipsy, Pete Wainwright's deputy and now caretaker manager, was subsequently drinking like a whale, giving captain's armbands to two players at once, his hand shaking so much he couldn't read back any written notes. He was stressed out by players hammering on his door, demanding to know why they hadn't been picked for tomorrow's match. During one game, centre forward Laddy Heywood mistakenly picked up Phipsy's water bottle for a swig and spat out neat gin.

Phipsy was petrified of Deansgate's Director of Football, rat-like Jarred Moreland, who ran the business side of the club. Jarred, who had hard dark eyes, short dark hair, and a black moustache and beard, emphasising a pointed nose and mean mouth, was known to the players as the Rodent Operative. Jarred was better at fiddling than Nicola Benedetti, charging for a non-existent scout touring the country in search of players, and similar vast expenses for his own mistress's house in Cirencester, dubbed 'Sirencester' by Dora Belvedon.

Like Ryan, Jarred got bungs off schools, garages and estate agents for fixing players up with cars, houses and the best education for their children. He was also in cahoots with a dodgy agent called Alan Garcia, who bunged him hugely whenever Jarred signed up one of Garcia's players or introduced a promising youngster to put on Garcia's books. Jarred was lazy and relied on Elijah Cohen, the brilliant coach who ran Deansgate Academy, to provide him with unknown stars he could sell on.

Jarred could get away with such skulduggery because he was always 'smarming up' (as the Deansgate staff called it) to Sir Craig, and telling the press what a wonderful, charismatic chairman he had.

Meanwhile, the circulation of the *Cotchester Times* was rocketing as Dora took readers behind the scenes at Searston and Deansgate, interviewing non-playing members of staff and getting them to gossip about the players. Last month, she'd done a glowing piece on sweet Tember, describing her as 'comforting as a hot-water bottle on a cold night'. Last week, she'd interviewed Kitsy, Searston's kit man, who always looked like a Christmas tree, wearing all the player's wedding rings, earrings, bracelets and necklaces to keep them safe during a game. He was also strict about players liberally giving away their shirts, and always made them pay for a new one.

Also, in early February, Dora had interviewed Mitchell Simpson, the groundsman at Deansgate, who kept the pitch like a billiard table and was nicknamed Groundsy, or Grounds for Divorce Man because he was so darkly handsome and nice.

Dora arranged to meet Groundsy for lunch at Bar Sinister, the wine bar on Cotchester High Street owned by Rupert's raffish, glamorous, polo-playing friend Bas Baddingham, and which had paintings of famous polo ponies and players all over the walls.

Dora had found an alcove in the garlic-scented, dimly lit dining room, so they wouldn't be overheard, and was already stuck into a bottle of Chardonnay. But actually, thought Groundsy, Dora was so young and pretty and fresh-faced, she had no need of dim lighting.

Before even sitting down, Groundsy said:

'Look, I've got to level with you: I've just got another job. I haven't told them at Deansgate yet, but there's no point in you interviewing me if I'm not working in the area any more, and I don't want to waste your time.'

'You won't be wasting it anyway,' beamed Dora, waving at the waiter. 'It was press day yesterday and I've got the afternoon off, so we can get pissed and have a lovely gossip. What would you like to drink?'

'I'll have some of that Chardonnay,' said Groundsy, taking off his overcoat and sitting down beside her.

'Why are you leaving, anyway?' asked Dora. 'You were Groundsman of the Year, last season.'

He really was a lovely-looking man, she decided, with a great body underneath his navy-blue-and-white-striped shirt and jeans.

'Because I love my family and don't see nearly enough of them.'

He was also particularly fed up with Sir Craig and Lady Grace being so rude and demanding before the big party they were giving to launch their new stadium, inviting all the Great and Good for lunch before a football match.

'Who've they invited?'

'Every celeb in the Cotswolds. Don't suppose they'll come.'

'Let us now prise out famous men,' giggled Dora.

'Sir Craig's having a statue of himself unveiled, and a stand across which he's going to have his name in huge letters in the future.'

As Dora refilled his glass, Groundsy added: 'I'm fed up with being called out in the middle of the night to mend Lady Grace's rollers or unblock one of the Wags' drains, or to remove a daisy from between the goalposts.

'And I'm fed up with Narcisco Romano, bloody little narcissist, fucking up the pitch, practising knee slides for when he scores a goal. And I'm so pissed off with Jarred Moreland taking bungs for any work I do.' Groundsy paused. 'This is off the record, isn't it? It won't look great if my new bosses read me slagging off the old ones.'

'Of course. If I write anything, you'll see copy first. What's Laddy Heywood like?'

'Lecherous, screws anything that moves. Takes the female staff into the disabled bog, which is known as the "Laddies" as opposed to the gents.'

'I know – such heaven! Aren't there any nice people at Deansgate?'

'Elijah Cohen, who runs the Academy. He's a great bloke, brings in and on fantastic youngsters.'

Over moussaka and a fine Beaujolais, they moved back to Craig Eynsham.

'Rupert loathes him,' confided Dora. ' "If you don't want the plague, avoid Sir Craig," sings Rupert, completely out of tune. And I loathe the way Craig culls boars. And changing Deansgate's name from Boars to Kestrels, who are far more evil. Poor Taggie was in floods the other day when a kestrel swooped down and tore one of her doves to pieces. Boars have been in the Forest of Dean since the days of Henry VIII,' said Dora.

'Wonder if they each had six sows,' said Groundsy.

Together, howling with laughter, she and Groundsy cooked up a scheme to sabotage Sir Craig's launch party.

'How can we round up the boars?'

'I've got a collie at home called Christian; he'll help us. I used to be a farmer.'

'Won't we go to prison for sabotage?'

'No one will know.'

'And I can use "Sa-boar-tage" as a headline.'

Tipsy Phipsy was so scared of losing tomorrow's game that he got even more drunk than usual the night before and passed out in his office, leaving the club keys on his desk and the gates open.

'Groundsy's very happily married,' Dora reassured Paris, as she set out with her hood pulled down to meet Groundsy and Christian the collie on the edge of the woods. It was a mild night, stars looking down on them through bare trees.

'What a blissful dog,' said Dora, stroking him. ' "Onward Christian soldier".'

Soon they heard grunting and, with a sack of nuts and Christian's help, rounded up a pack of boars.

'Aren't they delectable?' cried Dora, shining her torch on a little striped piglet. 'Couldn't we keep him? My Labrador, Cadbury, would love him and we could call him Chauvinist . . .'

At about three in the morning, as thick fog came down, the boars were let loose on the pitch, where, with a mass rootle, they dug up huge chunks until it resembled a ploughed field, before wandering off into the forest again.

By midday, the fog had cleared and Lady Grace was just wondering whether to sit Lord Waterlane on her left or her right. Sir Craig was just wondering which of his dashing hats to wear, when, looking out of the window, he caught sight of an earth-brown pitch and nearly had a coronary.

Jarred Moreland, Deansgate's Director of Football, had been pleasuring his mistress in Cirencester. Phipsy was laid low with a hangover and by the time the damage was discovered, Dora was back in her office writing her piece for Monday's paper, to be accompanied by great pictures with the opening sentence: 'Money is the rootle of all evil.'

Later, the celebs, football worthies and members of the press rolled up at Deansgate to a lunch of roast beef and Yorkshire pudding, lemon meringue pie and oceans of champagne, because there was no match to watch. The boar mascot, who had been sacked to make way for the kestrel one, however, turned up plastered in his obsolete boar costume and danced round the party to huge local and national mirth.

Barney Hughes, sports reporter from the *Cotchester Times*, rang Jackie Carslake, reporting a huge story of a big match being cancelled because boars had dug up the pitch, to be told that Dora had already filed copy with the headline 'Boarglar Alarm'.

Next morning, an incandescent Sir Craig first sacked Groundsy for not keeping an eye on the pitch, and secondly Phipsy, for leaving the gate open. The brilliant Academy coach, Elijah Cohen, was promoted to manager.

'Welcome to hell,' Phipsy told Elijah. 'The first decision you should make as manager is who to ask to your leaving party.'

Dora sent a card to Groundsy: 'Thanks for a terrific story. Hope you got lots of redundancy money because Sir Craig didn't know you were already leaving. Good luck with the new job. If things don't work out, come and work for Searston.'

25

Elijah Cohen, Deansgate's new manager, was the son of a very rich and eminent rabbi, Abner Cohen, and his wife, Ruth. Abner was an autocrat and hated Elijah playing football, particularly on the Sabbath, which must be kept holy, and, even as a teenager, turning first to the sports rather than to the business pages.

This also meant that a distraught Elijah could not watch his favourite football team, Tottenham Hotspur, on a Saturday because he wasn't allowed to turn on the television until after sundown.

Rabbi Abner was not wholly displeased, therefore, when a horrific cruciate ligament injury, caused by a rough tackle on his outstretched leg, later ended Elijah's very promising career as a player. Now the boy could get down to a proper job in business. Elijah, however, at twenty-four, was heartbroken to leave his North London football club, where he'd been devoted to his teammates. He therefore bravely defied his father and insisted on taking his coaching badges in order to become a manager.

As Elijah was an only child, his mother, Ruth, was already nagging him to find a nice Jewish girl and produce some grandchildren. Elijah, however, who had been repressing the fact that he was gay, was conscious of what Leviticus had said in the Old Testament:

'You shall not lie with a male as with a woman; it is an abomination . . . For everyone who does any of these abominations, the persons who do them shall be cut off from among their people.'

Despite a few discreet homosexual flings, Elijah was aware that his ultra-orthodox father would disinherit him if he came out, so he had taken up with a boyish non-Jewish girl called Madison. But when Elijah took her home to meet his parents, as possible future in-laws, it was a disaster. Ruth had gone to a great deal of trouble, making a delicious goulash followed by a fruit salad for dinner. This, Madison had hardly touched, instead drinking far too much and, as a very subversive token leftie, banging on and on about Israel's appalling cruelty to the Palestinians.

'They even deprive the poor folk of red, white and green paint, so they can't paint their national flag on their houses.'

As a result, Abner and Ruth detested Madison and when Elijah, at the age of twenty-six, impregnated her and honourably insisted on marrying out, he was totally disinherited.

This enraged Madison, who, despite being very left wing and from an impoverished background, was not averse to marrying a potentially very rich man, spending a lot of his money on charity and living in comfort for the rest of her life.

Qualifying as a manager, Elijah moved away from North London, buying a pretty little house called Buttercup Cottage on the edge of a Cotswold valley because he had got a job running the Academy of young players aged up to eighteen at Deansgate football club.

He turned out to be a wonderfully instinctive manager, appreciating each member of his team was unique. Even though one had to handle players with poor English, one should appreciate their needs and make them feel understood. If a player had a bad game, Elijah would go through the video with him afterwards.

Fair but firm, he wouldn't be kicked around but gave even the youngest members chances to play, many of them ending up in the England under-sixteen, -seventeen and -eighteen teams. He was constantly on the lookout for new talent, and spotted potential, costing next to nothing, hundreds of miles away. He built up his team on camaraderie and, because his young players adored him, they fought the opposition not each other.

Elijah was an intellectual, so he kept an eye on the Academy pupils' education. He was also a bad sleeper, dreading the agonising task of telling a young player he wasn't good enough to have a career at Deansgate.

Elijah was very attractive, tall and hunky, with thick hair the colour of dark chocolate, olive skin, kind sleepy eyes, a mouth never far from laughter and a deep husky voice. Determined to dispel the Shylock stereotype of grasping businessman, he was incredibly generous and was always the first to buy drinks in the pub.

As Deansgate players joked, Elijah got in so early and left so late that they'd never seen his car move, and they thought it hysterical that it was an old green VW Golf with a dent in it. Elijah was very brave in defeat, believing that 'the robbed that smiles, steals something from the thief', and always embraced any winning opposition managers. Sir Craig hoped Elijah would sneak on difficult players, non-playing staff and Jarred Moreland, Director of Football, whom he suspected of duplicity, but Elijah was too honourable to do so.

When Tipsy Phipsy was sacked, lazy, vicious, avaricious Jarred was thrilled. Now Elijah, at the age of thirty-seven, had been promoted to managing the senior team, Jarred could leave everything from a playing point of view to him, and he himself could deal in contracts and trans- fers, making fortunes selling on the players Elijah had nurtured and created.

This was heartbreaking for Elijah, but, worried about his job, he didn't protest. Madison, who had ambitions to become a Labour MP, didn't work except for helping out the odd charity; she expected to be supported and for their children, Isaiah and Naomi, now twelve and ten, to go to good schools.

Madison also resented Elijah working such long hours, watching videos and identifying the vulnerabili- ties and virtues of his players and future opponents late into the night. On the infrequent occasions Elijah made love to her, he could only get it up by fantasising about other men.

26

Elijah's nemesis and favourite player was Dolphy Carter, who came from Oakridge Court. This was the same horrible children's home in which Paris Alvaston had been imprisoned, and when Dora first visited the *Cotchester Times* she had been told they were running a story about troubled teenagers trashing the place.

Barney, the *Times* sports reporter, had, at the time, tipped off Elijah that one of the inmates playing football on the lawn showed huge potential. Cries of 'Pass to Dolphy, pass to Dolphy,' rang out continually and whenever he got the ball, despite being so small, Dolphy would dribble it down the pitch and into goal from miles away.

Dolphy Carter had no family, having been dumped around the age of one by an alcoholic mother. Far too many of the homeless are leavers from care homes, cast out on the world. Chucked out of Oakridge Court, joining Deansgate Academy at sixteen, Dolphy was now living in awful digs with a couple so indifferent they didn't even realise the boy had rescued a stray black greyhound he called Grandkid, whom he secretly kept in a nearby shed and took his own lunch every day. Grandkid was the love of Dolphy's life. Out walking him, Dolphy would look across the valley at Rupert Campbell-Black's beautiful house and long for a family. Dolphy was angelic-looking, with fair hair, huge blue eyes, a stammer and an incredibly kind heart.

Elijah recognised his potential, and the moment he was appointed manager at Deansgate in February, he gave seventeen-year-old Dolphy his first professional contract. Players bitched that Elijah had only taken on Dolphy because he was choirboy beautiful, but also soon recognised his talent. Having never been allowed to be hugged by the staff at his children's home, Dolphy took some time getting used to all the cuddling after goals were scored.

New players at clubs were subjected to initiation ceremonies, paying for a team dinner or singing a pop song in front of a group of players. Dolphy, who had only just started earning a salary, got caught stealing leftover chicken for Grandkid from the Deansgate kitchen. He was dragged off by one of the chefs, and handed over to a group of players including Laddy Heywood, ace centre forward and terrible letch, who went every which way and was also beady about Dolphy's incipient talent.

Returning to the club that evening to pick up his forgotten mobile, Elijah heard roars of laughter coming from the treatment room and found a terrified and whimpering Grandkid tethered to the door handle. Barging in, Elijah discovered Dolphy strapped down on the treatment table, a scarf tied over his mouth and Laddy Heywood threatening to ram a goalkeeper's glove, drenched in Deep Heat, up his arse. Dolphy was writhing in agony and terror.

'That will teach you to steal food,' yelled a grinning Laddy. Then, as Dolphy gave a muffled scream: 'Shut up, you li'el sod, and if you breave a word about this, we'll kill that fucking dog and you won't need to steal food for it no more.'

Elijah was so outraged that he hit Laddy across the treatment room, breaking his leg. Having untied Dolphy and Grandkid, and gathering up Dolphy's clothes, Elijah told the drunken but discomfited group:

'If any of you lay a finger on another player again, I'll tell the police exactly what you've all been up to.'

He then took Dolphy and Grandkid home to Buttercup Cottage. Madison and the children were away so he tucked him up in bed, and the next day found a nice older couple for Dolphy and Grandkid to board with. Dolphy was so grateful, he gave Elijah a bacon sandwich wrapped in Christmas paper as a present.

Jarred Moreland, Deansgate's Director of Football, was absolutely livid when he found out his star forward, Laddy Heywood, was out of action for a few months as a result of an unspecified fight at the club. He refused to sack Elijah, however, because he was so cheap and so good at his job. The players adored him and Jarred himself was making lots of money, selling on or loaning out the players Elijah had so dramatically improved.

Jarred dropped in on Laddy, who was lying on the sofa with his leg in plaster.

'I've got to keep it up for a fortnight.'

'You talking about your cock?' bitched Jarred.

Meanwhile, happy in his new digs, and hero-worshipping Elijah, Dolphy was playing beautifully.

27

Sir Craig Eynsham and Jarred had been only marginally pleased at the end of last season when a dramatically improved Deansgate had gone up to the Championship, because sixth-placed Searston had beaten Drobenham at Wembley and gone up too.

Lady Grace, however, had still decided to give her annual summer soirée to celebrate the fact and, once again, invited the Great and the Good and the press, one of whom was Janey Lloyd-Foxe, a very corrupt feature writer and wicked widow of Rupert's best friend, Billy Lloyd-Foxe. Janey had chatted up Sir Craig at the soirée and arranged a future interview.

Also among the press was the *Cotchester Times* reporter Jamie Abelard, who that evening had turned up with an incredibly good-looking man.

'He's fit – where did you find him, Abes?' asked everyone.

'He broke into my flat the other day,' giggled Abelard, 'and he was so pretty, he stole my heart, so I kept him.'

Lady Grace noted Jase the Burglar picking up and examining her silverware and photographing her pictures. There had been a lot of crime and hacking around football recently, and although she and Sir Craig intensely disliked dogs, they decided to invest in a trained one to guard them and their houses. They therefore forked out £15,000 for a long-haired Alsatian, who had the loveliest nature, but who had been trained to bite and show aggression on command. Calling him Duke, they neglected him appallingly.

Janey Lloyd-Foxe was busy writing her autobiography, *Billy and Me*, in which she intended, viciously, to bitch up Rupert. Hoping to gather more material, one boiling day in late June, she came down to interview Sir Craig. He took her in his new orange Maserati Quattroporte, with poor long-haired Duke dying of heat in the back, to lunch at Bar Sinister, and kept his panama tipped over his compelling hazel eyes throughout.

'You're so good-looking, Craig, I'm going to describe you as the Forest of Dean's answer to Rupert Campbell-Black,' teased Janey.

'That bastard,' stormed Sir Craig, remembering 'toupee or not toupee'.

'I loathe him too,' said Janey. 'He never mentioned me once in his speech at Billy my late husband's funeral, and he was such a stud before his marriage, there must be legions of women who'll come forward and accuse him of sexual harassment. Mind you, I can't cope with all this MeToo business. In my day, you said "eff off" if men were awful, and "eff on" if they were lush, like you, Craig.

'Sexy restaurant, this,' went on Janey, admiring the

portraits of polo players around the walls. 'Bas Baddingham, the owner, was an ace polo player and someone I said "eff on" to many years ago. Bas is a great mate of Rupert's. They both fancied Taggie. Have you seen her recently? She's got short grey hair.'

'Marriage to that bully Campbell-Black would turn any woman's hair grey,' hissed Sir Craig.

My goodness, thought Janey, *he is really psychotic about Rupert.*

After caviar, lobster and two bottles of champagne, they came out of Bar Sinister on to Cotchester High Street and joined poor panting Duke in the Maserati.

'Lovely car,' cooed Janey, surreptitiously spraying her wrists with Black Opium and undoing another top button.

'My chauffeur calls it a "statement vehicle".' Sir Craig put a caressing hand on a thigh fake-tanned more orange than the car. 'Shall we go for a drive, Janey?'

The Bar Sinister head waiter had tipped Dora off that they had been lunching there, so she'd lurked outside in the car park and, seeing them set off to a local wood, had driven after them. Leaving poor Duke imprisoned in blazing and direct sunlight, Sir Craig and Janey disappeared into a nearby glade for a shag. Having crept up and photographed them in flagrante, Dora was so incensed that she found a piece of Cotswold stone and smashed one of the Maserati's windows, setting off an alarm as she dragged Duke free, half carrying him to a nearby stream and drenching him in water. Hearing the alarm, Sir Craig and Janey came rushing out, pulling on their clothes.

'How dare you break into my car,' howled Sir Craig, 'and where are you taking my dog?'

'Away from you, you horrible disgusting man,' Dora howled back. 'And I'll report you to the police and Battersea Dogs Home and the RSPCA and Dogs Trust and the Queen and Paul O'Grady for letting that poor dog boil alive.'

'That dog's specially trained and cost fifteen thousand pounds. I want it back. Come, Duke.'

'I think not,' yelled Dora. 'I've got some lovely pics of you shagging Mrs Lloyd-Foxe.'

'Give me back my dog!'

But Dora had bundled Duke into her Mini and driven off. Later, she sent pictures to Sir Craig and Janey of themselves in the nude in the glade. Worst of all, Sir Craig was not wearing a hat.

Jackie, her editor, laughed immoderately when Dora showed him the pics.

'You can write a "shag-a-dog" story, but we'll have to watch it. Sir Baldylocks is in bed with the Chief Constable, Lloyd Dudsbridge, as well as Janey, so no one's going to book him for cruelty to anything.'

Nor was Sir Craig prepared to risk the scandal. Lady Grace would take him to the cleaners and all his other lady friends would pressurise him to marry them.

Fortunately, that week, Lady Grace was too glued to Wimbledon to notice Duke's absence. Even more so, a few days later, at Sports Day at Bagley Hall, she was so fit a granny that she won the mothers' race, with Dora describing it in the paper as the 'Gran National'. Lady Grace was so delighted, she had the cutting framed and hung in the downstairs loo. When Sir Craig informed her that Duke had gone to another home, she only felt relief that he wouldn't shed hairs everywhere any more.

So, Duke the Alsatian joined Cadbury, the ageing

chocolate Lab, and became utterly devoted to Dora, who renamed him Buddyguard and featured him in a lovely photograph in her 'Dog of the Week' column.

'How odd,' said Lady Grace, 'that Buddyguard looks just like our Duke.'

Sir Craig was insane with rage and vowed to get Dora and close down her paper. She had made an implacable enemy and would need Buddyguard to protect her.

Jackie Carslake only just stopped Dora captioning a nude picture of Janey Lloyd-Foxe 'Bitch of the Week' in her next column, and one of Sir Craig as 'Prat not in the Hat'.

28

As Searston had gone up to the Championship, where the average wage was £50,000 a week, as opposed to £10,000 a week in League One, they would be competing next season against much stronger clubs with huge budgets. Ryan, already feeling *deified* by his ongoing affair with Lady Emma, wanted a big increase in players and staff to cope with the new challenge.

These included a director of football, to free him up for more exciting activities, a goalkeeping coach, a throw-in coach, more masseurs, a second kit manager, a data analyst and a team of researchers gazing all day at computers, checking who ran furthest in training, who made the most assists and passes, plus nutritionists, fitness coaches and medical advisors.

As the leading manager in the Championship earned £3,466,000 a year, with an 'average manager's salary' of £900,000, Ryan wanted a huge raise himself so he could lavish superior trinkets on Lady Emma. He had also employed a beautiful counsellor called Gemini Coates, to whom players could take any mental health anxieties.

'My only anxiety,' Ludovic King told the dressing room, 'is whether she'll go to bed with me or not.'

Rupert, after a blazing row, had further enraged Ryan by saying such acquisitions were quite unnecessary and cancelling most of them.

'Players are not laboratory animals; they'll only suffer analysis paralysis. And why the fuck do you need a goal-keeping coach when you've got your father, the all-time greatest goalkeeper, to knock goalies into shape?' Which infuriated Ryan even more, as he loathed any adulation of Valent.

All Rupert wanted was for players to treat every game as though it were a cup final, and attack and attack and attack.

Meanwhile, the Searston Wags were still euphoric after the victory at Wembley and were well aware the average Championship salary was £200,000 a month, which in two months was enough to put down a deposit on one of the big Cotswold houses in the Rutshire Golden Triangle.

'Somefing like Rupert C-B's stately home,' sighed Sandra Pitt, and she, Rosalie Parkinson, Inez Griffiths and Bastian's girlfriend, Daffodil, were soon pestering their other halves to fork out.

'Just like Oliver Twist, asking for mor-gage,' observed Dora.

In between seasons, clubs were also caught up in the maelstrom of the Transfer Window. Football clubs used to be able to transfer players whenever they wanted, meaning they could buy players and sell them on to other clubs at will. However, FIFA decreed, because of the skulduggery and vast money annually scooped up by agents, well over £250 million, that there should only be two transfer windows a year.

A short window, lasting a maximum of a calendar month, took place in January, roughly in the middle of the season. The main transfer window in England, however, kicked off at the end of the season in late May, and ran for ten weeks until the beginning of the next season, towards the end of August. Other countries varied the times of their windows and, if still open, could buy players from other clubs whose windows were shut. It was all extremely complicated.

So now the pandemonium of the summer transfer window was in full swing, with all the clubs buying and selling. Poor Tember was never off the telephone, fending off avaricious agents or comforting players like poor Josef, desperate to get away from clubs where they were never played.

Other players wanted to leave but other clubs were not offering enough, or suddenly backed off. Some players were humiliated that their clubs wanted to dispense with their services and spent their time pestering their agents: 'Hasn't anyone come in for me?'

Everyone was loaning and swapping. Other clubs waited until the end of the three-month window, expecting prices would drop. Others wouldn't relinquish a centre forward like Downing until they'd found an adequate replacement. Every club wanted to buy Feral, who'd scored by far the most goals in League One this season and sold five times as many shirts in the club shop, but Searston wouldn't release him and Feral wanted to stay with Rupert. Other star players arrived at a new club and were greeted by flares and fireworks and thousands of cheering fans.

Wags were upstaging each other because their other halves were more sought after. Rosalie Parkinson, because her husband had secured a further year's contract, was never off the phone, wising up then sympathising with other wives when no one came in for their husbands.

As Deadline Day approached, all documents – some contracts running to twenty-five pages – had to be sent in to the FA before the window closed at eleven p.m.

Ryan felt Searston needed a supersonic forward to keep Feral on his toes. Without consulting Rupert or Valent, he had gone ahead and spent millions on an Argentinian striker called Facundo Gonzales, offering to pay him £300,000 a week, with a house in the Golden Triangle thrown in.

Rupert was incandescent. How could they possibly invest such a vast sum in one player, particularly when Valent countersigned the deal, saying, 'We need him, Rupert – he'll attract global sponsors, pull in more fans and push us up to the Premier League. And South American players need their egos boosted, so we moost all make him feel welcome.'

Another Portuguese player, a defender called Jesus, wouldn't come because he'd have to put his Great Dane, Lisbon, in quarantine.

'Right attitude,' said Rupert. 'We could get past it by getting Lisbon a passport.'

'Lisbon can be a girlfriend to Buddyguard,' crowed Dora. 'Just think what fun getting "Jesus wept" into a headline, although we won't if he brings Lisbon.'

Over at Deansgate, Narcisco, Deansgate's Moan of the Match, who always took down his man bun to talk to the press, was very smug because several clubs were after him.

'I am a commodity in demand, a true transfer target,' he told Sky Sports News, which irritated the rest of the Deansgate team so much they cut off his russet curls while he was having a siesta.

29

In late August, going into the last week of the window, a terrific tension was building up, as hours, minutes and milliseconds pirouetted on the right side of the television screen and constantly moving straplines reported which player was going where. Feral and Taggie, both poor readers, watching together at Penscombe, had to keep interpreting for each other. Taggie, who'd become really interested in football since Searston's victory at Wembley, was sad no one had come in for Josef and very upset when she saw Deansgate's Dolphy crying during an interview.

'Poor lad's being flogged to an 'orrible, very tough club up north,' explained Feral.

To keep Facundo, Downing and Feral up to the mark, Ryan had again defied Rupert and bought a very striking striker from America, called Orion Onslow, which excited all the Searston Wags and female staff. Orion's parents were divorced and, although his father was English, he had been brought up mostly by his American mother in Minnesota.

Little Wilfie Bradford had played so well last season

and so many scouts were hanging around his sweet mother's apartment in the Shakespeare Estate that Paris said it ought to be renamed Baden-Powell House. Several agents had also tried to sign him up, but his vile father, Dougie, wasn't going to put up with anyone else making a buck. Having earmarked a nice property in the Golden Triangle, Dougie was planning to move back in with his wife, Mary, and run Wilfie's career.

Older players were edgy about the future, particularly Griffy, who had spent the day on housework, looking after and feeding the four children, while Inez had been away filming a commercial for a local gymnasium. On Inez's return, just as she was claiming she was absolutely exhausted and ordering Griffy to pour her a large glass of white, the telephone rang. It was Rosalie Parkinson:

'I'm so sorry, Inez, I thought you'd like to know, but Ryan's just told Hubby he's not going to renew Griffy's contract. I didn't realise it ran out next month. Ryan's spent so much on Facundo and co., he needs to reduce the wage bill elsewhere, and poor old Iron Man's getting past his sell-by date. Thank goodness you've got your modelling career to fall back on, Inez. Inez!'

But Inez had hung up and was screaming at Griffy:

'Why the fuck didn't you tell me? What the hell are we going to live on? I can't support you all – I'm on my knees as it is.'

'Ryan hasn't said anything to me about it,' protested Griffy.

'Well, you'd better get on to the club first thing.'

Alarmed that she was going to punch him in the face or claw his eyes out, Griffy escaped to Deep Woods, saying he hadn't walked Mildred, their brown-and-white, tight-skinned, curly-tailed mongrel.

'And that bloody dog will have to go,' Inez screamed after him. 'We can't afford it.'

Outside, it was a boiling hot evening, stars crowding the sky like football fans, the air heavy with the sweet scent of roses, lavender and tobacco plants put in by Etta Edwards. Mildred bounded off into the woods, sniffing out foxes. Seeing lights still on in the office, Griffy decided to pop in, in case, miraculously, some other club was interested.

Even more miraculously, he found Tember, who had been working since eight o'clock that morning, fallen asleep at her desk, her lovely red hair spilling over her laptop. Beside her, in a jam jar, was a bunch of yellow roses with a note saying, 'Dearest Tember, thank you for kindness. Love, Galgo.' Griffy was startled and touched to see a photograph of himself, taken by Cadenza, taped to the wall.

Tember had tossed aside her olive-green cardigan, and her orange dress, held up by two straps, showed off her freckled shoulders. She looked so delectable, Griffy couldn't resist parting her hair and kissing her neck. Waking, she turned her head and smiled in amazement.

'Griffy, what a heavenly surprise.'

Next, they both jumped as the telephone rang. 'Don't answer it,' ordered Griffy and, drawing her up into his arms, kissed her sweet, trembling lips.

'I love you,' he muttered as they finally paused for breath.

'And I love you,' murmured Tember and, taking his head in her hands, running her fingers over his smooth dark hair, she again pressed her lips against his. They were so totally engrossed, they didn't even notice Mildred wandering in, nudging her master, then, getting no response, curling up on the moth-eaten carpet. Nor did they notice Ludo, who'd also popped in to see if anyone was showing an interest in him.

'Hush,' he whispered, to stop Mildred barking. 'Your master needs a break.'

'I've never stopped loving you,' Griffy was now telling Tember, as he stroked her face in wonder. 'I cannot believe anything so wonderful as you still loving me back. Do you really?'

'Oh, so much. I tried so hard to get over you when you married Inez, but I never could. Oh Griffy, what are we going to do?'

'Do each other as soon as possible.'

'I feel I'm going straight to heaven in a fast lift,' gasped Tember, and Griffy laughed, burying his lips in hers once more.

Retreating downstairs to the bar, Ludo found Parks, escaped from Rosalie, drinking a large whiskey and glued to the latest transfer window news on the television.

'Don't go up to the office,' said Ludo. 'Griffy's getting off with Tember at last. But he's bitten off more than he can screw. There's no way that bitch Inez will let him go.'

172

30

Over at Deansgate, Dolphy Carter had been playing so well in the Reserves that a lot of clubs were showing interest. Because he was a product of the Academy, Deansgate would reap all the profit, as there would be no sell-on fee owed to earlier clubs. Director of Football Jarred Moreland had therefore arranged for his crooked agent friend, Alan Garcia, to handle the boy. Sussing that Elijah had a very soft spot for Dolphy, still livid about the breaking of Laddy Heywood's leg, and determined that Dolphy wasn't going to enhance Searston, Jarred and Garcia sold Dolphy to a tough northern club called Lancs Rovers.

Elijah was utterly devastated when he heard the news, suddenly realising how crazy he was about Dolphy and thinking of Yeats:

'A pity beyond all telling / Is hid in the heart of love. / The folk who are buying and selling, / The clouds on their journey above, / . . . All threaten the head that I love.'

He went straight to Jarred and tried to change his mind, claiming Dolphy was much too young to be sent on his own up north, and it was insane for the club to risk losing such a potentially brilliant player. Jarred told him to mind his own business and not to interfere. Elijah once again didn't kick up a fuss because he so needed to keep his job to support Madison, who was making a name for herself in politics, and the children.

But he knew, and telephoned, Dolphy's new Italian manager, Pedro, to ask him to look after the boy.

Dolphy was equally heartbroken. How could he live up north without Elijah watching over him? Where would he live, who would look after Grandkid while he was playing? He was terrified of another initiation ritual. He'd always been scared of Jarred, but tried to plead with him.

'I don't want to go to L-L-Lancs Rovers. I'm r-r-really happy here.'

'You've been very lucky,' said Jarred. 'Only a few Academy graduates make the senior team. It's time to move on.'

Then, when Dolphy's huge blue eyes filled with tears, he added nastily:

'If you don't play ball, with no pun intended, Deansgate will fire you, and your career will be fucked.'

Elijah was away, so Dolphy didn't get a chance to say goodbye.

Deadline Day dawned, with Taggie and Feral still confused by the three moving straplines, but they again saw Dolphy crying, when interviewed, that he didn't know anyone in Lancashire and wouldn't be able to look after Grandkid up there. Returning home, Rupert found Taggie in floods. 'Oh, poor little Dolphy, he's been dragged up to

Lancashire with that horrible Alan Ghastly. He doesn't want to go and he's terrified of losing his dog. Feral says he's going to be a fantastic player.'

Enchanted by Taggie's great new interest in football, Rupert looked at his watch.

'Leave it with me.'

Alan Garcia, who still wanted to flog other players to Pedro at Lancs Rovers, flew Dolphy up to a nearby private airport for a medical so the deal could be done. Dolphy was in despair. He was petrified of Alan, who was short and fat with cruel eyes squinting behind rimless spectacles, and who hardly spoke to Dolphy and spent his time on his mobile sorting out other deals. Landing at the airport, they were just in the bar, waiting for a Lancs Rovers driver to collect them, when a large blue helicopter landed on the grass outside.

'Look at those film stars getting out,' cried Dolphy.

'Those aren't film stars,' said Alan Garcia. 'They're Rupert Campbell-Black, Tember West and Marti Gluckstein. What the hell are they doing here?'

The trio came straight into the bar.

'Hello, Alan. Hello, Dolphy,' said Tember.

'Can I have a word, Alan?' said Rupert.

'We've got to leave in a few minutes,' snapped Alan.

'OK, since we're short on time, come outside' – where Rupert explained that they wanted to buy Dolphy.

'He's already sold.'

'How much?'

'I'm not at liberty to say.'

'Oh, don't be so fucking wet.'

'A million. He's come straight from the Academy so there are no sell-on fees.'

'I'll double that,' said Rupert, which the avaricious Alan Garcia couldn't resist.

'Let me make a phone call.'

'Campbell-Black's here,' he told Jarred, a minute later. 'He's doubled our offer.'

Jarred was reluctant. 'Craig detests Campbell-Black, he'll go ballistic.'

'He needn't know. He's on a yacht in the Med. Tell him Rupert offered five hundred grand more. We'll split the rest. I'll draw up a contract similar to the Lancs Rovers one. Tember West, Campbell-Black and Marti Gluckstein are all here, so we can sign it.'

Jarred didn't need much persuasion.

In the bar, Rupert was showing Dolphy a photograph of Taggie's greyhound, Forester, lying upside down on the sofa, having kicked all the cushions on to the floor.

'He'll get on with Grandkid, and you can come and stay with Taggie and me until you've got settled.'

Time was running out. The sun was sinking into the dark-green late-summer woods and, an hour later, with contracts signed, Rupert, Tember, Dolphy and Marti piled into the helicopter and Eamonn flew them back to Searston.

On the flight, while Dolphy slept, Tember had several words with Rupert:

'Ryan doesn't like Griffy and plans not to renew his contract when it runs out next month. Griffy's such a kind and experienced player; while strengthening the defence, he feeds so many strikers great passes. I know he'll look after Dolphy and help him to adjust, and the other players love him.'

'And makes great passes at you, too,' grinned Rupert, tapping her pretty turned-up nose. 'He's a good player,

Griffy. He's not going anywhere. We need gravitas, or rather Griffy-tas.'

A blushing Tember glanced across at a sleeping Dolphy. 'And he's an adorable boy.'

Back at Deep Woods, a waiting James Benson gave Dolphy a lightning medical, and the contract was signed, scanned in and uploaded on to the online registration five minutes before the eleven o'clock deadline.

Then champagne was opened and Dolphy was in heaven. Not only was he now a Galloper, with Elijah only 22 miles away, but Dolphy's landlady turned up with an ecstatic Grandkid, who flashed his teeth in a smile at everyone and was treated to a steak sandwich from the bar.

A very cold Sky reporter who'd been hanging around outside, in case a late transfer excitement occurred, got a wonderful midnight interview with Rupert and Dolphy.

'Why did you especially want to go to Searston, Dolphy?'

'Well, Mr Campbell-Black knew the name of my greyhound, Grandkid, and he's invited us to stay at his mansion.'

Rupert then added he thought Dolphy was a very exciting player.

'And I hope I'm worf all that money,' said Dolphy, beaming up at Rupert.

Next day, Dora's story of Rupert's hijacking went viral and enraged both Sir Craig and Pedro, the manager of Lancs Rovers. An equally enraged Ryan tackled Rupert:

'Why on earth did you break the bank paying such a fucking fortune for that kid?'

'Well, I thought he'd get on with Jesus from Portugal, who's left his Great Dane at home with his mother,' replied Rupert. 'And I was only talking to my friend Sir Alex Ferguson last week, and he agreed how crucially important it is to have a big enough team, to keep players fresh and give every player a chance. I also took on board what you were saying about the need to buy and bring on brilliant young players like Jesus and Dolphy. Luckily, we've got experienced players like Griffy to share their knowledge and help them to get even better. So we're not sacking Griffy, either.'

Dolphy was enchanted to move in with Taggie and Rupert and spend time with Feral, who was one of his heroes. He also adored Taggie, who laughed one afternoon when the wind blew off the black wig covering her lank, short and grey hair, and Grandkid ran off with it.

'You still l-l-look beautiful, Mrs Taggie,' sighed Dolphy as he returned the wig to her. 'Why aren't all posh people as nice as you?'

31

Dora's boyfriend, Paris, also befriended Dolphy. Having just had huge success in *The Merchant of Venice* at Stratford, Paris was taking a break before starting rehearsals for *Julius Caesar*, so, a week before the football season began, he took Dolphy and Grandkid out for supper at the Dog and Trumpet, Rupert's local in Penscombe. Dogs were welcomed here, their photographs and portraits all over the walls. Grandkid promptly took up residence on the bench seat next to Dolphy, one paw over his eye to block out the light, the other to scrape Dolphy's arm if he stopped stroking him.

'He's a stroke-a-holic,' sighed Dolphy.

'Our headmaster had a white greyhound called Elaine, which Dora and I used to walk,' said Paris, putting a gin and orange for Dolphy, whiskey for himself and a bowl of crisps down on the table.

Sitting down, he then explained that he, like Dolphy, had spent several years at Oakridge Court, the same dreadful children's home.

'I have no idea who my parents were. My mother dumped me on the steps of some police station. They found my name, Paris, and a drawing of the Eiffel Tower tattooed on my shoulder, the only indication I was French. I detested Oakridge Court so much that I advertised for parents in the *Cotchester Times*, expecting Brad Pitt to roll up, but there were no takers.'

When Dolphy confided the horrors of his initiation ceremony at Deansgate, Paris admitted he too had been gang raped at Oakridge Court.

'Since I was four, I defended my ass in children's and foster homes all round the country. My life is recorded in social service files, not family albums. That's why I became an actor. I liked myself so little, I could at least play other people.'

A lovestruck young girl was hovering nearby.

'Could I possibly have your autograph and a selfie, Paris? I thought you were fantastic in *The Merchant*; so many lines to learn.'

Only after Paris had scribbled his name, and insisted Dolphy was included in the selfie – 'He'll be more famous than David Beckham one day' – did the enchanted girl drift away.

'Do you really act in the featre?' asked Dolphy. 'It must be scary in front of a live audience.'

'Stage fright revs you up, just like football. You have to star in front of thousands more fans. My next part is a character called Cassius, nasty piece of work.' Paris put on a deep voice. ' "Yond Cassius has a lean and hungry look; he thinks too much, such men are dangerous." '

Laughing, Paris held out the bowl of crisps to Grand-kid. 'So I've got to lose weight and look lean and hungry.' Then, as the waiter put down two plates of chicken and chips: 'You better eat my chips, too.' And he piled them on to Dolphy's plate.

'You ought to join Searston,' sighed Dolphy. 'They say the Championship's the toughest league, and pre-season's been brutal. Ryan makes us run miles every day. I've lost half a stone. He doesn't like me and says if I don't improve, I'll never get off the bench. Ouch!' as Grandkid, sniffing chicken, scratched Dolphy's arm again.

As Paris ordered a bottle of white, Dolphy said:

'D'you fink we should? Ryan's dead against drinking.'

'He won't know. Do you remember your parents at all?'

'No. My muvver was an alki, so Ryan wouldn't have approved. She didn't want me; she left me on a park bench as a baby wiv an empty gin bottle beside me. Nobody found her. I don't even know when my birfday is.' Dolphy's voice broke slightly. 'The auforities gave me a birfday, based on my development, but it wasn't my real one.'

'Things will get better.' Paris put a hand on Dolphy's shoulder. 'My Classics master was a terrific bloke, left me some money. Older parents adopted me and they're great. Then I met Dora – her father had died and her mother's a bitch, but she's my soulmate. So things will work out for you.'

Handing a piece of chicken to Grandkid, Paris went on:

'You're a fantastic footballer and you're bloody good-looking.'

Dolphy blushed. 'Elijah was the nearest fing to a farver I ever had. He was so kind to me and Grandkid. Taggie and Rupert are really lovely, and you and Feral and Shelagh and Eamonn. But I would like a family for Christmas.'

'You can have mine,' said Wilfie Bradford, the little redheaded Searston forward who'd just joined them. 'The pack's on the way. They've switched pubs, not wanting Ryan to catch them.'

'How are things?' asked Paris, noticing a bruise below Wilfie's left eye.

'Not great. I was saving up to buy a racehorse, now that I'm on good Championship money, but my drunken bully of a dad moved back home to thump me when I play badly and instead bought a Porsche for himself. I wanted to help poor Mum give up her job cleaning for another bully, Mrs Parks, but my dad says we need the money because he wants us to buy a home in the Rutshire Golden Triangle, so he's urging her to go and clean for Dinah-mite as well.'

'You poor sod,' said Paris. 'You need a drink.'

'I'll get them,' said Dolphy.

Next minute there was a 'woohoo', and in erupted a yelling gang of Searston players. Accompanying them, full of joy and alcohol, were Rupert's stable lasses, Lou-Easy and Marketa, who had a night off after a very successful week at York races, and were delighted to see Paris and Dolphy.

'How's Dora, Paris?' asked Lou-Easy. 'Fantastic piece she wrote about Rupert hijacking you, Dolphy. "Magna Carter" – what a great headline. How're you getting on, staying with Rupert and Taggie?'

Looking gorgeous but a little dishevelled in a turquoise minidress, Lou-Easy collapsed on to the bench seat beside a wagging Grandkid. 'Such a sweet dog, he's really palled up with Rupert's pack.'

'I fink Mrs Taggie put flowers in his basket when he arrived. She's so kind,' said Dolphy.

As the Searston players milled around being recognised by the locals, the landlord, thrilled by the invasion, put on the Gallopers' *Black Beauty* music and was offering drinks on the house.

'Rupert's buying in has been great for business,' he said. 'Fans from all over drop in here on match days.'

'And we'll be taking Safety Car and the Jack Russells over to do their demos on days we're not racing, to boost the crowds,' said Lou-Easy. 'That's them over by the window,' she told Dolphy, pointing to pictures of Cuthbert and Gilchrist. 'We must get one of Grandkid up there too.'

Next moment, Marketa tottered out of the ladies, looking stunning in a low-cut red dress, having put on even more red lipstick, taken the shine off her face, loosened her black hair over her shoulders and drenched herself in buckets of Coco Mademoiselle. She was just in time to embrace an incredibly good-looking dark-haired man who had entered the pub in jeans and a navy-blue polo neck. It was Orion Onslow, Ryan's new striker from Minnesota, known as 'Oh Oh' because he was so gorgeous. Both Marketa and Lou-Easy had the raging hots for him.

Orion was drinking tomato juice. 'Trying to prep myself for my Searston debut on Saturday,' he drawled.

'Against Midland Castle,' said Ludo, joining them. 'They're insane with rage they've been relegated from the Premier League. They'll probably lynch us.'

'Not if Facundo has anything to do with it,' said Barry Pitt. 'He should have arrived from Argentina by then.'

'We'll all three be making our debuts,' said Orion, raising his tomato juice to Dolphy and sitting down on the bench opposite, with Marketa and Lou-Easy lolling drunkenly on either side of him.

'Dora tells me you've got an online clothing range, Orion,' said Paris. 'What sort of stuff do you market?'

'Sweaters, cashmere like this one. Jeans for footballers – hard to find ones that fit when one's got such muscular thighs.'

Bastian, who'd just landed a television commercial for an aftershave, had finally proposed to his beautiful daffy girlfriend, Daffodil, who now rolled up with him, brandishing a huge diamond ring.

'So exciting,' she announced. 'We've just found a lovely property, Chaffinch Court, in the Golden Triangle.'

'Fucking hell,' sighed Wilfie. 'That's the one my dad's after.'

Glancing across the room, Paris started to laugh. While Orion had been talking football to Ludo and a newly arrived Angus, a plastered Lou-Easy and Marketa, slumped on either side of him, had both put a hand on his wonderful muscular thighs, and were stroking each other's hands, imagining they were his.

Meeting Paris's eyes, Orion laughed too, pretending to be playing the piano on their arms.

'Look,' whispered Paris to Dolphy, then realised the boy had dropped off, blond curls falling over his face. 'Better take you home,' he said, adding to the assembled company, 'pre-season and Ryan Edwards have really taken their toll; shame to wake him.'

Grandkid, however, cross about not being stroked, scraped Dolphy's arm again.

'Ouch, sorry!' cried Dolphy, jumping up and looking round. 'I must have dropped off.'

'Home,' ordered Paris.

'Two pretty rent boys off for a shag,' bitched Angus, as Paris shepherded Dolphy out of the pub.

'Delphinely not,' snapped an also woken-up Lou-Easy. 'Paris is dead straight and belongs to Dora.'

Dolphy's heart ruled his head. After their evening at the Dog and Trumpet, he hero-worshipped Paris, and bought him a dark-blue cashmere jersey from Orion's collection: 'For you to look "lean and hungry" in.'

'Orion's label's so smart,' quipped Paris, 'I ought to wear it inside out.'

Every time Dolphy saw an ad on television for ill-treated animals or children starved in Africa, he'd send them money. Later in the season, worried that Galgo was the only player in the club without an individual sponsor, he asked Tember if he could sponsor him. He was, in addition, totally dedicated, doing extra training every day, working to improve both his left and right feet, praying that if ever he made the first team and scored a goal, Elijah would notice.

Over at Buttercup Cottage, having watched videos of his own players half the night, working out ways to improve them, Elijah would invariably turn to one of Dolphy playing for the Reserves, then climb into bed beside a sleeping Madison for a few hours' insomnia.

'Oh, where is my wandering boy tonight, my boy who is sweetest of all.'

Ryan Edwards, on the other hand, was not pleased that people were so taken by blue-eyed Dolphy, and was not playing him in the team.

'No doubt his dog, Grandkid, will be giving football

demos with that effing Safety Car. You must have a word with Rupert,' he urged his father, Valent.

Valent had been working flat out all summer, extending the pitch and stadium at Searston Rovers to accommodate a Championship audience, building a dozen more hospitality suites for clients and VIPs to hire. Etta had not only opened their gardens at Badger's Court to over two thousand visitors, raising a great deal for charity, but had also transformed the gardens at Deep Woods.

Summoned for a drink on a lovely warm August evening, Rupert rolled up with Cuthbert and Gilchrist, who, thrilled to be back in their demo territory, shot off looking for rabbits. Breathing in the heady scent of roses and philadelphus, Rupert expressed admiration for all Valent had done.

'Looks terrific – you've worked bloody hard. Pitch looks fantastic, too.'

Valent took a deep breath and a swig of beer.

'Look, Rupert, we're in the Chumpionship now, things are mooch more serious. Don't think we ought to trivialise things by slapping down AstroTurf and putting on those animal demos any more. We can't have horses crapping all over the pitch, or that terrier' – he pointed to a racing-back Gilchrist – 'cocking his leg on the referee's leg.'

'Bloody funny, he was having a cock-leg party,' said Rupert, whistling to Gilchrist and lifting the little dog on to his knee. 'And those demos really pulled in the crowd – particularly children, tomorrow's audience. And Lou-Easy and Marketa are so pretty, they pull in all the blokes so the bar takings rocket. We've got to do something to save the billions a week spent on Facundo and all the star players, coaches, counsellors and computer buffs your beloved son's broken the bank with. Then he bellyaches because I spend a few bob to buy Dolphy Carter.'

'Facundo's a genius,' insisted Valent. 'As I've said, he'll win matches and push us up to the Premier League. I wish you'd try to get on better with Ryan, Rupe. He's a good kid, joost determined to do his best for the cloob.'

'He'd better buy a sheepdog, then, to make sure there are always sheep in the field.'

32

Facundo finally rolled up on a Thursday evening at the end of September.

Determined that his megastar would be welcomed in style, Ryan posted details on social media well in advance of his arrival. Consequently, a big crowd of press, fans, players and Wags in their glad rags turned up at Deep Woods, which looked sensational, with Etta's flower beds having been stripped of ruby and purple flowers to decorate the club inside and out, 'Welcome to Facundo' posters everywhere, and staff waving flags and banners.

Then, just as a big red sun was lurking on the horizon in hope of a glimpse, fireworks and flares soared into the rose-pink sky, a band struck up the *Black Beauty* theme and the Galloper landed on the pitch. Next moment, an ecstatic Ryan jumped out, shouting: 'Here's the answer to all our prayers! Three million cheers for Facundo Gonzales, the greatest, most powerful player in the world.'

This was followed by more fireworks and exploding flashbulbs, as out jumped a very tall, broad-shouldered, extremely handsome man with a deep tan emphasised by an off-white suit, glossy black curls, implants flashing below an ebony moustache, and dark eyes hotter than heaven or hell, depending on your persuasion.

'Oh, wow,' chorused his female audience. 'Isn't he macho?'

Fortuitously for Ryan, Rupert, who was violently opposed to Facundo's appointment, had pushed off to Newmarket with Taggie, so, briefed by Ryan, Facundo made a beeline for Valent, hugged him, and in a voice deeper than the ocean exclaimed: ''Ello, Valent Edward, my new chair and brozzer, who play great for England and vin FA Cup for Vest Riding, a leg-end like myself, it geeve me the duckbumps to shake you by ze 'and.'

So a delighted Valent hugged him back and introduced 'my wife, Etta', whose hand Facundo French-kissed, crying: 'Vot a beautiful lady, so perfect for a leg-end.'

'And I am so knocked out,' Ryan was now addressing the media, 'that this great player has been prepared to sign for a lower league for the adventure of leading us at Searston Rovers to greater glory.'

Then the band struck up to an accompaniment of popping champagne corks, with their lead singer launching into:

Facundo's a wonder
Who'll tear teams asunder.
Down the pitch he will thunder
And every goal plunder.
Privileged Searston
Will have nothing to fear soon.

This was followed by more deafening applause and laughter, and rockets soaring into the sky.

Having raised a glass of champagne to the press, telling them how happy he was to be in the Cotswolds, Facundo was then borne off by Ryan to meet the sponsors and then the players, each one of whom Facundo hugged and called 'brozzer' and said how he'd look forward to vinning with them.

Due to Tember's inability to keep secrets, however, every player knew Facundo was on £300,000 a week, with a splendid mansion in the Golden Triangle thrown in, and going to plunder their thunder, so they were much less keen.

Then Facundo moved on to the Wags and female staff, who were wildly excited as his smouldering glance stripped them of their clothes, as he kissed their hands and tickled their palms with his forefinger, assuring each one she was '*muy atractivo*'.

'Isn't he gorgeous?' whispered Daffodil to Charm. 'As we'll be neighbours in the Golden Triangle, I told him to drop in for a cuppa whenever he feels like it.'

It was noticed, however, that Facundo kept exchanging the hottest, longest eye-meets with Griffy's wife, Inez, who was looking ravishing in thigh-high boots, a slinky groin-level black dress, and full model make-up. Clearly, here was a man she found up to her weight.

Here we go again, thought Griffy, wearily, yet he felt far more excruciating pain and fury when Facundo progressed to Tember, asking her as club secretary to sort out numerous problems.

'I 'ope you vill come to my house tomorrow, water in indoor swimming pool not hot enough with vinter coming, we need plumber,' crooned Facundo, sliding his hand high round Tember's waist, so his long fingers could caress one of her lovely breasts.

'I'll get one of the club staff to drop by tomorrow,' gasped Tember, wriggling away from him, then raising her eyes to heaven and smiling briefly at an enraged Griffy, who was bearing down on them with clenched fists. Although touched by his reaction, fearing a punch-up, Tember hastily introduced Facundo to Dora, 'one of our press officers'.

'Oh, Dora,' beamed Facundo, 'who I shall call A-Dora-ble, we must have a long session to discuss my face book, I have many million followers. I 'ope you vill handle my publicity, do all my emails, and be my lovely leetle press officer.'

'Ker-iste,' said an escaping Dora, a minute later. 'He can't do emails, only females. He clearly thinks a press officer is someone you press very hard against.'

Bianca, on the other hand, radiant in dark red and on her fourth glass of champagne, thought Facundo was absolutely gorgeous.

'I asked him what the name Facundo means,' she told Dora later. 'He said it means "eloquent", which means "good at chatting", which he certainly is, and said his name was very popular in Argentina and Colombia. He was then thrilled when I told him I'm originally from Colombia, saying we were two South Americans and must have a little dance, and seal it with a little kiss. Feral was absolutely livid when he caught us.'

'I'm not surprised,' said Dora, who was watching Feral pushing his way through the party-goers and seizing Ryan's arm. Sidling up, she heard him say:

'Keep that bastard off Bianca.'

'Rise above it,' snapped Ryan. 'It's essential to make Facundo feel admired. Flattering a man's ego is all-important in Argentina. They have to demonstrate their virility.'

'Not over Bianca, they don't. He'd better watch it,' snarled Feral. 'Rupert'll pull a shotgun on him if he lays a finger on Taggie.'

The crowds had been sent home. Cheffie, Searston's chef, was putting out dishes of chicken Kiev on the boardroom table.

Facundo was back 'eloquenting' Inez. 'I love Engleesh television programmes,' he was saying, 'particularly *East Endaways.*'

Cadenza was rushing round taking everyone's photographs, when Lady Emma arrived to collect Harry.

A total contrast to Inez, Emma wore very little make-up, jeans and Harry's striped prep-school shirt, but looked so much more beautiful, thought Ryan. Then he winced as Dinah rushed up to welcome her and immediately introduced her to Facundo: 'This is Lady Emma, one of our dearest friends.'

'You are vife of vich player?' purred Facundo.

'No, no, I am mother of Harry, the blond one over there.' And Emma then winced as Dinah-mite interrupted her, announcing that Kayley was the squeeze of Harry and showing Facundo a photograph on her iPhone.

'Lovely leetle girl,' said Facundo, 'I look forward to meeting her.'

'I wonder if Ryan will banish Facundo to the bench,

like Josef, if he jumps on Princess Kayley,' muttered Dora to Ludo.

Ryan, however, was wondering if he'd been quite so wise to import Facundo, as he saw him whispering sweet everythings into Emma's pearl earrings. Inez was also looking daggers at Emma.

Next moment, Rosalie Parkinson swept in, bearing down on Facundo.

'Good evening, I'm your captain's lady, Facundo. Sorry I'm late; I got caught up in a meeting. Welcome to Searston.' She raised a glass of champagne to him. 'I hope you're pleased with your new home in the Golden Triangle. It's very near our property. You must bring your lady wife along to my boutique in the High Street. I've got my new range of winter clothes in and we don't want her to feel the cold. When will she be joining you?'

Rosalie had such a loud voice that everyone had stopped to listen.

'She vill not be coming,' replied Facundo. 'My vife, Zou Zou, stay in Buenos Aires with my cheeldren. I have three teenage keeds, all taking big exams next year, so I cannot take them away from their schools. I will mees them horrible, but education is more important.'

'What a caring parent you are, Facundo,' cried Dinah-mite, 'putting your children first. We feel just the same about Princess Kayley, who's taking her GCSEs next year.'

'I have two teenage daughters too,' said Inez, moving into the group. 'Their education is all-important.'

'Christ,' muttered Ludo. 'Leg-over, not leg-end. What the hell is Facundo going to do for sex without Zou

Zou? You'll have to provide him with a Wag a week, Tember.'

Dora was in heaven. 'Talk about Macho of the Day. I'll have copy for the Wag with the Dodgiest Tail for months to come.'

Inez then sought out Griffy. 'You'd better push off now and make sure the little ones are tucked up in bed and off their iPhones, and Ally and Gabriella have done all their homework.' She wouldn't be long, but one of the sponsors wanted to discuss some modelling job.

On the way out, Griffy passed Tember, muttering: 'I'll kill that Argentinian bastard if he ever gropes you again.'

There were too many people around for Tember to do more than murmur that she loved him and squeeze his hand, but what a miracle, she reflected, if Inez eloped with Facundo.

Shortly afterwards, fed up with Facundo making eyes at Emma, Ryan closed down the party, telling his players not to drink any more. 'I want you all in by ten thirty tomorrow, so you can start adjusting to Facundo.'

'That was a great success,' said Dinah-mite as she finished brushing her red hair a hundred times and got into bed. 'So glad Lady Emma came. She is a sweetie. And Facundo seemed to like her so much. So touching he's put his children's education first. Hope he won't be too lonely without his wife. We must ask him and Lady Emma to dinner – good to put lonely people together. Can you remind Mimi McLean about giving Kayley some English coaching? Goodness, I'm tired.'

The moment Dinah-mite's head touched the pillow, she fell asleep.

Resisting the temptation to throttle her, or to creep out and ring Lady Emma, Ryan suddenly had a brainwave. With him bringing in Facundo to push Searston up to the Premier League and even Champions League glory, he himself could easily be knighted, like Sir Alex Ferguson, for being such a great manager. Then Emma could marry him without relinquishing her title.

33

Facundo was indeed a marvellous player and knew it. His hat-trick at his first match the following Saturday enabled Searston to thrash top-of-the-league North Hattersley 4–0 and for Facundo again to tell the media: 'I am leg-end.'

He had also moved into his big house in the Golden Triangle, with a housekeeper, pool attendant, much-heated indoor pool – where Ludo quipped he could practise diving – and the yellow Lamborghini, plus a little yellow run-around, all provided by Searston Rovers.

As the season passed, if he felt like a lie-in, the team trained in the afternoon, and he sometimes missed away matches because he wanted a having-it-away match with one of the other player's women.

'Fuckundo anyone he likes,' observed Ludo.

He also hogged Charlie the masseur and, in addition, wanted to score more goals a season than any other player. As he earned not only appearance money but also a £10,000 bonus a goal, he tended to hog the goal as well as the girl opportunities.

An applause junkie, when the Searston coach drew

up at away matches, he insisted on being last off the coach so he could enjoy the loudest cheers from the fans of both sides.

He was a compulsive gambler as well, and spent his afternoons betting on the horses. Having heard that Rupert had promised the Searston players a racehorse if they went up to the Premier League, as principal scorer he felt Rupert should give him his own horse. And having clapped eyes on Marketa and Lou-Easy, he was annoyed, too, that Rupert refused to let him ride out at Penscombe.

Because he was the star player, Ryan told the rest of the team, particularly the strikers, that it was their duty to feed him the ball and boost his ego, even promising a £2,000 bonus to anyone who gave him an assist. But although Facundo did win matches, this wasn't helping team spirit.

As rivals to Feral, who was too devoted to Rupert, as were Josef, Wilfie, Dolphy and Galgo, Ryan was also regularly playing the gorgeous Orion, Harry Stanton-Harcourt (to please Lady Emma) and his own uppity son, Otley.

Otley took great pleasure in sneaking to his father that Rupert was being increasingly offensive on his visits to training or the dressing room. Last week, Rupert had lost his temper and called poor Jesus, in his first season with Searston, a 'stupid fucker' when he'd missed the easiest goal, enabling Dora to put 'Jesus wept' in her column. This week, he'd called Harry Stanton-Harcourt 'a useless little wanker' for passing for the second time to the opposition, who went on to score. This very much upset Lady Emma, and Ryan had to spend a lot of time in bed comforting her.

'Did you know, even worse, Dad,' reported Otley, 'when Facundo asked Rupert to go through the race-card and give him tips for Leopardstown next week, Rupert said he was far too busy and told Facundo to eff off.'

Ryan then disregarded Searston's mental health coun-sellor, Gemini Coates, who, claiming aggression was the result of insecurity, was avid to give Rupert some private sessions. 'Rupert did have five stepmothers and four stepfathers, Ryan.'

Instead, Ryan tipped off the General Football Coun-cil, who, in early March, summoned Rupert to appear before their Integrity Committee in central London.

'Don't worry,' Tember reassured Rupert, 'I'm sure they won't suspend you. Pop in on your way home and tell me about it.'

34

The Integrity Committee was packed with women to break the 150-year male stranglehold at the GFC's top table. These included a chief transfer negotiator, heads of physical performance, nutrition and coach placements, a mental health expert and the Executive Chair, called Susan Morecambe.

Rupert rolled up at the GFC in a beautifully cut dark suit and a suntan from racing abroad, and denied he was seriously abusive.

'I insult all my players if they screw up,' he drawled. 'I know I have a short fuse and yell at my players, but it doesn't last long, and I treat all my stable lads and lasses the same way.'

'You have some fine horses,' said the Head of Coach Placements, sternly. 'I gather you used to beat them up in the past.'

'That was when I was showjumping,' snapped Rupert. 'And considered it all-important to win.' Then, feeling he ought to be more conciliatory: 'But I regret it, and make sure now all my horses have the happiest of lives.'

'Didn't you have a stallion called Love Rat?' asked the Head of Physical Performance.

'I did,' said a delighted Rupert. 'He was so gentle my grandchildren used to sleep in his box.' And getting out his telephone he showed everyone pictures of Timon and Sapphire stretched out in the straw, with Love Rat gently nudging them. 'He was a guard stallion. Are any of you ladies thinking of buying a racehorse?'

Susan Morecambe, the Executive Chair, who'd intended to hang Rupert out to dry, asked him if he was thinking of taking his coaching badges. To which Rupert replied that he might, but he gathered it could take six years and he'd probably be dead by then.

The committee then adjourned and pointed out Rupert's track record: that when he was Minister for Sport, he'd dramatically reduced hooliganism when it was a huge problem. Searston had galloped from relegation to promotion in one season, and he must also have suffered a huge amount of stress coping with Taggie's cancer.

They all agreed that, with the shortage of English managers, Rupert would be a fantastic addition to the Premier League.

'He's even more handsome than José Mourinho, and watching the despair, rage and euphoria on a manager's face is part of the fascination of football,' said the Head of Nutrition.

'And seeing expectation become ecstasy would be like watching the sunrise on Rupert's face,' sighed the Head of Physical Performance.

'Steady on, Rita,' said Chair Susan Morecambe, 'but I'm sure he could get his badges more quickly. He's very successful at Searston Rovers.'

Fortunately, Searston had had a dazzling 3–0 win against Didcot Rangers the Saturday before, and, after warning Rupert to be more circumspect in future, the committee forgave him and reluctantly sent him home.

'Three chairs for me,' crowed Rupert.

Returning to Searston, Rupert, as promised, popped in to have a drink with Tember, who hugged him in delight when she heard the news.

'Oh, I'm so pleased. What were the Integrity Committee like?'

'Sweet. They want me to stop slagging off players and take my coaching badges, so I'm going to buy a stylish carriage and drive Safety Car round the Cotswolds.'

Tember's cottage, next to the antiques shop, looked from the front across the village green to the Running Fox and, at the back, had a little garden full of daffodils, bluebells and pink blossom.

Typically Tember, she welcomed Rupert into the sitting room with a blazing fire, a large bottle of Bell's, and a plateful of smoked salmon sandwiches.

'I bet you haven't had time to eat.'

She then drew the curtains, 'so all the regulars in the Running Fox can't peer in and see who I'm getting off with'.

She looked so pretty in her jeans and pale-yellow jersey that, in the old days, thought Rupert, he'd have whisked her straight upstairs.

'Mind you,' she went on, 'Ryan is always pestering me to report on any of our players drinking in the Fox.'

'Lovely cottage,' said Rupert, accepting a large mahogany whiskey and prowling round the room. Everywhere were piles of papers and boxes. 'You certainly bring a lot of work home with you,' he said, as Tember removed a pile from the sofa to provide room for Rupert beside a large snoozing black-and-white cat.

'His name's Riddance,' said Tember, 'because he's good. He actually belongs to my neighbour, but he likes dropping in.'

Rupert was still prowling. 'How long have you lived here?'

'About eight years, on and off. It belonged to Bobby Broadstairs, you know, the chairman before Stevas. He gave me my first job and became a real father figure. My dad had recently died, and my mother married again and moved to Scotland, and Bobby had just been widowed, so we sort of bonded – not sexually, but we had a lovely time building up the club and buying players, even keeping on bossy Ryan as manager.

'Then poor darling Bobby developed lung cancer, and I, well, sort of nursed and cared for him until he died.' Tember took a great gulp of white wine. 'And amazingly' – her voice broke – 'he left me this cottage. He had a big house near Cirencester and only used this place when he was on Searston business, and the proviso was that I stayed and looked after the team.'

'Which you certainly do – you hold the whole place together,' said Rupert.

Tember took another gulp of wine. 'That's Bobby there, with the Labrador, in the portrait over the fireplace.'

'Good-looking man.' Rupert was wolfing down the smoked salmon. 'And a very nice dog.' Then, turning to another portrait on the side of the fireplace: 'And that's Bobby Broadstairs again and, my God, that's Griffy – he looks about eighteen.'

'Griffy was another of Bobby's protégés. Bobby bought

him for the club about ten years ago. He was really excited, convinced Griffy was heading for stardom. Griffy adored Bobby and dropped in to see him a lot when he was dying. Griffy was playing really well then, both scoring and defending. When Bobby died, I couldn't stand Stevas when he took over, and I've never been wild about Ryan,' Tember said, peeling off a piece of smoked salmon and giving it to Riddance the cat. 'So I really only stayed on . . .'

'Because you loved Griffy,' said Rupert, putting another log on the fire.

'Y-Yes,' stammered Tember. 'Griffy was very shy, from a minor public school, with a terrible bully of a father, and found it difficult bonding with a rowdy, confident, mostly working-class Searston. He and I had only held hands a bit, but it was going really well. Then Inez rolled up on a shoot in Cheltenham. She was much older than Griffy, beautiful, a successful model, divorced with two girls. Griffy seemed the perfect answer: a handsome footballer destined for the Premier League and stardom.

'Griffy fell for her like a whole forest of logs. So they got married and, to cement the relationship, had twin daughters, who Griffy absolutely adores. He loves his stepdaughters, too.'

'And it broke your heart,' said Rupert.

'The tragedy,' sighed Tember, 'is that Inez is an absolute bitch. Having to put modelling aside while she was having the twins, she found Griffy wasn't progressing as a footballer – Ryan wasn't keen on him – and she demoralised Griffy physically and mentally by making him do everything, getting up in the night for the babies, feeding the family, doing the washing, the school runs, so she could go back to her career. Because he adores his children, he's terrified she'll push off with some rich man, like Facundo, and take them with her. She torments him with these possibilities all the time.'

Tember blew her nose and wiped her eyes. 'I'm so sorry, Rupert. You shouldn't be such a good listener.'

Rupert had picked up a scrapbook on a side table and smiled, finding it stuffed with newspaper pictures of Griffy.

'At least your boy's got a good cuttings service. On the other hand,' he went on, 'I see another side of the picture. The first time you and I met at Searston and you gave me your smoked salmon and cream cheese sandwiches, I noticed that Griffy, when he was supposed to be playing, couldn't keep his eyes off you in the stands. He may be worried about his children, but he's as bats about you as you are about him.'

Tember got to her feet and, looking in the mirror, wiped away her smeared mascara.

'Well, actually, last transfer window, bloody Rosalie rang Inez and said Parks had told her Griffy was for the chop. Inez was so furious that she was going to have to support the family that she flew at Griffy and nearly clawed his eyes out. He's too much of a gent to hit her back, so he fled to Deep Woods with Mildred, their mongrel, to see if anyone had come in for him, and I was working late and we ended up in each other's arms. It was the most wonderful moment of my life.' She gasped. 'I'm so sorry, Rupert, I must be boring you.'

'Not at all,' said Rupert, absolutely riveted. 'You two must get together.' He stopped stroking Riddance and held out his glass. 'Can I have another drink?'

'Of course, I'm so sorry. Shouldn't you get back to darling Taggie?'

'No, she's got my daughter Tab staying, so we won't be dining until eight thirty or nine. Look, if Griffy isn't going to leave Inez, don't you think you ought to look for someone else? There'll be plenty of takers.'

'I'm nearly thirty-two,' sighed Tember, 'but I've never really loved anyone else.'

'Then we must get Inez to run off with Facundo.'

'He's got lots of others,' said Tember. 'Do you know what Ludo calls him? The Great Dick-tator, because he's ruled by his cock.'

Rupert laughed. 'I used to be like that in the old days, before I fell for darling Taggie. I'd have had you upstairs in a trice.'

'How heavenly. I love it that we're such good friends, Rupert. Griffy's very jealous of you. I'm so sorry, I've banged on and on about myself. I've not asked you anything more about the Integrity Committee.'

'They were OK. I asked if any of them would like to buy a racehorse. They seemed quite keen. All the same, I wonder who tipped them off.'

'You must go home to Taggie,' whispered Tember, looking furtively round the room. 'Promise not to tell Otley, who sneaks on anyone, but it was Ryan who shopped you.'

35

Rupert bided his time. He sent some flowers to thank Susan Morecambe and the Integrity Committee, and he also had a run-in with Etta's ghastly son, Martin Bancroft, who raised money for charity and himself. One of his charities was WOO, which stood for War on Obesity and was sponsored by Sir Craig Eynsham's No-Bese. Martin had dropped in on Taggie one March afternoon and tried to persuade her to join his campaign to raise money for WOO by inviting the public to visit Penscombe Court one Saturday for tea and a look around the grounds.

'I call them "Chari-Teas". Isn't that rather fun?'

A returning Rupert didn't think so, and summoned bouncer Eamonn, who threatened to throw Martin in the lake.

Etta Edwards, Valent's wife and Ryan's stepmother, tried very hard to understand football, but although she'd made the flower beds at Searston Rovers look beautiful, she tended to get the players' names and the language all wrong, calling pre-season 'in season' and football congestion 'indigestion'.

On Mothering Sunday, 31 March, Ryan was missing his own mother, Pauline, who had died in the Paddington train crash. As Valent was abroad, and Lady Emma was having supper with her son, Harry, Ryan rolled up to see Etta at Badger's Court bearing a bottle of champagne, and, as it was a lovely evening, they sat out on the terrace, admiring white magnolia and pink cherry blossom, and breathing in the heady scent of bluebells, lilies of the valley and hyacinths.

'It looks wonderful, Etta. You've completely transformed the place.'

'And you're doing so well at Searston; your father's so proud.'

'I wish Arsy-B thought so. He never stops putting me down.'

Etta agreed Rupert was a terrible bully. He'd been so rude to her son, Martin, when he'd dropped in the other day, and he'd been horrible to Etta's rescued mare, Mrs Wilkinson, who'd won the Grand National.

'He put the poor darling in a ring bit, which made her mouth bleed, and a cross noseband to make her run straight. I hated Wilkie going to Penscombe. And Rupert always insisted on having his way with Master Quickly, although we co-own him. I'm so disappointed the Integrity Committee didn't suspend him.'

'He's so, so irrational,' grumbled Ryan as they started on a second bottle. 'Thank God, Dad's sidelined those ridiculous animal demos and letting that infernal Safety Car come into the dressing room. Rupert even thought it funny when we caught Charlie the masseur massaging

Grandkid on the training room couch last week. He still won't accord Facundo sufficient deference, and he's always interfering with the players, telling them to do something when I've told them not to. He's so against any counselling. He made Otley cry the other day, said he wasn't training hard enough.'

'Poor Otley,' stormed Etta, 'he's such a creative dribbler. Rupert should go back to racing and leave you to get on with things.'

When Ryan drank a lot, his Yorkshire accent increased and he sounded much more like Valent, which endeared him even more to Etta.

'Dad was so lonely without Mum,' said Ryan, putting his hand on Etta's, 'but you've made him so happy.'

Next day, a delighted Ryan stirred it. Driving to training, he told Angus and Barry Pitt that Valent's wife, his stepmum, couldn't stand Rupert and thought him a terrible bully, whereupon Barry and Angus told all the other players – 'Dew know what?' – who then told all the non-playing staff, until Charlie the masseur told Rupert, who snapped:

'Ryan's an arsehole and Etta's a stupid bitch who should keep her nose out of things.'

So Charlie the masseur told Kitsy, the kitman, and round went the 'Dew know what?'s again until, during training the next day, Otley repeated it back to his father, Ryan, who, in joyous indignation, decided to relay it to Valent.

Valent had had a bad night, kept awake by rheumatism in his hips and back. No amount of thrusting under the coolest pillow could ease the arthritis in his goalkeeper's hands, out of which the soap kept slithering in the shower. Etta was sleeping so peacefully in their double bed after a long day's gardening that he merely pecked her on the cheek before leaving for morning training at Searston. He was delighted that his grandson Otley and Harry Stanton-Harcourt were responding so well to his coaching. He was cheered by a lovely day. Lambs skipping in the fields, a pale-green blur on the trees, the first cow parsley on the verges. Then his mobile rang.

'Dad, Dad, where are you?' shouted Ryan.

'On my way. I'll be with you in twenty minutes.'

'You've got to do something. That bastard Campbell-Black told Charlie the masseur and several players in the treatment room that I'm an arsehole.'

'We bluddy know he thinks that. I've told him to back off. I'll have another word.'

'There's worse. He said that Etta was a stupid, interfering bitch who should keep her nose out of things.'

'He wh-a-a-a-t?' exploded Valent, nearly driving his dark-blue Bentley into a seven-foot Cotswold-stone wall. 'He called her a wh-a-a-at?'

'A stupid, interfering bitch.'

'Fooking bastard! How dare he! That's it, then.'

Jamming on his brakes, narrowly avoiding the car in front and the cars coming the other way, Valent stormed back to Penscombe and up Rupert's drive. Even Etta's magical gardening at Badger's Court couldn't compete with the languid beauty of Penscombe Court in the spring sunshine. Bugger Rupert!

Irish Shelagh answered the front door.

'Mr Edwards, how good to see you.'

'Where's Rupert?'

'Down at the yard. The horses are off to Windsor any minute.'

But Valent had gone.

He found horses being loaded into the big blue-and-green Rupert Campbell-Black Racing lorry, and more horses looking over their dark-blue half-doors at Rupert and his dogs, talking to Lou-Easy.

'You bastard,' howled Valent. 'I can't work with you any more.'

'What on earth have I done now?' asked Rupert.

Gilchrist and Cuthbert started yapping, and the heads of the stable staff, readying the horses, came over the half-doors.

'You bastard,' repeated Valent. As he advanced on Rupert, purple in the face, eyes bulging, fists clenched, sixteen stone of geriatric but formidable muscle, Rupert thought he was going to hit him. So did Lou-Easy.

'Leave the boss alone,' she screamed, brandishing her pitchfork in Valent's face.

'How dare you tell Charlie and half the players my Etta's a stupid, interfering bitch? How dare you accuse her of poking her nose into everything? My wife's never been unkind to anyone in her life.'

'That's debatable. According to Charlie, she called me a terrible bully.'

'Too bluddy right, and you called my son an arsehole.'

At that moment, a beautiful grey stallion called New Year's Dave, who Valent three-quarters owned, put his head over a half-door and started whickering.

'At least he's pleased to see you,' mocked Rupert.

'It's not bluddy foony, Rupert,' roared Valent, so that even gentle Labrador Banquo started growling. 'If you know so mooch about footy, you can bluddy cope on your own. Ryan and I are out of Searston. Just see what a cock-oop you'll make.'

'We'll do all right, YOU great bully,' shouted Lou-Easy, thrusting her pitchfork even closer.

'And we'll win the fucking Champions League,' yelled Rupert, as Valent turned and stumbled out of the yard to his car.

There was a long pause. Rupert looked round at his flabbergasted staff.

'I'd better start divorce proceedings,' he drawled, 'and you'd better get off to Windsor. Thank you for defending me, darling,' he added to Lou-Easy.

'You'd better start taking those coaching badges, boss,' urged Lou-Easy.

At that moment, Safety Car trotted into the yard to see what all the noise was about, and started nudging Rupert's pockets for treats.

And you can go back to your football demos, Safety darling, thought Lou-Easy, *and I can see gorgeous Orion again.*

Taggie, meanwhile, was in the kitchen making ratatouille, frying onion and garlic on the Aga, when Rupert broke the news. She was absolutely horrified. She was so fond of Etta and Valent.

'It's just Ryan winding people up. I'm sure it's just a hiccup. Valent adores you, he'll cool down and you'll be able to make it up. You can't split up when you're doing so brilliantly. At least send Etta some lovely flowers and say you didn't mean it.'

'I did. She called me a horrible bully. It's over. I'm not working with Valent or Ryan any more.'

'It's all my fault,' wailed Taggie, putting her arms around him, feeling his body rigid yet quivering with rage. 'I was the bully nagging you into buying Searston, because I was so desperate for Bianca and Feral to come home. And it's all Ryan's fault for stirring things.'

'We could do with some stirring round here,' observed Rupert, as the sickening smell of burnt onion and garlic invaded the kitchen.

'Oh bugger, there goes my ratatouille,' moaned Taggie, whipping the frying pan off the Aga, before collapsing on the sofa. 'But seriously, oh darling, what are you going to do?'

'I ought to sell Searston Rovers but I'm going to buy Valent out and fucking show them.'

'You can't run a huge yard as well as a football club on your own.'

'Try me,' said Rupert as he looked up at a framed photograph to the right of the window, of Eddie on Master Quickly winning the World Cup, wearing his sapphire and emerald colours. 'And screw that awful ruby and purple. Searston are going to play footy in my colours from now on. I also told Valent we'd win the Champions League.'

'I thought Searston came third last year?'

'No, that was to get us into the Championship. Champions League is the biggest competition in football after the World Cup and pays infinitely more, with several hundreds of millions to the winners and picking up fifty million in the group stages. So that's what we're going to do.'

'What'll the players think?'

'At least I'll be able to play Josef and Dolphy and Feral and Griffy and Ludo when I want. I'd better go and ring a few people. You're not to worry, angel.'

But, slumped at his desk, Rupert gazed up at the

Stubbs of his ancestor Rupert Black on Third Leopard, which he'd probably have to sell. As he put his head in his shaking hands, gentle and kind black Labrador Banquo, who never complained about the Jack Russells stealing the limelight, put his head on his master's knees, gazing up with big brown eyes: 'You still have me.'

Then the telephone rang.

'Are you OK?' It was the sweet, soft voice of Tember West. 'I've heard the news, Rupert.'

'I'm fine. You will stay with me, won't you, Tember?'

'Wild Gallopers wouldn't keep me away. And here's something to cheer you up. Griffy's just texted me. The players heard about it after training and they're cracking open the champagne and letting off fireworks. I didn't realise quite how much they loathed Ryan. The dressing room will no longer be the depressing room. We're going to be fine without them.'

Rupert felt even better when Feral came home with a bottle of whiskey from the lads.

'Sorry you had to go fru that, Rupe.'

'I need a caretaker manager to keep us at the top for the last few games.'

'I got just the guy. Remember Pete Wainwright? He managed Larkminster Rovers, then Deansgate before Craig Eynsham fired him. Well, he's just retired but he's bloody good, he's kind and he'd steady the ship.'

Rupert remembered Pete Wainwright, a tough, bluff Lancastrian who'd liaised with Taggie on coursework when they had both been teaching GCSE – Taggie in cookery – at Larkminster Comp. Pete, who'd had a bit of a crush on Taggie, but who'd also given Feral his first football trial and set him on the road to stardom.

'I'll give him a ring,' said Rupert.

Rupert then proceeded to buy Valent's share of the club for £40 million. Several of his most beautiful pictures were seen to be missing from the walls of Penscombe Court, as he now had to pay all the club wages, including Facundo's £300,000 a week. Thank God, he'd stopped Ryan going completely crazy buying non-playing staff – nutritionists, statisticians, medical advisers and second goalkeeping coaches – at the beginning of the season. And at least the ones he had brought in were self-employed or casual workers who didn't need paying off.

'And tell that bossy-boots Gemini Coates to bugger off,' he told Tember.

Fortunately, Ghengis Tong, a trillionaire aeroplane manufacturer from Hong Kong, the brain behind the Green Galloper and whose sweet son Bao had done work experience in the yard a year ago, agreed to lend Rupert a few million to tide him over.

To the heartbreak of the yard, New Year's Dave was moved to another stud. In retaliation, a sculpture of Valent, just completed by Dora's sister, Emerald Belvedon, to stand outside the club at Deep Woods, was dumped outside the Cockpit at Badger's Court.

36

Amazingly, the GFC, after due-diligence tests, let Rupert carry on without Valent. There were only a handful of games until the end of the season, and if Searston players didn't like the new set-up, they could hopefully get their agents to find them new clubs in the three months of the summer transfer window.

All big Eamonn's bouncer skills were needed to keep the press from descending in droves to discover the ins and outs of the Great Divorce, or the Vend-Etta – particularly when naughty Dora posted a picture, taken on one of the stable lads' iPhones, of tall, lean, blond, handsome Rupert confronted by vast, fist-clenching, apoplectic Valent, entitled 'Beauty and the Beast'.

There was also much media mockery of how a football ignoramus like Rupert could run Searston on his own, particularly when it was leaked that he had boasted to Valent he'd go on and win the Champions League, which was, the *Guardian* claimed, as likely as Searston climbing Everest in bare feet.

Searston were so incensed that they proceeded to thrash Drobenham 4–2 the following Saturday, with

Dora posting a headline: 'Multiple Scoregasm'. They then kept on winning, to end the season top in the Championship and go up to the Premier League, with Deansgate only coming third.

Despite his massive debts, Rupert rewarded his players with a hefty bonus and gave them his lovely chestnut filly The Story So Far.

Searston proceeded to receive £200 million for going up to the Premier League. But this was supposed to cope with increased players' salaries, club bills and acquiring the new players needed to contain the growing pressure, rather than paying off Rupert's debts.

At the dawning of the summer transfer window at the beginning of June, to the world's astonishment, the majority of Searston players, with the exception of Otley Jepson-Edwards and a rather reluctant Harry Stanton-Harcourt, who still violently disapproved of his mother's continuing close friendship with Ryan, opted to stay with Rupert and didn't ask their agents for transfers.

Rupert had always given them great racing tips as well as a chestnut filly. He made them laugh, and they were all a little in love with Taggie, who was slowly regaining her beauty. Her lustrous hair, although still grey and curly, now flowed down her back again. Recovering from the after-effects of chemo and radiotherapy, she had much more energy and, with Shelagh's help, she was already transforming the food at Searston. Now she was hooked on football, and, remembering Czech Josef's mother's tears at Wembley when Searston had gone up to the Championship, she was determined to look after any player who was lonely or finding it difficult adjusting. She had therefore found a lovely tenant's cottage, overlooking the lake at Penscombe, for Jesus from Portugal, Wilfie, Dolphy and Grandkid to share, which they were all enjoying.

'Although tell Jesus he mustn't turn the lake water into too much wine,' quipped Rupert.

Another reason many players stayed at Searston was because their other halves were loath to leave their splendid new mansions with electric gates in the Golden Triangle. All the Wags were thrilled no longer to be bossed about by Dinah-mite, and Rupert was very touched to get a thank-you card from sweet Mimi McLean: 'Such heaven not to have to coach Princess Kayley any more.'

Rupert also had to admit that, before storming out, Valent had hugely enhanced the club. Not just the Boardroom, as the Directors' Lounge had now been renamed, and the hospitality suites; he had, in addition, completed covered seating all round the stadium, which would vastly increase match-day takings.

'We bloody need it,' grumbled Rupert to Pete Wainwright, his new caretaker manager, 'to cover that fatuous three hundred grand a week his idiot son agreed to pay Facundo. I'm going to fire him if he ducks out of any more games.'

'Better not,' sighed Pete. 'Cost a fortune to break his contract, and we need his ferocious left foot for when he's having an Alpha Male day.'

'Alpha mule,' snapped Rupert, 'he's so fucking stubborn. And can we play Dolphy Carter in the first team soon? He hasn't sulked and he tries so hard in training.'

Searston were dying to make their Premier League debut in their dazzling new kit in Rupert's racing colours; the shirts with their horizontal emerald-green and sapphire-blue stripes made their shoulders look even broader. But, sadly, their opening game at the beginning of September was away to Durham, whose kingfisher-blue-striped kit was so similar that Searston had to play in their white-and-grey away kit.

Before they flew north, Rupert gave them a rousing pep talk:

'You've probably all read that when we split up with our co-chairman, Valent Edwards, I bet him we'd end up winning the Champions League. Well, I like winning bets, so, to qualify, we've got to end up in the top four this season. And that means you've got to attack and attack and win every match, starting today.'

Searston, as a result, were so fired up and mad to attack that they left their own goal dangerously exposed, and, despite Rupert's bawling-out at half-time and Pete Wainwright's attempt to calm them, they lost 2–3.

This absolutely enchanted Sir Craig, particularly when Deansgate, inspired by Elijah Cohen, won their Premier League debut 2–1. So Sir Craig burst into verse and texted:

> Poor old Searston,
> You'll end in tears soon,
> Nor will Pete Wainwright
> Help you in your fight,
> No time for celebration,
> You're off to relegation.

37

Searston's first chance to flaunt their new kit was a home game, a local derby against hated Deansgate, which was being televised on Sky. This meant Searston, as the home team, earning £100,000 and Deansgate only £10,000, and resulted in fans unable to get tickets scaling trees in the surrounding woods to witness the Cotswolds grudge match.

As Jesus had torn a calf muscle, and Facundo was still in bed with a so-called groin injury – 'Probably someone's wife,' said Rupert – he and Pete formed a strong attacking front four of Feral, Orion, Downing and Josef, with Galgo and Wilfie as midfielders, Parks, Griffy, Ludo and Angus defending, and Barry Pitt in goal.

Feeling Dolphy should be fed in gently on his Premier League debut, they started him and Jesus on the bench. Dolphy was already in a panic about his debut in the first team. After his hideous sexual initiation, he was terrified of confronting Laddy Heywood again. On the other hand, he was longing to see Elijah, and put in hours of extra training to impress.

*

Deep Woods was looking great. Everyone in the hospitality suites was raving over Taggie and Shelagh's fantastic ratatouille, chicken supreme and sticky toffee pudding.

'At least I didn't burn the onions and garlic this time,' giggled Taggie, who was deliberating with Tember, who'd become such a friend, whether she ought to go and welcome Lady Grace, who'd just arrived in the Boardroom for lunch with Sir Craig, Chief Constable Lloyd Dudsbridge, Jarred Moreland and Alan Garcia.

'Why not serve them up fish bones stewed in arsenic,' suggested Tember.

'Sir Craig's been so endlessly vile about Rupert,' said Taggie, 'I can't be nice to him. I suppose I could say hi to Lady Grace and the Chief Constable.'

At that moment, Rosalie Parkinson swanned in in an apple-green coat and skirt and sapphire silk scarf. 'What are you ladies stressing about?'

'Whether we should go and welcome Sir Craig and co.'

'I'll greet them,' cried Rosalie, 'I am the captain's lady, after all,' and she whisked off to the Boardroom.

'Let the silly bitch get on with it,' muttered Tember. 'Do you know why her right boob seems much larger than the left? It's all the cards advertising her awful boutique, stuffed into her right-hand top pocket.'

The Wags had taken up their places in the stands, and Bianca had chummed up with Bastian's daffy new wife, Daffodil, who was showing her pictures of their new home in the Golden Triangle, eighteenth-century Chaffinch Court: 'It was so exciting when Bastian carried me over the flesh-hold and said how he loved holding my flesh. This is the library, which won't have any books in until Bastian finishes his *Hauteur Biography*.'

'It's all gorgeous,' sighed Bianca. Perhaps she and Feral should find a house, but life was so cushy at Penscombe.

Behind them sat Charm, saying how she and Midas loved their new home, also in the Golden Triangle. 'We're having our drayve done and now I'm faynding it so relaxing wray-ting my kiddies' book about dayno-saurs in the orangery.'

'That's such a pretty house,' said Bianca, handing Daffodil back her phone.

'That's Chaffinch Court, isn't it?' said Rosalie. 'Have you seen the ghost yet?'

'Ghost?' gasped Daffodil in horror. 'What ghost?'

'Oh, some sobbing lady who's supposed to wander round the house at night.'

'Don't be ridiculous,' snapped Bianca, 'stop frighten-ing Daffodil. No one's ever seen a ghost at Penscombe and that's miles older than Chaffinch Court.'

Rosalie was livid, but reluctant to bawl out the chair-man's daughter. Fortunately, they were then interrupted by a deafening roar as three referees followed by the teams came out on to the pitch, accompanied by mas-sive cheers, boos and wolf-whistles at Searston's new blue-and-green-striped strip.

Lou-Easy and Marketa had meanwhile been dying to get another crack at the Searston players, particularly Orion, but Rupert had rejected another Safety Car and Jack Russells demo.

'There's too much going on today. Leave it till later in the season.'

As the yard had won the St Leger the previous Satur-day, Marketa and Lou-Easy had taken the afternoon off to go to the match. As they weren't invited into the Boardroom, Tember had got them two tickets in the

Fan Zone in the south-west corner of the pitch. This was where a large embattled block of Searston fans was separated from Deansgate fans by a couple of dozen policemen in orange sleeveless jackets, waiting for fights to break out.

'It's all male, you'll enjoy it,' laughed Tember.

Scented and gorgeous, Lou-Easy and Marketa turned out to be the only women, but the men, mostly in bomber jackets with fur-lined hoods, were far too keen on the game and insulting each other to show a flicker of interest. The loathing between the two teams could have set the pitch on fire.

Sitting in the front row, on a level with the goalposts, the two women realised how vast the pitch was. And the din was unbelievable, both sets of fans singing, shouting, clapping hands above their heads, thrusting fists and a barrage of abuse back and forth.

'Rupert Black, cut your losses, just go back to racing hosses.'

But that was equalled by the yelling on the pitch. Anger Management shouting at the young midfielders, Wilfie and now Dolphy, like a military policeman; Captain Parks and Ludo yelling at everyone; Barry Pitt howling at the Searston defenders for not defending him.

'We're not Real Madrid, we're not Barcelona,' sang the Searston fans, 'we're Searston Rovers and Rupert is our owner.'

Next moment, Orion came racing down the pitch, passing to Downing, who skyed the ball above the bar. A returning Orion, seeing glamour in the front row, smiled seductively at it.

'Wow, isn't he edible,' cried Lou-Easy. 'We must get

him into bed soon. And look at little Dolphy racing about! Oh, come on, Dolphy.'

'That Deansgate coach, Elijah something, is fit too,' raved Marketa.

Though Elijah had miraculously guided Deansgate up into the Premier League, he was fed up. He was still expected to carry on winning even though players he'd brought on and loved kept being sold on, so Sir Craig could pay himself several million a year. Elijah also had difficulty with Laddy Heywood, who had never forgiven him for breaking his leg, and since Narcisco's russet locks had been cut off, he'd refused to head the ball in case it flattened the curls growing back.

Elijah's cross, however, was arrogant but useless Lyall Dudsbridge, who had to play every game, with Jarred nagging the rest of the Deansgate players to feed him the ball. This was so he might score in front of his illustrious father, the Chief Constable.

On the other hand, Elijah was enchanted to see little Dolphy racing around looking for gaps in the defence or unmarked players to pass to, but no one seemed to be giving him the ball.

It was a very tough game, both teams frantic to win and equalling each other in cussedness. Feral, Orion and Downing, normally lethal in attack, found it infuriatingly difficult to penetrate Elijah's rock-solid defence and constant marking. So, although by clouting the ball to each other they were dominant in the first half-hour, they failed to convert possession into goals.

Narcisco was racing down the pitch when Downing came in from the right, edging up and taking the ball from him, so Narcisco stumbled, and started screaming before he hit the ground, then writhed around in simulated agony. As the ref rushed up waving a yellow card, Downing lost it:

'I hardly touched the fucker, he fucking dived!'

As players closed in, fists raised, Narcisco gave another scream.

'Get up, you wanker,' yelled Downing.

'That's enough,' shouted the ref, brandishing a red card, and Searston were down to ten men.

Nothing Elijah or Pete Wainwright yelled at their players could be heard over the din of the crowd. Just before half-time, Dolphy's nemesis Laddy Heywood picked up the ball, and, not so fast since his broken leg, lofted a lovely diagonal pass across the pitch to a Deansgate midfielder, who passed in turn to a miraculously recovered Narcisco, who, galloping down, dropped the ball sweetly between Anger Management and Griffy, so a Deansgate striker was able to whisk it past Barry Pitt into goal.

1–0 to Deansgate.

'He's lush,' said Lou-Easy, consulting her team sheet. 'I don't blame all those Deansgate players jumping on top of him. Orion will have to look to his laurels.'

Then Orion vindicated himself by scoring an exquisite goal to thunderous applause, which died away when it was declared offside.

Several balls were dutifully passed to Lyall Dudsbridge, the Chief Constable's son, which he missed and passed to the opposition. Searston's defence was reassembling, when a missile, fired by Laddy Heywood, thundered past Barry Pitt into the net. 2–0 to Deansgate. And the half-time whistle went.

'Go easy on them,' Pete Wainwright pleaded with Rupert, as a depressed Searston returned to their dressing room. Rupert didn't. Dolphy, who'd hardly touched the ball, huddled in the corner, waiting to be subbed.

Though chided by Jarred that Lyall Dudsbridge hadn't scored yet, Elijah, on the other hand, told his players they were doing brilliantly. In the hospitality suites, everyone enjoyed delicious Lemon Dribble cake.

'It's all over, Searston Rovers,' sang Deansgate down in the Fan Zone. 'Take a hit, you're fucking shit.'

'Hardly songs of praise,' giggled Lou-Easy.

On his way to the bar, a handsome Deansgate fan asked Lou-Easy what she'd like to drink, then, seeing her blue-and-green shirt under her coat, said: 'On second thoughts, I'll just buy my own.'

Searston's mascot, based on Safety Car – brown and white with a straggling mane and tail, one ear, huge eyes and a great toothy smile – was, however, a huge hit with fans, as he handed out packets of Taggie's fudge.

Rupert's pep talk had also fired Searston up. Ten minutes into the second half, Feral scored a beautiful goal, taking them to 2–1, which Bianca, chattering to Daffodil, didn't notice at all until Charm tipped her off, whereupon she screamed with delight, particularly when the fans started singing: 'If you're in peril, send for Feral.'

Eight minutes to go, most of the players were down at the Searston end, when Dolphy, miserable that he hadn't scored, noticed a fluffy marmalade cat that had wandered on to the pitch in front of the yelling Fan Zone. Next moment, a grinning Lyall Dudsbridge had sidled up and was about to boot it out of the ground.

'Stop it, you horrible man,' yelled Dolphy. 'Stop the game please, Mr Ref, there's a ginger pussy on the pitch.' And, racing 80 yards up the field, in front of laughing, cheering fans, he gathered up the terrified cat, stroking its orange fur, crooning to it and then, when it struggled, tucking it inside his shirt, so its head peered out of the neck.

'All right, pussy, you're safe now.'

Looking round, the referee blew his whistle and stopped the game.

Returning to the benches along the touchline, Dolphy caught sight of Lou-Easy and Marketa.

'Isn't he lovely?' he called. 'Could you take him and keep him safe?'

'Bit difficult here,' yelled back Lou-Easy, 'they'd probably eat him.'

'For God's sake, Dolphy,' bellowed Rupert, 'put the fucking cat down.'

'Book him,' roared Jarred. 'Give him a red card.'

Everyone else was laughing their heads off. Dolphy had just reached the technical area, hoping to hand the cat over to Elijah, when Dora jumped down from the press box and, taking the cat, wrapped him in her beautiful new blue-and-green-striped Searston scarf.

'I'll look after him, Dolph.'

'Just till the end of the match,' panted Dolphy. 'Perhaps you could find him a saucer of milk. I'll take him home later.'

'Send him off,' roared Jarred.

Most other people were still laughing as Dolphy returned to the game. The ref was looking at his watch. Seven minutes' stoppage time, most of those due to Dolphy's cat rescue. The din was deafening. Still 2–1, Deansgate had seven frantic minutes to bank their win.

One Deansgate defender, who'd always pinched Dolphy's sandwiches, had the ball and passed it to Lyall

Dudsbridge, who passed it by mistake to Josef, who dribbled it down the left side, then kicked the ball across to Orion, who belted in a beautiful goal to screams of delight from Marketa and Lou-Easy.

2–2, with two minutes left.

A Deansgate striker kicked off. Little Jesus, who'd been subbed for Wilfie in midfield, snatched up the ball and galloped down the pitch, weaving in and out of Deansgate players, before sending a beautiful assist to Feral, who was poised to finish, when, catching sight of Laddy Heywood pounding towards him, he flicked the ball to Dolphy on his right, who, with the outside of his left foot, somehow coaxed it between Byron Stopwell and the right-hand post. There was a pause. Did it go in? Then the net shivered.

3–2 to Searston, and the full-time whistle blew.

'The ginger pussy brought us luck,' cried Dolphy as an avalanche of cheering fellow players descended on him.

Taggie was enchanted to see the blaze of triumph on Rupert's face as he sprinted out to congratulate his team. Elijah was thanking the refs and consoling all his furious players, who felt they'd been robbed and that Dolphy should have been sent off. But when he came face to face with Dolphy, Elijah couldn't resist giving him a hug.

'Brilliant, Dolphy, fantastic finish, and your first Premier League goal.'

'And my first for Searston.'

'And well done for rescuing that cat.' Elijah pushed a lock of damp blond hair off Dolphy's forehead.

'He brought us luck.' Dolphy thought what a lovely smile Elijah had and how tall, dark and handsome he was, and how proud he seemed.

'He did. What are you going to do with him?'

'Take him home.'

'To join Grandkid?'

'You remembered his name.'

'Of course I did. How is he?'

'Fine. I live in a cottage wiv two uvver players so he gets lots of treats.'

'Elijah,' howled Jarred, 'come back and talk to the press. Why the hell are you chatting up that little sissy?' Then, seeing the fury on Elijah's face: 'Running after that cat, he completely disrupted our rhythm. We were robbed. He should have been red-carded.'

Sir Craig was also hopping mad.

'Why's Elijah Cohen wasting time talking to that Searston schoolboy?'

'He used to play for us.'

'Why did you let him go?'

'Elijah sold him,' lied Jarred.

'It's the Curse of the Ex,' mocked a passing Rupert.

'Come on, Lady Grace,' snarled Craig. 'We're leaving.'

'Oh no,' protested Grace. 'Can't we stay for a noggin?'

'No, we bloody can't.'

38

Sir Craig was so outraged by the defeat – particularly embarrassing in front of the Chief Constable, who'd specifically beefed up police security, knowing it was a grudge match, and who then was furious that his son Lyall didn't score – that, in the morning, he sacked Elijah.

This was promptly pounced on by the media, and Sir Craig, who adored publicity, donned a light-brown-and-sky-blue baseball cap to tell a packed press conference that Elijah had to go because he was a wimp.

Poor Elijah had to pile his office belongings into his battered Golf and go home to pretty Buttercup Cottage to tell an unsympathetic Madison he'd been fired.

'Not man enough,' she sniped. 'I presume you got a massive severance package? No – only a couple of months' salary?'

Having kicked off as coach of the Academy, Elijah had never negotiated a contract when he became manager.

'What the hell are we going to live on? How on earth are we going to pay the mortgage?'

Madison was obsessed with becoming a Labour candidate for Cotchester, and marriage to a successful football manager would have been a great plus. Elijah's children, Isaiah and Naomi, were also relentlessly teased at school: 'Your dad's a wimp.'

Dolphy was distraught. The marmalade cat hadn't brought Elijah any luck and when he took it home, Grandkid mistook it for a rabbit and tried to eat it.

So, the cat had moved in with Dora and Paris and was now called Mew-Too. It had bonded with Buddyguard the Alsatian, who was very sad – as the whole household was – at the passing of Dora's beloved ancient chocolate Labrador, Cadbury, who was now buried in Rupert's animal graveyard.

The following week, after the match, determined to save Elijah's career, and having checked Rupert's engagements in Tember's office diary, Dolphy dragged Rupert out of a black-tie racing dinner.

'Oh please, Mr Rupert, Elijah's the best manager I've ever known – he's brilliant, and he's so kind if you screw up and helps you play better. He gives young players a chance, explains fings to the foreign ones and never spends lots of money on players, so he'd be miles cheaper for you than Ryan.'

A sleepless Elijah was in total despair, wondering what the hell to do with his life, imagining his father, Rabbi Abner, thinking, *I told him so*, when, at two in the morning, the telephone rang. 'How would you like to come and manage Searston Rovers?' drawled a voice.

'I'd like it very much,' stammered Elijah. 'Are you quite sure?'

'Quite. I'm such a bully and you're such a wimp, we should cancel each other out.'

'How did you get my number?'

'Dolphy gave it to me, gave you an excellent reference as well.'

Dolphy was so enchanted, he went out and bought Rupert a pair of long diamond earrings.

After being sacked by Sir Craig, Elijah had been too traumatised to unload any of his Deansgate manager crud out of his ancient, dented Golf, but early on the morning of Rupert's call, he drove over to Searston, where two of the club cleaners, Nadia and Roxanne, showed him to his office, which they had just cleaned.

'It looks marvellous,' gasped Elijah. 'My last office was a spiders' hotel, and you've even cleaned the windows.' He could see the woods turning gold outside. 'Thank you so much.'

Roxanne and Nadia were therefore delighted to help him unload the Golf, sticking up posters saying 'Side Before Self' and 'Marching Together' beside the wall sculpture of a galloping grey horse and the club slogan, 'Horse Power', in blue and green letters.

'I want to put up a picture of all the Searston staff,' said Elijah, then, as Nadia brought in a huge picture of Team Deansgate, 'but I guess that's one for the scrapheap.'

'I might keep it,' giggled Nadia. 'That Laddy Heywood is so good-looking.'

'Where do you want this CD player putting?' asked Roxy. 'And you need a little cupboard for all those CDs and for all your aftershaves. Are those your kiddies? They're cute.'

'Isaiah and Naomi – here, let me!' Elijah took a pile of books, including a copy of the Old Testament, from Nadia.

When Roxy brought in several medals and three cups Elijah had won previously as a player and a manager, he said: 'I'd better take those home; it's a bit showing off to display them.'

'Not when I've given them a good polish,' said Nadia.

The word got around. Next minute, another cleaner had rolled up with a cup of tea and biscuits, and then another with a cup of coffee and cake.

The next arrival was Tember.

'Oh goodness, you've beaten me to it. Welcome to Searston! It's all looking gorgeous.'

And so do you, thought Elijah, even without any make-up and her lush long hair scraped into a ponytail.

'I hope you can find room for these.' She put a big vase of agapanthus, bright-blue bell-shaped flowers with green leaves like ribbons, down on the edge of his desk.

'Wow, they're great – and in Searston colours, too. Thank you so much.'

Tember looked around. 'Goodness, you've been working hard.'

'Roxy and Nadia have,' said Elijah. 'I thought I'd better get ensconced quickly in case Rupert changed his mind.'

'He hasn't, he's thrilled, he texted me in the middle of the night. He's getting Marti Gluckstein, his ace lawyer, to sort out your contract.'

'Ask for lots of money, Elijah,' urged Roxanne, coming in with more CDs and Elijah's dark-green quilted jacket, which she noticed had split at the shoulders and vowed to mend.

'Not too much,' said Nadia. 'Rupert's bankrupted his-self buying the club, wiv hundreds of people dependent on him and all his racing yard. The *Daily Mail* said we've got to win every match this season to save Rupert and Taggie. She's a lovely lady.'

'Push off, darlings, I need to discuss things with Elijah,' said Tember and shut the door with rare firmness. 'Everyone is over the moon you've joined Searston.' She added, giving him a hug, 'Rupert wants you to get started training the lads tomorrow and Pete Wainwright wants to stay on as consultant, if you're happy with that.'

'That's marvellous. Pete's great.'

'We've got a biggish game against North Wilts on Saturday – not far, the coach will be back here around seven. Taggie wants to give a little party at Penscombe to welcome you.'

'That's too much for her; she hasn't been well. I was thinking of giving a little do myself in the Running Fox, just to celebrate.'

'No, Taggie really wants to, she's got so hooked on football. And she wants you to bring your wife.'

'Bit of a downer if we lose on Saturday.'

Tember laughed. 'You won't if Dolphy brings his lucky ginger pussy. He'll be distraught he wasn't here to welcome you with fireworks and flares.'

The moment she left, Roxy and Nadia were back.

'Here's a pile of chewing gum for you,' said Nadia. 'You'll need it for matches. It calms nerves, decreases stress, improves concentration. D'you like peppermint or juicy fruit? Oh look, one of your CDs is the showjumping music. Rupert was a great showjumper, wasn't he?'

'The greatest in the world. Olympic gold with a trapped nerve in his arm,' said Elijah. 'Let's play it.'

And Nadia slotted the CD into the machine, the brass band booming through the building, making everyone jump.

Elijah turned it down. 'Thank you both so much. I think I'd better do some work.'

In the big general office next door was a large screen to play videos of matches and a chart of the pitch, covered in arrows and crosses, telling players where to go. Out of the window, he could see a groundsman painting in the white touchline and waved at him. *The pitch itself could be better*, he thought.

Back in the kitchen, Nadia and Roxy were wondering whether to take Elijah more coffee or put some sandwiches in his fridge.

'Lovely guy,' sighed Nadia. 'So handsome, and he's really nice too, and so grateful. Ryan never said thank you for anything.'

Elijah was just identifying the forty players in the team photographs when a very pretty blonde swept in with a large Alsatian.

'Hello, hello, I'm Dora, Rupert's press officer. I also write for the *Cotchester Times*. I want to do a first big interview about you joining Searston before it gets picked up by the nationals.'

'I haven't really got to know the players yet, or had my first game.'

'You're one of the youngest Premier League managers and were responsible for getting Deansgate up there too.'

'I'm not sure Jarred Moreland would agree.'

'Oh, he's as bent as a paper clip, and I'm so pleased you've escaped from Sir Craig – he's such a bastard. I rescued Buddyguard from him.' She patted the Alsatian, who wagged his tail as she gave him one of Elijah's biscuits. 'And now Rupert's rescued you. Cadenza's going to come and take a really good photo of you. She'll probably make a pass at you. Her hobby is other people's hubbies.'

Elijah laughed. 'I still think we should check with Rupert.'

'And did you know that the Deansgate players are so livid you've been sacked, and they didn't get a chance to say goodbye, that they're threatening not to play on Saturday? Isn't that a great story? Strikers on strike. And Taggie's giving a party for you on Saturday. That's so cool. She's going to ask the Wags to meet your wife. Does she love football?'

'Not hugely. She's called Madison and she's hoping to be adopted as Labour candidate for Cotchester.'

'Oh goodness,' squeaked Dora. 'My brother Jupiter's the Tory MP. She'll have a job to oust him. He's tough. He's also an art dealer' – Dora lowered her voice – 'he's been selling a lot of poor Rupert's pictures, and taking a huge percentage for himself.'

Twenty minutes later, a tearful Dolphy rushed into Tember's office, finding her talking to Dora, and cried out:

'I wanted to let off fireworks to welcome Elijah. We must keep this from him: that b-b-bastard Sir Craig is so furious about Deansgate players frettening to go on strike, he's posted the most horrible fings about him and Rupert. Calling them Elijah Doolittle and Prince Charmless and how they'll be even more harmless, wiv a big headline "Gone with the Wimp" and horrible big pictures. I hate hate hate Sir Craig.'

'So do I, and so does Buddyguard,' said Dora. 'We will get our revenge.'

Getting home to Buttercup Cottage, Elijah found Madison weeding round the red geraniums filling their front garden and told her Rupert and Taggie had invited them to a party after the match on Saturday.

'Rupert Campbell-Black is the worst kind of arrogant, right-wing bastard,' snorted Madison.

'He is my new boss, Maddie, so please at least be civil to him. He can't be that much of a right-wing bastard – he did sort out football hooliganism when he was Minister for Sport, and Searston going up to the Premier League in two seasons was miraculous and has done amazing things for the area, hotels and shops really flourishing. When he fell out with Valent Edwards, he really stretched himself buying Valent's share when he could easily have put the club up for sale and left everyone to stew, and ninety-five per cent of the players opted to stay with him. The party should be fun.'

'He's still an arrogant right-wing bastard.'

Lou-Easy, unlike Madison, was desperate to come to the party, which would be a chance to see gorgeous Orion again. She hadn't slept with anyone else since she'd developed a major crush on him.

'Can Marketa and I come to the party on Saturday and hand round nuts?' she begged Rupert.

'As long as it's only nuts,' said Rupert.

'And can we bring Safety Car?'

'As long as he wears a tie.'

*

In the days before the party, Elijah toured the building to meet the staff and began one-to-ones with each player to discuss how they felt about their role in the team.

'This guy is clever, he really listens,' said Ludo. 'Ryan Edwards never did.'

39

Ryan Edwards, on the other hand, although he'd caused his father, Valent, to pack it in with Searston Rovers back in April, had not been happy about the split-up.

'It's a bit drastic, Dad,' he had protested to Valent at the time. 'I'm out of a job now, and what about Otley and Harry Stanton-Harcourt still in the Searston Academy, and poor Facundo left to Rupert's lack of mercy.'

Ryan had also forfeited all those bungs from estate agents, schools and car manufacturers he had enjoyed at Searston and, even more importantly, he no longer had work as an excuse to escape from home and make love to Lady Emma.

He was irritated that although he'd taken Searston nearly up to the Premier League in two seasons, the press hadn't reported any regret on the part of the players at his departure.

With Elijah moving to Searston, Deansgate were now without a manager, and, as Jarred pointed out to Sir Craig, they needed one who would win matches and who would be ace at bringing in young players for them to sell on. After a recommendation from the League

Managers Association, Sir Craig had invited Ryan to lunch at the Ivy in Cheltenham.

Here, over a delectable Pouilly-Fumé, truffled wild mushrooms and lobster linguine, they shared their loathing of Rupert Campbell-Black.

'He was so evil about my lovely stepmother,' said Ryan, 'and even boasted that Searston are going to win the Champions League.'

'Not a hope, with Wimp Elijah in charge.'

Ryan then spoke of his access to two very gifted young players looking for a new club: his son, Otley, and Harry Stanton-Harcourt.

'Ah, Lady Emma's son,' sighed Sir Craig. 'Such a beautiful woman.'

'And a very good friend,' purred Ryan.

'We must all have dinner.'

By the end of lunch and several brandies, Ryan had become the new manager of Deansgate and made a mutual vow to bring down that bastard, Rupert Campbell-Black.

40

Contrary to Sir Craig's and Ryan's predictions, Wimp Elijah's first game was a triumph, with Searston thrashing North Wilts 5–2, which put everyone in a joyous mood for the party at Penscombe. This was held on the big lawn behind the house backed by Rupert's beech woods, their leaves turning a rich gold in the autumn sunshine.

Everyone was now guzzling champagne and devouring Taggie's delicious canapés. After quick showers, a lot of the players had come straight to the party on the team coach, their other halves arriving separately but just as competitive sartorially, having taken the opportunity to wear pretty summer dresses before winter set in.

Bianca, ravishing in a rose-red mini, Griffy's wife, Inez, in peacock blue with slits in her skirt showing off her endless legs, and Marketa in shocking pink, open-top bust form, were all being chatted up by Facundo, very up himself, having again scored three goals and received the match ball.

Orion, who had scored another two goals, was already plastered in both senses. The blood from a cut on his upper arm caused by the studs of a North Wilts centre back was already seeping through its dressing and he was knocking back the booze to deaden the pain.

Lou-Easy, handing him most of a plate of prawns wrapped in smoked salmon, was in heaven because he had expressed a hope she and Safety Car would soon come back for another demo.

'You're so pretty, Lou-Easy, you brighten up every game.'

Dolphy was also in Heaven. He'd provided an assist for Orion and nipped home to fetch Grandkid, who'd flashed a toothy grin and nudged Elijah, remembering when they were rescued and spent the night at Buttercup Cottage.

Dolphy had hoped Rupert might have worn his diamond earrings.

Taggie had specially invited Wilfie Bradford and his sweet, gentle, pretty, redheaded mother, Mary, but was outraged when Dougie, her evil drunken bully of a husband, gatecrashed the party as well. He turned up sober for once, in a suit and Searston tie, his hair brushed smoothly, intending to charm everyone.

Wilfie promptly escaped to the stables to talk to The Story So Far. Taggie swept Mary off to another part of the garden to talk to Charm and Angus's wife, Mimi. Almost instantly, spying them laughing together, Rosalie Parkinson swanned up, waving a finger. 'Now now, ladies, don't you dare poach my daily. As working wives we need our backup. Can you get in a little earlier tomorrow, Mary, and pick up *Country Life* and the *Sunday Times* on the way?'

Mimi, exchanging a horrified glance with Charm at Rosalie's tactless cruelty, tried to change the subject:

'Oh, there's Safety Car, in a new Searston tie like Dougie.'

'You've met Mary's husband, Dougie, haven't you, Mimi?' demanded Rosalie. 'I think he's delightful.'

'He is a nayghtmare,' snapped Charm with rare aggression.

'I don't agree,' said Rosalie. 'I get on with him, but then I get on with most people.'

'Get on most people's nerves, more likely,' muttered Mimi.

Elijah, meanwhile, was working the room, dressed in his lucky green-checked shirt and jeans, congratulating victorious players, telling the ones on the bench they'd be playing soon, introducing himself to the wives and ground staff, hugging and saying thank you to Roxanne and Nadia.

'Isn't he nice and fit?' murmured the Wags. 'Such a lovely deep voice and great body, and a lovely smile.'

'Vitch von is his wife?' Marketa asked Lou-Easy. 'I vouldn't let him out of my sight for a moment.'

Staff were putting out vast shepherd's pies and home-made ketchup in pots on the tables.

'We're going to have supper in a moment,' Taggie told Elijah.

'Can I just say a few words?' asked Elijah. Where the hell was Madison? He clapped his hands.

'Ladies and gentlemen, horses and dogs, I just wanted to say how happy I am to be your new manager. I can't thank you enough for so tactically staging such a great win today, so hopefully your chairman, Rupert Campbell-Black, won't feel he's made a gha-a-astly mistake.'

Then, as Rupert started to laugh: 'You all played brilliantly and all deserve to be Man of the Match, and your beautiful partners' – Elijah smiled round at the Wags – 'must be so proud of you. I'd also like to thank Rupert and Taggie for giving such a wonderful party to welcome me and my wife, Madison, and providing such buckets of champagne and fantastic food, and inviting the sun along as well, who is having such a good time he doesn't want to set.

'I must apologise to you all that Sir Craig Eynsham, not my greatest fan, has been so vile about Searston and particularly your chairman since I joined you. But he's certainly got egg on his face after today's game.' Then, breaking into a deep baritone, he sang, ' "Don't be vague, just avoid Sir Craig like the plague." And finally, huge congratulations to Rupert's colt Lady Killer for romping home in the Cambridgeshire this afternoon. So, we are all winners, and huge luck for the coming season. Thank you all so much.'

And the cheers rang around the valley.

Hearing the cheering did not improve Madison's mood. Bicycling to Rupert's, she had been pushed into the nettles by several footballers in flash cars hurtling towards the party. She bristled even more when confronted by the splendour of the ex-Tory Minister for Sport's estate, particularly by the length of his drive.

Unlike the other Wags, with their long shining hair and their flowery floating dresses, Madison had clearly made no effort. She hadn't bothered to brush her short, light-brown curls, she wore no make-up, and her slim boyish figure was not enhanced by a sleeveless grey T-shirt with a button missing, hanging outside calf-length grey cords showing off unshaven legs and grubby white trainers.

'Go home,' ordered Eamonn, as, having leaned her bike against a statue of a cantering horse, Madison stalked towards him. 'This is a private party.'

'To which I have been invited,' snapped Madison. 'My husband, Elijah Cohen, is the new Searston manager.'

'I'm so sorry, mam,' said Eamonn. 'Congratulations, your husband did brilliantly this afternoon – everyone's over the moon. Come through the house; the party's outside. Have you come far?'

'About six miles.'

'Do you need the ladies' room?'

'Certainly not.'

'Ah, here's Mrs Campbell-Black. This is Mrs Madison Cohen, Taggie.'

'Madison Holtby,' said Madison firmly. 'I go under my given name.'

'How lovely to see you,' cried Taggie. 'Your husband just made the sweetest speech; they did so well today. Come on in and meet everyone.'

Outside, a rip-roaring party was in full swing. Guests, having moved on to red or white wine, were tucking into huge helpings of shepherd's pie. Elijah, talking to Pete Wainwright and Rupert, looked up and waved but, grabbing a glass, Madison made a beeline for Feral.

'I am your new manager's wife. How long have you been playing for Searston?'

'This is my third season, ma'am,' said Feral, and Madison was off. Had Feral been given decent accommodation? Did he feel isolated? Did he feel racially abused by his colleagues on Instagram? Did Searston have a regular counsellor to deal with players' mental health problems?

'I think she's left,' said Feral.

'And what is your country of origin? Do you get home-sick, and do your folks live far away?'

'Only a few miles.'

'So where do you actually live?'

'I live here, ma'am, wiv Rupert and Taggie. Their daughter Bianca, over there in the red dress – she's my girlfriend.'

'You live in this house!' shouted Madison. She was just assimilating this, then gave a scream as Safety Car, wearing a blue-and-green Searston tie, wandered over to nudge his friend Feral.

'Make that horrible beast go away.'

'Safety's a star, ma'am, he brings in the crowds doing demos at matches.'

As Safety wandered off, Madison accepted another drink and moved on to the importance of embracing biodiversity, telling a bemused Feral he must ensure a variety of animal and plant life.

'Plenty of animals here,' said Feral, as Buddyguard, Cuthbert, Forester and Banquo charged across the lawn in pursuit of Gilchrist, who was brandishing a rubber rabbit.

'Do you embrace biodiversity, Feral?'

'No, I'm not bi, I'm straight, ma'am.'

Lou-Easy, who was topping up their glasses, tried not to laugh.

Now Madison was banging on about the need for more affordable houses in the Cotswolds: 'This valley would be perfect.'

'Not sure Rupert would see it like that.'

'Of course not.'

'Rupert provides work and accommodation for thou-sands of people,' snapped Lou-Easy, 'and Feral here is one of your husband's best players. It must be fun being a manager's wife with access to all those fit guys.' And, noting Madison's look of disapproval, she shimmied off to chat up Orion.

Elijah had been waylaid by Bastian: 'When I retire from football, I'm going to be a writer. I'm already working on my *Hauteur Biography* – I'm well into a chapter on your arrival – but, like all artists, I need to feel supported in my creativity and hope I will be in the line-up next Saturday.'

'Sure, sure,' said Elijah, as he noticed poor little Dolphy being bawled out for taking a glass of white rather than red to Anger Management, and Feral still pinned against the wall by Madison. He ought to rescue him before he died of boredom or fell asleep.

Music was drifting out of the house now, and couples were dancing.

Bianca was chatting to her friend Dora.

'Facundo's just made a pass at me, asked me to drop by tomorrow afternoon.'

'Both on and off the pitch,' observed Dora, 'he's making more passes than any other player. He's clearly having an affair with Inez, and this evening he's come on to you, Lou-Easy and Marketa, and Tember. The *Telegraph* called him a ferocious left-footer' – Dora gave a scream of joy – 'and so is Madison, she's a *very* ferocious left-footer. God, she bangs on – you must rescue Feral.'

'She'd be quite pretty if she didn't look so cross,' said Bianca. Then, as Rupert passed them: 'Daddy, can you go and rescue Feral? Oh hell, he's fallen asleep. He'll be far too tired to make love again tonight. Perhaps I should get off with Facundo.'

Dougie the bully, meanwhile, was dancing with Rosalie Parkinson.

'As the captain's lady, I hope you have a word in Hubby's ear about regularly playing little Wilfie. And I hope you're happy with my Mary. If you want her to put in more hours, just let me know.'

Madison had had three large glasses of white and not eaten.

'Who are you?' she asked as Rupert strode up with the light behind him.

'Your husband's new boss, Rupert Campbell-Black. Welcome to Penscombe. I gather you're planning to become an MP?'

'In time,' said a slightly thrown Madison.

'What would be your plans to improve the area?'

'Much more socially affordable housing. We could get half a million properties in this valley alone. We need better, safer cycle lanes. I was pushed into the nettles' – she waved at her mottled calf – 'by half the drivers coming in their flash cars, none of them electric, to your party. We've got to address climate change, so you ought to rewild a lot of your land. And you should care much more for older and younger members of society.'

'Which am I?'

Madison let her eyes travel upwards. 'Neither.' Then she gave another shriek as Safety Car wandered over to nudge his beloved master.

'Take him away.'

'He wants to know if he's an older or younger member of society.'

'Don't be fatuous.'

'Your husband is an extremely nice man,' said Rupert.

'And this is an extremely nice party,' said Lou-Easy, topping up their glasses.

'I don't think Madison wants to dance with Safety Car,' said Rupert.

'I'll take him away,' said Lou-Easy, vaulting on to Safety Car and riding off across the lawn. She was in heaven: a well-away Orion had kissed her most passionately behind a willow tree before murmuring, 'As you fed me a prawn cocktail earlier, why don't you drop in to the Shaggery tomorrow afternoon for a porn cocktail?'

'Only if you get that shoulder sorted,' Lou-Easy had teased.

She wasn't going to tell Marketa, who would be heart-broken, having spent all evening trying to make Orion jealous by flirting with Facundo, who was now sitting on the lawn making hot eyes at Inez.

'Why don't you send your husband 'ome?' he murmured to her. 'Then you can come back to my 'ouse.'

So Griffy, who was in despair having spent the afternoon on the bench, was ordered home to relieve the babysitter. In the hall, he bumped into Tember, who'd been so busy helping to organise the party that she hadn't had a proper chance to talk to him. She looked so beautiful in her orange sleeveless dress. Had he been dreaming? Did this beautiful creature *really* fancy him?

'I miss you,' whispered Tember, drawing him into the downstairs loo with all Rupert's showjumping photos on the walls and pulling him into her arms. 'We MUST see more of each other.'

'I never think of anything else but you,' gasped Griffy. 'I absolutely adore you.'

'Not as much as I adore you. Can't you stay on for a bit?'

248

'I've got to get home for the little girls, but' – Griffy buried his lips in hers for a long, searching kiss, then, when they paused for breath, stroked her slender bare arms – 'all I want to do every night is to fall asleep counting your freckles.'

They both jumped as someone banged on the door.

'It's engaged,' shouted Tember. Then, smiling up at Griffy: 'Oh, I so wish we were engaged to each other.'

It was so lovely seeing him laughing as he took her back into his arms and slid his hands inside her dress to caress her breasts.

Only after he'd written 'I love Tember' in the misted-up mirror did they finally emerge, not noticing a lurking Cadenza, who took a quick snap. It might come in useful one day. She wasn't keen on that bitch Inez.

'Drive carefully, won't you, darling,' Tember called after a departing Griffy. 'Never forget for a second how precious you are to me.'

Oh God, why couldn't they run away together into Rupert's back woods? She was so tempted to follow him home.

In the drawing room, as people were leaving, Elijah went up to a very drunken Madison.

'We ought to go, Taggie must be tired.'

Dougie was now chatting up Bastian's pretty wife, Daffodil, who was laughing her hair extensions off.

'Who's she?' asked Lou-Easy.

'Daffodil Clark-Rogers. Someone told her she had a lovely laugh and she's been acting like a hyena ever since,' sneered a passing Inez.

'That's unkind, Inez,' reproached Rosalie Parkinson. 'Daffodil's just got a lovely sense of humour.'

'That's because she laughs at your jokes,' snapped

Inez, who was insane with rage to discover Facundo had pushed off with Marketa instead of herself.

'Come on, Rosie, we must go,' said Parks, sensing trouble.

Outside, the coach was waiting to take home couples who hadn't got drivers. A departing Ludo gave Taggie a hug.

'You've done brilliantly, duchess. Want to come upstairs for a bit of rough?'

Taggie giggled. She loved Ludo.

Rosalie was now introducing herself to Madison:

'I'm the captain's lady. May I call you Mad?'

'I'd rather you didn't,' said Madison, cannoning off the front doors so Elijah had to grab her.

On her way out, Rosalie passed Mary, who was still enjoying chatting to Shelagh, and shouted, 'Go home, Mary, you need to be fresh in the morning.'

'I'll make sure she is there on time, Rosalie,' called out Dougie.

'Have another drink, Mary,' said Rupert.

'Mary's a star,' said Taggie, giving Mary a hug. 'So thrilled you came. Come and have supper with Shelagh soon.'

Czech Josef was sad. He had watched his flatmate Orion chatting up Lou-Easy and snogging not just her but several other girls behind the willow tree. He knew he could never be as attractive to women as Orion, but he so didn't want Lou-Easy to be hurt.

He had been touched, however, when Rupert took him into his study and showed him the big silver cup awarded to Penscombe Pride, the gelding who had won the Czech Grand National, known as the Pardubice. He had also been cheered up by Elijah's compliments. No longer locked out by Ryan's dislike, he was able to display more and more flair, contributing two crucial assists today.

'You put the ball exactly where a player needs it,' Elijah had told him.

Next minute, Orion had sidled up:

'My shoulder's giving me hell, Josef, and I'm too drunk to drive. Can you drop me off at casualty on the way home?'

41

Everyone agreed it had been a great party. Next day, the Searston players were glad to work off their hangovers before returning to training on Monday. Lou-Easy and Marketa had to get up early to do their horses, Lou-Easy having not drunk much last night, wanting to look luscious for Orion.

Marketa, who had gone home with Facundo, was full of chat.

'His place is so gorgeous – games room, Jacuzzi, indoor svimming pool and a pool attendant waiting up for us. Garage for six cars. Vot's not to like?'

Lou-Easy, who was polishing Cambridgeshire winner Lady Killer's sleek dark-brown coat, asked what Facundo was like in bed.

'Huge villy, but not much before-play. Vot about you?'

'I went to bed; I was tired.'

'Vot are you up to this afternoon?'

'I'm going to see my sister,' lied Lou-Easy. If Marketa had been off shagging Facundo, she couldn't be that smitten with Orion. Lou-Easy felt less guilty and asked: 'What are you up to this afternoon?'

'Catching up on some sleep, and I might pop into Vaitrose – ve are out of eggs.'

'That was a good party,' said Lou-Easy. 'Isn't Elijah heaven? But that Madison is awful; it was hysterical her not realising Feral had fallen asleep. Wilfie's dad's even worse. He shouted at poor Wilfie for riding Safety Car. Safety was more pissed than Madison.'

Six hours later, Lou-Easy rolled up at the Shaggery, the house in Cotchester Market Square in which the Searston poster boys, Orion, Downing, Josef and Galgo, now had the top two flats. A silvery-grey mini-tunic clung to Lou-Easy's pretty figure and she was drenched in Marketa's Coco Mademoiselle, her ash-blonde hair newly washed, not much make-up because her hands were shaking too much to apply eyeliner and almost to press the doorbell. She'd never been so much in love in her life. This was the Real Thing.

Josef, going to the flat's front door, nearly fainted with delight to see Lou-Easy on the indoor security camera. Pressing the button, he bid her come up to the third floor, and hastily patted his hair, pulled down his T-shirt and splashed on some of Downing's aftershave.

'Hello, Orion.' Tearing up the stairs, trembling with excitement, Louisa was startled to see his flat-mate Josef.

She looked so ravishing, Josef wanted to take her in his arms.

'Orion is not 'ere. He'll be back soon, I expect.'

Steering her away from the kitchen, where Downing was breakfasting on Alka-Seltzer and watching porn, he led her into the sitting room, which was furnished with huge black leather sofas, a vast television, two exercise bikes and, on hangers, rows of clothes that Orion sold online.

Throwing a cushion over a pink sequinned shawl left on one of the sofas, Josef said to Lou-Easy:

'Vait vile I get you a glass of vine and some Scottish shortbread. How is your Jack Russell terrier? How are your horses?'

'None of them are running today,' said Lou-Easy, who was admiring the photographs of Orion on the wall. What a beauty he was.

'I vill be back in a minute.'

Back in the kitchen, he asked, 'Vere the hell is Orion?'

'God knows,' said Downing.

Then Josef jumped and spilt the Sancerre he was pouring, as the doorbell rang again.

'Thank Christ, that must be Orion. Must have lost his keys again.'

But after he had handed over the glass of wine to Lou-Easy, the doorbell rang again.

And, oh God, on the security camera was a ravishing redhead in a blue-and-white nurse's uniform, who said she was Lucille and she had come to see Orion.

'He's not back yet,' stammered Josef.

'Oh, let her in,' said a hovering Downing.

The pretty nurse, when Josef did, explained that Orion had popped into A&E last night to get his shoulder dressed, quite a nasty wound.

'He asked me to pop in this afternoon, but made me promise to wear my uniform, naughty boy.'

'Let me get you a drink. I expect he vill be here soon,' gasped Josef, ushering her into the games room, which had a sofa but was filled with more exercise bikes, dumbbells, cardio machines, empty bottles and photos of Orion looking virile.

'This is vere ve vork out, but I expect you know all that,' said Josef. 'May I get you a drink?'

'I'd prefer a cup of tea, I'm driving.'

Scuttling back into the kitchen, where Downing was laughing his head off, Josef wailed:

'Vot are ve going to do?'

'Orion must've got so pissed, he's forgotten he asked either of them back.'

They were then joined by Galgo in striped pyjamas, who said:

'Orion's upstairs, pulling the Czech one with long dark hair – Maria?'

'Marketa. She teach me English – the bastard,' stormed Josef. 'Poor Lou-Easy; we better say he's gone to London.'

'We could have a foursome or a fivesome,' said Downing. 'They're both pretty.'

But poor Josef couldn't laugh, he was so worried about Lou-Easy. Having taken Lucille the nurse a cup of tea, he took the bottle of wine into the sitting room, where Lou-Easy, straddling an exercise bike, was touching up her face in its mirror.

'I like your new manager,' she said.

'We all like him,' said Josef. 'He give me game time, and explain when I don't understand English.'

'You must have fun here now. How long have you known Orion?'

'About one year. He play so vell yesterday. So did your horse, Lady Killer. Funny name, vot does it mean?'

Lou-Easy laughed. 'A man who is successful at seducing women – sounds like Facundo.'

And Orion, thought Josef.

'Lovely view,' said Lou-Easy. 'I like that statue of Charles I, and I think you can see Penscombe from here.' Opening the window, she peered out. 'I hope Orion will be back soon, I don't want to waste your afternoon.'

Then she gave a shriek and burst into tears. 'There's Marketa's blue Mini down in the car park – she must be here. She said she was going to Waitrose.'

Then, almost on cue, out of the open window above came ecstatic moaning, which was followed by shrieks of pleasure.

'I'm coming, I'm coming, go on, Orion, go on.'

'She must be upstairs,' said Josef, in horror. 'I didn't see her come in.'

'She's clearly coming now,' sobbed Lou-Easy. 'Orion said he wanted to make love to me so much, I can't bear it; I've had a crush on him for so long, I didn't realise how much I loved him.'

'Come here,' said Josef, pulling her into his arms. 'You are most lovely voman in the vorld.'

'Orion doesn't think so. I didn't tell Marketa because I didn't want to hurt her, and perhaps she didn't tell me because she didn't want to hurt me, and I'm wearing her scent . . . Oh God, I'm so sorry, I must go, Josef.'

Next moment, Lucille the nurse walked in.

'Oh, hello. Sorry to interrupt, but Orion still hasn't turned up. I'm off.'

'I can't bear it,' wailed Lou-Easy, breaking away from Josef and, grabbing her bag, she fled out of the flat.

42

Rupert's lunch with Elijah to assess the current situation and make plans for the future was delayed by yearling sales and Lady Killer getting beaten into fourth place in the Arc de Triomphe at Longchamp – not an auspicious boost to his future stallion career, nor to Rupert's bank balance.

So, it was on the Monday after Elijah's second match – against Andover, in which Searston only equalised because Orion scored in stoppage time – that they met at the Bear Inn at Bisley, fifteen miles from Searston.

Happily, so they were not overheard, it was still warm enough to lunch outside over a bottle of red, boeuf roulade, roast potatoes and broccoli. Once again, Elijah thanked Rupert for the party at Penscombe:

'It was such a great way to meet everyone, particularly your enchanting Taggie. She is so sweet and even prettier in the flesh. I hope it didn't tire her too much.'

'No, she enjoyed it, and your thank-you letter,' said Rupert, not adding that she couldn't read it.

'I can't imagine what a nightmare it must have been for you.'

'Not exactly a day in the country.'

Once again, Elijah was blown away by Rupert's beauty. Not just his body, as powerful and solidly muscular as one of his stallions. There was no grey in the sleek blond hair, hardly a wrinkle in the smooth tanned face, not even crow's feet around the hard, unsmiling blue-eyed stare, which suddenly softened when a smile lit up his face like the sun. Catching a waft of his aftershave, Galop d'Hermès, Elijah steeled himself not to drink too much, in case he left a hand too long on Rupert's arm or, even worse, his thigh.

Elijah himself, having got even less sleep than usual, poring over videos of past Searston games and future opposition teams, looked pale and drawn.

'Everything all right, sir?' asked Lydia, the pretty hovering waitress who couldn't take her eyes off Rupert. 'Would you like some horseradish or French mustard?'

'French Mustard's a nice name for a horse,' reflected Rupert. 'No, we're fine, sweetheart.'

Once she'd gone, Elijah apologised for Searston only drawing on Saturday.

'I gather Facundo didn't show,' said Rupert.

'Said he felt some discomfort in his groin.'

'Probably kneed by some jealous husband.'

'We've got to face the fact,' said Elijah, 'that staying in the Premier League is much harder than going up to it – far more travelling and playing against teams with massive budgets to buy players.'

'I know this,' Rupert said, irritably.

'Therefore, it will be a miracle if Searston, in their first season, finish in fourth place and qualify for the Champions League,' continued Elijah. 'However, I'm aware of your bet with Valent Edwards. We'll need to aim for three points in every game, and score as much as possible, so we don't get pipped at the end by goal difference.

'As we haven't got a huge amount to buy players, we've got to improve those we've got and purge those who have nothing to offer. The crucial thing is to strengthen our defence. I know you believe attack is all-important, Rupert, but it's vital to defend as a whole team. Any opponent should have to fight to get past our front four, and then past our midfielders, before they even reach the back four and our goalkeeper.

'Yesterday, for example, we were all on the counter-attack in their half, when their centre forward grabbed the ball, weaved down the touchline and scored before any of our boys could catch him. We must never leave our goal unprotected.'

Christ, Rupert ate fast – his plate was nearly empty. Elijah noticed his left hand curled round his second glass of red, his gold signet ring shining on his little finger, and found himself blurting out:

'What does it say on your crest?'

'Rage begets arms,' drawled Rupert.

'Ah,' mused Elijah. 'Is that your philosophy? Rage at being beaten? Rage at another player coming in and taking your place, urging you to play better or more aggressively? Hatred of the other side making you pull your socks up?'

Rupert laughed. 'Downing won't. He wears his socks round his ankles and the shortest shorts to show off his chorus-boy legs.'

Elijah took a slug of wine.

'I think that's the problem – forgive me – at Searston. Too many players competing with each other rather than the opposition. I prefer camaraderie, putting side before self. I know you won Olympic gold, Rupert.'

'No, that was part of a team.' Rupert put his knife and fork together. 'Now, eat up and let's go through the players.'

'Orion's brilliant,' Elijah observed, 'but he relies on natural talent. Likes to party, leads the other players astray. He's just got a modelling job for some hair shampoo, plus millions of followers for his clothes range. Not sure he doesn't get a bung from the local implant team every time he puts an elbow through another player's teeth.'

'And,' butted in Rupert, 'I'm going to throttle him for breaking the heart of my favourite stable lass, Lou-Easy. I keep finding her sobbing into Lady Killer's shoulder because he's screwing Marketa, another of the stable lasses.'

'Doesn't believe in exhausting himself in training' – Elijah was making notes – 'saves himself for the big occasion.'

'Or Marketa. You'd better sort him out, then. Downing?' asked Rupert.

'Huge potential, but we must curb his aggression. He got red-carded on Saturday for swearing at the ref and calling him "Deaferee" because he wouldn't listen. Playing against powerful teams, we cannot afford to go down to ten men.'

'He's always been short-fused. Once, when the opposition were booing him for a dodgy tackle, he kicked the ball straight into the crowd and gave an OAP a bloody nose.'

'I'm very happy with Galgo and Josef. Galgo is faster

than lightning. Josef needs confidence but he does the work of two players, defending and attacking, feeding the ball exactly where a player needs it, skips around opposition players. He can take the ball on the run with both feet.'

'He's so delighted to be playing,' said Rupert. 'Ryan left him on the bench. Taggie is very fond of him. How about my Feral?'

'Best of the lot, potentially.' Elijah cut up a roast potato but didn't eat it. 'But if you'll forgive me, he seems a bit off form. Not very happy and easily distracted.'

'He paid enough attention to your wife the other night.'

'Yes, sorry she earwigged him. Some of the players regard him as the partner of the chairman's daughter – teacher's pet, sort of.'

'Mother's in rehab. And although I adore my daughter, she's not the ideal support. Keeps him up at night with her chatter.'

'We must get his form back; we need him badly. He's probably fed up with Facundo and Orion hogging all the glory.'

'And the cash,' sighed Rupert. 'Fucking Ryan bankrupted us buying bloody Fuck-Can-Do. His three-hundred-thousand-a-week wages are higher than the rest of the team put together. I'd sell him but he is a goal machine, so we'd better hang on to him till we make the top four, although it doesn't make for cama-raderie, him screwing the players' women and insisting on taking every penalty. You've got to be brave and stop him. How about Bastian?'

'Narcissistic. Intellectual snob. I'd dump him straight away but he's just bought a house in the Golden Triangle and his wife's expecting a baby.'

'That's his problem. Let's get rid of him.'

'He might improve. I'm much more worried about our senior players.'

'Let's get a forger in to lop a few years off their passports,' grinned Rupert. 'Then we can sell them on for a profit.'

Elijah put together his knife and fork.

'So sorry,' he said to Lydia the pretty blonde waitress, as she took his half-eaten food away.

'Do you want pudding?' asked Rupert. 'Then bring us the cheese board and another bottle of red,' he added to Lydia.

'I've got to work,' sighed Elijah.

'We are working.'

'I think the squad is top-heavy. Some of the senior players are terrible bullies. Barry Pitt never stops yelling, unnerving the younger players who don't know who he's yelling at. Unreliable too, wants to prove he's a player and won't stay in goal. Andover scored on Saturday, taking the ball off him when he ran halfway up the field. And Angus McLean.'

'Anger Management is an absolute shit and a sadist.'

'God, yes! He terrorises young Wilfie and Dolphy.' There, he'd said Dolphy's name. 'He was foul to them at your party, bawling them out for getting him the wrong drink, taking the piss, humiliating them in training. And he's insanely jealous of Facundo and poster boys like Orion, Downing and Feral for attracting the fans, particularly the female ones. I noticed him chatting up Midas's wife, Charm, and that dangerous photographer,

Cadenza. I'd watch her – she was taking photographs when people didn't realise it. I bet she sells them on.'

'Mrs Management, Mimi, on the other hand, is a darling,' said Rupert. 'She teaches in a secondary school. Pity she can't teach him some manners.'

'On the other hand,' mused Elijah, 'Angus is a good player, reads the game well. If I could tame that aggression and turn it into authority . . .'

'He's almost as bad as poor Wilfie's sadistic father, Dougie.'

'Oh my God, he came to the match on Saturday and bawled poor Wilfie out for missing a goal. Wilfie had a black eye this morning at training.'

'What are you waiting for?' demanded Rupert, cutting off a slice of Brie. 'We're supposed to have a zero-tolerance policy towards any form of violence or abusive behaviour. Bastard turned up uninvited at our party, and in the past he walked out and left Mary penniless to bring up the children, then moved back in to blow Wilfie's Premier League wages on a house and a flash car. Claims he's Wilfie's agent. Not a gent. If he starts beating Wilfie up, I'm going to get him arrested and banned from the club. Wilfie's divine.'

'Very good player.'

'Very good rider. I'm tempted to poach him as a jockey.'

'Then there's the senior players. I had Captain Parks in for a one-to-one last week. Lovely bloke.'

'Got us up to the Premier League.'

'But his sight's deteriorating, his back's playing up. He also defends very cautiously and he's really slowing up.'

'He's very popular in the area' – Rupert filled up their

glasses – 'does a lot for charity, going into schools and care homes and tedious council dinners. Anything to escape that gha-a-a-astly wife. She's always trying to frog-march Taggie into her boutique.'

Elijah rolled his eyes. 'Rosalie told Madison she ought to smarten herself up as a manager's wife, particularly to stand out as a Labour candidate. She had just the perfect red dress.'

Rupert had been wondering how such an attractive man as Elijah could live with such a charmless killjoy. He was dying to ask about his marriage, but felt he might be too rude about Madison, so instead helped himself to another slice of Brie and put a slice on Elijah's plate.

'Do you think you could fire Parks up, rather than fire him?'

'I'm going to try. Pitt Bully is well nicknamed, but he's a good goalie. Midas Channing used to be a great striker but he hasn't scored this year. Probably too busy putting shelves up in his new house in the Golden Triangle. Not sure about Griffy.'

'"Almost damned in a fair wife." Inez is even more of a bitch than Rosalie Parkinson. The Wags have nick-named her Meanest. Griff has to do all the housework, cooks, looks after the kids, ferries them back and forth to school. He's absolutely exhausted and he's totally lost his confidence.'

'He's a lovely bloke, but perhaps we should think about selling him on in the January window? Although I doubt he'd get another job.'

'He's still a good player. Perhaps you could gee him up. I'd like him to stay.'

'So would lovely Tember.'

'You don't miss a trick,' mocked Rupert.

'Here's a doggie bag for you, Rupert,' said Lydia, putting a plastic bag with the remains of Elijah's boeuf roulade on to the table.

'What about Ludo?'

'Adore him,' said Elijah, 'funniest man in the side, but he's slowing down too. Doesn't defend fiercely enough and drops off the pace. He's got cruciate ligament trouble, too.'

'He's brilliant with the media, and the fans would lynch us if we sold him. Problem is an ex-wife and two kids who are really greedy for maintenance since he's gone up to the Premier League.'

'He's so articulate, he should become a pundit. Perhaps you could have a word with Sky. That's the nightmare of being a player, having to retire at thirty, mobbed in the street, thinking you're invincible, then nothing. As Ian Herbert wrote in the *Mail* last week, "The image of bravado and fame surrounding professional football belies the prospect of struggle . . . when the floodlights begin to fade."'

'"O, the fierce wretchedness that glory brings us!"' Rupert shook his head. 'You had to retire at twenty-four. But you managed.'

'Or managered. But I know what hell it is, so I'll try and let them down gently, or fire up the ones I can.'

'Any ideas for replacements?'

'I've got feelers out for two cracking African players, a striker and a full back, and I'm keeping an eye out for Harry Stanton-Harcourt.'

'Emma's son.'

'Right. He doesn't like Deansgate and he detests Ryan knocking off his mother.'

'Pretty woman,' observed Rupert. 'Terribly funny. Ryan evidently was on the way to a smart black-tie dinner the other night and, first making sure Harry Stanton-Harcourt was at training, popped in to show off his finery to Emma. He was just giving Lady E a seeing-to, when Harry came home early, and Dasher, Emma's golden retriever, welcomed him with one of Ryan's shiny black dress shoes. Although Lady E pretended Ryan had just dropped in for a drink and was mending her bedside light, by then Harry had chucked Ryan's shoe into some nearby woods, so he had to go out to dinner with one shoe missing.'

'Cockadoodle-do, my Ryan has lost his shoe,' sang Elijah. As both men howled with laughter, Rupert filled up their glasses.

'I've got to drive, ought to go back to the office.'

'Eamonn'll take you; he's picking me up. What d'you feel about Jesus?'

'Such a sweet boy, but not really happy here, desperately missing his dog, who I gather is living with his mother back in Portugal. His team there want him back.'

'So he can go back in January. What about Dolphy?'

'Oh, Dolphy is going to be a star, weaves through any pack of players, kicks with his left foot and right straight into goal, trains harder and longer than any of the team.' *I must keep my voice from shaking*, thought Elijah. 'His only problem is he's too humble and unselfish, feels he ought to give the ball away to better players instead of racing on and scoring himself. He's a god-send to Orion and Facundo. And he's so brave, he'll take on any thug.'

'He speaks very well of you,' said an amused Rupert. 'He tells me that you not only tell him what he can do, but how to do it, and that the players not only love you but respect you, too.'

'That's so kind.' Elijah looked down so Rupert couldn't see he was blushing.

'What else?' asked Rupert, as Lydia arrived with two cups of black coffee.

Elijah took a deep breath.

'This may sound presumptuous – I know how busy you are – but I think you could pay more attention to the fans at matches and the sponsors and the people in the hospitality boxes.'

'Whatever for?' snapped Rupert. 'Tember does that brilliantly.'

Elijah took another deep breath.

'I don't think you realise that it's you people come to see. You're the star. I read that piece about the postman having a hernia delivering all your valentines. I just watched those Wags drooling over you at the Penscombe party.'

'Except your wife,' said Rupert, coldly.

'No, I'm sorry about her, she's . . .'

'Allergic to right-wing bastards. You're a fine one to talk. Look at Nadia and Roxanne and all the female staff at Searston force-feeding you cake – no wonder you can't eat any lunch.'

'No, sorry, what I mean is we need the gate receipts to rocket even more, and the hospitality boxes, and more companies fighting to sponsor and invest in us, and TV companies to film our matches. If we're going to go up to the top four and win the Champions League next year, we need the dosh to buy more players. Managers like Arsène Wenger used to chat to every table in the restaurant, talking to fans. You just need to take five minutes to talk to them and the sponsors in the Board-room, then they can name-drop that they've met you.'

'And find I'm not such a bastard as they expect.'

Oh God, thought Elijah, but he must cash in on the opportunity.

'And finally, I know you've often had a dramatic effect shouting at our players at half-time. It can fire them up but it also unnerves them. Like the time you evidently said, "Are you Midas Channing's brother?" "No, boss, I'm Midas Channing." "Why don't you fucking play like him, then?" And all the dressing room cracked up with laughter, but Midas was mortified. The hairdryer treat-ment worked with Alex Ferguson.'

'Who's a friend of mine,' said Rupert, icily.

'Might galvanise the older players, but the juniors don't need a half-time blasting.'

'I see,' said Rupert. 'As I've said, we have a zero-tolerance policy on abusive behaviour at Searston. So, I'd better watch it or Chief C-word Dudsbridge will arrest me. Although, if I'm wrecking Searston, he'll probably let me stay.'

Oh God, I've totally screwed up, thought Elijah.

Then Rupert laughed and the sun came out again.

'I must remember to wear Dolphy's diamond earrings when I come to matches.' He looked at his watch. 'We'd better go.' He waved at Lydia for the bill.

'Let me do this,' said Elijah, reaching for his wallet.

'No, save your money for a new coat before the winter. Sorry to have kept you, sweetheart,' Rupert added to

Lydia, who gave him another plastic bag with the remains of Elijah's cheese. 'Thank you. Forester adores Brie.'

When he'd signed the bill, Lydia produced a note-book. 'Can I possibly have two autographs, one for me and one for Julie, my mum?'

'See what I mean?' laughed Elijah as they went out.

43

Elijah was a huge success. Tember adored him, so did the players and the background staff. There was a feeling of camaraderie. Bastian started calling senior players 'grand' rather than Grandpa. Downing stopped yelling at referees; players out of form recaptured it.

Elijah's training methods were so varied, like roping Barry Pitt to his goalpost so he couldn't wander off up the pitch, that players couldn't wait to go in every day. Even on the coldest, wettest days, Elijah would be out on the pitch, staying on afterwards to help any player needing advice.

One day's training a week would be devoted to practising set pieces. These were free kicks, throw-ins and corner kicks, which contributed to around 22 per cent of goals scored in a season.

Unlike Ryan, Elijah took the blame for losses and was livid with any media who slagged off his players unfairly. And victories came, one after the other.

The following January window, to the regret of everyone, saw the departure – after a riotous farewell party – of Jesus back to Portugal and his Great Dane. The window also saw the arrival of the two African players Elijah had earmarked. The first, Ahmed Nelson, was from Sierra Leone, with the whole country watching his every game. In one of his first matches, against Lancs Rovers, Ahmed missed a crucial penalty, losing Searston a vital two points, as they only drew after they'd fought back hero-ically from 3–0 down.

In the dressing room afterwards, Anger Management bawled Ahmed out: 'You lost us that game. Why aren't you more gutted? That must be the worst fing that's ever happened to you.'

'No, it isn't,' replied Ahmed. 'Back in Sierra Leone, my father, my mother, my wife and two of my children were all murdered, and another child died of Ebola. I'm sorry I screw up today, but those killings were the worst thing that ever happen to me.'

There was a long pause. Then, hard-as-nails Angus went over, shook Ahmed's hand and hugged him, and all the players followed suit and took Ahmed to their hearts. Dolphy and Wilfie insisted Ahmed join them in the tenant's cottage to replace Jesus, and Ahmed and Angus became the greatest of friends.

The other player was Ezra Matta from Nigeria, known as Super Sub because he came off the bench and scored in the closing seconds of the game.

Ezra, although a good player, was always losing his car keys, his wallet, his mobile and himself. On one occa-sion at an away match, when the team had been out on the town, Ezra rang Ludo:

'I cannot find Queen Hotel.'

'You're in it, you berk,' shouted Ludo from the bar.

Later in the evening, an inebriated Ezra had to be rescued when he misread the number of his hotel room and was found getting into bed with a startled honeymoon couple.

But, apart from Ahmed and Ezra, no more players were bought in the January window, because even though match attendance was rocketing – as were the merchandise sales – as Searston won match after match, Rupert was still having sleepless nights about money. To cancel out his massive debts, it was essential Searston finished in the top four and qualified for the Champions League next season.

One evening, towards the end of the window, he was gazing at the Stubbs of Rupert Black on his office wall, wondering in despair whether he'd have to flog it, when Feral wandered in.

'Can I have a word, Rupe?'

'You can have several and a drink.'

'No, I'm fine.' Feral joined Banquo and the Jack Russells on the sofa.

'Manchester Rovers have been putting feelers out. Amazin', they've offered fifty million for me. I'm a bit fed up playing second fiddle to Facundo and Orion, and I thought the dosh would get you out of a hole, and you wouldn't have to sell no more paintings.'

'You're not going anywhere,' said an unbelievably touched Rupert. 'You're easily the best player in the side, and we've just got to stop Fuck-Awful and Orion hogging the goal opportunities. Elijah thinks the world of you. That's amazing Man Rovers are so keen. Bianca must be proud. Come on, let's have that drink.'

What Feral didn't say was that he and Bianca weren't getting on. Bianca hated him being a poster boy and, increasingly desperate to have a baby, was insisting on sex morning and night, and becoming even more hysterical when her periods arrived every month. Clean sheets were great in football and also in life.

As a result, Bianca was also flirting outrageously with other men and, when Feral got furious, taunting him that it could be his fault she wasn't getting pregnant and she might do if she slept with someone else, whereupon blazing rows would follow.

Leaving Rupert that evening, Feral went upstairs to find Bianca going into the shower. She was not particularly interested when Feral told her that despite Man Rovers' big offer, he was going to stay with Rupert and Searston. 'And as they're not going to get fifty million to buy players, I'll have to work even harder this season to make sure Searston qualify for the Champions League.'

Suffering from a very painful thigh injury picked up in training earlier, Feral then crawled into bed and was dropping off, when Bianca emerged from the shower. Wafting Diorissimo, golden skin smoothed with body lotion, wearing the prettiest, shortest white lace nightie, she couldn't have looked more adorable.

Next moment, she was nudging him. 'Wake up, Fer.' Then, running her hands over his dark muscular chest, she knelt down, caressing his testicles, taking his cock in her mouth, her flickering tongue trying to bring it to life, whispering: 'Come on, make love to me.'

'I've gone, babe,' muttered Feral. 'Gotta 'uge game up north tomorrow, crucial we win.'

So Bianca burst into tears. 'Every other man fancies me – why don't you?' And she stormed out of their bedroom, running slap into her mother, Taggie, on the landing.

'Darling, what's the matter?' gasped Taggie.

'Feral won't make love to me. I'll never have a baby, and I want you to be a real granny, not just a step-granny.'

As Rupert was still out in the yard, Taggie drew Bianca into their bedroom and wrapped her in the beautiful, flowered cashmere dressing gown from Perth.

'I so know what you're going through.' Taggie sat down beside Bianca on the huge red four-poster.

'I'll never forget the agony I felt not being able to conceive and provide Daddy with children of our own. It was only after endless miscarriages that Daddy and I crossed the world to that convent in Colombia, where I fell hopelessly in love with you.' She pointed to a photograph of baby Bianca on the dressing table. 'And Daddy fell in love with Xav, who was only two, and it was the happiest day when we brought you back to Penscombe. You were the most beautiful baby' – Taggie stroked Bianca's cheek – 'and you're even prettier today. I'm sure you're going to get pregnant soon, darling, but you can always adopt.'

But still Bianca refused to be comforted. 'You had Grandpa Declan and Granny Maud as real parents who brought you up,' she sobbed, 'but I didn't. I've no idea who my first parents were. I want my own baby, to carry on my genes and establish my own bloodline.'

Nor were matters helped in the following weeks by Bastian's wife, Daffodil, becoming even more noticeably pregnant, nor by Bianca's brother, Xav, and his wife expecting a baby in Pakistan, and Rupert and Taggie making secretive plans to fly out and see them for a few days at Easter.

44

Over at Deansgate, on the edge of the vast forest, Ryan Edwards and Sir Craig were united in their loathing of Rupert and their determination to make the top four ahead of Searston and qualify for next year's Champions League.

Arriving at the club as manager, however, Ryan was horrified by his loss of freedom. In the past, Jarred, the lazy, avaricious, rat-faced Director of Football, had left everything from a playing point of view to Elijah, so he could concentrate on contracts and transfers, making a fortune selling on players, like Dolphy, whom Elijah had discovered and nurtured. Because of Elijah's skill as a manager, Deansgate got away with underinvestment, which meant more money in Sir Craig's pocket. Jarred was also able to take the bungs, as Ryan had at Searston, from schools, car manufacturers and estate agents.

Ryan now discovered he wasn't at liberty to buy players independently any more, certainly no Facundos at £300,000 a week. He was deeply irritated by Jarred demanding the list of players for tomorrow's match by lunchtime the day before, because Chairman Craig liked to peruse it. This meant Ryan had great difficulty making last-minute changes and spying opposition clubs had time to adjust their teams.

It infuriated Ryan in meetings when the telephone rang with a big agent, like Alan Garcia, or GFC's Susan Moreland on the line. 'Put them through,' Jarred would say, insisting on taking the call.

And although Ryan was desperate to be more successful than Valent, he missed the support of his famous father. Still devastated by the break-up with Rupert, but detesting Eynsham, Valent had backed off to spend more time with Etta.

Worst of all, Craig was hand in football glove with the Chief Constable, Lloyd Dudsbridge, who was turning a blind eye to Craig's financial and property malpractices, which meant that Lloyd's smug but useless son, Lyall, whom Rupert had nicknamed 'Lout', had to be fed the ball in every match.

The curtailing of Ryan's freedom meant that he had less opportunity to slip away and spend time with Lady Emma, his passion unabated, and as her son, Harry, and his son, Otley, had both joined Deansgate, it meant both Dinah and Lady Emma were likely to turn up at games to cheer on their sons.

Lady Grace was also very keen on Lady Emma, as was Sir Craig, so Ryan was also encouraged to play Hooray Harry, as he was nicknamed, in every game.

Having irrationally benched poor Josef for months for making a tiny pass at Princess Kayley, Ryan was only too happy to let Kayley get off with Harry. If Harry got her up the duff, he'd have to marry her and Kayley would be the Hon Mrs.

Equally irrationally, Sir Craig, unaware of Valent's

dislike, had been impressed by the Valent Edwards Stand at West Riding, so, in March, Deansgate were going to unveil the new enlarged South Stand with 'Craig Eynsham' painted in three-foot-high red letters across royal-blue seats. After some debate, Craig had decided to leave out the 'Sir', as he might get a peerage soon.

Once painted, the stand was covered in dark-green felt and would be unveiled after a big game against Drobenham. Lady Grace had planned another soiree and invited local celebs and the media, and was delighted to include Lady Emma.

Dora, however, had not forgiven Sir Craig for nearly suffocating Buddyguard. She had been at work with Groundsy's keys and, with the help of her colleague Abelard's new love, Jase the burglar, had invaded the stands the night before.

To the delight of Lady Emma, who'd turned up looking ravishing in Ryan's sapphire pendant, Harry scored a goal against Drobenham and provided an excellent assist at the edge of the goal, which enabled lumpen Lout Dudsbridge to boot one in.

The Chief Constable, Lloyd Dudsbridge, was very taken by Lady Emma, and delighted to have been asked by Sir Craig to open the stand. Smoothing his thick grey hair and bushy moustache, he ordered all the celebs, media and Deansgate staff to gather around the great green-felt-covered stand with full glasses of champagne.

'Ladies, gentlemen and luminaries, I am very proud to unveil the Craig Eynsham Stand. Craig is as great a chair as he is an inventor of groundbreaking products. He is also chair of the most exciting football club in the country, well on their way to the Champions League, and I am very proud and emotional that my son, Lyall, a leading member of the team, scored another fine goal this evening.' Then, as the Deansgate players exchanged looks of incredulity: 'Thank you too, Lady Grace, for your excellent refreshments. Finally, let us raise our glasses to the new Sir Craig Eynsham Stand.'

As the band broke into the Deansgate signature tune, the green felt covers were untied and drawn back to reveal, in three-foot-high red letters, the words 'Craig Eynshambolic'. There was a long pause and then gasps of amazement, stifled laughter and a bellow of rage from Sir Craig.

'How dare they? A saboteur's been at work. How dare they? You've got to nail the bastards, Lloyd.'

The press was going berserk, cameras flashing everywhere, capturing a yelling Craig about to have a coronary, and the guests and players trying not to laugh.

'We need a graphologist to get rid of the "bolic", which must have been painted on in the night,' shouted Jarred. 'Go and find one,' he ordered Ryan.

'We need some Tipp-Ex,' quipped Laddy Heywood.

'My boys won't rest until we track down the criminal,' the Chief Constable reassured Craig, whose dark-red sombrero had been knocked askew in the scrum.

'How dare they!' For a moment, Craig looked as though he was going to cry. Then Lady Emma, who had a kind heart, went up to him and straightened his hat before putting her arms around him.

'I'm so sorry, Craig, it was a wicked and evil thing to do, but only done by someone jealous of your huge success. Everyone knows you're the most unshambolic person in the world, and all your millions of fans will be furious this has happened. They'll come out in your defence and the "bolic" can be painted out in a trice. Now, have a huge glass of fizz.'

'Thank you, Lady Emma,' mumbled Sir Craig. 'I'd better address the media.'

'Well done,' said Laddy Heywood, handing Lady Emma a full glass and drawing her apart from the crowd. 'It'd be quicker if they painted in the letters "un" before the "shambolic".'

'Hurry up and find that graphologist,' Jarred kept nagging Ryan, who was fed up with being bossed around and even angrier to see Emma adoring being chatted up by lecherous Laddy.

The players were also fascinated.

'I thought Lady E was being shagged by the boss,' protested Narcisco, at which goalie Byron Stopwell laughed, insisting: 'Ryan tries too hard to be posh. Lady Emma likes her rough trade really rough.'

'And why does Jarred keep asking Ryan to find someone to graffiti Sir Craig's stand?' asked thicko Lout.

Searston were vastly amused when they learnt of Deansgate's Shambolic crisis, with Rupert in particular being caught on camera laughing his handsome head off. But although aware that Dora and Jase the burglar had been responsible, they denied any involvement and, travelling round the country, won match after match.

Dora celebrated this with a big piece in the *Cotchester Times* about 'the most beautiful team in the beautiful game'. Cadenza, the gifted but naughty photographer, had taken ravishing pictures which justified Elijah pinning up one of Dolphy in his office, alongside a poster which said: 'Beware of the Underdog', i.e. complacency.

Cadenza had also crept into Penscombe one night

and captured one of Rupert fast asleep in the huge red-curtained bed, entitling it 'Four-Poster Boy', which resulted in a multitude of likes that infuriated the insanely jealous Sir Craig even more.

Dolphy actually had become a poster boy, with millions of female fans, but he was still terribly shy of girls and always went out with his cottage mates, Wilfie, Ezra and Ahmed.

'Get him some Glitteris,' mocked Angus.

Ostensibly, the team star was Facundo Gonzales, who'd scored the most goals this season because the other players still felt they had to supply him with the ball. He was also frequently missing training without permission, leaking confidential data on social media and staying behind to enjoy having-it-away matches with his most frequent squeeze, Griffy's bitchy wife, Inez.

Elijah was outraged:

'We need a clear-out of egos, Rupert. We can't afford a three-hundred-thousand-a-week superstar like Facundo ducking out of games with pretend illnesses and shagging other players' women. We've gotta sell him for a fortune.'

And, once again, Rupert admitted they could use it, but felt they should hang on until the summer transfer window to make sure of getting into the Champions League.

45

And again Elijah delivered, strengthening Searston's defence and revving up their attack, so that by the end of April they had climbed to fourth place in the Premier League with only two matches to go. Way above them were two mighty Manchester teams and one from London, so far ahead on points that all three had already qualified for the Champions League. Searston, with 66 points, looked likely for qualification. Deansgate were three points behind on 63, with Drobenham one point behind on 65.

Also, Searston's penultimate match was against Durham City, a team at the bottom of the league, who were desperately battling to avoid relegation.

'Understandable they want to stay up,' posted naughty Ludo, 'because it's so much easier to pull birds if you're in the Premier League.'

On arrival at their Durham hotel, assuming an easy win the next day, Orion, Downing and a pack of other Searston lads, instead of going to bed sober and early, went secretly out on the town, even having a bet on who would pull the prettiest barmaid – so they were not in the finest fettle the following day.

Durham City proceeded to throw everything at the game and thrashed Searston 3–1.

Even more disastrously, Deansgate won their match and Drobenham drew, bringing each of them to 65 points, just one point behind Searston on 66 points. Deansgate and Drobenham also both had easy fixtures for the final game, whereas Searston were pitted against brutal West Mids, one of the few teams who'd slaughtered them in an away game earlier in the season.

Rupert, also regarding the match in Durham as a formality, had gone instead to see The Story So Far and Lady Killer lose at Newmarket. Enraged at the prospect of no longer making hundreds of millions of pounds in the Champions League, he'd rung and bawled out Elijah.

'What the hell were you playing at? Certainly not football. How could you fucking lose such an easy game? I'll have to sell the fucking club, not that I'll get anything for it after today's cock-up, and you'll all be out on your ears.'

Elijah was devastated. Not only would he lose his potential huge bonus for nailing the Champions League, but never had the 'Beware of the Underdog' sign in his office been more appropriate. The confidence of his players was shattered by such a humiliating defeat and a vicious mauling by the media, who loved a chance to knock Rupert.

'Who's Shambolic Now?' shouted the headlines.

'Do you think Searston can beat West Mids on Saturday?' asked talkSPORT.

'No, West Mids aren't that bad.'

Yesterday's most exciting team and youngest manager had become the most useless. The players were distraught at the prospect of losing bonuses and their mansions in the Golden Triangle being repossessed. The Wags were particularly upset, having bought new outfits for a celebratory party after the game.

Fed up with Elijah watching videos of West Mids late into the night, Madison was at her most bitchy. The kids had been teased again at school and the two Labour grandees for whom she'd demanded tickets on Saturday were not sure they could be bothered to come – 'They so detest RC-B, anyway.'

She had also been reading in the *Guardian* that big football owners evidently love getting into the Champions League because of the hundreds of millions in extra revenue, the global prestige, the huge appeal to sponsors and the fact that they can buy players much cheaper, because they all want to play for Champions League clubs.

'I know this,' snapped Elijah, surreptitiously throwing his boiled cod and cabbage in the bin.

'Worse of all,' Madison read on, 'big bosses often pull the trigger on managers who miss out. So don't expect that shit Campbell-Black to be any exception. You'd better start looking for another job.'

And I won't see Dolphy every day, thought Elijah in anguish.

Looking in the mirror, he was horrified by how tired and old he looked. *Man-ages*, he thought wearily.

Going to bed after midnight, he heard sobbing coming from Naomi's room.

'What's the matter, darling?'

'The whole class is laughing at me and singing, "Elijah Cohen'll soon be goin'."'

Having comforted her and gone downstairs to pore over yet another video, Elijah put on Grieg's Piano

Concerto; such a slow, lethargic Second Movement leading into the joyful, rampaging racing over the keys of Movement Three. That's what his players must do.

Insomnia among the players that night was universal. Even Orion was incapable of giving Marketa an adequate seeing-to and they had a blazing row because she resorted to her vibrator.

'Vy-not-brator,' snapped Marketa, 'if you're not up to it.'

46

Saturday 23 May – the last day of the season – dawned warm and sunny. Throughout the country, under bright skies, every Premier League team kicked off at three p.m. Deansgate, a point behind Searston but with a match against a much weaker side, happily anticipated victory and fourth place.

Despite a large home crowd shouting them on, Searston started appallingly. Confidence shattered, frantic to score, not pausing to think, missing goal after goal, passing straight to West Mids players – who were soon one goal up.

Feral, who'd wrenched his thigh again in training, was slumped in great pain on the bench.

Caught up in traffic, Rupert arrived just before half-time with Lou-Easy, who couldn't resist coming along to have a last match glance at adored Orion.

'Is it hurting any less?' Rupert had asked her.

'Not much,' half laughed Lou-Easy. 'For the first time in years, I'm celibate, and getting past my sell-by date.'

Josef didn't think so, noticing how beautiful Lou-Easy looked, rolling up in a striped Searston shirt, with their blue-and-green flag painted on her emaciated cheeks. If he played his heart out, it might hurt less.

But still-panicking Searston showed no composure. By half-time, West Mids were three goals up.

Rupert was prowling towards the dressing room when Elijah stopped him, standing outside the door:

'No, Rupert, you're not going in; they're wobbly enough as it is.'

For a moment, he thought Rupert was going to hit him. 'For fuck's sake, let me in. Someone's got to talk some sense into them.'

Next moment, they both jumped as Taggie appeared, putting a hand on Rupert's arm.

'Please, darling, leave it to Elijah. He's your manager.'

'As you point out,' said Rupert, icily, 'and, as he is my manager, I'm entitled to tell him to do what I like.'

'Please don't; your players need comforting and reassuring, so they can fight back.' She took Rupert's hand. 'Please come back upstairs.'

And, after a pause, Rupert did. Tight-lipped, they returned to the stands.

In the dressing room, Elijah clapped his hands. 'Come on, lads, you've got to save Rupert, and Taggie too. He's nearly bankrupted himself saving us and now we've got to save him. You're all great players, just go out and prove it.'

In the second half, Josef played brilliantly. One moment patrolling the area in midfield, the next acting as shield to the defence, then taking the ball upfield, he lofted it over the West Mids brutes lined up in defence and into the goal. 3–1.

Drobenham were also losing their match, but Deansgate were two goals up and each time they scored

Searston could hear boos coming from their own fans up in the stands, watching Deansgate on their phones.

Play was in the West Mids box. Ludo got the ball and was belting it upfield to Griffy when he slipped, and a brutal West Mids striker called Seb Bridport stamped on his knee. Ludo gave a howl, tears streaming down his sweating face, as he registered that the crunching seriousness of the injury could put him out of the game for ever. Griffy stayed close, trying to console him, until he was finally stretchered off by six medics. The ref gave a penalty, which Facundo insisted on taking and which would have made the score 3–2, but instead he hit the woodwork, and the booing became thunderous.

No one put a consoling arm around Facundo's shoulders, as he never hugged other players when they scored. Expecting all the players to put the ball on a plate for him, he shouted so nastily at little Wilfie for making an assist instead to Midas, who missed it, that a furious Elijah subbed Facundo. Then, turning to Feral, who'd been gingerly warming up to test his injured thigh, he asked:

'Are you up for it?'

'Yes,' said Feral.

There were only five minutes more, followed by injury time.

'Come on, lads,' Feral ordered the players, who'd been taking a water break. 'We've got to slaughter these buggers.'

'We've got to play gooder and stronger,' said Josef, or he'd be sold to another club and never see Lou-Easy again.

We've had the Adagio, now it's time for the Allegro, prayed Elijah.

Over at Deansgate, as the final whistle blew, mass euphoria took over: fans cheering their heads off, flourishing cuddly kestrels, and whirling scarves round and round, a breeze ruffling the spring-green leaves as though every tree in the forest was dancing for joy.

On the big screen was evidence that Searston were losing 3–1. Drobenham had already lost 2–0, and were no longer in the race for the Champions League. Deansgate had won 3–0, which put them at 69, three points ahead of Searston.

Overjoyed by his son Lyall's assist, the Chief Constable joked that they mustn't count their chickens until the final whistle had blown on every game, including Searston's, but this didn't stop a pitch invasion of ecstatic dancing fans, and loudspeakers belting out 'Sweet Caroline' and 'Deansgate's Coming Home'.

Ryan was smugly telling Sky how pleased he was with the squad he'd chosen, and that he was particularly delighted that the young players he'd brought on had performed so well:

'Harry Stanton-Harcourt; Lyall Dudsbridge, the son of our Chief Constable; and, forgive me for boasting' – Ryan gave a little smile – 'my own son, Otley Jepson-Edwards.'

He longed to go and hug Lady Emma, who was looking particularly beautiful, wearing his sapphire pendant and flushed from champagne in the boardroom, but Dinah was present, hoarse from shouting for Otley. At least, now they were in the Champions League, playing matches all over Europe, Ryan felt he'd be able to take Emma with him to cheer on their two sons.

Sir Craig, in a dashing new blue trilby, was in heaven. He could hear fans singing his song: 'Don't be vague, insist on Sir Craig.' Lady Grace, waving a cuddly kestrel, was having a little bop with the Chief Constable.

Lady Emma was now pecking handsome Laddy Heywood on the cheek: 'Thank you for giving Harry that assist. He thinks the world of you.'

'I fink the world of 'is mum.'

'And it's thrilling we're on sixty-nine points.'

'That's soixante-neuf – can't be bad.'

'I must go and find the ladies, I've had so much fizz,' giggled Lady Emma.

'I'll find you one,' said Laddy, taking her hand.

As Searston were still 3–1 down, legions more bottles of champagne were being lined up at Deansgate for a big celebration.

The Deansgate players, who'd been singing a song in a circle, glanced across at Ryan, still talking to the press. 'Bastard's taking all the credit. If we have to throw him in the air, let's drop him,' said Byron Stockwell.

'We've bloody won!' shouted Hooray Harry.

Unable to contain themselves, the Deansgate players all joined hands and raced off, stopping to bow and clap the cheering fans on all four sides of the pitch. On the big screen, the results were being listed. Deansgate 3–0, full time. A great cheer went up.

Over at Searston, Ludo had been rushed to hospital. With Parks also injured, Angus was now wearing the captain's armband.

'Come on, lads, we've got five minutes. We've got to avenge our mate Ludo,' yelled the normally reticent Griffy.

But the clock was ticking away; the ref kept glancing at his watch. Dolphy, desperate to go on, was warming up in front of Elijah as an injured Midas came off.

'Please put me on, guv.'

'Oh, OK,' said Elijah. Was it subconscious, his reluctance to subject Dolphy to such a bear pit? Feral, heavily marked because he was their best player, was trying to rise above the pain in his thigh. Then Josef thundered down the field, kicking directly to Feral's good leg so he was able to whack it straight into goal, instantly howling: 'Don't waste time hugging me.'

The goal had given him belief again. Gathering the ball after kick-off, he hurtled goalwards. 'I'm here,' cried little Wilfie, and Feral passed to him; then, as hulking West Mids defenders closed around him, Wilfie passed to Dolphy, who whipped it back to Feral, who clouted it in. 3–3.

'Don't blow your whistle, please, Mr Ref,' pleaded Dolphy.

'Shut up, Dolphy,' roared Angus.

A second after kick-off, Feral gathered up the ball again. He had to save Rupert from ruin. Racing down the field, agonising thigh forgotten, in and out of the opposition, like a gymkhana pony in a bending race, and, in the last seconds of the game, whisking it to Dolphy, who glanced round, for once deciding to be selfish and score himself, took it on the volley and flicked it past the goalkeeper. Then, after an eternity, the net fell backwards.

4–3 to Searston, and a grinning ref blew his whistle.

'We've won!' screamed Dolphy, as players fell on him.

Next moment, Rupert jumped down from the stands and charged on to the field, wrapping Feral in a big bear hug.

'Fucking marvellous! Christ, you did well.'

'Well enough to marry your daughter?' grinned Feral.

'Not sure she's good enough for you now.'

'Goodness, I've never seen RC-B hugging a man before. Is he bisexual?' asked Madison.

There was another pause as Sky, the BBC and all the media worked out the results.

'We did it!' cried an overjoyed Tember. 'And weren't Feral's two goals and the ones from Dolphy and Josef just marvellous?'

Gradually, it dawned on the world that Searston had snatched victory, and were fourth in the Premier League. Sir Craig's roar of rage must have reached outer space.

At Searston, the stands emptied and the pitch became an ecstatic sea of green and blue.

Elijah, who had prayed for an hour in the synagogue that morning, was battling through the fans, hugging his players. For a blissful moment, his arms went around Dolphy.

'You won, you saved our club. Your goal clinched it.' He could feel the boy's beating heart, how slender yet strong he was.

For a moment, they just gazed at each other. *I don't ever want him to let me go*, thought Dolphy. Then a voice said, 'Fantastic result, Elijah,' and Rupert was clapping him on the back. 'Sorry I was so bloody earlier. Well done, Dolphy. Sky want to talk to you, when they're finished with Feral.'

Dolphy really enjoyed talking to Sky: 'I had a dream last night that I scored a goal, and when I was young I was told Friday's dream on Saturday always comes true, however old. So, at the end of the game, I warmed up in front of Elijah and begged him to put me on, and he did and I scored. Elijah's the most wonderful manager in the world, and we all love our chairman, Mr Rupert, and we're going to try and pay him back all the money he's spent on us by winning the Champions League for him and because he knows the name of my greyhound, Grandkid, and I've got my own song now: "Try to be smarter, don't be a martyr, our Dolphy Carter will take you aparta." Good, isn't it?'

'Very good,' said the Sky interviewer, at last getting a word in. 'Well done, Dolphy.'

Over at Deansgate, Lady Emma and Laddy Heywood came out of the 'Laddies' to find Jarred shouting at Ryan, and Sir Craig and the Chief Constable looking like matching thunderclouds.

'We can celebrate now,' said Laddy. 'Bring on the Bolly.'

'No, we can't,' snarled Jarred. 'Searston pipped us to the post. Take away all those bottles,' he told the waitresses. 'We're going home.'

'Can't we stay for a noggin?' cried Lady Grace. 'I'm sure Lady Emma would like one.'

'I'd better go and have a shower,' said Laddy.

Twenty minutes later, Ryan was checking the showers at Deansgate to see if anyone had left their bags or phones behind, when he overheard a departing Laddy Heywood talking to Byron Stopwell.

'I'm gutted Searston robbed us, but at least Lady E gave me the best blowjob I've ever had.'

And I've lost the Champions League and Emma in one

evening, thought Ryan, and went home and cried his eyes out all night.

Dinah, assuming it was just not making the Champions League, said, 'There's always next year,' before going to sleep in the spare room.

47

The group stages of the Champions League began the following September, which involved Searston in home and away matches against three different European clubs. The trouble with high-league football is fixture congestion. Teams, competing for several trophies at once, including the Premier and Champions leagues, the League Cup and the FA Cup, often play nearly sixty matches in a season, many involving travel around the world and all getting in the way of each other. Other teams bigger than Searston had twenty-five or thirty top players on their books and didn't need to play every player every week, so could give them each an occasional rest.

Ghengis Tong hadn't helped. The Hong Kong trillionaire, having lent Rupert so much money and wanting publicity for his Galloper plane, insisted they play two matches in China. This tired the players out before the season began, while other sides like Deansgate were on relaxing bonding trips in the Maldives.

Searston had also, back in May, been devastated to lose Ludo, who'd always boosted morale. Bearing chocolates and Ian Rankin's latest novel, Elijah dropped in to see him at Cotchester hospital. He found Ludo surrounded by flowers and hundreds of get-well cards, but still in great pain and battling depression.

'James Benson's told me my race is run. Even with another op. I'm never likely to play again or dance round the Running Fox.'

'That bloody Seb Bridport, he should have been banned for good for ramming those studs into your knee.'

Ludo shrugged. 'Evidently enough bricks have been chucked through his windows for him to build a second home.'

'Not much compensation for you. Christ, I'm sorry, too effing unfair. When I had to retire at twenty-four, I seriously thought of topping myself. I know what you're going through. But you're the funniest, best-loved guy in football, and one of the cleverest. We must find you work as a pundit.'

'Ludo – Lion King of the Cotswolds. I've got to support my ex and the kids somehow.' Ludo reached out for a large bottle of tonic on the bedside table, filled up his glass and half drained it.

'Do you want some ice and lemon?' asked Elijah.

'No, it's neat gin. Dolphy brought two bottles in: "I fort you might be firsty." God, he's a sweet kid. You must look after him, Elijah. Do you think I could make some dosh as a pundit?'

'Without a doubt – you're a fundit.'

Elijah was still gunning for Facundo, who he'd tried to offload during the summer window. Not only did he cost fortunes, terrify young players and duck out of matches and training to pleasure Inez et al., but he'd recently told the *Sunday Times* that 'Searston ees so lucky to 'ave me to ween matches for them', and loved his nickname, 'Macho of the Day'.

Facundo also had no desire to leave his glorious Golden Triangle mansion, with its housekeeper and pool attendant and yellow Lamborghini, where he was now angling to have an ice rink installed. Also, his ruthless agent had originally negotiated with Ryan such a watertight four-year contract that it would cost a fortune to get rid of Facundo unless he committed some dreadful crime.

But, as luck would have it, on 15 September, a huge General Football Council awards ceremony was taking place in London to honour the stars of last season. To add excitement, the shortlists for each award were only revealed on the night, although the clubs were privately alerted in advance, so they could ensure potential winners would be present.

Rupert was delighted that Elijah, Feral, Dolphy, Josef, and – less so – Facundo had all been shortlisted.

'But why didn't they select Safety Car as the Fans' Favourite?'

'If Facundo gets Footballer of the Year or the Lifetime Achievement Award, he'll be even more insufferable,' sighed Elijah.

The big excitement, however, was that Idris Elba, the marvellous actor who was supposed to be master of ceremonies, couldn't make it at the last moment, so the job had been secretly handed to Ludo.

'Make sure you don't have too much of Dolphy's tonic water beforehand,' warned an overjoyed Elijah.

Also in the Searston party at the Awards were Taggie,

Bianca, Lou-Easy, who Rupert felt needed cheering up, Madison, who felt it was useful for her Labour candidate credentials to be seen at a football function, and Dora and Paris, who was now playing Hamlet at Stratford and had been asked to do a reading.

Tember had cried off with a tummy upset, but so that they wouldn't worry about the dress code, she'd arranged for all the shortlisters to hire black-tie kit, except Facundo, who, determined to outshine, was wearing a cream satin suit with a midnight-blue shirt.

Bianca, who was still desperate to get pregnant, and despite having given up Maths at eleven, had worked out she might be ovulating, and was glad the Searston party was overnighting at the nearby Hilton. She therefore put on a ravishing shocking-pink minidress to entice Feral back to bed.

The Awards were held at the Royal London Hotel, starting with a champagne reception in the foyer. Screaming fans milled around outside to catch glimpses of their heroes arriving in flash chauffeur-driven cars with their Wags glittering with jewels, the necklines of their spangled, sequinned designer dresses plunging to their navels, and slits up the sides to show endless legs glowing from sunbeds.

'Wow,' giggled Dora, discreet in a pale-blue silk trouser suit, 'why don't they just turn up in their bikinis?'

' "Continuous as the stars that shine, And twinkle on the milky way",' observed Paris, who was holding her hand. 'None of them are as pretty as you.'

'Or you,' beamed Dora, standing on tiptoe to peck him on the cheek.

'Who does that guy play for?' murmured the Wags. 'He's absolutely gorgeous.'

Amid such beauty, Taggie, who'd been the greatest head-turner in the past, tried not to regret her curly grey hair and still-scant eyelashes, and the feeling that she couldn't wear anything plunging or too clinging after her operation. How could she be attractive enough for the handsomest man in England? Taggie so wished Tember had been able to make it; she always cheered everything up.

Dora, who was writing a fashion piece for the *Mail*, noticed that many of the footballers had hair like goalposts, cut in a horizontal line above their foreheads and falling at right angles to their earlobes. Others absurdly topped black dinner jackets with peaked white beret caps, worn back to front and with long diamond earrings.

'I did hope Rupert might wear his,' sighed Dolphy.

Sir Craig Eynsham felt very much at home in a new dark-green velvet trilby decorated with a diamond kestrel, but was still fuming that they had been denied a place in the Champions League back in May by Searston Rovers.

Also in his party were Lady Grace, Ryan and Dinahmite, Janey Lloyd-Foxe, Jarred and his partner, Laddy Heywood and goalie Byron Stopwell, both of whom had been shortlisted. Young Harry Stanton-Harcourt had also been shortlisted for Best Debutant, to the ecstasy of his mother, Lady Emma, exquisite in midnight-blue lace:

'So appropriate when I was Deb of the Year myself.'

'Five minutes please, ladies and gentlemen,' shouted a General Football Council official. 'Please take your seats.'

The Searston Rovers party was well placed, ten rows from the front and between the two aisles. Facundo insisted on sitting on the edge of the row, so he could leap out easily to accept his grand award.

'I don't need to, I won't win,' said Feral, whose thigh was aching after a rough match yesterday.

'Nor need I,' said Josef, wearing a new black velvet Alice band and thrilled to be sitting next to Lou-Easy.

Technicians were still scuttling about, checking camera angles, locating celebs and possible winners. The stage itself looked ravishing, like a town lit up by a thousand stars on Christmas Eve, with blue flares rising to the ceiling. On a plinth on the platform, awaiting the first winner, was a silver football on which the name of the recipient could be engraved. A huge overhead camera captured all the footballing greats and on-message celebs as they poured into the hall, holding up their faces to be singled out: 'I am recognised, therefore I am.'

Everyone recognised Rupert, who ignored the lot of them as he stalked in, hand in hand with Taggie, before settling her next to Feral and telling him to look after her.

Ryan had been desperate to sit next to Emma, but Sir Craig had bossily insisted she sit on his right, with Lady Grace on her other side. Laddy Heywood had nipped into the seat behind her with his protégé, Harry Stanton-Harcourt, beside him. Laddy, who had been at the booze, kept whispering in Emma's ear. Ryan wished he could lip-read. He was livid to have journalist Janey Lloyd-Foxe, always looking for trouble, on his left, and Dinah, who was driving him more and more crackers, on his right, particularly as she kept noisily referring to Harry as 'our daughter Princess Kayley's BAE', which, in the latest school parlance, stood for Before Anyone

Else – something that Ryan suspected horrified Emma, who leapt up to kiss a passing Rupert on both cheeks, crying, 'Darling, you must know Sir Craig and Lady Grace.'

'Not if I can help it,' snapped Rupert, stalking off down the aisle and disappearing through a door on the side of the stage.

'Prince Charmless as ever,' smirked Sir Craig.

In a dressing room, Rupert found Elijah tying Ludo's bow tie, and shouted with delight:

'Christ, you look knockout!'

Ludo was tanned from a summer convalescing. With his drooping lion's mane replaced by a blond crew cut, long shaggy beard shaved off to reveal the strong lines of a very handsome, laughing face, expensive new top and bottom teeth showing off a genial Labrador grin, booze belly concealed by a black velvet smoking jacket and pale-blue cummerbund, he was almost unrecognisable.

'Is it really you, Ludo?'

'No longer scruff trade,' admitted Ludo. 'Still, I can't let you fork out for all this gear and gnashers.'

'Yes, you can,' said Rupert as he straightened Ludo's tie. 'As long as you slag off all the other teams and only say nice things about Searston now you're a pundit, Gary Lionkinger. Come on, they want you on stage.'

48

Up on stage, Susan Morecambe, Chair of the GFC Integrity Committee, in a lovely gold midi-dress to wow Rupert, was waiting to introduce Ludo.

'Ladies and gentlemen, we're here tonight to celebrate greatness in football, and we'd like you to shout and applaud as much as possible.'

'Hurrah,' yelled Dolphy, clapping like mad, 'hurrah, hurrah, hurrah.'

'Please be quiet,' snapped Madison, who'd pinched Rupert's seat next to Feral.

There was a great roll of drums.

'Pray silence for your captain, everyone,' cried Susan, 'master of ceremonies, Searston left back and fans' favourite, Ludovic King.'

There was a long pause, because no one recognised him, followed by roars of laughter and deafening cheers. Deeply saddened that Ludo had been forced into early retirement by such a hideous injury, they were overjoyed to see him again.

'Wow-ee! Poster boy! Heart-throb! Hunky!' yelled the Wags.

'Come upstairs – what d'you think I married you for?' yelled Lou-Easy.

Ludo laughed. 'Wait a few hours, darling. Ladies and gentlemen, welcome to the Oscars of football. People grumble we're paid far too much, but our beautiful game' – he patted the back of his crew cut – 'gives more pleasure and excitement than anything else in the world – even sex.' He paused for laughter. 'I have to confess, I'm far more nervous tonight than ever I was on the pitch, so let's get on with the first award, Best Player of the Season.'

Having read out the six shortlisted candidates, Ludo shouted for the room to make some noise for a Manchester Town centre forward, who scored endless goals for the Premier League winners and was so revered that everyone cheered a lot.

'Thank goodness Facundo didn't win it,' murmured Elijah to Rupert.

'I do hope you brought a box of tissues with you, Emma,' advised Lady Grace, 'and remembered to avoid putting mascara on your lower lashes, because football award ceremonies are so tear-jerkin'.'

In fact, they usually aren't. Too many teams have no desire to cheer for bitter rivals who've caused them to be relegated, played dirty or fucked up their best player. Too many players are irritated when rivals in their own teams beat them, as are the five disappointed shortlisters who, when they lose out, are expected to smile and applaud to show what good sports they are. Equally, throughout the evening, to fill time, the mood is destroyed by endless clips of finals and semi-finals of big tournaments with teams ecstatic that they won, or in floods that they didn't, or pop stars singing and swaying along for twenty minutes with all the audience expected to sing and sway along with them.

So it needed all Ludo's charm and skill to move things on and keep the audience alert and amused.

The next award was for Best Debutant of the Season, with the camera rolling over the six young hopefuls, including Harry Stanton-Harcourt and Dolphy, who was slightly flushed from several slugs from Feral's hip flask.

God, he's delectable, prayed Elijah. *Please let him win it.*

'And the winner,' beamed Ludo, 'trains longer and harder than any young player I know, so please make a thunderstorm of noise for Searston Rovers' Dolphy Carter.'

Dolphy's mouth fell open. 'Did they say me?'

'Yes, darling,' said Taggie, hugging him. 'Up you go.'

'Really me?'

'Yes, darling,' said a delighted Rupert, standing up to let him through.

Mouth still open in bewilderment, Dolphy slowly mounted the steps, where Ludo pulled him into a massive bear hug, before handing him his silver football.

Dolphy gazed in wonder at the cheering tumult.

'I'm so frilled to be given this prize, fank you so, so much. Sadly, I haven't got a family of my own to fank, but I'm so lucky to have Searston Rovers as my family and our brilliant, kind, wonderful manager, Elijah Cohen, who keeps us togevver and remembers all our families' names and even our pets' names. I've got a greyhound called Grandkid, who helps me run fast when I go for runs, so fank you, Grandkid. And I'd like to fank our wonderful chairman, Rupert Campbell-Black, and his wonderful wife, Taggie. Rupert flew his chopper all the way to norf of England to buy me last year, and fanks to his horse, Safety Car, who's a terrific footballer and a fans' favourite, and fanks to Lou-Easy, who brings him to demos wiv Rupert's Jack Russells, Cuffbert and Gilchrist, and, oh yes, I'd like to fank all the fans as well, they're so kind to us at Christmas, this year they . . .'

The audience was in hysterics.

'That's great, Dolphy, terrific speech,' said Ludo, removing the mic. 'Grandkid will be so over the moon, he'll take up jump racing soon.' And, giving Dolphy his football, he waved to an official to take him off to a press conference.

'Do you think I ought to keep an eye on him?' Elijah asked Rupert.

'No, he'll be fine. Lucky he hasn't got a family or he'd buy each one a huge house in the Golden Triangle.'

Sir Craig and Deansgate were livid. Why had Dolphy beaten their own Harry? Why had they let him go so cheaply?

The next award was for Best Young Foreign Player, for which Josef was shortlisted but which went to a charming Italian, who mounted the stage, grabbed his silver football and said, 'I am so excited to have won that I have no words to express my 'appiness, thank you all very much,' and walked off the stage.

'What a relief to have a winner who doesn't drone on,' said Sir Craig, rather too loudly.

Lou-Easy was touched by how bravely Josef took the disappointment and genuinely applauded the winner. Later, he was blown away when his mother texted him from the Czech Republic, saying how proud she was to see him praised on British television.

'Next year you'll win,' said Lou-Easy, giving Josef a slug out of her hip flask.

'And you never let that poor lad off the bench,' Jarred sniped at Ryan.

Another roll of drums was for the Manager of the Year, presented by the great player, manager and Tottenham Hotspurs legend, hunky golden-haired Glenn Hoddle. Dolphy, back from his press conference and a couple of glasses of champagne, shouted:

'It's got to be Elijah!'

'Be quiet,' hissed Madison, who'd got out her diary. 'Now, Feral, when can you come and visit that school for pupils with learning disabilities in Stroud?'

Feral laughed. 'I'm afraid it would be coals to Newmarket, ma'am.'

'You wouldn't have to speak.'

'Pack it in,' Rupert ordered. 'It's your husband's turn.'

Ludo then read out and praised all the top managers, including Searston's Elijah Cohen:

'Who took Searston up to fourth place in the Premier League, thus landing a Champions League place, despite a ginger pussy invading the field.'

The audience giggled nervously and held their breath. This one was huge.

'And the winner, I am once again delighted to announce, is Elijah Cohen of Searston Rovers – such a good guy and always charming to the opposition, whether he loses or wins.'

And Dolphy led the screams of delight.

'"Well done, thou good and faithful servant",' murmured Rupert.

As Elijah mounted the steps to accept his football

from Glenn Hoddle, the band broke into the Gallopers' *Black Beauty* signature tune, and the applause was genuine, because he was so popular.

'And you sacked Elijah, you naughty Craig,' chided Lady Grace.

Lady Emma, sitting between them, froze, convinced for a moment that Sir Craig was going to punch his wife in the face.

Elijah's speech, in his lovely deep voice, was very short.

'It's such an honour to accept an award from Mr Hoddle, one of my greatest heroes and one of the greatest and most gifted and creative footballers and managers of all time. And I'd like to thank another hero of mine, my chairman, Rupert Campbell-Black; and every member of staff at Searston Rovers, and all the fans; my wife, Madison; my children; and, of course, my players, for a manager would be nothing without his players . . .'

'But,' observed Ludo, 'your players would still be worth a fortune without you – look at Facundo.'

Elijah laughed, said, 'Thank you very much,' and took his football back to his seat. But with everyone thumping him on the back, he still felt a deep sadness that he didn't dare thank the Rabbi and a family that had rejected and disinherited him.

'Why didn't you mention my surname?' grumbled Madison, 'and you missed an opportunity to mention my candidacy.'

'It's Elijah's award, not yours,' cried Bianca, who was fed up with Madison waving her diary at Feral. 'That was brilliant, Elijah. We must push off soon,' she urged Feral.

'Bianca,' reproved Dora, 'we've still got the most important award to come.'

Deansgate were slightly cheered by Byron Stopwell winning the Gilded Glove, the award for the goalkeeper who'd kept the most clean sheets.

'Goalkeepers should be "six foot tall and thick-skinned", to quote my ex-boss, Rupert Campbell-Black,' announced Ludo, 'because their mistakes are so fatal. Byron plays in the Cotswolds, like I did, and he's a really nice guy and keeps so many clean sheets.'

I only want clean sheets, thought Bianca, then, turning, hissed: 'Let's go back to the Hilton.'

But Feral had rushed off to get the autograph of his all-time hero, Glenn Hoddle, before he left, and Macho of the Day Facundo had turned to Bianca.

'Your are veery beautiful. Perhaps you will have deener with me at my 'ouse zis week and dreenk out of my Gilded Boot.' Dropping his already-written acceptance speech, he thrust his hand between Bianca's thighs to retrieve it.

'Oh, I wish poor Tember was here,' sighed Taggie. 'I do hope she's OK.'

'She's such a trouper,' agreed Dora. 'Her tummy upset must be a shocker to keep her away.'

Back in her cottage in Searston, Tember lay in Griffy's arms, her red hair spilling over the pillow. Inez had taken all four children away to Bristol for the night for a photoshoot on 'Loving Mothers'.

'I shall be punished for telling lies, Griffy,' murmured Tember, 'but this is the loveliest tummy upset I've ever had.'

'Liar, liar, you've most certainly set my pants on fire,' Griffy murmured back. 'No one's ever set me alight like you do.' Then, wonderingly stroking her face, he quoted: ' "Who would have thought my shriveled heart / Could have recovered greenness?" '

'Sounds like the pitch at Searston after a grudge match,' said Tember and they both shook with laughter.

Looking at the big bunch of pink scented freesias on a nearby chest of drawers and fighting jealousy, Griffy asked: 'Are those from another admirer?'

Tember smiled. 'No, they're from darling Taggie, saying how sorry she was I couldn't make it to the Awards. I adore floral tributes.' Then, wriggling down, taking Griffy's cock in her mouth, caressing it with her tongue, she added: 'And this is an oral tribute.'

Rejoicing in her licking and loving expertise, Griffy came in a trice.

'God, that was heaven,' he shouted, pulling her back into his arms. 'I don't ever want to come back down to earth.'

He couldn't ever remember Inez going down on him. Hearing him shout, Mildred the mongrel, thrilled to have been invited along, left the sitting room fireside and leapt on to the bed.

'Do you think she's reminding us we ought to check if awful Facundo's won the Gilded Boot?' asked Tember.

'Certainly not.' Griffy moved down, kissing her freck-led thighs. 'It's my turn to give you an oral tribute.'

49

Back at the Awards, another clip had been shown of Drobenham players weeping when they didn't qualify for the Champions League.

'Tournamental health,' giggled Dora, 'they'll all need counselling.'

'That's trivialising,' accused an outraged Madison.

'However wealfy I get,' muttered Dolphy to Lou-Easy, 'I'll always vote Labour, but I couldn't vote for Elijah's wife, Madison.'

'Nor could I,' agreed Lou-Easy with a shudder.

To hold up proceedings even further, Dancer Maitland, huge rock star and polo patron, then came on and sang 'Sweet Caroline' and other hits for fifteen minutes, and the audience swayed and sang along with him.

Rupert was watching racing on his telephone; Taggie was asleep. A star-struck Feral had just got back from acquiring Glenn Hoddle's autograph and slid into his seat, not thinking he'd have a hope, as Ludo urged the audience to make a vast amount of noise for the winner of the Gilded Boot and Footballer of the Year.

'And the winner is . . .'

Next minute, Facundo had leapt into the aisle, brandishing his reworked speech and punching the air, when the huge overhead camera sent him flying back into the stalls.

'And the winner this year,' continued Ludo with a smirk, 'is not the player who scored the most goals, but the one who, despite crucifying injury, scored two goals and a dazzling assist, which qualified Searston Rovers for the Champions League this season. So, everyone, please make some noise for Feral Jackson.'

'Feral's won,' screamed Bianca and Taggie. 'Feral's won!'

'Good boy.' Rupert stood up to let him through, handing him over to an official who helped him on to the stage, where Ludo joyfully embraced him.

'Gilded Boot and silver football – well done, boyo.'

Feral, tall, dark-skinned and incredibly handsome, took the microphone.

'Ladies and gentlemen,' he tried to make himself heard over the tumultuous cheers, 'I didn't think I was going to win, so I didn't prepare a speech. Thank you all, but most of all I'd like to thank my single mum, Nancy, who worked her arse off to bring up my brothers and sisters and me and put food on the table. Wivout her, I'd never be here today' – he brandished the glittering, silvery-gold boot – 'so, thank you, Mum. I'd like to thank all the players and ground staff at Searston Rovers, particularly Ludo, who's always good for a laugh, and Elijah, who's a terrific manager, and all the fans, and my beautiful fiancée, Bianca.'

As Bianca gave a scream of excitement – was that a proposal? – Feral put down the Gilded Boot and stretched open palms towards her. 'An' who else? Oh yeah, Bianca's triffic mum and dad, Rupert and Taggie Campbell-Black.'

'Boooo,' shouted Sir Craig. 'Rupert Campbell-Black's the biggest shyster in football.'

'Rupert's not shy,' cried Dolphy.

'You beast,' cried Taggie.

'Shut up! You're one to talk,' yelled Feral, 'Mr Shambolic!'

And the crowd cheered and howled with laughter.

'I think we'd better get on,' grinned Ludo, handing Feral his Gilded Boot and sending him off to talk to the press.

Then suddenly a voice roared, 'There must be some meestake,' as Facundo, having picked himself out of the stalls, stalked up the aisle and, vaulting on to the stage, seized the microphone from Ludo.

'It's a fucking deesgrace,' he yelled. 'I score thirty-three goal for Searston Rovers this season, Feral Jackson only twenty-two, and the only reason he ween the Gilded Boot ees because this country is so sheet-scared of appearing racist, and not having enough Black winners tonight, so they geev Gilded Boot to Black player who is fucking second-rate.'

There was a horrified pause and gasps of shock. Then the hall went crazy, with a firework display of flashing camera lights, press fighting to get near the stage and the audience yelling their heads off.

'How dare you,' shouted Dolphy. Leaping on to the stage, he advanced on vast Facundo with his little fists clenched. 'Feral's awesome, he got us into the Champions League when he was horribly injured. He's the bravest person, and you're just a rotten loser and a bully and an adultery.'

311

'You leetle sheet,' bellowed gigantic Facundo, who'd completely lost it.

'Stop it, Dolphy,' yelled Ludo, who, despite his wrecked knee, leapt between them.

'Leave me alone,' Dolphy cried, pummelling Ludo's blue cummerbund.

'That's enough!' Terrified the boy might get seriously hurt, Elijah had also jumped on to the stage and, grabbing Dolphy, pulled him free, clamping his slender, quivering body against his own.

In the end, it took half a dozen plain-clothes policemen and several officials to get Facundo off the stage and into the foyer, where he shook them off and stormed into the night.

'I think that calls for another divorce,' said Rupert, as he and Elijah settled back into their seats. 'Couldn't be better publicity for Ludo's debut as a pundit.'

Ludo was calling everyone to order. 'I must apologise for such a vicious, unforgivable interruption, and I don't think I need to ask you to make any more noise for Feral and Dolphy, except well done, both of you. And to restore some calm, I'd like to ask actor Paris Alvaston, who's playing Hamlet, Prince of Denmark, at Stratford, to deliver one of Shakespeare's most beautiful speeches.'

'Oh, that's who he plays for – Denmark,' cried the Wags as Paris mounted the stage.

'He's a Great Dane, like Jesus's Lisbon,' sighed Dora.

'Paris was the first boyfriend I went to bed with,' confided Bianca. 'We did it in the woods at Bagley Hall, and in the science lab. He used to help with my homework, too, and write me poems which I didn't understand.'

'I know, I was there,' said Dora.

'And now I'm going to marry Feral – did you hear him call me his fiancée?'

'I did. Now shut up.'

'"To be or not to be,"' began Paris, and really made the words sing.

'Isn't he great,' said Ludo as the tumultuous applause ended. 'We certainly had to "take arms against a sea of troubles" tonight. You must all go and see him at Stratford.'

Then he grinned round at the audience. 'My version's a little different, but since I gave up the beautiful game, I've been piling on the pounds' – he patted his blue cummerbund – 'so it's tubby or not tubby, that is the question.' And the audience, including Paris, howled with laughter.

'And that brings us to one more award to end the evening,' said Ludo. 'Playmaker of the Year, to the player who's made the most assists, and that is . . .'

There was a roll of drums.

'Make a huge amount of noise for Laddy Heywood.'

To a squeal of delight from Lady Emma, Laddy swayed up the aisle, tripped up the steps, fell flat on his face, and lay there shaking with laughter.

'Have you hurt yourself, Laddy, or are you just diving so you can accuse me of a bad tackle and get me red-carded?' asked Ludo, then, pulling Laddy to his feet, shouted to the audience, 'Should we give him the Laddy Go-Diver or the Playmaker award?'

'Playmaker,' roared the crowd.

'Thanks, guys,' said Laddy, taking his silver football. 'I think we should all congratulate Ludo the Lion King for his very impressive debut as a pundit.'

And everyone gave Ludo a standing O.

The media were hard-pushed for who to interview now Facundo had scarpered. They tried to pin down Feral, whom everyone wanted to photograph with his defender Dolphy and his future bride, Bianca, who adored being photographed but for once was frantic to escape to her and Feral's double bed at the Hilton.

'Don't drink any more,' she said, removing Feral's glass of champagne. 'I'm sure I'm ovulating.'

Taggie put an arm round Bianca's shoulders. 'Good luck, darling. I know it'll happen soon.'

The *Sun* started asking Feral about his single mum and why wasn't she at the Awards, but before Bianca could chip in that she was a heroin addict in and out of rehab, a hovering Elijah whisked them away, saying Nancy hadn't been very well lately.

Back at the Hilton, a half-naked Feral held up his Gilded Boot for a second in the mirror. Did he really win this? It would be nice if Bianca were more delighted for him. Bianca, her shocking-pink dress chucked on the carpet, was lying, slender, naked and beautiful, in the huge double bed, looking at the Awards on her phone.

'That's a good one of us, and one of me. I'm so glad you beat horrible Facundo. He deliberately dropped his speech on the floor so he could bury his face in my crotch, trying to find it, and said he'd love to take me to bed.'

'So would I,' said Feral, stepping out of his boxers.

'Did you really call me your fiancée, Fer?'

'I did, my darling.' Feral removed her phone. 'You can put that thing away. We're not going to fight any more, we're going to make love and, fingers crossed, and legs uncrossed, we'll make a baby and keep clean sheets for nine months.'

Then he kissed her on the lips, and carried on kissing her down her slender body, till he found her tiny clitoris, reducing her to gasping ecstasy, before plunging deep inside her.

After they'd both come gloriously, Feral, who'd been up training vigorously at the crack of dawn, immediately fell asleep, only to be shaken awake by Bianca: 'As I'm ovulating, can we do it again to make doubly sure of making a baby?'

'Where are Bianca and Feral?' asked Rupert when he and Taggie got back to the Hilton.

'Gone to bed,' said Dolphy. 'Bianca must have been very tired; she kept talking about Ovaltine.'

50

After the Awards, Rupert and Elijah sacked Facundo for racism and extreme misconduct. Officially, they couldn't get rid of him until the January window, but behind the scenes his Machiavellian agent sold him to Vermelho, a vast and mighty Portuguese team, for £90 million, a nice whack of which went to Searston. This meant they no longer had to fork out his massive £300,000-a-week salary.

They also sold off his £20 million mansion in the Golden Triangle and his yellow Lamborghini, which helped Searston's bank balance, but Rupert hung on to the little yellow run-around, which would be cheap to whizz about his land, impress people he was economising and prove useful when the grandchildren started learning to drive.

The Searston players, meanwhile, not having to cater for Facundo's needs any more, really perked up.

The only person devastated by Facundo's departure was Inez, who'd found him a most exhilarating and prestigious lover, particularly as he'd lavished so many presents on her. She'd also lied so often that she was off on modelling jobs, when she was actually spending days and nights in bed with him, that her private account had been drastically reduced. She was consequently taking great chunks of money out of her and Griffy's joint account, as well as taking it out on Griffy himself, who Elijah was playing less regularly in the first team.

'No wonder you weren't nominated for a General Football Award,' she sneered.

This particularly devastated Griffy, who, after spending the night of the Awards with Tember, wanted only to spend the rest of his life with her. But Inez was in such a vile mood, terrorising the children, particularly the two little ones, that he didn't dare rock any boats at the moment.

Elijah was also showing steel in other directions:

'We've got to strengthen the defence and get rid of Parks, Rupert. He just plods along, shows no leadership and has slowed up appallingly. Players need direction. We need a leader. I think Angus McLean is the answer.'

'Angus!' exploded Rupert. 'ANGUS! He's a total shit. Poor Dolphy was in floods yesterday, because he missed an easy goal and Angus yelled: "We've got enough sprinklers on the pitch, we don't need you blubbing all over it as well."'

Forbearing to mention that Rupert had often been just as vitriolic to the players, Elijah said, 'I know he's a shit, but if he were given some authority officially, he might feel more secure and stop bullying.'

'And you're obsessed with camaraderie?' stormed Rupert. 'Always bawling me out for bawling out the players, now you're promoting the chief bawler. Are you going to install a second changing room for leopards to change their spots?'

'He's been very good to Ahmed and he's as able in defence as he is in attack, and knows where everyone is on the field.'

'And yells at all of them.'

'Leave it with me.'

That afternoon, Elijah called Angus into his office:

'I've decided to make you team captain.'

'Captain? Are you sure?' Angus's red hair clashed with his blushing face.

'Quite sure.'

'You'd really put your trust in me? With all these huge matches coming up?'

'Yup, it'll be a challenge.'

The ecstatic smile on Angus's face really touched Elijah, particularly when the Scotsman, who so rarely embraced anyone, seized his hands and briefly hugged him.

'What about Parks?'

'He's tired. He can play the odd game, particularly for the Reserves, helping the young players, and perhaps find another club in the January window. He's a good guy. We'll let him down gently.'

But Angus was too excited to dwell on Parks.

'My God, boss, I'd definitely like to accept. Can I go and phone Mimi? She'll be so delighted.'

The players were absolutely horrified at first. Was Elijah going to grow stinging nettles along the touchline? But Angus was so knocked out by his promotion that he became an excellent captain overnight, encouraging and praising as much as he commanded. He loved the attention from the media and particularly the female fans. Cadenza took some ravishing photographs,

318

which Dora captioned 'Angus McLean Sweep', because Searston were winning so many matches.

And everyone was thrilled to have lovely Mimi McLean as the new captain's lady, who got on so well with Tember, Taggie and Shelagh, and kept an eye out for any lonely players and Wags. All her pupils at her secondary school made and signed a big black-cat good-luck card for Angus.

Parks, in turn, seemed happy to spend more time warming the bench and would probably retire in the summer, when Rupert said they'd give a big testimonial party for him.

The only person insane with rage was his wife, Rosalie Parkinson.

'If Parks had stayed on another year, he could easily have been knighted and I could have renamed my bou-tique The Lady Rosalie.'

'Never maynd,' comforted Charm. 'You'll probably become a dame in your own rayght.'

Bianca, meanwhile, back at Penscombe, after her and Feral's epic lovemaking following the Awards, was des-perate to discover whether she'd fallen pregnant.

At first, she raced back and forth to the loo every five minutes, to check whether her period had arrived. Then, overjoyed when it didn't, she went rushing off to Cotchester to empty Boots of pregnancy test kits, and, on the way home, popped into Cotchester cathedral, where her parents had got married, to beg God to grant her a baby.

Back home, she spent her days in the loo, weeing on one pregnancy test kit after another, praying that the capital letters 'PREGNANT' would appear on the blank screen.

As the days passed, Taggie tried to comfort her. 'I know the waiting's agony, darling. I was so desperate to get pregnant, and so devastated every time my period arrived. It used to be called the Curse in those days – the curse of not becoming a mother. Then we adopted you and Xav and our lives were totally transformed.'

Whereupon Bianca would shout back: 'How many times do I have to tell you? I don't want to adopt someone else's baby.'

Feral, who was frantically busy training, playing matches and giving interviews about being Footballer of the Year, and announcing his engagement to Bianca, was relieved that Bianca no longer wanted sex all the time, in case it might dislodge a possible baby.

Then, late at night on 7 October, Feral, after a punishing Premier League victory, had fallen into a deep sleep; Bianca, however, was still wide awake. A slight breeze was ruffling the pale-blue bedroom curtains, the floor littered with discarded pregnancy test kit boxes. Picking up another box, Bianca crept down the landing to the loo, sitting down to wee on yet another test, then putting it down on the edge of the bath.

Awaiting the result, she picked up a copy of *Hello!*, temporarily distracted by a glamorous photograph of herself and Feral at the Awards. That shocking-pink dress had really suited her, and Feral looked gorgeous. Then her eyes slid back to the pregnancy test and she gasped. For there, clear as day, in capital letters was the word 'PREGNANT'.

Next moment, Bianca was shrieking her head off,

grabbing the test, racing down the landing into their bedroom.

'Feral, Feral,' she screamed, shaking his shoulders. 'Look, look, we're having a baby!'

Woken from deep sleep, Feral took a few seconds to register, then, peering at the screen, he gave a shout of joy: 'Oh my God, my darling!' And, drawing her into his arms, he hugged her and then gently stroked her tummy.

'You've got our baby in there. That's so fucking marvellous.'

'You mustn't swear in front of him or her,' giggled Bianca.

Down the landing, hearing the screams and shouting, Taggie, fearing the worst, wriggled out of a sleeping Rupert's arms and, putting on her flowered cashmere dressing gown, ran down the landing, banging on the door. 'Are you OK?'

'Come in,' shouted Feral. 'We're more than OK! Bianca's pregnant!' Then, as Taggie came into the room, he held out the test. 'Even you and I can read this.'

'Oh, oh, oh,' screamed Taggie in ecstasy, putting her arms round both of them. 'Oh well done, darlings, that is so wonderful.'

Next minute, a yawning Rupert, exhausted after a long day at Tattersalls yearling sales, wandered in, followed by his dogs.

'What the fuck is going on?'

'I'm pregnant, Dad!' cried Bianca. 'You're going to be another Grand Dad, Dad.'

Feral was almost the happiest to see the delight on Rupert's face as he yelled: 'That's fantastic! That

Ovaltine at the Hilton really worked. I'm so pleased for you both, and for us.' He gave Taggie a huge hug.

'I must ring and tell Dora,' said Bianca, seizing her phone, which Rupert promptly removed from her. 'It's one o'clock in the morning, darling. Too late to wake Dora and too late even for a bucket of champagne.'

From then on, an ecstatic Feral, having wrapped Bianca in cotton wool at home, was out scoring goal after goal. Dolphy, Wilfie and Josef, no longer petrified of Angus, were all playing well. Barry Pitt was shouting less and Downing, who was slightly in awe of Angus, didn't throw a temper tantrum when subbed and hadn't been red-carded for punching a player or a ref all season.

Another huge piece of excitement was that Ludo had been such a success at the awards ceremony that all the big television companies were offering him work as a pundit.

'Can you manage not to plug Searston Rovers every five minutes?' begged Sky. 'There are other clubs.'

'I'll try,' said Ludo.

This was hard because Searston were on a roll. In November, after punishing home and away matches against three other leading European clubs, they won their way out of the group stages of the Champions League, notching up an extremely welcome £100 million. In February, they would enter the last-sixteen knockout stage, with the final on 29 May in St Petersburg.

They were also fourth in the Premier League and doing brilliantly in the early rounds of the FA Cup, beating one of the big Manchester sides, who admittedly played with a weakened team, saving their best players for a big Premier League game on Monday.

With Angus as captain, the world saw how fondly Feral, Orion, Galgo, Ahmed, Ezra, Downing, Wilfie, Dolphy, Midas, Barry Pitt and occasionally Griffy blended together. Yet on the pitch, they were animals, who'd do anything to slaughter the opposition.

Ahmed, who worshipped Angus, was becoming a big star; the whole of Sierra Leone watched him weekly and followed his every move. Despite his not being a candidate, two million people voted for him to be prime minister. Ahmed also liked bigger girls and had started dating Rupert's assistant head lass, Harmony Bates. Harmony's heart had been broken some years back when Jan Van Daventer had pretended to be in love with her so he could gain access to Taggie and sabotage Rupert's horses. As Ahmed had lost all his family, he and Harmony found great comfort in consoling each other and mending each other's hearts.

'We go to Tesco's supper market,' Ahmed told Angus, 'to buy supper to take back home.'

The press also noted how well Rupert and Elijah were getting on, with Oliver Holt writing a big piece in the *Mail on Sunday* on how Elijah had 'tamed the Golden Beast'.

In the FA Cup semi-finals in the middle of April, however, Searston played West Riding, Valent Edwards's former club, at a beautiful ground in the valley below Ilkley Moor. Valent, Etta and Ryan had all been invited along as honoured guests to lunch in the boardroom, where a splendid portrait of Valent as Footballer of the Year, a very rare award for a goalkeeper, smiled down on them. To avoid confrontation, Rupert, Dora and Elijah had a quick lunch in a nearby hotel.

A very tired Searston were losing 2–0 at half-time, with an overjoyed Valent, Etta and Ryan cheering their heads off in the stands. Television pundits, except Ludo, were writing Searston off, the crowd singing:

'Poor Prince Charmless really is harmless, what a ghastly bore, his side can't score.'

They then launched into 'On Ilkla Moor Baht 'at', which made Dora laugh: 'Sir Craig would loathe that, he hates going anywhere without a hat.'

The Golden Beast, however, bored of being tamed, invaded the dressing room at half-time, yelling at the players, which Dora managed to record and post online: 'This programme does not contain weak language.'

With all the pundits except Ludo saying West Riding were home and dry, Searston rallied, going out in the second half and scoring four goals. Dolphy nearly got a hat-trick, but sweetly passed to Ahmed, who was having a temporary goal drought and who then scored the winning goal in the final seconds.

As the ball settled in the net, Ahmed whipped off his shirt and rushed to celebrate with the travelling fans, including his overjoyed new girlfriend, Harmony, before disappearing beneath a mob of jubilant teammates.

Three million people in Sierra Leone now voted for him to become their prime minister.

Flicking a victorious V-sign at Valent, Rupert was flabbergasted to receive a vigorous middle finger from Etta. Her stepson, Ryan, was half appalled and half delighted.

51

Having progressed from the last sixteen of the Champions League, Searston now faced a massive challenge: the first and second legs of the semi-finals of the Champions League against a mighty German team, Union Beethoven, who were based in Nachtburg, a new town near Bonn, which had been Beethoven's birthplace. Composed of powerfully built, mostly blond players, their run-out music was 'Ode to Joy' from Beethoven's Ninth Symphony.

The first leg, on 24 April, was at home for Searston, who were increasingly being nicknamed the Comeback Kids, because they tended to start slowly, conceding goals in the first half and much of the second, before storming ahead to snatch victory in the closing minutes.

'Union Beethoven will be expecting this,' Elijah told his players, 'so we've got to wrong-foot them.'

This Searston did, by providing a defence as impenetrable as a hawthorn hedge. Barry Pitt, revved up by his mate Angus, stopped everything. Galgo and Midas policed the midfield and Orion and Downing banged in a goal apiece in the first ten minutes, followed by two more from Feral, so by seventy minutes Searston were four up.

They then proceeded to irritate Union Beethoven by playing possession football, passing back and forth to each other all around the pitch, not letting UB get a toe on the ball, until their best player, a vast blond hunk called Wilhelm Walter, lost his temper. Charging into the Searston pack, scooping up the ball, he clouted it straight as an arrow past Barry Pitt's fingers, making the score 4–1.

With five minutes to go, Wilhelm Walter captured the ball again, hurtling towards goal, but he was brought down by a vicious tackle from Downing and stretchered off in terrible pain. Whereupon Downing was red-carded and banned from the second leg.

In six minutes' injury time, an enraged UB scored again, making it 4–2, whereupon little Wilfie broke away, dancing the ball through the opposition defence until Ludo, as a pundit for BT Sport, forgetting to be impartial, howled:

'Come on, Wilfie, you can effing do it!'

And Wilfie effing did as the whistle blew. 5–2, and Feral was made Man of the Match.

Union Beethoven then returned home to Bonn absolutely furious. They were not even amused by Dora posting a large picture of Buddyguard in a UB scarf, captioned:

'Of course he's devastated you lost. He's a German shepherd.'

Matters weren't improved by an interview a jubilant Angus gave to Janey Lloyd-Foxe, having had a few drinks after the match. Although he just answered a brief 'yes', 'no' and 'perhaps' to her questions, she quoted back these questions as his actual answers.

So the piece stated that he was 'absolutely delighted Searston had improved so dramatically since he'd taken over as captain', and how he 'had no worries about the second leg against UB next week'. When asked about Searston's great Premier League rivals, Deansgate, he quipped back, 'Never heard of them.'

The piece, which was taken up by all the media, was accompanied by another glamorous Cadenza photograph of Angus stripped to the waist, with a strawberry-blond rinse softening his ginger hair. All this infuriated UB, Deansgate and particularly Elijah – how could Angus be guilty of such hubris?

As a result, when Searston flew out to Nachtburg for the second leg a week later, they were greeted at the airport by hostile fans who smashed the windows of the coach that drove them to their hotel.

Cheffie, who'd accompanied them, insisted on taking over the hotel kitchen in case UB tried to sabotage their food before tomorrow's match. As a result, the Searston players, who'd been looking forward to a rich and lush German nosh-up and the odd glass of hock, were incensed to be fobbed off with boiled chicken and no booze. An apologetic Elijah then sent them to bed early, which was another fiasco as they were kept awake by blazing flares and fireworks deliberately let off outside their hotel rooms all night.

Next day, all the little shops put up metal shutters and bouncers took up residence at the door of every pub, with hostile fans lining the route all the way to Club UB, where Beethoven himself might have been conducting the booing, chanting and drumming when Wilhelm

Walter arrived to watch the game in a wheelchair and the home fans realised their star player had been put out for the rest of the season.

At kick-off, Searston were leading 5–2. Determined that Feral shouldn't score any more, UB set three of their toughest defenders to constantly mark him, while a frenzied pack of their fans resorted to monkey chants and pelting him with missiles if he ever got near the ball.

As UB proceeded to score twice, making it 5–4, Elijah was so furious at Feral being the victim of such racist abuse that he metamorphosed into Rupert as he gave Searston a blistering half-time pep talk:

'It appears that effing UB want to get to St Petersburg even more than you do. You've got forty-five minutes left to get off your fucking arses!'

This astounded his players so much, they fought back like hellhounds, with Orion scoring before Super Sub Ezra came off the bench in injury time and, striking a blow against racism, banged in a further goal.

7–4 to Searston, who had scored the most goals so came out on top.

'We've won, we've won!' screamed Dolphy as the whistle blew. 'We're in the final of the Champions League and we're going to St Petersburg to make millions and millions of pounds to save Rupert.'

And no one could've been more delighted than Rupert who, after winning the 2000 Guineas, had only just arrived in Bonn, because the Green Galloper had been held up at the airport.

During a joyful celebratory dinner at their hotel afterwards, where the Searston players didn't get too plastered because of a big Premier League match in three days' time, Orion sat next to Rupert, who still disliked him intensely for breaking Lou-Easy's heart.

'Can I ask you something, boss?' said Orion. 'You must know you're the hottest guy on the block. All the Wags and the women fans are crazy about you.'

'That's kind of them.'

'Particularly when you must be getting on a bit, it's amazing you haven't lost any of your hair.'

'Odd when I tear out so much of it watching you play football.'

'And, even more amazing, you haven't got a single grey hair and it's a great colour. I was just wondering what shade you dye it?'

'Dye it!' said Rupert in outrage. 'I don't touch it.'

The table had gone silent, everyone desperately trying not to laugh, but Orion ploughed on:

'And you don't even get your barber to colour it for you? You must use a tinted conditioner to make it so golden and glossy.'

There was a long, long nervous pause, then Rupert laughed. 'You'd better have a word with Safety Car. He uses something called Mane 'n Tail.'

52

As a result of their brilliant first-leg victory against
Union Beethoven, Feral, Angus, Wilfie, Dolphy, Orion
(who, because his divorced father lived in England, was
considered eligible to play for this country) and Downing (despite being red-carded and not making the
second leg) were all picked as possibles to take part in
an England friendly against Turkey in Istanbul in early
May. Dolphy was blown away.

'I fort they was joking when they called and asked me
to go straight to St George's Park, near Burton-on-Trent,
training ground of the England football team.'

'The publicity will transform you and Orion into
global poster boys, Dolphy!' cried Dora.

The medical team at Searston, however, advised by
Rupert's star doctor, James Benson, pretended Feral
wasn't fit enough to go because his left thigh was playing up again. They couldn't afford to let him get injured
when they had the most important Premier League
game coming up. Feral was distraught, but Rupert reassured him: 'It's only a friendly; the England manager

will be trying out all sorts of combinations. Safer to wait for the real thing.'

Bianca, who was due to have her baby in a few weeks' time, in early June, was very put out not to be the partner of an England player. Poor Dolphy was so excited but, tragically, three days later, injured his Achilles tendon in a nasty tackle during training and also had to pull out.

The four other players, particularly Angus, who at thirty-two had been selected for the England squad for the first and probably last time, pleaded with Elijah to let them go. Persuaded in turn by Elijah, Rupert reluctantly agreed, but added that the four were not staying on for any celebratory party afterwards.

He would send the little Galloper to bring them straight home from Istanbul so they would have a day's rest before the huge game on Saturday. This was being televised by Sky Sports Main Event, which would bring in the cash and crowds and help Searston in their qualification for next year's Champions League, as well as pleasing any sponsors. The publicity for the Galloper would also delight Ghengis Tong.

'And you're not to chew gum during the National Anthem,' added Rupert.

The media praised Searston for having so many England possibles, particularly congratulating Elijah for engineering this. Elijah was delighted for Searston but still miserable that his father, the rabbi, refused to acknowledge him.

'What son?' snapped Abner Cohen when questioned by the press, who tracked him coming out of his synagogue in North London. 'I have absolutely no comment to make.'

Naomi, Elijah's daughter, saw a clip on the BBC and Elijah came home to find her sobbing in bed.

'Everyone at school wants to know why Grandad doesn't recognise us. I thought rabbis loved everyone. What have we done wrong?'

With Searston still having four England players and Deansgate, with Laddy Heywood, only one, naughty Dora kept gloating online that Searston were 'Four to One, Four to One', which enraged Jarred and Sir Craig.

She was also working late on the Wednesday evening before the Searston players flew out. Climbing up a tree in the Forest of Dean to spy on one of Ryan Edwards's training sessions, she discovered another journalist, Ian Herbert from the *Daily Mail*, also spying from the next-door tree. This triggered a frenzy of barking from Buddyguard, beneath them. Dora, Ian Herbert and Buddyguard then fled into the forest before an alerted and enraged Ryan could catch them.

Later, Ryan reported to Sir Craig that Dora was using kidnapped Buddyguard for spying, which made Sir Craig even more determined to bury her.

Dolphy was still miserable his injury had stopped him playing for England. He was also worried about Elijah, who seemed so depressed and was also rumoured to be going to Istanbul with Rupert to watch the game.

The same evening Dora was spying on Deansgate, Paris took Dolphy and Grandkid out for a drink at the Running Fox to cheer Dolphy up.

'Who was Elijah, anyway?' asked Dolphy.

'He was the most popular of the Old Testament prophets,' replied Paris. 'Fought as a soldier of the Lord against heathen gods, championed the downtrodden, performed loads of miracles and vanished up to heaven in a chariot of fire. He was evidently walking on water on the River Jordan when this flaming chariot appeared, Elijah jumped into it and a whirlwind took him up to heaven. The Jews don't believe he died, and at Passover an extra cup of wine is poured for him and families draw up an empty chair at the table for him.'

'That's nice,' said Dolphy, drawing up a chair from a nearby table. 'I wish I could cheer him up. If I was playing for England, if I scored a goal . . .'

'They'll ask you again.' Paris was half amused to see that all the girls in the pub, who usually stared at him, were gazing longingly at Dolphy and patting Grandkid, hoping to decipher Dolphy's phone number from his collar.

After several drinks, they wandered home singing 'Jerusalem': 'Bring me my bow of burning gold . . . Bring me my chariot of fire.'

'*Chariots of Fire* was a good film,' said Paris. 'You must watch it.'

When Elijah discovered Dolphy had been out drinking with Paris, unable to overcome his jealousy, he bit Dolphy's head off next morning, shouting, 'You're supposed to be resting that ankle, not getting pissed.'

Not playing for England, no longer Elijah's special pet, Dolphy was utterly miserable.

333

53

Another person totally fed up was Inez Griffiths. Wags – even those with important jobs – derived kudos from the success of their partner. Because they had all been victims of her sharp tongue, the Searston Wags therefore made no attempt to hide their delight that their other halves had been picked for Champions League and Premier League matches and now for England, while Griffy, although they loved him, was showing a dramatic loss of form and was no longer a regular member of the team.

Inez was very much missing Facundo, not the greatest correspondent, who, speedily settling into Vermelho, his mighty Portuguese club, was notching up goals and all over social media, looking macho.

Because Inez had spent so much time pretending she was modelling when she was actually jogging over to the Golden Triangle to sleep with Facundo, she and Griffy, since he'd been demoted, were both short of cash.

As a result, Inez was regularly bitching up Griffy and the children. Never eating much, to keep her weight down, she'd be plastered after a couple of drinks, getting worse and worse tempered. The theme was always the same: why wasn't Griffy playing in the Champions League and the FA Cup and for England, why was he the only one on the bench at Searston? She was at her most vicious on Easter Monday night:

'Why are we living in a grotty little house in Cotchester instead of the Golden Triangle? Why aren't the kids going to Bagley Hall? I've been a victim of false pretences. I thought I was marrying a star, but you're just a has-been, or rather, a hasn't-ever-been.'

'Please, not in front of the children,' murmured Griffy, as he loaded the dishwasher. If he shouted back, Inez might resort to violence.

Mildred the mongrel, however, started whining querulously in her master's defence, whereupon Inez threw a book at her.

'Don't hurt Mildred,' screamed the little girls.

'Go to bed and shut up,' howled Inez.

Griffy longed to escape and walk Mildred, but he daren't leave Tilly and Minnie alone with Inez in such a volatile mood. He and Tember had had endless discussions on what to do about 'the situation', but Griffy was terrified that a ruthless Inez might manipulate custody of the little girls.

The only Wag Inez had a semblance of a friendship with was Rosalie Parkinson, because she modelled for the catalogue Rosalie sent out for her boutique.

The Tuesday after Easter, which was also the day the six Searston players learnt they had been selected for the England friendly against Turkey, Rosalie dropped in on Inez to discuss the boutique's summer range.

Griffy was at training; Gabriella and Ally had gone back to school with GCSEs lurking in four weeks' time;

Tilly and Minnie, jittery about their mother's short fuse, had retreated to *Peppa Pig* on their laptops, with play-group starting next week.

Putting a bunch of rather tired daffodils on the kitchen table and accepting a cup of tea, Rosalie said how thrilled she felt for Mimi McLean that Angus had been picked for England.

'I remember how bowled over I was when Parks was selected. So precious to get an England shirt. I must get it framed.' As she added it was a shame Griffy'd missed the boat, the little girls noticed their mother's scarlet-nailed fingers drumming on the kitchen table.

'And I'm delighted Sand Pitt's got a modelling job for some travel company. I thought I might ask her to share promoting my summer range with you, Inez. She's young, still in her early thirties.'

'And so lifted,' snapped Inez. 'She'll soon be wearing her pubes as a moustache.'

'That's very unkind, Inez,' reproached Rosalie. 'You must have had some work done in the past to look so good. Let's face it, you're no spring chicken.'

'I have NOT!' exploded Inez. 'I've never had Botox.'

'Yes, you have, Mummy,' reproved Tilly, looking up from *Peppa Pig*. 'You've got two buttocks. Look,' and she pointed at the framed blow-up of a naked Inez's back view next to the oven.

'Don't be fatuous,' hissed Inez, but Rosalie had burst out laughing: 'Two buttocks – that's priceless, Tilly.'

And Inez lost it, shouting at Tilly not to be so bloody silly, until Mildred began whining again, and Inez's hurled mug only just missed her.

'Don't hurt Mildred,' screamed Tilly again, bursting into tears.

'Go to your room,' yelled Inez, calling after them, 'and tie that bloody dog up outside.'

'You're so lucky, Inez.' Rosalie, still laughing, drained her cup of tea. 'Living in such a small house, you don't have to shout up miles of stairs like a fishwife. I'm off. Thanks for the cuppa. I'll liaise with Cadenza and find a date for you and Sand Pitt to model the summer range. Such an exciting collection, and I can't wait to share "two buttocks" with everyone!'

The following day, having bitched at Griffy all night, Inez took a vast chunk out of her and Griffy's joint account and, leaving a note in the drawing room telling him she was leaving him for Facundo and their marriage was over, took a plane to Portugal. She left no messages for the four children.

Returning from training in the pouring rain and finding the note, a shattered Griffy was just bringing Mildred in from her kennel, when the little girls returned from playing with a friend.

'Mummy's gone away for a holiday to Portugal,' he told them, and nearly broke down when Tilly piped up:

'How lovely. Jesus has just gone back to Portugal – perhaps he'll bump into Mummy and she'll meet Lisbon, his big dog. Are you crying, Daddy?'

'No, it's just the rain.'

Later, when the teenagers returned from school, Griffy told them too that their mother had gone away for a break in Portugal.

But he was totally panic-stricken. How the hell was he going to cope with football, family, school runs, babysitting, as well as all the shopping and a totally depleted bank balance? After cobbling together a very scrappy supper, the larder was bare. He longed to ring Tember but he felt he shouldn't lumber her with such a disaster.

Elijah, meanwhile, after Easter, had called Griffy in for training, seriously thinking of bringing him back into the first team. Now Ludo had gone, Feral was grounded with a pretend injury to avoid the England friendly and Midas was off with a sprained knee, he must restore Griffy's form so he could add calmness and reassurance to the team when so much was going on.

On the morning after Inez walked out, Tember was in the office wading through a pile of post. There wasn't a moment she didn't miss Griffy, but she tried to let him do the contacting, in case Inez rumbled something.

Picking up a magazine called *Women Matter*, she discovered a big piece on Inez, which must have been written when she'd taken the four children to be filmed in Bristol. There was a lovely picture of Inez wearing very little make-up, a white shirt and jeans, with a twin on either knee, and Gabby and Ally behind each shoulder; they were all laughing.

'Caring Mother,' said the headline, with the piece beginning: 'Despite her demanding career as a top model, Inez Griffiths always puts her footballer husband and her four children first. "They're what really matters," says Inez.'

'Hypocrite,' stormed Tember. 'You utter bitch.' Getting out a red Pentel, she turned the headline into 'Scaring Mother' by adding a large S.

It was that same evening, when Inez had taken all the children to Bristol, that she herself had ducked out of the awards ceremony to stay at her cottage with Griffy and he'd said the biggest award in the world was to spend a night in her arms.

She jumped and shoved the magazine into her desk as Elijah popped his head round the door.

'As Griffy hasn't turned up for training and I want him for Saturday's match, can you give him a ring?'

Tember knew his number by heart. Why did her hand shake every time she dialled it?

'Griffy, it's Tember. Are you OK? Elijah wondered why you hadn't come in.' There was a long pause. 'Are you OK, Griff?'

'Inez has left me,' said Griffy.

'Oh my God, I'm so sorry. When, how?'

'She's gone to Facundo in Portugal. Left a note in the drawing room – ought to rename it Departure Lounge. Tilly and Minnie haven't gone back to playgroup yet.' His voice broke. 'I can't leave them. Could you apologise to Elijah? It's been hard, trying not to upset the girls too much. I've got to go shopping and get some supplies in.' As his voice broke again, he half joked: 'I'm trying to keep a stiff upper lip.'

'I want your upper lip to do much more exciting things,' said Tember. 'You're not to worry about a thing. I've got a meeting in five minutes, but I'll be round to you about six, and I'll bring supper for everyone, including Mildred. I'm going to take care of you, darling.'

That evening, Tember rolled up, weighed down with carrier bags of delicious food for everyone, including Mildred, and a big scented bunch of pink roses for the kitchen table. Thinking that even distress and utter exhaustion couldn't destroy Griffy's beauty, she took him briefly in her arms. Realising he was shivering, she said: 'It's very chilly – why don't you light a fire in the kitchen? Everything's going to be OK, darling.'

She then comforted and fed the two little girls, tucking them up with a bedtime story, before hugging and listening to teenagers Gabriella and Ally, who were struggling with GCSE revision for exams in a month's time.

'I'll never get good enough grades to have a career,' sighed Gabriella. '*Macbeth* is so boring.'

'You're both so pretty, you can always model to make ends meet,' reassured Tember.

Then she cooked them a gorgeous chicken casserole accompanied by a glass of white wine each, and understood when their father, Griffy, was too strung up to eat much.

'Don't worry, Mildred can finish it up; it'll be a nice change from Butcher's Tripe.'

Mildred, blissful to be allowed back inside, was stretched out in front of the fire.

'Please stay the night,' Griffy begged Tember, as he helped clear supper away.

'I shouldn't – it might upset the children, and you need a decent night's sleep.'

'Stay in the spare room, if you'd prefer.'

The spare room was the bleakest room in a very bleak house, covered in mirrors and blow-ups of Inez, with grey walls and curtains. Every drawer was filled with her clothes, and hundreds of shoes and bags and hats.

Sir Craig would love to get his hands on all those Easter bonnets, thought Tember, noticing several copies of *Women Matter*, featuring Inez, on the bedside table. She also thought it sad that Inez had appropriated the next-door

340

room for more clothes and her mass of make-up, while the teenagers and the twins were squashed into two tiny rooms.

She was very touched when Gabriella came in with a hot-water bottle:

'Thank you for cheering up Dad. He's pretending Mum's gone off for a holiday, but we know she's left him.'

'We'll all look after him,' said Tember, giving her a hug.

Despite the hot-water bottle, it was a very cold room. Tember longed to be in the main bedroom with Griffy, but was comforted when Mildred wandered in and curled up on her bed, and she was woken up by Tilly and Minnie joining them.

'Why don't we all get into Daddy's bed? There's more room,' said Tilly.

Next night, Tember did, and in the days that followed, all the family cheered up and felt cherished.

Griffy, who for the first time was not exhausted by shopping and housework and school runs, was so thrilled when Tember and the girls came and watched him playing on Saturday that he scored three goals.

'Geri-Hatric' was Dora's huge headline in the *Cotchester Times*, and Mildred was thrilled with the match ball.

Tember was exhausted but blissfully happy. *How on earth does such a slender body contain such a huge heart?* wondered Griffy.

'We must make plans for our future,' he told her.

54

But alas, Inez was not finding it easy living with Facundo in Portugal. Expecting a bed of roses, she was horrified to find it full of thorns. Zou Zou, Facundo's wife, and his three children had been staying for Easter and only just returned to Buenos Aires, leaving the place a total tip.

Facundo, although initially pleased to see Inez, expected her to clean the place up and do everything for him. His house was beautiful and on the seafront, but then other women kept ringing, but instantly dropping the call if she picked up.

In England, she'd had masses of time to make herself look beautiful; here, after a night of sex, she was expected to get up and cook Facundo breakfast – admittedly only coffee and croissants, but he wasn't keen on instant coffee and got very crossant when she burnt the croissants.

He also expected a three-course dinner in the evening but discouraged her from coming to matches to meet all the other players and their wives – 'You must stay and relax here, Inez.' Finally, he was incandescent when she singed his midnight-blue silk shirt and shrank his cashmere jerseys in the washing machine.

After ten days and a particularly blazing row, Inez returned to the Cotswolds to pick up some clothes and visit her bank manager, and bumped into Nemesis, in the form of ex-captain's lady Rosalie Parkinson, who whisked her into a coffee bar.

'Are you still with Facundo, Inez? I hope the naughty boy is behaving himself, but I do want to reassure you not to stress yourself about Griffy. You know Tember West has moved in? They seem so happy. Tember dropped the kids off at school this morning and she's often bringing their dog, Mildred, who seems devoted to her, into the office. Griffy's back to playing really well, so you mustn't feel guilty about them.'

Inez had always suspected goody-goody Tember had a crush on Griffy. 'Now she's stolen him and my children and my dog.'

So while Tember was at the office and Griffy was out, Inez went back to the house and sobbed all over Gabriella and Ally when they returned from school, telling them how lonely she was and how she'd made a terrible mistake and how much she was missing them and wanted to come home. 'Being away made me realise how much I adored you.'

Gabriella and Ally were stunned; they'd never experienced their mother being so vulnerable and totally loving before, her make-up streaked with tears.

Matters weren't helped when Tember returned from the office, weighed down with shopping for supper, and the little children rushed to hug her and Mildred the mongrel bounced around ecstatically.

Seeing Tember's car in the drive, Inez retired upstairs to have a shower and repair her make-up. She was tracked down by Tilly and Minnie.

'Now that you've come back, Mum, can Tember stay too?' begged the little ones. 'Daddy's always laughing and Mildred loves sleeping on their bed, and she doesn't want to put her down and she cooks such lovely food and reads us lovely stories and helps Gabs and Ally with their homework.'

But alas, simultaneously, Gabriella and Ally had sought out Tember in the kitchen:

'So sorry, but we never realised Mum loves us so much. We never knew she felt like that. She is missing us all and wants us to be a family again. Daddy really does love her and she wants to try really hard to make their marriage work.'

So, an utterly heartbroken Tember packed and left, leaving a note for Griffy in the rechristened Departure Lounge: 'I love you more than anything else in the world, but I can't break up your marriage. Please take care of yourselves. All my love, Tember.'

Inez promptly tore up Tember's letter, telling a broken-hearted Griffy when he came home that she'd walked out.

'Just buggered off,' she sneered. 'She obviously realised everyone wanted me back.'

A devastated Griffy retreated to the top of the house. Paradise utterly lost. He would have jumped the forty feet down on to the paved stone terrace below, if he hadn't had all his children to look after.

Tember retreated to her cottage and cried so continuously that Riddance the cat couldn't get any sleep and flounced off back home.

Tember's and Griffy's hearts were not the only ones shattered. Orion, famous for taking dives near his sponsors' advertising board on the pitch, had landed a huge ad for tinned sweetcorn, so whenever poor Lou-Easy went into Tesco, she saw his handsome face adorning rows and rows of tins.

Marketa and Lou-Easy no longer shared a flat and communicated as little as possible at the yard. But one evening, before the players left for Istanbul, Lou-Easy, after two wins at Kempton, was persuaded into the Dog and Trumpet by Rupert's lads, who thought she needed cheering up. She'd just settled on to a barstool, getting stuck into a large gin and tonic and checking the day's results, when Marketa walked in in a sapphire-blue dress. For a moment, she and Lou-Easy stared at each other, then, overwhelmed with joyful memories, they fell into each other's arms.

'Oh Lou, I've missed you so much.'

'And me you. We mustn't fight any more. What do you want to drink?'

'Oh, anything – red, vite, champagne. Ve must celebrate; I can't wait to tell you. Look, look.' Marketa flashed a huge sapphire circled with diamonds on her ring finger. 'Orion and I are getting married, and ve both vant you to come to our vedding and be our bridesmaid.'

Next minute, a shattered Lou-Easy felt an arm round her waist and a kiss on her cheek and, swinging round, encountered a laughing, impossibly good-looking Orion.

'We want you to be our chief bridesmaid, babe,' he murmured, 'but only if you come on honeymoon with us.'

Somehow Lou-Easy managed to laugh rather than cry and, hugging them both, saying she was so happy for them, feeling she ought to get a BAFTA for acting, muttering that she had to check on Story, fought her way out of the pub. Sobbing her heart out as she ran back to Penscombe, she wished Josef was around to comfort her, but he had flown to the Czech Republic to take part in an international friendly against France. Lou-Easy texted him a message wishing him good luck and was touched when a message came winging back instantly: 'Deer Loo, your messidge make me so happy. I try and scaw for you. All luv, Josef.'

Lou-Easy liked being 'Deer'. They could have a stag party when Josef came home.

55

On a beautiful sunny May morning, Eamonn drove to Deep Woods in a people carrier to pick up the four chosen Searston players and take them to Birmingham airport to join the rest of the England team flying out to Istanbul.

A crowd of excited fans brandishing England flags and banners had turned up to cheer them off. Inside, the walls of the club were papered with good-luck cards bearing red crosses or the three blue lions with their scarlet tongues hanging out.

Tember had taken a few days off, pretending to have flu but constantly in tears, trying to get over splitting up with Griffy, continually praying that after reading her farewell note he might ring or text her – but nothing. She found herself worrying about Mildred the mongrel and whether Inez would chuck her out.

She had to steel herself to return to Searston to wish her four boys luck. Adorning the foyer was a big bunch of wallflowers and forget-me-nots. *That's me*, she thought, *a forgotten wallflower.*

On the way in, she was drawn aside by Wilfie's father, Dougie, in an England scarf, asking what fee Wilfie would get for playing for England.

'Only two thousand pounds,' said Tember, then adding to Dougie's horror: 'And players often donate this to charity.'

Taggie was feeling so much better and stronger that she needed Shelagh's help less at Penscombe, and because Tember had been away, Shelagh had been seconded to help out in the office at Searston. She was now appalled by how much weight Tember had lost and how red and swollen her eyes were in a drawn and deathly pale face.

'Shouldn't you still be in bed, little darling?'

'I'm fine.' But, breathing in a soapy, sickly sweet smell, Tember bolted past Shelagh into the Boardroom, where she gave a little scream on finding a huge bunch of hawthorn, rising in white rockets, on the big table. Gathering up the entire bunch, she stumbled downstairs, along the passage and out through the back door, and threw them into the dustbin.

'What are you doing?' cried Shelagh. 'It's lovely hawthorn!'

'It's also called May,' sobbed Tember, her hands dripping blood from the sharp spikes, 'and it's desperately unlucky to bring it into the house. It always brings disaster, and with the boys flying out it couldn't be at a worse time, and with Rupert and Taggie flying back from Pakistan having been to see Xav and Aysha's new baby.'

'Are you really OK?' persisted Shelagh, wiping the blood off Tember's face and hands with a piece of dampened kitchen roll and handing her some dark glasses.

Outside, the crowd of fans had been joined by an army of press, including Cadenza. Usually clad for work in jeans, a shirt and trainers, with her hair in a ponytail, she had rolled up as if she were going to a party, in very high heels and a short sleeveless yellow dress patterned with gold leaves, freshly washed curls dancing in the breeze and her big yellow eyes enhanced by long false eyelashes.

She was now busy photographing Angus, Downing and Wilfie, all in their dark England tracksuits. Wilfie, who'd nipped into Penscombe to give The Story So Far his morning carrots, was quaking with nerves.

'I'm so excited but scared, Boss.'

'You'll be marvellous.' Elijah hugged him. 'Keep calm and look around before you kick.' Then, putting an arm around Downing, who, despite legions of girls turning up to wave him off, was looking apprehensive: 'Don't forget, there are twenty England players going out there, so don't stress if you don't get much game time or even play.' Elijah laughed. 'You're a great player – just be a hit, not a hitter.'

Tember, having hugged each of her boys and wished them good luck, was still praying Griffy might turn up, but he was probably far too busy ferrying children about, shopping and ironing Inez's dresses.

Glamorous Cadenza was still taking pictures, concentrating on Angus:

'Look towards the woods, darling, that's your best side.'

'How's lovely Mimi, Angus?' asked Shelagh, pointedly.

'She wanted to come and wave us off,' said Angus, 'but she's got GCSE revision all day.'

Her pupils were less conscientious. Escaping Cotchester

High, a couple of dozen of them had rolled up, waving England flags and iPhones, crying:

'Selfie with Wilfie, hurrah for our hero, we want a selfie with Wilfie.'

And Wilfie, who'd shot up in the last year and could no longer be mistaken for one of the child mascots that players lead on before matches, beamed round in amazement. This was slightly irritating to the nearby Downing and Angus, who were not averse to adulation from gorgeous schoolgirls.

Nor was Dougie, who promptly sidled up, putting his arm around his son's shoulders:

'Even better, a selfie with Wilfie and his dad.'

'We don't want you,' screamed the girls, 'we only want selfies with Wilfie!'

Pretty girls really fancying me, thought Wilfie. He wished his mother, Mary, was there, but there was no way she would be let off by that bitch Rosalie, who complained to Dougie if Mary missed a minute. The moment he got back to England, Wilfie vowed he was going to talk to Marti Gluckstein about making sure a vast chunk of his £50,000 a week went to Mary, and, if he was brave enough, to kick out his father.

Marketa and Lou-Easy were also really upset that they'd had to go racing in Exeter instead of saying goodbye.

The fans were showing no sign of dispersing and were now holding up a huge placard saying:

'Godspeed to our four England stars.'

Journalists were trying to get last-minute questions over loudspeakers booming out the *Black Beauty* music.

'We're off to play for England!' cried Wilfie.

'Come on,' roared Eamonn, opening the doors of Rupert's people carrier. 'We've only got two hours to get to Birmingham airport, or you won't be playing for anyone.'

And where the hell was Orion, who wasn't answering his phone and who always arrived at the last minute?

Only when Wilfie, Downing and Angus were all ensconced did he finally roll up.

'Oh hurrah,' cried Wilfie, glancing round. 'Rupert's got back from Pakistan to come with us.'

'That ain't Rupert.' Downing burst out laughing.

And, as he whipped off the sunglasses concealing his dark eyes, it could be seen that Orion had dyed his dark hair blond and styled it exactly like Rupert's, with a side parting and brushed-straight back and sides to show off his beautiful man-tanned forehead and cheekbones. Grinning round, he drawled:

'I thought if I looked a bit more like Arsy-B, I might compete with Angus's pink rinse. Do you think it comes orf?'

And even Eamonn howled with laughter as Orion jumped into the back beside Angus, adding: 'And I might be able to pull a few birds in Istanbul.'

'You won't have much time,' retorted Angus. 'The Galloper's collecting us immediately after the match. And I thought you were engaged to Marketa.'

'Any room for a little one?' cried a running-up Cadenza, batting her false eyelashes at Eamonn as she slid her overnight bag into the boot and herself into the back, in between Angus and the window, before the people carrier moved off.

'Good luck, boys. We're all so proud of you,' shouted Tember.

'Where's Istanbul?' asked Wilfie.

'It's the capital of Turkey, an ancient city once called

351

Constantinople,' replied Angus, sliding a surreptitious hand with his thumb moving upwards between Cadenza's thighs. 'It's on a harbour midway between Europe and Asia, with great buildings and endless markets. We might have an hour or so to explore tomorrow. And you can put that fifty-grand watch two hours forward, Orion. It's two o'clock in Turkey.'

'I'm glad we're going to Turkey,' piped up Wilfie. 'We can have a Turkey dinner tonight, like Christmas.'

56

There wasn't much time to admire Istanbul, because Kim Chatterley, the England manager, supervised a brief training session in the morning, giving him time to look at new and untested players and various combinations for possible international games in the future. Laddy Heywood was the only Deansgate player, but Orion was intrigued to glimpse Lady Emma among the spectators, and amused when she rushed up and embraced him, then shrieked with embarrassment, 'Oh my God, I thought you were Rupert,' whereupon Laddy snarled at him to 'bugger off'.

In the afternoon, England won easily – 4–1, with all the Searston lads playing well. Angus, forgetting he wasn't captain, bossed the players around too much, to the irritation of the current captain, but he defended and attacked with equal competence, blocking several Turkish goals. Orion whipped in a goal in the top corner. Downing scored too and didn't sulk when he was subbed after twenty minutes. Finally, Wilfie hurtled up to the touchline, providing an assist for Laddy Heywood.

Wilfie was also thrilled to be given a white shirt which

had the red Turkish flag across its chest, with a crescent moon and a star slightly left of centre. This came from a young Turkish player whose goal Wilfie had warmly applauded, and whom he had helped up after a rough tackle.

'I'm going to wear it at all times,' vowed Wilfie.

When the Searston players left immediately after the match, the England manager congratulated all four, saying he'd be in touch in the future.

'Next time you must stay for the after-party!'

'I wish we could,' they chorused.

This was all excellent publicity for the Green Galloper, of which Cadenza took great shots both at Istanbul and at Heathrow, where their South American freelance pilot, Alphonso, stopped to refuel, and where passengers on private planes could go through the back door with no passport control.

While the Galloper was refuelling, its passengers retreated to the Transmission Lounge for a quick drink and were gratified when several people congratulated them on their England victory. Orion, who'd put on a green-and-blue Rupert Campbell-Black chairman shirt, was also delighted when a very pretty blonde sidled up to him: 'How amazingly fit you look, Rupert – can I have your autograph?' which Orion naughtily signed with a flourish.

Next moment, a ravishing brunette rushed in, pushed her aside and threw herself into the arms of her future husband.

'Vot a vonderful goal you score,' cried Marketa.

'How on earth did you get in here?' asked an astounded Orion.

'I flash bosom and passport at some security guy,' laughed Marketa. 'I could not vait to see you, and I'm not leaving naughty boy for a second longer on his own.'

Then, as another beauty sidled up to Orion to ask for Rupert's autograph, Orion turned to Downing:

'You see, gentlewomen do prefer blonds.'

'Come on,' ordered Angus, draining his drink. 'Or we'll never get back to Deep Woods.'

It was a beautiful warm evening, with a full moon.

'We do moons better than the Turks,' said Wilfie, thinking of the little crescent moon on the Turkish flag.

Back at Deep Woods, Ludo, Dora and Elijah were tracking the Galloper's return on a flight radar app.

'Incredible one can identify our little plane from all the other planes in the sky,' crowed Dora. 'Can you see it, darling?' she added, holding Buddyguard's face up to the screen.

'Shouldn't be long now,' said Ludo.

'And we've got Bolly at the ready for them.'

'Not too much,' said Elijah, 'they've got a big match on Saturday – no, it's tomorrow now.'

'Goodness, it's dry,' observed Dora, looking down at the cracked ground beneath their feet. 'I must remember to water Etta's plants.'

'Galloper's nearing Rutshire airfield,' said Ludo. 'Here in half an hour.'

'Little plane's done so well,' said Dora. 'It loves having an outing. And your boys have done so brilliantly.' She turned to Elijah.

'They have, and the best thing is they've all escaped injury,' said Elijah, who was recovering from a row with Madison, who wanted to spend any bonus he got for being in the final of the Champions League on a flat near Westminster, so she'd have somewhere to stay when she was 'in the House'.

'Sir Craig'll be livid the Galloper's getting so much more publicity than his stupid Battery Ram,' said Dora. 'I bet he won't acknowledge that wonderful assist Wilfie gave Laddy Heywood.'

'I'll mention it,' said Ludo. Then, glancing at his phone: 'Fucking hell, we spoke too soon. Angus has just texted to say the pilot's not happy with the Galloper, and he's going to land her as near to Rutshire airfield as possible. And can we arrange for someone to collect them from there.'

Fortunately, the passengers in the Galloper had had enough to drink to cushion them against too much panic when the pilot announced he was going to crash-land in a bumpy green field, particularly when he did so successfully and they discovered they were only a few hundred yards from Rutshire airfield. By then, Angus had received a text from Elijah saying a woken-up Eamonn and the people carrier would be along as soon as possible to bring them back the fourteen-odd miles to Deep Woods.

Having humped their luggage over to the airfield HQ, however, they were irritated to discover that the bar was closed.

'Hello, Mr Campbell-Black,' one of the airport officials hailed blond Orion, thinking he was Rupert. 'Any tips for the Guineas? Congrats on England beating Turkey today. Your car's in car park C.'

Turning to the rest of the party, Orion reported: 'Arsy-B's little yellow run-around is parked over there.

Why don't we take it, instead of waiting ages for Eamonn?'

'Yes, let's,' said Downing. 'It's one o'clock in the morning and I need another drink.'

'So do I,' said Marketa, 'and Rupert always leaves his keys behind the sun visor.'

'Won't Rupert need it when he gets back from Pakistan?' asked Wilfie.

'I don't think they're back till later tomorrow,' said Marketa. 'Taggie's so crazy about her new grandchild.'

'And we can always text Eamonn to wait for them,' said Orion.

So they all piled joyfully into Rupert's car, Orion driving, Downing in the passenger seat with Marketa sprawled on his knee, and Angus, Wilfie and Cadenza crowded in the back with their luggage crammed into every inch of space. Off they went, music blaring, shrieking with laughter, Cadenza leaning out of one of the open windows to take pictures of the occupants.

An ace driver, Orion was complaining that he was having great difficulty steering the car and that the brakes weren't great. This was not helped by Downing, who, with his arms round Marketa's splendid bosom, was trying to restrain her as she kept lurching sideways to kiss Orion, while he, Downing, simultaneously tried to read doting messages from his scores of girlfriends.

Wilfie, having checked on the evening's racing, was texting his mother, Mary: 'Can't wait to see you, Mum, coming back in Rupert's car, bringing Turkish shirt home for you.'

Angus was texting Mimi: 'Missed you babe, home around two-ish.' Then he switched his phone off and turned to Cadenza: 'Going to miss you, babe, but I'll try and get away as much as possible.'

'I'm going to miss you too,' said Cadenza, 'but my pics are going to turn you into the next England poster boy.'

'That's Jarred's house to the right,' shouted Orion as he hurtled out of Cirencester, 'which Arsy-B claims is called the Bungalow, because Jarred takes so many bungs.'

'We missed the after-party, so now we're having a laughter-party,' crowed Wilfie. 'Isn't this the best night ever?'

'People carrier's not arrived,' announced Ludo. 'So Angus says they've bloody cheekily nicked Rupert's yellow run-around and should be here very soon. We better warn Eamonn that he'll need to pick up Rupert and Taggie later instead.'

'What a beautiful night,' sighed Dora, breathing in the sweet scent of Etta's lilies of the valley as they went outside. 'The moon looks just like a silver football – we should engrave it with our four boys' names.'

'That sounds like them,' said Ludo, looking up, as a blast of loud music and revelry echoed round the valley, and a little car chugged along the top road, its white lights followed by its red tail lights, then disappeared behind a copse of trees covered in new spring leaves.

'Look, there's Deep Woods with the lights on. Bolly ahoy,' shouted Cadenza. 'Smile, stars of the future!'

They had reached a very sharp bend in the road. Lurching violently to the right to navigate it, Orion lost control before hitting the right-hand grass verge, then, despite frantically trying to straighten and slow the car down, finding the brakes weren't responding, he couldn't prevent it lurching back across the road and hitting the left-hand verge before ricocheting over it into a vast sycamore.

Instantly, a mighty crash rocked the valley, deafening, terrifying, trees crashing, windows smashing, fragments of car and debris flying everywhere, a vast cloud of smoke rising out of the wreckage as the fuel tank blew up, setting the surrounding desperately dry woods on fire.

Giving great bass-baritone barks, Buddyguard plunged off into the trees.

'Come back, wait for me,' screamed Dora.

But as she, Ludo and Elijah tore after Buddy, fighting their way up the wooded hill, tripping over fallen logs and bramble cables, desperate to rescue the passengers, they were beaten back as the entire woods ahead caught fire and became a towering inferno of flames.

'Buddy, where are you?' sobbed Dora.

'Come back.' Ludo grabbed her arm. 'I've rung nine-nine-nine; we've got to wait for the fire engines.'

'We must check if there's anyone alive.'

'It's too dangerous,' said Elijah, taking her other arm, pulling her away from the blaze. *It's my fault*, he thought in anguish. *I should never have persuaded Rupert to let them go.*

Next moment, two fire engines came roaring up, sirens blaring.

'Car's blown up,' yelled Ludo. 'You gotta try and rescue the passengers.'

'We'll do everything we can, but it's not looking good,'

shouted back a fireman, leaping out and recognising him instantly. 'It's not safe here, Ludo, fire's still raging. Get back to the club. Nothing more you can do.'

A heartbroken Elijah and Ludo, and a wildly weeping Dora and desperately worried Buddyguard with his fur singed, then retreated to Deep Woods, which was festooned inside with congratulatory posters and good-luck cards, plus a huge blow-up of Angus, Downing, Orion and Wilfie, ironically captioned: 'Godspeed to our four England stars.'

God goofed on that one, thought Ludo, tearing it down.

After an agonising wait, the fire brigade confirmed there were no survivors. Elijah, Ludo and Dora were then faced with the nightmare of telling everyone.

'We must wise up Rupert immediately,' said a stricken Elijah, 'and before anyone else does. His plane was due to land at Rutshire airfield sometime around dawn. If we alert air traffic control, they'll get word to him.'

'And they were having such a lovely time,' sobbed Dora, 'and now they are going to get this horrendous news, which will turn their world upside down. Oh, poor Rupert and Taggie. We must break it to the players' families before they hear it online.'

'I'd better drive over and tell Mary and Mimi,' said Ludo.

'That leaves Downing's parents, who live in Wiltshire,' said Elijah, who, to distract himself from the utter heartbreak, was making a list. 'Orion's father lives in London, but he's split up from Orion's mother, so we will need to tell them individually. Cadenza's got a lawyer boyfriend, Hughie Winston, who lives in Cheltenham.'

'And we've got to tell Marketa's family,' wailed Dora, who was tearing down good-luck cards, 'but they live in the Czech Republic, and I don't speak Czech.'

'We'd better ring Tember,' said Elijah. 'She's got everyone's numbers. She'll know what to do.'

For a blissful moment, Tember thought the surprise caller at 3.45 in the morning must be Griffy. When instead Elijah told her about the car crash and the deaths, she said she'd come in at once. Just pulling on an old yellow T-shirt and jeans, she didn't bother to shower, nor did she need to wash her face, as tears were streaming down it.

Outside, the moon had set, the stars were fading, cow parsley foamed along the verges as she drove. Oh, her poor darling boys.

Ludo, who was knocking back a large whiskey, greeted her with a hug.

'I'm so sorry to drag you into this, but if you could inform a few rellies and make sure Elijah's got through to Rupert, and we need to get on to Marketa's parents, but none of us speak Czech.'

'Josef could do that,' suggested Tember. 'He's in Prague on that international friendly against France. He'd be ideal, he's so kind.'

From a next-door office, they could hear wild sobbing as, clutching Buddyguard, Dora tried to compose a press release:

' "It is with infinite sadness that we have to announce that four of our greatest players . . ." Oh, I can't go on.'

'You'd better ring Paris,' Ludo told Tember, 'and tell him to come and take her home. She's only a baby.'

'Poor child,' wept Tember. 'God, isn't it awful.'

'Fucking awful,' said Ludo, 'and I've got to go and break it to Mary and Mimi.'

Mimi McLean, in her and Angus's cottage on the edge of Cotchester, was still up and dressed. She had finished marking her pupils' essays on their GCSE set text, *Macbeth*, which they disliked intensely, and Mimi was taking the opportunity to play her favourite Brahms symphony, which Angus disliked intensely, preferring jazz or pop music.

As her pupils were taking their exams in a few weeks, Mimi was now flipping through *Macbeth* itself, trying to find poetry to inspire them. The ones who had acne had liked the line: 'Out, damned spot.'

'Out, out, brief candle,' read Mimi. 'Life's but a walking shadow, a poor player that struts and frets his hour upon the stage, and then is heard no more' – which was so beautiful, although if Shakespeare were writing today, he'd probably have put 'rich player'.

In the past, she'd often dreaded Angus coming home, particularly if Searston had lost. He could be a terrible bully, short-fused and picking on her about everything. But since he'd been made captain, he'd cheered up so much, loved all the media attention and had been utterly ecstatic to be picked for England.

Mimi glanced at her watch. Heavens, he was late. She prayed he hadn't enjoyed being with glamorous Cadenza so much he'd decided not to come home. Cadenza had posted a lush picture of him from Istanbul, stripped to well below the waist, a strawberry-blond rinse softening his ginger hair.

As she gathered up her pupils' essays, Mimi smiled to remember how many of them had skipped an English lesson to cheer little Wilfie off when he left for Istanbul. A lovely selfie of them and him, appearing on the *Cotchester Times* website, hadn't amused Mimi's head-mistress. It was a pity they couldn't take Wilfie for GCSE rather than *Macbeth*.

Where on earth was Angus? He'd said he'd be back in an hour. Then, hearing a bang at the door, she hastily switched off Brahms.

Answering it, she found one of her favourite people. 'Ludo, I was expecting my hubby. Would you like a drink?'

'No, I'm fine, love.' She'd never known him to refuse one before and he wasn't his usual grinning self.

Perhaps Angus has run off with Cadenza, she thought with a lurch of fear.

Following her into the sitting room, which was lined with books, Ludo patted the sofa and drew her down beside him.

'Mimi, I'm so sorry, there's been an accident. The Galloper bringing back Angus and the rest of the lads was playing up, so the pilot landed at Rutshire, and your boys transferred to Rupert's little yellow run-around, which crashed on the road above Deep Woods and set the woods on fire. We tried to rescue them, but it appears there were no survivors.'

There was a long pause.

'Survivors?' yelped a bewildered Mimi. 'Angus texted me he was nearly home; he sounded so happy. You mean my Angus is dead?'

Ludo took a deep breath. 'Yes. The fire brigade con-firmed that none of the crash victims were found alive.'

' "Out, out, brief candle," ' intoned Mimi. ' "Life's but a walking shadow, a poor player that struts and frets his hour upon the stage, and then is heard no more." '

For a second, she gave a hysterical laugh, then her sweet, gentle face was consumed with rage.

'And bloody Rupert insisted they flew home before the rest of the team. He's murdered my Angus.' She burst into such a flood of weeping that Ludo put his arms around her.

She was still so distraught that he called Shelagh to come over and comfort her, because he still had to break the news to Mary.

Having moved out of the Shakespeare Estate, Mary now lived in a block of flats near Cotchester railway station. On the front door, she had pinned a big picture of Wilfie, and underneath had painted: 'Welcome Home International England Star Wilfie Bradford, the Great Assister.' From inside, but not loud enough to keep the neighbours awake, drifted the *Black Beauty* music.

'Oh God, poor little Mary,' groaned Ludo, banging on the door. Instantly, she opened it.

'Wilfie, love, what took you so long? I was so worried.'

She was still dressed in jeans and an old darned grey jersey, but with her short red hair, which she cut herself, all tousled, Ludo thought how pretty she looked.

'Ludo,' she cried, 'how nice to see you! Didn't our boys play well? I thought you were Wilfie. He texted ages ago saying he was bringing me back a Turkish shirt. I thought he might be hungry so I made him some chicken soup – would you like some?' Then, when he shook his head, she was about to offer him a drink, but remembered that Dougie, on his last visit, had drunk it all.

She led Ludo into the kitchen, which was attached to the sitting room, where, on the back of an ancient sofa, a duvet cover and pillows lay folded – waiting for dastardly Dougie, thought Ludo. All over the walls were photos of Wilfie, and his younger brother and sister as well – Mary was always anxious not to favour anyone – and on every shelf, brightly polished cups and medals shone like stars. On the table was yesterday's *Sun*, from which Mary was cutting out a photo of the four Searston boys and a forecast of the match with a big headline: 'Go and Roast Turkey, England.'

'They didn't expect to win by so much,' she told Ludo proudly. Then, seeing how tired he looked: 'Are you sure you wouldn't like a cup of tea?'

'Sit down,' said Ludo, taking her little hands in his huge ones. 'I'm afraid it's bad news.' And he set off on his tragic preamble again. 'The Galloper was playing up, so the players landed at Rutshire airfield and trans-ferred to Rupert's little yellow run-around.'

'I know, Wilfie texted me.'

'But it crashed and caught fire on the way home, and set the surrounding woods on fire. We tried to rescue them, but the blaze took over and, according to the fire brigade, there aren't any survivors.'

'You mean my Wilfie's dead?' whispered Mary. 'My Wilfie, my little lad.' Her head fell back, her mouth open as she let out howl after howl.

'Oh, my poor child,' said Ludo, pulling her into his arms.

57

By dawn, firefighters had finally put out the blaze and a helicopter circled overhead, assessing the damage. The police had set a perimeter security cordon around the area; forensics had taken over, trying to piece together any body parts and car wreckage to find out what had happened.

At 6.30 a.m., having been alerted mid-flight, Rupert and Taggie flew in from Pakistan bearing photographs of their first adorable grandchild, Liyana, which Taggie had been so longing to show everyone. Instead, they had to face up to the crash.

At midday, an utterly devastated, grey-faced Rupert, still wearing the dark-blue checked shirt and light-brown cords he'd flown home in, was giving a press conference on the pitch at Searston, which was already filling up with distraught fans and bunches of flowers. He had tried to persuade Taggie to stay away. She'd been in such floods of tears and he felt she should catch up on some rest after such a long flight, but she'd insisted on accompanying him and now stood in the background, her arms around a stricken Mary.

Among the police presence, to Rupert's fury, was the Chief C-word, Lloyd Dudsbridge, flanked by Sir Craig Eynsham in a black tie and black homburg and Lady Grace in a black dress, 'sorry for your loss'-ing around, all keen to show their caring and compassionate face to the media and the bereaved.

Rupert then slowly read out the list of the players who had died: Angus, Orion, Downing and Wilfie, as well as Cadenza Westerham, a press photographer, and Marketa Melnik, one of his stable lasses.

'They were all marvellously talented,' repeated Rupert, 'and we have absolutely no idea what caused the crash.'

'Why did your players come home before the rest of the team?' asked the *Telegraph*.

'To rest them before a crucial match on Saturday.'

'Feral Jackson, your star player and your daughter's partner, was selected for England but didn't go,' shouted ITV.

'He was injured.'

'He trained for three hours yesterday,' accused *The Times*.

'He must have recovered.' As an ever-increasing pack of media closed in on him, and all around relations and fans were sobbing so loudly, Rupert was having difficulty making himself heard.

'Was it normal, having women travelling with them on the plane?' asked the *Sun*.

'Cadenza was a brilliant photographer who wanted a scoop and who'd already posted some incredible pictures. Marketa was engaged to Orion Onslow and boarded the plane at Heathrow because she wanted to travel home with him,' explained Rupert.

'Why were your players travelling in your car, when they'd left Istanbul to fly home to Deep Woods in the Galloper?' shouted the BBC.

'Because the pilot reported the plane wasn't quite right and managed to bring it down near Rutshire airfield, so they transferred to my car, which was parked there.'

'And then what happened?'

'I honestly don't know. The emergency services have appealed to anyone with any information to come forward. Skid marks on the road suggest the driver lost control of the car before it hit a huge tree and burst into flames.'

Dolphy, meanwhile, was still injured and very sad that Elijah hadn't been in touch since he'd bollocked him for going out drinking with Paris. Perhaps he had gone to Istanbul to watch the Searston players.

After a long lie-in, driving into Searston for rehab, Dolphy first heard about the crash when he turned on his car radio. In the breaking news that followed, the newsreader wasn't sure who'd been in the car, which was bringing back the Searston Premier League players from an international friendly, but a report claimed there were no survivors.

Dolphy gave a scream of horror. Could Elijah have been in the car?

Police cars were streaming past him towards the club. A single magpie for sorrow flew across the road. *Elijah's gone up to heaven in a chariot of fire.*

Screeching into the car park, Dolphy hobbled on to the pitch and suddenly spotted Rupert and Elijah, a tiny island in a growing ocean of press and public.

Bursting into tears, trampling on flowers, Dolphy pummelled his way through reporters, sending cameras flying. Then crying, 'Oh Elijah, Elijah, I fort you was dead and I love you so much,' he took Elijah in his arms and kissed the life out of him.

'It's OK,' stammered Elijah, appalled to be momentarily so ecstatically happy in the middle of such a horrific nightmare.

Dolphy collapsed sobbing on his shoulder.

'I can't live wivout you, I fort you was dead.'

'That's enough, Dolphy,' said Rupert, prising him off, giving him a hug and handing him a handkerchief.

'Stop now, leave him alone,' he snarled at the paparazzi, who clamoured to ask Elijah if he'd been shagging Dolphy.

'Going to call the match off tomorrow, Rupert?' asked Sky.

'No, we must play it to honour our players who died.'

Such was Rupert's superhuman courage and determination to stay strong for everyone that he managed not to break down and later insisted on taking Dolphy home with him, although Elijah desperately wanted to, because Rupert felt Taggie would be infinitely better at comforting Dolphy than Madison.

Later that night, after a sobbing Dolphy had finally fallen asleep, Taggie returned to her and Rupert's bedroom and found a stony-faced, still-dressed Rupert gazing out of the window.

'Oh, Tag.' His voice broke. 'If I'd let them come home with the rest of the team, they'd still be alive now.'

'You only did it,' cried Taggie, 'because we must win tomorrow, because we so desperately need the gate receipts to save our club and our players' jobs.' Then she put her arms around him. 'It's not your fault, darling. Please come to bed.'

Despite his utter anguish, Rupert was so touched that Taggie referred to Searston as 'our club'.

58

Next day, however, the press was murderous, 'The Don't Comeback Kids' appearing in every headline.

Terrible messages, including endless death threats, were posted on social media, particularly by Angus McLean's normally sweet and gentle wife, Mimi.

'You're a bastard, Rupert, forcing the players to fly home in that grotty little plane, just to satisfy your lust for silverware, but saving your future son-in-law Feral Jackson by stressing a minor injury diagnosed by a private doctor, and the boys we love will never come home again.'

Dougie Bradford gave an interview to the BBC, bursting into tears and wailing:

'I've lost my beloved son Wilfie; he was on the way to being one of England's greatest players.'

'Bastard's only upset because he's lost his cash cow,' stormed Laddy Heywood, who was very fond of Wilfie, particularly after he'd provided him with that brilliant assist in Istanbul.

'I Thought You Was Dead' was also headlining every paper, accompanied by pictures of Dolphy kissing Elijah and emphasising the huge difference in their ages, the *Sun* even pointing out that Elijah lived at 'Buttock-Up Cottage'.

The outrage at such a display of unbridled passion in the middle of such an appalling tragedy was so great that Rupert told Dolphy and Elijah to stay apart for the moment.

'Rupert wouldn't worry about Elijah getting off with Dolphy,' announced Janey Lloyd-Foxe on *Loose Women*. 'He's always regarded failure as a much worse crime than sodomy. Look at his own son Marcus, who lives with his husband in Russia!'

Dolphy was insane with rage and, forgetting he mustn't talk to the press, told the *Daily Mirror* when they rang:

'How dare you accuse Elijah of being a paedo? I was dumped by my muvver so I've no idea when my birfday is, so I might easily be a lot older than Elijah. And he's never laid a finger on me or any of the uvver players. He's a farver figure to all of us. It was me wot laid a finger on him because I fort he was dead.'

This of course went viral, with pictures of schoolboy Dolphy with his 'younger' boyfriend, Elijah.

Tember was devastated. Who had put the vase of May in the Boardroom? So many of her beloved boys had gone, and it had been agonising trying to console their bewildered and equally devastated parents.

Against her will, she was avoiding Griffy, although she longed for them to comfort each other. But if he had opted to stay with Inez, she must accept it.

Nor could she bear all the flowers covering the pitch dying from lack of water, and wept when she saw Dolphy going round with a watering can.

*

Jarred, meanwhile, had been feeding poison to the media – so Rupert, for ruthlessly flying his boys home for a big game, and Elijah, for seducing Dolphy, were billed everywhere as the most detested men in football. *The Times* quoted Giraudoux:

'One of the privileges of the great is to watch catastrophes from a terrace.'

Many of the press reprinted Jarred's anonymously posted photo of a cardboard effigy of Rupert hanging from a gibbet near the statue of Charles I and his horse in the market square at Cotchester. An incandescent Eamonn stormed into town, tugged it down and shredded it back at Penscombe before Taggie had a chance to see it.

An even more devastating moment for Rupert was when a forensic scientist from the Crash Investigation Unit turned up at Penscombe to report on the latest findings. 'We've found and analysed the wreckage of your car. It seems the steering and the brakes had been tampered with, and the fuel tank punctured; someone clearly wanted to take you out. Seeing Orion with his hair dyed your colour, the official at Rutshire airfield must have thought he was you and directed him and the players to your car. We're determined to find out who's responsible.'

A horrified and utterly shattered Rupert then had to deal with both the guilt and the sadness as the enormity of what had happened sank in.

Despite Ghengis Tong, incensed about the terrible publicity afforded the Green Galloper, demanding his loan back, Rupert, in a blind fury, decided to sell the Stubbs and pledged £6 million to the dependants of each of the people who had died.

'That's nothing,' scoffed Caring Sir Craig. 'He can flog Feral Jackson for that in the next transfer window.'

Wilfie's father, Dougie, however, got very excited. Six million would buy him a very nice property in the Golden Triangle.

With the paps lurking everywhere, Dolphy and Elijah were obeying Rupert's orders to stay well apart. Although Dolphy was staying at Penscombe and being cossetted by Taggie, he cried himself to sleep every night thinking of his lost comrades 'burning to deaf'. He was also devastated he had tarnished Elijah's career. 'I only ran up and kissed him because I was so fankful he was alive.'

'You did it the wrong way,' chided Bastian. 'If you're going to come out, do it on *Soccer Saturday* or *Match of the Day* for maximum effect. When I finish my *Hauteur Biography*, I might come out for the hardback and go back in for the paperback.'

Madison, predictably, gave a huge interview to the *Guardian*, exuding righteous indignation.

'I've never felt truly loved or desired over the years. Now I know why.'

At Buttercup Cottage, she was giving Elijah hell, drinking, shouting, tearing up happy family snaps and his precious football photographs, hurling the silver football he'd won as manager into the red wallflowers and geraniums outside.

'Did you ever love me, or did you just marry me to appear straight? You've wrecked our family, and the poor kids are being crucified at school. They'll be too traumatised to go in, which'll screw Isaiah's GCSEs, and what's it going to do to my political career? Nothing wrong with being gay, it's you living a lie that matters. How long have you been shagging Dolphy?'

'I haven't,' shouted Elijah, 'he's just one of my players. Don't!' he cried as Madison tugged another framed photograph of him and the team off the kitchen wall and smashed it on the edge of the table.

'I can't leave you,' she yelled, filling up her glass again, 'because I've got nowhere to take myself and the kids. Now your star players have gone, you're not going to win any silverware and get a fat bonus, so we can't buy that flat in town. The only thing I can flog is my wedding ring.'

It was even worse comforting the children:

'You know pupils get crushes on senior pupils and teachers? Well, Dolphy doesn't have a family, so Rupert and I are sort of like parents to him, and he was terrified we'd been killed in the car crash.'

'Trolls called Dolphy a "catamite, or rather a Carter-mite". That's evidently a boy kept by an older man as a sexual partner. Do you love him, Dad?' asked Naomi.

'I love all my players. Dolph's a sweet boy, he just needs a family,' protested Elijah, thinking: *Oh God, should I level with them and confess I'm gay?*

He also felt shy around his players; he'd always hugged them to show his appreciation and wandered into the showers to chat to them. Now he noticed them hastily covering their nether regions with towels.

Worst of all, he felt responsible for the tragedy. Rupert may have insisted his players flew straight home in the Galloper, but it was he, Elijah, who had pestered a reluctant Rupert to let them go to Turkey in the first place.

But he still had to carry on managing, desperately trying to comfort and keep up their spirits. Ironically, because he'd been so focused on camaraderie, persuading the players to support and like each other, reserving their animosity for the opposition, they were now more devastated by the loss of their comrades, even Angus, about whom Ahmed was heartbroken that his protector was no more. The glamour boys, Downing and Orion, had gone, so Elijah had lost two brilliant strikers, as well as little Wilfie, who could shimmy through any defence.

Back at Penscombe, Feral was also feeling desperately guilty for not being in the car, yelling at Rupert:

'You and James Benson shouldn't have exaggerated my injury.'

'Don't be ungrateful,' shouted back Bianca. 'Dad saved your life.'

Bianca, on the other hand, couldn't help feeling jealous of Rupert and Taggie staying on longer in Pakistan because they'd been having such a lovely time with her brother, Xav, his wife, Aysha, and baby Liyana, particularly when she found photographs in Taggie's handbag.

Due to have her baby in June, Bianca, being tiny, was not only scared about the birth, but couldn't get comfortable in bed at night, and with the baby kicking around – 'He's clearly going to be a footballer like you' – she had to keep getting up for a pee. None of this helped Feral get any sleep, when, as best player, he needed to carry the team.

Despite his pledge, Rupert had called off the match on Saturday – the players simply weren't up to it – so Searston were in danger of not qualifying for next year's Champions League.

He and Elijah also had to decide who was going to captain the side. Griffy was back with Inez, looking hollow-eyed, exhausted and utterly suicidal. It would be hard for Pitt Bully, stuck in goal at one end of the pitch. Midas lacked authority. The only answer was Parks, who had been playing for the Reserves but was overjoyed to be asked back. Alas, this meant the return of Rosalie, giving captain's lady interviews outside her boutique, saying it was so good that her husband, Parks, had returned to restore grace and dignity to the team. Then, seeing Mimi McLean in Cotchester High Street, Rosalie promptly told her she'd been so upset to see the picture of Angus, naked in bed except for his captain's armband, which Cadenza had posted from Istanbul.

'But at least it must make you feel more able to accept his loss, Mimi.'

Whereupon gentle Mimi yelled at Rosalie to shut up.

Poor, heartbroken Mary, although utterly crucified by her son Wilfie's death, had to carry on working for Rosalie because Dougie insisted they needed the money, while he carried on getting bungs for interviews about being Wilfie's desperately grieving dad.

Almost as devastated as Mary was Lou-Easy. Not only had she lost Marketa, her best friend, with whom she'd shared so many laughs and lovers, but also the love of her life, Orion, her knight in shining Armani. She could imagine him up in heaven, wowing the angels, selling sustainable jeans to the Holy Ghost, and asking God to sponsor him.

To make matters worse, she had to comfort poor Safety Car who, desolate without Marketa, whinnied for her constantly, while little The Story So Far still waited hopefully for Wilfie and his carrots every morning. Lou-Easy was also upset by numerous reports that Josef had played so brilliantly for the Czech Republic against

France that several big European clubs were keen to buy him in the summer transfer window. After Saturday's Premier League match was cancelled, he still hadn't returned to Searston.

'He's so good-hearted, he's evidently staying with Marketa's parents to comfort them,' said Shelagh.

I want him here to comfort me, thought Lou-Easy.

But who was behind the fatal and clearly premeditated crash? Could it be someone who had seen Cadenza's photographs from Istanbul of Orion with Rupert's hairstyle, assumed Rupert was on the Galloper or in his yellow run-around when the players transferred to it, and somehow sabotaged both plane and car? Or could it be someone who wanted to destroy Team Searston? Or was it some desperado craving everlasting notoriety? But no one came forward to claim responsibility.

Unimaginable horrors had been found, like one of Cadenza's charred legs in a thick tangle of undergrowth. But until such body parts were released by the police, there could be no burial.

Sir Craig Eynsham, however, appeared delighted by events, urging Jarred to keep up the malevolence on social media. He was sure Rupert had engineered the boars digging up the pitch and 'Eynshambolic' being painted across the stands at Deansgate. The beastly little Green Galloper, which, as a flying taxi, had been in direct competition with Craig's electric Battery Ram, would be stigmatised for having been unable to complete the journey from Istanbul, not only destroying the planet with carbon emissions but six humans as well.

Above all, Craig resented Rupert's contempt and Dora's constant mockery. Infernal Dora, who had stolen

Buddyguard and still had the 'Boobs in the Woods' photo of Craig shagging Janey Lloyd-Foxe. Her latest jibe in the *Cotchester Times*, before the crash, had claimed that the climbing frame which Lady Grace had had built in the garden for visiting grandchildren was really for social climbing.

The Chief Constable seemed equally delighted Rupert was being stigmatised. He'd never forgiven him for nicknaming his son Lyall 'Lout', and for telling *The Times* that the reason Deansgate were falling behind was because they had to expend so much energy feeding the ball to 'Lout', so he could hit the woodwork.

Caring Sir Craig finally took every opportunity to express sympathy to those mourning lost loved ones, even putting up a huge poster of himself surrounded by Deansgate players, saying:

'Dear Searston, your Cotswold neighbours are so sorry for your loss.'

'That was made by the same people who created Rupert hanging from a cardboard gibbet,' stormed Dora. 'We've got to get them.'

59

Searston had four games to come, starting with a penultimate Premier League match against a Wiltshire team facing relegation. As half the Searston players still didn't feel up to starting, the Wiltshire team were delighted to win 3–0 and take the three points. This meant Searston dropped more places and were the victims of more mauling by the media.

This still left a final Premier League game and two other colossal matches: this year's Champions League final in St Petersburg at the end of the month, and the FA Cup final next Saturday, 15 May, at Wembley against a very tough northern side – Cumber West, known as the Westies, with a little white West Highland terrier as their mascot.

Elijah was in despair. How could he protect his boys from mass humiliation?

'For a start,' said Rupert, 'anyone not injured must bloody well play. I know it's hard for them – for us all – but it's the only way to restore morale, and we owe it to the fans.'

*

Dora, utterly fed up with Searston – and particularly Rupert and Elijah – being so vilified for destroying their players' lives, had defended them on Instagram.

'Rupert Campbell-Black,' she wrote, 'is a wonderful family man, and he and his wife, Taggie, have recently returned from Pakistan, where they were visiting their son, Xav, and Xav's wife, Aysha, and meeting their new granddaughter, Liyana.'

The piece then included pictures, pinched from Taggie, of the whole family, including one of a beaming Rupert holding adorable Liyana.

'Rupert and Elijah Cohen,' continued Dora, 'have transported little Searston Rovers from near-relegation in League One to the top of the Premier League in three seasons, in a miraculous climb which has brought both wealth and glory to the Cotswolds. Finally, Rupert has nearly bankrupted himself, offering millions to the dependants of the six people who tragically died when his car crashed and blew up returning from Istanbul. So please give him, Elijah Cohen and Searston Rovers all your support in the FA Cup final this afternoon.'

'Great stuff, Dora, but did Rupert know you were posting this?' asked her editor, Jackie Carslake.

'No, of course not. But we've got to stop Caring Sir Craig, the Chief C-word and Jarred demonising Searston.'

Team Searston, edgy about all the death threats, and fearful that the mystery saboteur, who had not been identified, might strike again, travelled up to Wembley on the club coach, dropping to the floor in a panic when a nearby car backfired.

*

Among the team were Parks, back as captain, Griffy and Midas, plus Ahmed and Ezra, who'd all pulled themselves together and been vastly cheered by fan letters and sympathy gifts pouring in.

Also on the coach were Galgo, who'd carried on training and going on long runs, and Josef, back from the Czech Republic after reaching stardom in the game against France. He'd also had a haircut and chucked away his Alice band, so light-brown curls fell becomingly around his face.

'Suits you, Josef,' said Bastian, who had dyed his hair black in sympathy, and was busy scribbling his *Hauteur Biography* on the coach. ' "Wembley Again" – should be a good chapter,' he went on. 'The last time we played there we went up to the Championship and Angus and Wilfie were in the team.'

'Shut up, Bastian,' snapped Griffy. 'Don't upset the lads, reminding them.'

Dolphy, sitting by himself, was already panicking he might betray his love, particularly as Barry Pitt had warned him: 'The paps will be everywhere, so don't go snogging Elijah.'

Behind Dolphy were Mattie and Rollo, two young players from the Academy, wildly excited to be on the bench with a chance of being brought on.

And finally there was Feral, dozing after a sleepless night, worrying that the team depended on him, the one star striker, to get them out of trouble. But just as the coach reached Swindon and was swinging on to the motorway, he was woken by a call from Taggie.

'Bianca's gone into labour. James Benson and the midwives will be here in a minute.'

'That's a mumf early. Is Bianca OK? Lemme talk to her.'

'Please, please come back, Fer,' sobbed Bianca. 'I need you. I can't go through this without you. Please, please.'

'Don't worry, babe,' soothed Feral. 'You'll be fine. I'll come straight back. I love you.'

Taggie then took back the telephone.

'I'm so sorry, Feral. Eamonn can collect you in the chopper from Swindon.'

So Feral then rang Rupert, who was in the yard checking horses going off to Doncaster and Newmarket.

'Sorry, Rupe, but I must be wiv her.'

Oh bugger, thought Rupert, but said: 'Of course you must, but when the chopper drops you off at Penscombe, make sure it brings Safety Car back up to Wembley to replace you. All the luck to you and Bianca. Keep me posted.'

But as the Searston coach trundled on past cherry trees in white and pink blossom, and new green leaves silvered by a shower of rain, spirits plummeted and the players were reminded once again of the comrades they had lost.

'We're in peril without Feral,' sighed Midas, glancing at his iPad. 'Cumber West are five-to-one to win now. Lucky buggers came up yesterday afternoon, stayed at the Hilton and had a nice walk along the river after breakfast, so they'll be well prepared.'

Bastian put down his pen and burst into beautiful song:

' "Abide with me, fast falls the eventide, The darkness deepens Lord, with me abide. When other helpers (like Feral Jackson) fail and comforts flee, Help of the helpless, oh, abide with me." They always sing "Abide With Me",' he explained to the bemused foreign players, 'before kick-off at FA Cup finals.'

'Who wrote it?' asked Griffy.

'Some Scottish Anglican minister called Henry Lyte. He was dying of TB, poor sod. They used to play "Alexander's Ragtime Band" at Cup finals, then, in 1927, they switched to "Abide With Me", because it was King George's favourite hymn.'

Elijah's my favourite him, thought Dolphy longingly. *And I'd so love to be* his *favourite him. I* must *remember not to hug him.*

'There's the Wembley arch rising out of the trees,' said Griffy, sitting down beside Dolphy. 'How are you getting on at Penscombe?'

'It's fine. Taggie's the kindest person in the world, and Grandkid loves all the other dogs.'

Then Griffy couldn't resist asking:

'Do you ever see Tember there?'

'Sadly no,' sighed Dolphy. 'She's the second kindest person in the world. I really miss her.'

Oh God, so do I, thought Griffy.

Sitting behind them, Josef was tempted to ask Dolphy if he ever saw Lou-Easy down at the yard at Penscombe. She'd be at the races today. He was flipping through emails from his agent listing the several European clubs who were really keen on buying him – very gratifying. If he left Searston, it might be the one way to get over Lou-Easy.

Still trying to improve his English, he had picked out a book of poems from the shelves at the Shaggery and, finding one called 'Love in the Valley', read:

She whom I love is hard to catch and conquer,
Hard, but O the glory of the winning were she won!

Said it all, really. He'd so much rather win Lou-Easy than the FA Cup.

Although most of the Searston players were too nervous to eat much lunch, they were thrilled to go into their dressing room and find all their kit laid out, including new blue-and-green-striped shirts, each adorned by their name and a badge saying 'FA Cup Wembley'.

Outside on the vast pitch, newly watered and smooth as green suede, lay the crests of each team, like two vast table mats, with Searston's galloping horse on the left and Cumber's perky little West Highland terrier on the right.

'That dog will have trouble keeping up with our horse,' said Bastian.

Already the red Wembley seats were filling up, a block of Cumber West fans in yellow like a great slab of butter, and Searston followers in a sea-green sweep where the blue stripes merged with the green. All around, wives and girlfriends, who'd come along to support the Searston players mourning for their lost comrades, and to catch a glimpse of Rupert, were going 'Aaaaaaahhhh,' as they discovered the photo of him and Liyana on their iPhones. They were also intrigued to see Mimi McLean had rolled up with Cadenza's lawyer boyfriend, Hughie Winston; they'd been comforting each other.

Quite incongruously, in the face of so much tragedy, Rupert, who'd flown up to Wembley in his helicopter, was now hiding in the gents, checking up on Bianca, who was still in labour, and watching his horses running at Newmarket on his iPhone. He was hiding because he'd just caught sight of a vast blonde with an enormous bosom jumping out of a Rolls-Royce and being greeted by FA Cup dignitaries. It was opera singer Dame Hermione Harefield.

'She's a monster,' announced Rupert, when Elijah tracked him down. 'She joined the hunt to gatecrash my sixtieth birthday party. She's a nympho who's been trying to shag me for centuries.'

'She's got a great voice – she's come to sing "Abide With Me".'

'In bed with me, more likely.'

'We'll avoid her if we creep round the back. I need you to wish the lads good luck. Please, Rupert. They're going on soon and they're terribly uptight and sad to be reminded of Orion and co. the last time they were here.'

Oh, so am I, thought Rupert.

Rupert revved Searston up, telling them all would be fine, and they must honour the players who had died. 'I know how tough it's been and still is. But I want you to go out there with your heads held high and do it for those who can't any more – I know you've got it in you.' Just as he finished speaking, an ear-splitting burst of song made them all jump. On the edge of the pitch, with conductor, choir and the band of the Royal Gurkhas, Dame Hermione had launched into 'Abide With Me'.

'Christ, she'd wake the dead,' gasped Midas.

'Pity she can't,' sighed Ahmed, thinking of Angus.

'Come on, fifteen minutes to kick-off,' said Elijah. 'Remember what Rupert just said. We believe in you. And don't forget: look around and think before you kick.'

The huge FA Cup glittered silver and glorious on its plinth as the players ran out.

On such a hot, muggy day, it was hard to tell if the

Searston players were sweating or crying as, all wearing black armbands, they lined up with three refs in red between them and the Cumber West players. Then, after a minute's silence, with both sides standing round the centre circle, to remember the dead, pictures of Angus, Orion, Downing and Wilfie came up on the big screen and all the crowd clapped and cheered their heads off.

'Man up,' shouted Parks. 'It's going to be OK.'

But, from then on, it was carnage, with Cumber West breezing through Searston's defence as though it didn't exist, yet providing a defence of their own so impenetrable that Searston couldn't find a single gap. Barry Pitt, unable to see where any ball was coming from, let in goal after goal. The rare moments Searston captured the ball, Cumber took it off them, contemptuously passing back and forth to each other.

Fans on both sides who'd come a long way to see an exciting match were booing from boredom. All the noise was coming from the Cumber West supporters, who were constantly drumming and singing 'Poor Prince Charmless'. On the rare occasions Galgo or Josef made long-distance crosses, there were no strikers to take them into goal.

At half-time, Cumber West were 6–0 up.

'Oh God,' said Josef to Galgo, 'Mr Rupert is going to murder us.'

But as Rupert was walking towards the dressing room to administer a rocket, Dame Hermione emerged from the Royal Suite and, seeing Rupert, cried:

'There's Rupert Campbell-Black, my favourite poster boy.'

So Rupert fled back to the gents, leaving any pep-talking to Elijah.

In the Cumber West dressing room, the manager was saying he felt almost embarrassed to be so ruthlessly ahead: 'But well done, you completely outplayed them. They ought to be called Tortoises rather than Gallopers.'

The pundits were ruthlessly dismissive.

'It's a bloodbath. Searston are useless – they couldn't even pass the parcel, and their defending is shocking,' pronounced footballing icon Alan Shearer. 'The record win in any cup final is seven–nil, and Cumber might just be on track to break it.'

'That's monstrously unfair,' snapped Ludo. 'They're heartbroken they've lost their three star strikers as well as their captain. Angus dominated the midfield, but he also told the players exactly what to do. Don't forget what Searston has done this season, easily winning all their matches in the FA Cup, nearing the top of the Premier League and off to the Champions League final in a fortnight. Finally, their most powerful striker, Feral Jackson, opted out because of some family matter – so it's no wonder they're being annihilated.'

'Why don't you put on a blue-and-green shirt and pop down on to the pitch and help them out, Ludo,' reproved anchorman Gary Lineker, 'or acknowledge Cumber are playing rather well?'

'Good old Ludo,' said the Searston players, who'd been watching him from the dressing room. 'We've got one fan.'

Expecting a bollocking from Rupert, they were relieved that only Elijah came in and reassured them: 'I know you're trying your best. It's so hard to adjust when so many players have gone. But, as Rupert exhorted you, we must honour their memory.'

In the corner, he could see a huddled Dolphy trying not to cry and longed to comfort him.

'You've played your hearts out, Griffy and Parks, but it's such a boiling day, I don't want to risk you having heart attacks – I need you for St Petersburg. So I'm going to give the lads from the Academy a chance and give you that captain's armband, Pittsy.'

'You sure?' said Barry Pitt. 'If I let in any more goals, we'll have the dirtiest sheet in history.'

'Quite sure. Now go out and play your socks off.'

As they set off, Elijah sent up a prayer from *Henry V*:

'Oh God of battles, steel my soldiers' hearts; possess them not with fear.'

60

In the second half, Searston answered Elijah's prayers. Galgo received a pass from Bastian and, spotting Josef racing ahead, curled a beautiful ball in front of him, whereupon Josef picked it up with his left foot, flicked it on to his right foot and, a few yards from the goal line, at the tightest of angles, caressed it into goal with his left.

So the score was 6–1, and not a record any more.

Nothing cheers a desperately losing side more than a goal. Searston fans bellowed and burst into song. Drums thundered as the players fell on Josef. Seeing the delight on his manager's face, Dolphy thought, *I want to delight Elijah.*

'Don't think you're going to get your hands on that trophy,' sneered a Cumber forward, edging towards goal with Barry Pitt howling at his defenders to protect him. As the sneering forward let loose an Exocet, a flying Barry stopped it and, before Cumber could regroup, pounded up the field, like Charm's 'knayfe through butter', and, with massive might, nutmegged the smug Cumber goalie, belting the ball between his legs and straight into the net, shouting: 'I hope that got you in the balls, you bastard.'

Somehow, Searston continued to keep Cumber at bay, even the two little Academy players getting a few touches, until the board, announcing four minutes' stoppage time, went up.

'Come on, let's make it seven,' yelled the Cumber captain.

'No, you can't,' screamed Dolphy. Removing the ball with a sliding tackle from the sneering forward, he swung round, dancing down the pitch like a gazelle. Seeing two brutally roaring Cumber defenders closing in on him, he chipped it over their heads to a hurtling-down Galgo, whose running every day had paid off as he gathered up the ball and, with a long greyhound paw, flipped it into the net.

'Go Galgo, go Galgo, go Galgo, go go go,' yelled the Searston fans, as the full-time whistle blew. And Galgo was made Man of the Match.

Immediately, Rupert emerged from a corner of the stands, where he'd been hiding from Dame Hermione, and ran down on to the pitch, hugging each of his players, telling them they were effing marvellous, shaking hands with the opposition, then hugging Elijah.

'You're a bloody marvel! We'd have been seven–six up if we'd had another half-hour.'

'It was more difficult than the score suggests,' admitted the Cumber West manager, who was delighted to win some silverware – as were the overjoyed Cumber fans, who, lighting red flares everywhere, had turned Wembley into an inferno.

'They played their broken hearts out,' Rupert was telling the cameras. 'I'm so proud of my boys. When you think what they've been through in the last fortnight, losing teammates to whom they were devoted, but they lit up the second half this afternoon.'

'Where's Feral Jackson?' asked the *Guardian*. 'We're told he had to withdraw because of some family crisis.'

Rupert's telephone rang.

'Excuse me if I take this.' Then he said, 'Great, that's really great. I'll ring you back in five minutes, that's fantastic.'

'What's happened to Feral Jackson?' persisted the *Mirror*. 'Is he still injured?'

'No, he's just become a father,' grinned Rupert. 'My daughter Bianca, his partner, has just given birth to a boy, who's going to be called Teddy.' And everyone cheered.

'Are you going to pay Teddy appearance money?' joked the *Mirror*.

'As Teddy's a Saturday's child,' called out Alyson Rudd from the *Sunday Times*, 'he'll have to work hard for his living.'

'He'll jolly well need to,' cracked back Rupert, 'to keep Searston solvent and keep his mother in designer gear.'

'And you've become a grandpa again, Rupert,' called out the *Sun*. 'Your son Xav's just become a father, too; his wife's had a baby girl. I've just seen a picture of her and you on Instagram.'

'You did,' answered Rupert. 'She's called Liyana. And Teddy can take her to dances when they grow up. Will that do?'

And the press laughed and gave him a round of applause.

*

Normally the supporters of losing teams slope off, but the Searston fans were so proud that they stayed on. And the whole of Wembley gave the team a standing O when they went to collect their losers' medals and shake hands with Prince William.

'How was it for you?' asked talkSPORT, noticing how long Dolphy had held up the queue chatting to the prince.

'Oh, he seems a nice bloke. He said, "Well played, Dolphy," and he knew Grandkid's Christian name and wanted to know all about him. So I told him about Grandkid shoving his head into hedges for so long looking for rabbits that I call him a hedge fun manager. Prince William liked that. I can't wait to tell Grandkid.'

Rupert was on the telephone to Taggie, who, although rejoicing over the birth, was telling him how gruelling it had been. 'Poor little Bianca. Thank goodness Feral was there. He was marvellous, and so thrilled to be a dad. So lovely to see them so in love. They've named Teddy after you: Rupert Edward Algernon. They thought Teddy was nicer than Algy, and he's so adorable.'

'So are you. I'll be home soon; the lads are going to have a bit of a party at the pub when they get back.'

When they returned, Searston were amazed to find fans lining the streets of Cotchester, cheering them home.

Earlier, the Wags had travelled up to Wembley in a small team coach, with Rosalie Parkinson wearing a huge blue-and-green hat from her boutique.

'People sitting behind her won't be able to see a thing,' grumbled Daffodil.

Charm had made sandwiches for everyone, but Rosalie said she was too devastated by the deaths of all the players and Cadenza and Marketa and too nervous about the game to eat anything on the way up.

'People always worry that I'm too highly strung to partake.'

On the journey home, however, having told the media how her captain husband had taken charge of and transformed Searston, she asked:

'Have you still got any of those sarnies, Charm?'

'Yes, they're still here with your name on your special packet, Rosalie,' said Charm.

Rosalie, having wolfed the lot, conceded: 'They're surprisingly tasty, Charm. Where did you buy them from?'

'I made them mayself.'

'You must give me the recipe.'

Next moment, Rosalie's phone rang.

'Hello. Yes, Hubby did play well,' she said, walking away up the coach. 'They subbed him in the second half so he'll be fit for St Petersburg.'

Daffodil and Sand Pitt turned to Charm.

'What was in her sarnies that was so special?' asked Sand Pitt.

'Promise not to tell her,' whispered Charm. 'Promise, promise. It was Butcher's Traype.'

'Traype? Oh, tripe,' gasped Sand Pitt. 'Butcher's Tripe? That's a dog food.'

Next minute, Daffodil's lovely laugh rang out and out and out.

61

Back at Searston, the post-FA Cup party was in full swing – everyone was so relieved to have something to enjoy after the tragic recent events. Even Deansgate winning at home and almost certainly qualifying for next year's Champions League didn't upset them too much. Rupert and various fans provided plenty of booze. Jackie Carslake, who'd been to the match, stayed for an hour or two to celebrate with them. Everyone was drinking to Feral's new baby boy.

Returning to the *Cotchester Times*, Jackie found Dora at work.

'Amazing match,' he told her. 'Incredible that Rupert and Elijah can go from zero to hero in one day. Your piece on Rupert helped a lot, too.'

'I've just got even better gossip now,' cried Dora. 'You'll never guess what. Ryan Edwards has just been sacked, with only one Premier League match to go. Deansgate were being thrashed by Drobenham and Ryan finally lost it and said he couldn't win matches if his players had to cater for Lout Dudsbridge – and all the fans were yelling "Lout out, Lout out." But when

Ryan subbed him ten minutes after· half-time, Lout ignored him, so when Ryan marched on to the pitch and dragged him off, there was nearly a punch-up, before Laddy Heywood and several players pulled them apart. So Lout went up and sulked in the stands with the Chief C-word. Deansgate, no longer stymied by Lout, turned the game around and won four–three, securing a possible fourth place in the Premier League.

'Whereupon Caring Sir Craig marched into the dressing room and sacked Ryan, and all the players cheered because they hate him for always criticising them and taking credit for any win. So, I've got the perfect headline.' Dora got out her laptop. ' "Fired with Enthusiasm".'

Jackie laughed. 'It's a great story, but I think we'll lead with Searston fighting back and getting a standing ovation at Wembley. Why don't you go round and interview Ryan?'

'He wouldn't see me. He hates me almost as much as Rupert.'

'He'll have been so bloody humiliated, he'll want a good moan. It was a home game so he'll probably have gone home. Take a bottle of Bolly and see if you can get some serious dirt on the Chief C-word and Craig.'

Jackie glanced up at the noticeboard.

'In fact, Dinah is at some charity bash with Lady Grace and Lady Emma, so he may well be on his own.'

'Isn't it a bit late?'

'Only half eight; I don't expect he's in sleep mode.'

Returning to Paris at Pear Tree Cottage, Dora rang Ryan, who picked up, hoping by some miracle it might be Lady Emma.

'Ryan, it's Dora Belvedon.'

'Fuck off.'

'No, please. Ryan, I'm so, so, so sorry. How dare Craig show you the door after such a sensational victory? Who's going to be skilled enough to guide them through the Champions League next year? Craig's a lunatic. Let me bring a bottle of fizz round and give me your true version of events before that bastard Jarred starts pouring poison on Twitter.'

Ryan felt so suicidal, he said she could drop in.

Having wised up Paris, who was sitting on the sofa with ginger pussy Mew-Too, learning lines for Petruchio in *The Taming of the Shrew*, Dora changed into a pretty periwinkle-blue dress and drenched herself in Penhaligon's Bluebell. Just as she was leaving, Buddyguard bounced in from the woods and, with a flurry of tail-wagging, dropped a turquoise leather pouch at her feet.

'Oh, you good boy.' Wiping off the mud, Dora gasped with excitement. 'Omigod, it's Cadenza's iPhone, and it's still working. Must have flown into the trees after the car crash. Paris!' she shouted. 'Look what brilliant Buddyguard's brought in. It's Cadenza's. I must catch Ryan before he changes his mind, but we can look at it later. Can you give Buddyguard a really scrummy supper?'

'Then he's going to hear my lines,' said Paris, who doted on Buddyguard. 'He's such a good listener.' Then, bursting into song: 'The God of love, my German shepherd is, his goodness faileth never.' Paris handed Dora the bottle of Bollinger from the fridge. 'Don't let Ryan jump on you. You look gorgeous, by the way. If you're not back in an hour, Buddyguard and I'll come and get you.'

Dora gave him a hug. 'You're the only person in the world I'll ever fancy.'

'Let's go to bed, then,' said Paris.

'Later. It's too hot a story.'

Dinah, Princess Kayley and Otley were all out, so Ryan had got seriously stuck into the whiskey. Checking the result of Deansgate's game, however, Dinah had read the news of her husband's sacking and rang home:

'I'd come back, but I can't let Lady Grace and Lady Emma down when I've organised so much of this charity function for them. You must make sure you get a decent severance package and find another manager's job soonest. I'm too involved in my charity work to take on a full-time job any more. And what about poor Otley, still playing for Deansgate. And poor little Kayley, who'll be so upset not seeing Harry Stanton-Harcourt.'

And what about me? Thinking his wife was distinctly lacking in charity, Ryan hung up and, with another large glass of whiskey, sat slumped on one of the vast sitting-room sofas. All around him, silverware glittered in big glass cabinets. The walls were covered with photographs: Kayley looking ravishing, Otley scoring goals, Ryan surrounded by all his Deansgate players, Dinah and Lady Emma at some charity do, which gave him the chance to have Emma on display. Now he'd been sacked, he'd probably never see her again.

By the door was a sweet picture of his mother, Pauline. If only she were alive now to hold him, a sobbing little boy, in her arms. And would his father, Valent, who'd always detested Sir Craig, say 'I told you so'?

Masochistically, Ryan was playing back the afternoon's match against Drobenham, and had just watched himself

398

frogmarching Lout off, and Deansgate's subsequent four goals, when the doorbell rang.

It was Dora, waving the bottle of Bolly and some beef sandwiches.

'You need to keep up your strength.'

Seeing the antagonism on Ryan's face, she went into suck-up mode and, as they took their drinks into the sitting room, cried out:

'What a gorgeous picture of Princess Kayley. And that's today's match – how wise you were to sub Lout Dudsbridge.'

'Little shit, keeps pressurising Kayley to go out with him,' snarled Ryan. 'Thinks he's posher than the other players because his father's Chief Constable.'

'And there's the full-time whistle. Four–three – what a brilliant turnaround.'

The sofa was so big that Dora's little legs couldn't reach the edge of the seat, so she had to lie almost horizontally.

'Oh look, there's Laddy Heywood, whipping off his shirt to flaunt his hunky body, then giving it to that little kid, so everyone'll think he's both caring and sexually attractive at the same time. He's such a wanker.'

Ryan smiled – he liked Emma's suitor being slagged off.

'And there's another wanker,' Dora pointed out, as Sir Craig, in a panama with a Deansgate-colours hat-band, was shown welcoming back his players.

'He hates me,' she went on, 'ever since I surprised him shagging Janey Lloyd-Foxe in the woods.'

Noting his eyes were red from crying and the dark rings beneath them so black they looked like upside-down eyebrows, she felt almost sorry for Ryan.

She pleaded: 'Forgive me, Ryan; I know we're enemies on paper, but I recognise greatness and you've done such a wonderful job at Deansgate. Where would you like to go now? Real Madrid? They'll all be after you.' Then, as Ryan filled up her glass: 'Here's to life after Deansgate; you deserve so much better. Craig's a prat.' Dora went on, 'Did you have any idea beforehand that he was going to sack you?'

'No, it was only because I'd subbed the beloved son of the Chief Constable, whose blessing Craig needs to carry out all his dodgy practices.'

'Craig's never forgiven me for pinching Buddyguard, and you'll never guess what. They're still finding wreckage from the car crash around Deep Woods, and just as I was leaving to see you, Buddyguard brought in Cadenza's iPhone, with photographs she must have taken at Heathrow. Let's have a look.' Dora got it out of her handbag, and started jabbing away at the pictures.

'Look, there's that earlier one in Istanbul of Angus naked except for his captain's armband.'

'Christ!' said Ryan. 'Poor Mimi.'

'And that's interesting,' went on Dora. 'Gosh, look, while they were refuelling at Heathrow – that's a gorgeous picture of Downing, Angus and Wilfie, and Marketa, and Orion looking exactly like Rupert with his blond hair, having a drink in the Transmission Lounge. And, look, look, Cadenza's videoed Jarred – what's he doing at Heathrow, lurking in another part of the lounge? He seems to be arguing, and now he's topping up the glass of a very dark-haired man.'

'Jarred's too stingy to top up anyone's drink,' said Ryan, snatching the iPhone. 'Fucking hell, Jarred's talking to Alphonso Pachino. Why are they having a private conversation?'

'I know that name – Alphonso Pachino was our pilot that day,' cried Dora.

'He's a freelance. South American, often flies for us too,' explained Ryan.

'And after that conversation with Jarred,' persisted Dora, 'he claimed the Galloper wasn't safe to fly and crash-landed it next to Rutshire airfield, dumping all the players so they transferred to Rupert's car, which subsequently crashed and burst into flames on the way home. Where does Alphonso live?'

'Well, he's currently flying for Deansgate, so he's lodging at Craig Eynsham's estate.'

'Which Rupert calls the Launderette, because Sir Craig launders so much money.'

'Exactly – and I heard later that the Galloper was found to have nothing wrong with it.' Fuelled by booze, Ryan picked up his car keys. 'Let's go and confront him.'

'Is it safe to?' asked Dora, dickering between fear and the prospect of a massive scoop.

Passing huge blow-ups of swooping kestrels and advertising boards of beautiful male and female models extolling the wonders of No-Bese and Spot Kick and Glitteris, Ryan drove into Craig Eynsham's estate. Alphonso, who was staying in a ground-floor apartment on the edge of the car park, took some time to answer the door. He turned out to be tall with dark eyes, sallow skin and dark hair in a ponytail, and looked very apprehensive.

'Mr Ryan Edwards, what can I do to help?'

'We're coming in,' said Ryan, marching into the kitchen, which was very sparse with peeling paint and only a cooker, no fridge or dishwasher. On the dresser was a photograph of a pretty woman and two little boys.

'Why did you lie about the Galloper being fucked, crash-landing it down in a field next to Rutshire airfield?' demanded Ryan.

'I never go to Rutshire.' Alphonso had a very strong foreign accent.

'Look at this.' Ryan produced Cadenza's iPhone. 'Here you are arguing with Jarred Moreland at Heathrow, and here's Orion Onslow looking exactly like Rupert Campbell-Black.'

Ryan was bigger and stronger than Alphonso, who slumped down on a kitchen chair, shaking violently, as Ryan shouted: 'What murderous plot were you firming up with Jarred?'

'N-No, I never,' stammered Alphonso.

'You bastard!' cried Dora. 'If you'd flown the Galloper a further fourteen miles to Deep Woods, which it was perfectly capable of doing, six innocent people would be alive today. Did you sabotage Rupert's car?'

'I never touch Mr Rupert's car,' repeated Alphonso, his dark eyes darting around the room in terror. 'It is terrible to kill people. I not sure if Galloper was safe, and I wasn't making plot with Mr Jarred.'

'You didn't?' Ryan raised a sceptical eyebrow. 'Then come with us and talk to the forensic team leading the investigation. If you didn't lie about the Galloper being unsafe, of course you'll be let off.'

But the next moment, Alphonso had leapt to his feet, opened a nearby drawer, and taken out a gun.

'Put hands up!' he shouted. 'I no go to any police.'

'Don't be crazy, Alphonso,' said Ryan, grabbing Dora

and shoving her in front of him. 'You don't want to be done for any more murders, especially of an innocent young lady like Dora.'

'Lemme go,' screamed Dora as, still pointing the gun at them, Alphonso edged towards the front door and flung it open, howling:

'Get out of my house, get out.'

Letting go of Dora, Ryan bolted through the door.

'You go too,' Alphonso bellowed at Dora.

Following her, he seized the photographs of the pretty woman and the two little boys, locked the door behind him, raced out to his parked car and screeched off into the night.

'Murderer!' Dora howled after him. 'Murderer! And you're not much better.' She turned on Ryan. 'This'll make a great last paragraph in my glow-job about you. "Ryan Edwards used me as a human shield, or rather a bulwark." I've always wanted to work the word "bulwark" into a piece.'

'I'm sorry,' said Ryan. 'I thought he'd be too chivalrous to shoot a young woman. We'd better go to the police.'

'Not the Chief C-word – I don't think he'd be very receptive.'

Then, as they got into Ryan's Ferrari, Dora, trembling more violently than Alphonso, got a diary out of her bag and started scribbling.

'Do you think Sir Craig and the Chief Constable are involved?' she asked.

'Very probably, if Jarred is.'

'I wonder how Lady Grace will enjoy being married to a mass murderer, or Lout having a corrupt dad, and,' she gabbled, 'what will happen to Deansgate without a chairman? You're well out of it, Ryan. Did you know any of this was going on?'

'Course I didn't. Part of our agreement this evening was you were going to defend me in this piece, putting my case, saying I was as powerful a manager as Dad was a goalie.' Ryan was really shouting now as he hurtled the car at hundreds of miles per hour through the dark woods. 'There was no way I was implicated in that car crash. You've got to defend me utterly.'

'I already did,' quavered Dora, 'as a bulwark between you and Alphonso. I'm not entirely sure Alphonso sabotaged Rupert's car.'

'Course he did.' Then, as Ryan swung into the lane leading to his house: 'Christ, there's another car beside yours outside. Wonder if Alphonso's wised up Sir Craig.'

'No, no,' gasped Dora, hearing barking and catching sight of a man with white-blond hair, 'it's Paris. Oh, thank God.' And stumbling out of the car, she fell into his arms.

'The most terrible things have been happening,' she sobbed. 'I thought I might never see you again.'

'What the fuck have you been doing to her?' Paris turned on Ryan, then, as Ryan clenched his fists: 'Don't go trying anything.'

Holding Dora tightly, Paris stroked her hair.

'You were away so long and you left your mobile behind. What happened, sweetheart?'

'We found videos on Cadenza's phone of Jarred at Heathrow, arguing with Alphonso, the pilot who was flying the Galloper, and when we confronted Alphonso, and I accused him of sabotaging Rupert's car, he pulled a gun on us.'

After all three had calmed down a little, Ryan invited them inside, and they discussed what to do next. They decided not to go to the local police dealing with the case, because the all-powerful Chief Constable, particularly if he was in league with Sir Craig, would immediately scupper any accusations. They needed more evidence.

'But we must stop them murdering Rupert and any more players,' wailed Dora.

'I think it's better, at this stage, until we know more, not even to involve Rupert or Elijah or anyone at Searston,' said Paris.

'I know a wonderful Chief Inspector Gablecross, based in the Midlands, who's brilliant at tracking down murderers,' volunteered Dora, wiping her eyes. 'His team saved Rupert and Banquo, his Lab, when Jan Van Daventer tried to murder them because he wanted to marry Taggie. I'll get in touch with him first thing tomorrow morning.'

62

On a happier note, Lou-Easy, who had had two winners at Doncaster, had watched the FA Cup intermittently on her mobile. At first, she hadn't recognised the handsome player with light-brown curls, then realised it was Josef with a new haircut and without his hairband. Wow, he looked fit, and he had such a lovely strong face.

'Lots of clubs are after Josef,' said Gav, Rupert's assistant trainer, as they travelled in the lorry back to Penscombe. 'Even more after today. He should have been Man of the Match.'

'I must make a plan,' vowed Lou-Easy.

Over at Searston, the post-FA Cup party was breaking up. Elijah had collectively and individually praised his players:

'You were true Comeback Kids, and I want you to recapture your second-half form when we go to St Petersburg in twelve days' time. I know you're all exhausted; it's been a long, cruel and incredibly sad season. So get some sleep, because you need to be back for hard-graft training at ten a.m. on Monday.'

'You were fantastic,' Elijah told Josef privately. 'Stunning goal, and you defended like a whole pack of guard dogs. Not being weighed down by that great mane of hair must help you run faster. And playing so well back home in the Czech Republic must have boosted your confidence.'

'My vill to vin,' grinned Josef.

He had just received two texts, one from his mother saying how proud she was, and one from Alan Garcia: 'Terrific game, well done. Several more clubs after you. Talk tomorrow.'

'I vant Lou-Easy after me,' sighed Josef.

He looked around for Galgo, but his flatmate, loser's medal glittering round his neck, was joyfully bopping with a gorgeous redhead.

Breaking away from her, Galgo told Josef: 'She's asked me back to her place, so I might not be home till sometime tomorrow. Sorry to desert you, mate.'

Galgo didn't look sorry, he seemed to be laughing his head off. Josef felt overwhelmed with black gloom. Without Orion and Downing, whom he missed terribly, and now Galgo tonight, it was bleak going back to an empty Shaggery, where there had always been high jinks of some kind.

Driving into the Market Square, however, Josef was irritated to see a light on in his bedroom and the yellow curtains drawn. He must have left it on this morning. Or could it be burglars?

Letting himself in, he found lights on on the landing and in the bathroom as well.

'Anyone here?' he yelled, grabbing a walking stick. Then, going into his bedroom, he breathed in a heavenly scent, as though he'd wandered into a rose garden,

407

then gave a gasp. For on his bed, in a short pink lace nightgown showing off endless brown legs and painted pink toenails, her golden hair spilling over the pillow, lay Lou-Easy.

'How did you get in here?' he stammered.

'Galgo left me a spare key under the doormat. I wanted to surprise you.' Lou-Easy slid off the bed, glided towards him, then raised her arms to ruffle his new short curls.

'You're such a beauty now.'

Then, pulling down Josef's head, she pressed her lips to his. Their first kiss seemed to go on for ever, until they collapsed on to the bed.

'You played so well,' whispered Lou-Easy, 'and now you're going to play even better.'

But Josef was confused.

'You no just drop inside for quick visit?'

'No, no. We had two winners today. Rupert's given me tomorrow off, so I'm going to stay all night and day and night making love to you.'

Josef couldn't take it in. Running his finger down her cheek in bewilderment, he said:

'You like me – in that vay?'

'Oh God, yes. Orion was love at first sight; with you it started slowly and built up. I missed you so much when you were in the Czech Republic.' Lou-Easy started unbuttoning Josef's shirt. 'Every day I missed you more and more. Suddenly I wanted you around all the time.'

'I cannot believe it,' stammered Josef, crossing himself before running his hands over her lithe, whippet-slim body, fondling her lovely high breasts, their jutting-out nipples and the warm river bubbling between her legs, showing how excited she was. Now they were both naked and Josef was moaning as her quick tongue darted everywhere.

'Come inside me, Josef.'

'You sure?' protested Josef. 'Perhaps I not good enough at sex. I have not had many vomen.'

'Hush,' chided Lou-Easy. 'I've had far too many men, but from now on, I'm not going to open my legs to the public. I'm Louisie, not Lou-Easy.' Then, taking his face in her hands: 'I want to be the only woman in your life, and you to be the only man in mine.'

Any tiredness evaporated as they fell back on the bed, Josef joyfully driving into her with such power and confidence until the coming of dawn, by which time they themselves had both come numerous times.

Waking, Louisie found Josef smiling down at her:

'Am I dreaming or did it really happen?'

'It did, and I want it to happen again and again for evermore. I love you, Josef. I never realised what proper real love was before. You've caught me unprepared.'

Putting her hand up, she smoothed his thick brown eyebrows.

'You're so gorgeous now, and I must say, those very few women you went to bed with taught you exceedingly well.'

Josef couldn't stop laughing.

'Jewel shops are not open today,' he told her, 'but tomorrow after training, I go to buy you a beautiful ring, a diamond or emerald, or vun you like best, and then I vant to go down on vun knee and ask you to be my vife.'

'Oh yes, please,' sighed Louisie, 'but could you ask me now?'

'Vill you marry me, Louisie?' Josef's voice broke. 'And can ve have vedding very soon?'

'Yes, please. And I'll be a VAG,' giggled Louisie, 'and you'll be Bennet's stepfather. We'll have to find a house with a field and a stable. We may not be able to afford a place in the Golden Triangle, but had you noticed I've shaved my pubes in a golden triangle, and you can stay there as long as you like.'

Fingering her blonde bush, Josef was in stitches.

'We might have to go to St Petersburg for our honeymoon.'

'That's OK.' Louisie laid a hand on Josef's rising penis. 'Evidently, the Lakhta Center there is the tallest skyscraper in Europe, so your lovely cock will give it some competition.'

63

To the despair of the fans, Searston lost their last Premier League match against West Putney and fell to sixth place, so no longer qualified for next year's Champions League. Only this year's Champions League final in St Petersburg lay ahead, against Vermelho, the mightiest Portuguese side. This was being staged at ten o'clock in the evening – eight o'clock English time – so as much of the world as possible could watch.

'You'll have to wear Dolphy's diamond earrings,' Taggie teased Rupert. 'Oh, I so long to go to Russia with you, darling, but I feel I truly ought to stay home and help Shelagh look after Bianca and baby Teddy.'

She was also uptight about future test results, which would tell her whether she was clear of cancer.

With equal heroism, Louisie was not accompanying Josef to St Petersburg because she felt she must not abandon The Story So Far, who was the only filly competing in the Derby on the afternoon of the match. Rupert, finding Louisie singing, 'I'm getting married in the morning,' at the top of her voice to Story, had also asked her to postpone her wedding.

411

'Darling, it's not just Story needing you, Searston does too. If you were planning to spend the honeymoon in St Petersburg with Josef, he'd be far too exhausted to kick a single ball.'

In compensation, Rupert had promised her and Josef a slap-up wedding later in June.

'Where Safety and Bennet can deliver you to the church in a stylish carriage.'

Team Searston were gutted not to be at the Derby to cheer Story on, and all had made vast advance bets on her. Remembering Rupert's generosity in giving them the filly, they vowed to try to win the Champions League for him, which would also bestow legendary status on Elijah as manager.

Fat chance, thought Elijah. With everything they'd all been through recently, how could they possibly not be annihilated by Vermelho? Alone on the Thursday evening before they flew out, he was overwhelmed by despair. Someone, probably Jarred, had posted his landline number on Instagram, so he had been bombarded by such vitriolic abuse after losing their last match that Madison had taken Isaiah and Naomi away for half-term to some undisclosed woman friend and was not answering his calls.

The cottage felt horribly empty. Madison had removed any happy photographs from the walls. Some enraged fan had poured petrol all over the red flowers in the front garden and set fire to them. There was only a moribund quiche and a three-quarters-empty bottle of white in the fridge.

Elijah could not resist turning to social media, all predicting a bloodbath in Russia for Searston, as well as

Rupert, who was only interested in silverware, selling up to maintain his vast yard, and Elijah and all the players getting the sack, the thought of which would utterly demoralise them before they flew out.

Also trending were media reports of his father refusing to recognise any connection with Elijah, which then praised Abner as one of the most hard-working and admired rabbis in the country. Overwhelmed with longing, Elijah googled Dolphy, finding Cadenza's ravishing photograph of him, all big blue eyes and windswept golden curls, with a horribly disparaging caption written by a troll – 'Cotswold's Searston have changed their name to Queerston' – followed by gallons of even worse vitriol. Oh, poor, poor Dolphy.

He must concentrate on St Petersburg and turned to videos of Vermelho matches, finding them terrifyingly good.

To dilute the terrors, Elijah switched on Classic FM and the room was flooded with Brahms – the lovely horn arpeggios at the end of his first piano concerto, one of his father's favourite pieces of music.

Suddenly, Elijah was filled with longing for his childhood and his strict but loving parents lighting candles at the start of the Sabbath at sunset on Friday. Both of them laying a gentle hand on his head as they prayed, followed by a fireside supper of egg dumplings in chicken soup. If only he could take Isaiah and Naomi to meet them – he was sure they'd all adore each other.

He was appalled to find tears pouring down his cheeks and furiously ordered himself to stop wallowing in self-pity. He must concentrate on the videos, so he could brief his players.

' "Oh God of battles," ' he quoted *Henry V* once more, ' "steel my soldiers' hearts; possess them not with fear." '

He knew they were petrified of the four-to-five-hour flight tomorrow, even though Rupert had hired a private jet in case saboteurs struck again.

The only players who weren't jumpy were Rollo and Mattie from the Academy, who were so excited at having been picked for the first team in the biggest match of the year that they were wondering whether to cover themselves in tattoos and each buy a Ferrari before setting out.

64

Because the police were still trying to work out who was responsible for the car crash, they still hadn't released any of the few remaining body parts to be buried. Rupert had therefore arranged for plots to be reserved in the local graveyard at Penscombe church, now known as the Griefyard, so their families could plant flowers there in anticipation and decide what to put on their gravestones.

Mimi, already devastated by the revelations about Angus and Cadenza and various other women coming out of the woodwork, describing how they'd had flings with her husband, was still being comforted by Hughie Winston, the sweet solicitor boyfriend of Cadenza, whose plot was next door. Together, they were planning a communal rose garden with Wilfie's mother, Mary, who was still crying herself to sleep every night. Worst of all for Mary was waking up in the morning and finding her darling boy was no more. Then, during the day, she kept forgetting and picking up her mobile to ring him.

Although Rupert had already forked out six million to each of the dependants of the people who'd been killed in the crash, Wilfie's father, Dougie, was still nagging Rupert's office to hand out an extra six million to himself.

'Horrible man,' stormed Dora, who meanwhile was worried stiff that Sir Craig and the Chief C-word might strike again. She and Ryan hadn't notified the police yet, because they were still convinced the Chief C-word would kibosh any accusations, and Dora had only just managed to track down Chief Inspector Gablecross and was meeting him tomorrow. She had also been so frantic fending off hate mail against Searston, Rupert and Elijah that she didn't find time to walk Buddyguard until dusk on the Tuesday before Searston flew out.

Setting out round Deep Woods, breathing in the sweet scent of lime tree flowers, battling with wild garlic, she shrieked in terror as a figure emerged from behind a large oak tree, calling out: 'Mees Dora, can we talk?'

'Don't shoot my dog,' Dora screamed.

'No, no, not armed.' Alphonso held out empty hands. 'Only use gun for protection. I must explain. Since I come to England and join agency for pilots, sometimes I fly Green Galloper, sometimes Battery Ram or other plane for Sir Craig. I work very long hours to make money to bring my wife and keeds here from abroad.'

All the birds seemed to have stopped singing to listen as Alphonso went on: 'Mr Jarred, who work for Sir Craig, learn this and offer me very big money to tell not-true thing that when I fly Searston players back from Istanbul, the plane become not safe when leaving Heathrow and I must land it sudden in rough field near Rutshire airfield. Searston then send people carrier to collect, which do not arrive, so players take Mr Rupert Campbell-Black's car parking there.'

'I know all this,' snapped Dora, still trying to control an increasingly growling Buddyguard and thinking the stench of Alphonso's sweat was overcoming any wafts of wild garlic.

'Next day,' continued Alphonso, 'I learn terrible theeng, that all Searston happy players and their pretty ladies are keeled and burnt to death when Mr Rupert's car crashes, but when I go to Sir Craig and Mr Jarred and ask why terrible theeng happen, because I was told to make claim that Galloper not safe to fly them to Deep Woods when it was perfectly safe to do so, Sir Craig and Mr Jarred go mad with rage. They refuse to give me any of the very big money they promise to bring here my family. They say if I do not keep trap shut and tell anyone they made me to lie, they will tell police it was my decision to crash-land Galloper, and I will be jailed for long time for keeling and I will never see my family again.'

And collapsing on a fallen log, Alphonso burst into tears.

'Yes, you will,' cried Dora, putting an arm around his shuddering shoulders, 'if the police learn that, just to discredit the Galloper, Sir Craig and Jarred bribed you with vast sums to say the plane wasn't right, then you landed it very cleverly in a bumpy field and didn't hurt anyone. I know a wonderful Inspector Gablecross who will help us once we explain you only told a tiny white lie to save your family.'

As Dora patted Alphonso's clenched fist, and Buddy stopped growling and laid a fawn paw on his thigh, Alphonso drew back in terror, then relaxed, muttering: 'And I theenk it was Mr Jarred who sabotage Mr Rupert's car.'

'Do you really?' gasped Dora.

'Because little yellow car was waiting for Mr Rupert returning from Pakistan, Mr Jarred had time to make it not safe, and official at Rutshire airfield, seeing Mr Orion with yellow hair, theenk he is Mr Rupert and direct him to little yellow car and Mr Orion and players and their girls climb into it and get keeled instead. Jarred want to please Sir Craig, knowing he is so mad with hating of Mr Rupert, and Sir Craig say C-B stand for Completely Bastard.'

'Come on,' urged an excited Dora, 'we're going to see Chief Inspector Gablecross and make sure you can bring your family to England.'

On Thursday evening, before flying out with the team, the Completely Bastard, having sorted out which of his horses were running in tomorrow's Oaks and Saturday's Derby and other big races, came into the kitchen to find his grandchildren Timon and Sapphire watching television and eating Taggie's divine chocolate tart. They were staying for half-term – another reason Taggie wasn't coming to St Petersburg with him.

'What's erectile dysfunction?' asked Sapphire, who was looking at the ads.

'It's when your willy won't stick up and go into a woman's hole,' explained Timon. 'Like a weeping willow.'

'Or like a weeping willy,' crowed Sapphire.

Rupert tried not to laugh. 'Where's Granny?' he asked.

'Upstairs doing your packing,' said Sapphire.

'Why can't I play for Searston?' complained Timon. 'I was playing forward at school last term and they really need decent strikers. Online, they all think it's selfish of Feral not to go.'

So did Rupert. He'd been tempted to order Feral to

go himself, but Bianca, despite having a whole household to look after her, was feeling needy after a difficult birth and frantic for Feral and Taggie to stay in case the plane blew up.

'I'm sure Feral could make Searston win,' persisted Timon.

'Winning's rude,' announced Sapphire, giving the rest of her chocolate tart to a drooling Forester.

'What you talking about?' snapped Timon.

'Winning's rude. It's unkind to the poor team who come second.'

'I think that'll probably be us, darling,' said Rupert, 'so don't stress yourself.'

Feral was utterly torn. He was besotted with Teddy, his little baby son, with his down of ebony hair and huge brown eyes, who always seemed to be gurgling with happiness. He was thrilled Bianca seemed madly in love with him again, not wanting him to leave her side for a minute, particularly to risk his life on a plane. But he was desperate to fly out with the lads on Friday. He still felt so guilty for not having perished in the car crash, and now he felt worse not honouring those who'd died. Every day he sloped off for a couple of hours to train at Deep Woods, booting goal after goal into the net, dreaming of the stands rising to the Russian skies to cheer him on. Worst of all, he felt he was letting Rupert down.

65

On Friday morning, Team Searston set off in their private jet from Rutshire airfield, reassured that Rupert, Elijah and non-playing staff, including Cheffie, Kitsy and Charlie, were flying with them. But they were irritated to learn that Sir Craig was giving a media party that afternoon to celebrate Deansgate getting into next year's Champions League.

Elijah was devastated he hadn't been able to track down his children to say goodbye. After a lunch of poached salmon, asparagus and fruit salad, he gave the team another briefing about tomorrow's opposition, Vermelho, showing pictures of the players on a big screen.

'They are very motivated,' he began, forbearing to add that each player would receive a bonus of £3 million if they won.

'Their manager, for a start, is called Zeus Martinez. Zeus, in Greek mythology, was the supreme god, the cloud gatherer and hurler of thunderbolts, and this Zeus expects his players to do the same into the net.'

'Isn't that an 'andball?' called out Dolphy.

The team grinned.

'Zeus thinks he's a god. He wears very sharp suits and so much aftershave that if you don't want to get asphyxiated, you'd better run out quickly. His team is bristling with alpha males, not great on camaraderie and each determined to go down in history as record goal-scorers.

'Facundo, who you know, is their star player; he's already scored nineteen goals in Champions League matches and is hell-bent on revenge because we sacked him. He'll charge around the pitch leaving open spaces, so watch him for gaps. Bruiser Big Ben Martin also joined them at the beginning of the season and is still trying to justify his massive purchase price. Jean Jacques Voltaire from France, known as Jeanius, is arguably their best player, but Facundo's been hitting on his wife, so neither will pass to the other if they can help it.

'Also watch out for their central midfielder, Ruben Carlos, a world-class finisher and a little weasel. He'll tug at your clothes and wind you up until you lose it and get red-carded.'

When he'd run through the rest of the team, Elijah stressed that Vermelho were so obsessed with attacking and scoring, they weren't that bothered about defending.

'And we're great on that now, so we've got to man-mark them insensible. I know you can do it.'

While he was speaking, Elijah noticed Parks fighting sleep, Josef looking longingly at iPhone pictures of Louisie, Griffy gazing wistfully out of the window, Barry Pitt doing the *Daily Mail* quick crossword, and Bastian writing his *Hauteur Biography*. Elijah was worried that Parks had slowed up hugely and in the final Premier League game hadn't marshalled his fellow backs aggressively enough, nor tackled anyone himself, and hardly seemed to notice what was going on on the rest of the field.

Elijah was seriously thinking of making Griffy captain instead.

Elijah also found himself avoiding Dolphy's eyes, because he was so desperate not to betray his hopeless longing. In turn, Dolphy, hurt that Elijah seemed to be deliberately ignoring him, had palled up with Mattie and Rollo, who were the same age as him.

'I'm sure you're going to be really excited by St Petersburg,' concluded Elijah.

Bastian, who'd dyed his hair in blue and green stripes, put down his *Hauteur Biography*.

'Let me tell you about it,' he announced. 'St Petersburg is the world's most northern city and we're going into twenty-four-hour daylight called the White Nights because the sun blazes all night long and doesn't go below the horizon enough for the sky to go dark, so the authorities never have to provide street lighting.'

'Poor dogs with no lamp posts to lift their legs on,' sighed Dolphy, and blushed when everyone guffawed.

'Never mind,' went on Bastian, 'there are two hundred museums and one of the finest art galleries in the world. There are lots of canals and rivers to walk along, past houses and palaces with gold roofs, a cathedral where all the tsars are buried, and one of the tallest skyscrapers in Europe, the Lakhta.'

'That's the one not as tall as my cock,' muttered Josef – he must text Louisie yet again.

'You might not get much sleep tonight,' went on Bastian, 'because, as I said, the sun blazes and the bells ring all the time. One clock has a bell that plays six different tunes.'

'Well, you'd better get some kip now,' said Elijah. 'Thank you, Bastian.'

Just as they were nodding off, they were woken by a shout of excitement from a separate section at the front of the plane.

Wandering up there, Elijah found Rupert delighted that one of his colts had sauntered home in the first race at Epsom.

'Then you've got the Oaks and the Derby tomorrow. The lads will be over the moon if Story does well.'

'Are they OK?'

'Bastian's been giving them a geography lesson so they're all dropping off. Taggie provided a marvellous lunch.'

'I don't know what plans you've got this evening,' said Rupert, 'but my son Marcus is meeting us at the airport. He's flown up from Moscow.'

'How marvellous,' said Elijah, who'd got all Marcus's CDs.

'Wonder if you'd like to join us for dinner.'

'I'd adore to, but won't you want to spend time alone together?'

'No, no, he's bringing his, er, husband, Alexei Nemerovsky. Along with Nureyev and Nijinsky, he's known as one of the Three Ns, the world's greatest ballet dancers.'

'How long have he and Marcus been together?'

'About twenty years. Marcus won the Appleton piano competition, emerging from hospital after some ghastly asthma attack. He was brilliant. I only got applause like that at the Olympics. In his acceptance speech, he came out, extraordinarily praising me for accepting that he was a homosexual, and thanking me for it. I was knocked out. We'd always had a tricky relationship – he was much closer to my first wife, but at last I felt he was truly mine and we were going to have an opportunity to get closer. Then, on the very same night, he announced he was buggering off to Moscow into the arms of Nemerovsky – now his husband – and despite Nemerovsky being more than twenty years older, it's been a real love match. But I don't know a thing about ballet, so you can rabbit on to him about *Swan Lake* at dinner.' Rupert drained his drink. 'I must watch the next race.'

And Dolphy's twenty years younger than me, thought Elijah.

As they went through the barrier at St Petersburg, Elijah noticed two very good-looking men waiting surrounded by a hovering mob of autograph hunters and fans seeking selfies. Shrugging them off, the younger man, who had dark-red hair and freckles, came forward and hugged Rupert in delight, then beckoned forward the older man. *Marcus Campbell-Black and Alexei Nemerovsky*, thought Elijah, and, overwhelmed with shyness, he joined a gawping Team Searston and escaped to the coach which was taking them to the hotel.

'Who is that with Rupert?' said Bastian.

'It's his son Marcus,' said Griffy. 'One of the best concert pianists in the world.'

'What's a concert penis?' asked Dolphy.

'It must be a crowing cock,' said Bastian, and he and Dolphy cracked up with laughter.

66

Meanwhile, back in the Cotswolds, Tember had rolled up at Deep Woods after some weeks away, desperately pale and thin from missing Griffy and mourning the death of so many of her beloved players.

'Come to Russia with us,' begged Dora. 'The Wags and I are flying out first thing tomorrow. It would cheer up the lads so much to see you. They've missed you terribly.'

'Is Inez going?' asked Tember.

'I expect so, but we'll just ignore the stroppy cow.'

'I bet she leaves darling Mildred the mongrel alone in the house with no food.'

'You must rescue her,' laughed Dora. 'You have a duty of cur. I'll organise you a seat on the plane.'

'I'll need to get my hair cut and find something to wear,' wailed Tember.

'I'm off to gatecrash another of Lady Grace's soirees,' said Dora. 'I'll keep you posted.'

The moment Tember had left the office, Dora texted Griffy: 'Tember's coming with us to St Petersburg.'

*

Sir Craig was still in heaven because Deansgate's last win had put them in next year's Champions League. Tossed in the air by his victorious players, Sir Craig had managed to hang on to his dashing dark-red sombrero.

The following Friday, as Searston were landing in St Petersburg, Lady Grace had invited the media to a super soiree to celebrate both Deansgate's victory and the launch of the Battery Ram. Landing the little pale-blue-and-fawn plane on the big lawn behind the house, Sir Craig jumped out. Then, seizing a glass of champagne, he toasted the assembled company, raising his red sombrero with a special smile for Lady Emma.

' "Red hat, no knickers," as my grandmother used to say,' muttered Dora to Jackie Carslake.

Leaving Buddyguard in Jackie's car with the window open and in deep shade under the trees at the edge of Sir Craig's car park, they had smuggled their way into the reception, lurking behind a large rose bush.

'I am so proud,' continued Sir Craig, 'to be a pioneer in clearing the skies with my electric plane: the Battery Ram. With him, I'm going to help eliminate carbon from aviation. Three hundred engineers in my factory are already working all hours to produce a battery which will enable the biggest jumbo jets to fly by electricity. But my Battery Ram' – he patted the little plane – 'is the harbinger.' And everyone cheered.

'Any other new creations?' asked the *Telegraph*.

'Well, I'm delighted with Kwik-Dri, a glass tent in the bathroom which will dry you in a trice, and Whisk-a-way, a crème which will remove any superfluous hair in another trice. There are samples' – he pointed to a nearby table – 'for all the ladies present.'

'He could use it on his head,' whispered Dora.

'And you must be delighted Deansgate finished above your Cotswold rivals, Searston Rovers,' called out the *Western Daily Press*.

'Delighted. Particularly as our young players Lyall Dudsbridge and Harry Stanton-Harcourt scored and provided fine assists in our last game. It looks as though Searston are going to get lynched in St Petersburg tomorrow evening. Seems extraordinary that Rupert Campbell-Black cannot even get his daughter's partner, Feral Jackson, ostensibly his best player, to take part.' The sudden hatred in Craig's voice sent a shiver through the guests.

'Are you going to take a bit of a break now?' suggested Katie Jarvis of *Cotswold Life*.

'Indeed. Lady Grace, my wife, Chief Constable Lloyd Dudsbridge and his lady wife, Lady Emma Stanton-Harcourt, and Jarred Moreland and his partner and I are off on a cruise on my yacht, also called *Lady Grace*, which is moored in Monaco.'

'Thank havens for little tax,' sang Dora. 'Bloody name-dropper.'

'Keep your voice down,' hissed Jackie.

'And I'd finally like to announce' – Sir Craig smiled around at everyone – 'that my Director of Football, Jarred Moreland, who has been so instrumental in helping Deansgate to qualify for next year's Champions League, will be joining the board of Craig Eynsham. So, let's hear it for Jarred.'

Amid rather half-hearted cheers, the players could be seen exchanging glances of absolute horror.

'And the Battery Ram, the finest flying taxi in the world, is taking us to Birmingham airport,' concluded

Sir Craig. 'It's been a long year, but the next one's going to be even more exciting.'

As the garden was flooded with a group singing, 'Don't be vague, insist on Sir Craig,' Dora whispered: 'Look, look, Chief Inspector Gablecross has delivered.'

For two plain-clothes men were fighting their way through the guests:

'Could we have a word, Sir Craig?'

'You'd better have a noggin first,' cried Lady Grace.

'We'd like you to come down to the station,' said the older man, as they both displayed their badges.

'What on earth for?' demanded Craig. 'Who authorised this? My friend Chief Constable Dudsbridge will have something to say about you barging in like this.'

'Come on, sir.' The younger man seized Craig's arm. 'Car's outside.'

'I'm not going anywhere,' said Craig, haughtily. 'Lady Grace, Lady Emma and I have to leave shortly for Birmingham airport, to join Chief Constable Dudsbridge.'

'You can't hijack Sir Craig in the middle of our soiree,' cried Lady Grace. 'We've got a plane to catch to Monaco.'

The other guests were looking startled, wondering whether to come to their hosts' rescue. Craig himself, who'd noticed the several uniformed police now lurking on the end of the lawn, and that two of them were addressing Jarred, was pondering whether it might be easier, rather than revving up the Battery Ram, to escape in his Statement Vehicle, the bright-orange Maserati, which was standing in the car park. He was just nodding at his chauffeur when he caught sight of Dora, creeping round her rose bush to have a look, and, rage overwhelming him, promptly lost his gentlemanly composure.

'You evil, scheming little bitch,' he yelled, 'how dare you gatecrash our soiree!' Then, turning to Gablecross's plain-clothes men: 'She's the one you ought to arrest – she stole my guard dog, Duke, who's worth fifteen thousand pounds. She graffitied my stand at Deansgate, and let in wild boars to dig up the pitch before a crucial game, and she does all that bastard Campbell-Black's dirty work for him.'

'Don't let him escape,' shouted Dora. 'He's murdered six innocent people; you've got to stop him murdering Rupert.' And she leapt bravely into the path of an approaching Craig, who, completely losing it, seized her little shoulders and shook her violently.

'Help, stop him!' shrieked Dora.

Next moment, Craig had punched her in the face so viciously that he'd knocked her to the ground, and was about to kick her in the ribs.

Hearing her shrieks, Buddyguard managed to wriggle out of Jackie's car window and hurtle across the car park, leaping over a yew hedge and dashing across the lawn through the flabbergasted guests. Catching sight of his loathsome, bellowing ex-master assaulting his beloved mistress, Buddy flew through the air, crash-landing on Sir Craig's back, growling furiously and knocking him to the ground, standing over him and tearing off his sombrero. He then growled even more ferociously when Gablecross's boys tried to drag him off, until Dora, still lying on the grass, quavered, 'It's OK, Buddy, drop him, come here, brave boy,' and Buddy turned to his mistress, licking away the tears and the blood, nudging her better, offering one paw after another.

Gablecross's men, meanwhile, had lost no time in

slapping handcuffs on Sir Craig and frogmarching him off to join Jarred in their police van.

'Wait till your Chief Constable hears about this,' he could be heard howling. 'You'll all be fired.'

'Are you all right, love?' As a uniformed policeman reached down to help Dora on to a nearby bench, Buddyguard started growling again.

'It's OK, good boy, you rescued your mistress,' said a shaken Jackie Carslake, joining Dora on the bench and putting an arm round her shoulders. 'You really OK, love?'

'I'm fine.' Dora fingered her battered, bleeding face. 'In future, I must avoid Sir Craig like the plague.' Then, brightening, 'But wasn't Buddy brave?' she asked the assembled company and, groping for Sir Craig's red sombrero, plonked it on Buddy's head, tucking his pointed ears in. 'Doesn't it suit him? Red hat, furry knickers.'

And the crowd, bewildered about how to react to events, burst out laughing and clapping, until Buddyguard waved his fluffy black-and-fawn tail in delight.

'You ought to go to Gloucestershire hospital and have those bruises looked at,' said a uniformed policeman.

'I haven't got time,' insisted Dora. 'I've got to fly to St Petersburg first thing in the morning to look after Searston, and masses to do before that.' She turned to Jackie. 'Promise, promise you'll write a wonderful piece about Buddy, praising him to the skies for his valour, and insisting he gets a dog VC for his bravery. And you must publish a picture of him in Craig's hat.' She hugged her still-wagging dog. 'Then he can take up modelling as a second career.'

67

The Searston Rovers' hotel in St Petersburg, at which Rasputin and Tchaikovsky had once stayed, had wonderful views over the Baltic Sea, a forest of spires and gold-turreted buildings. The players decided to have a wander round the city before dinner, strolling along the canals, enjoying the extra sunshine and the streets bustling with excited tourists.

A returning Elijah found an unusually cheerful-looking Griffy asking a receptionist if she knew anywhere he could get a tattoo.

'I'm going to have dinner with Rupert,' Elijah told him, 'but I won't be late. I do hope the boys will be able to get some sleep with all those bells ringing and the sun shining and Instagram predicting we're going to get slaughtered.'

'Pity we can't give them some Mogadon and take away their phones,' said Griffy.

'How do you feel about captaining the side tomorrow?' asked Elijah.

Griffy's face lit up. 'I'd like that very much, but what about Parks?'

'His calf strain's really slowing him up. I'll talk to him tomorrow. And without Feral, you must try to bang in some goals, Griffy.'

'I will.'

Thinking how handsome Griffy was when he was happy, Elijah then had a shower, put on a dark suit and a white shirt he'd brought for the match tomorrow, and lots of his new aftershave, Yves St Laurent's La Nuit de l'Homme, which Searston cleaners Roxanne and Nadia had bought him as a good-luck present.

If only he could take Dolphy along too. Then, on the way out, he passed him and Rollo and Mattie, who were sharing a room, having a pillow fight and sternly told himself he mustn't cradle-snatch.

He joined Rupert, Marcus and Alexei at the legendary restaurant known as the Literary Cafe, which had portraits of great writers like Dostoevsky and Lermontov over the red walls, a waxwork of Pushkin sitting at a table on the top floor and a stuffed bear on his hind legs in the foyer.

They dined in an alcove, so hovering press and autograph hunters couldn't bother them, and drank a lot of superb red wine.

'Elijah has all your CDs,' Rupert told Marcus.

'I'm a huge fan,' confessed Elijah. 'My father's favourite is Brahms One.'

'What does your father do?' asked Marcus.

'He's a rabbi.'

'He must be excited about tomorrow. Is he coming to watch?'

'No. He doesn't approve, because I married out and manage football so often on the Sabbath.'

'No Sabbath here,' said Marcus, 'because the sun

never sets – so you've no need to feel guilty tomorrow. I didn't get on with Dad when I was younger either, and now my only regret is that I don't see nearly enough of him and adorable Taggie. He thinks the world of you, and Alexei and I are mad about Searston – we watch whenever we can. Horrendous tragedy about the massive car crash. Such dazzling players, losing their lives at the beginning of their careers. Talk about the paths of glory leading to the grave.'

Marcus was so charming, thought Elijah, and he could see a likeness to Rupert, like blond and russet greyhounds. Marcus was slighter, but they had the same lean, broad-shouldered bodies.

Feeling they must have so much to catch up on, as soon as the main course of boeuf stroganoff arrived, Elijah turned to talk to Alexei, 'the treat from Moscow', who was shy-makingly gorgeous with his deep basso profundo voice, grey-black curls, eyes slits of amused malice beneath heavy lids, and a half-smile playing over his big mouth. He was also as keen to talk about football as ballet.

'Searston do so well before car crash took so many of your players. Do you live in Vest Country?' he asked. 'I meet Marcus when I came there to dance in *Le Corsaire*.'

'Byron,' said Elijah. ' "There was a laughing devil in his sneer." '

'Very good.' Alexei was surprised. 'I didn't know footballers read poetry.'

'I'm a manager. Fucked myself as a player, but I couldn't bear to leave the game.'

'Me the same. Deeficult to retire as dancer, no more bravoes, no more centre of attention.'

'You'll always be the centre of attention – look how you were mobbed at the airport.'

433

'Marcus can go on playing for another thirty years, but to do it, he has to travel around. I am directing ballet now. Like being a manager, exciting in different way, more responsibility, I have to not be too autocrat. I think you should get new captain; that Parks is past it.'

'Actually, I'm replacing him tomorrow with Griffy.'

'Good choice. Greefy control game from central midfield.'

'Telling Parks is the hardest part. His bitch of a wife'll give him such hell.'

Across the table, Marcus and Rupert had so much to catch up on.

'How's darling Taggie?'

'She's really good. Hates having grey curly hair, but it's long now, and she looks just as gorgeous. She's cooking wonderful food for Searston and, as usual, looking after all the poor wives and girlfriends of the players who died. She loves football now. She desperately wanted to come to St Petersburg. But Bianca's suffering from one of those women things, the birth was tough, and she's so needy. She pleaded with Feral and Taggie to stay home with her.'

'Searston needs Feral far more than she does,' said Marcus, angrily. 'It's only for forty-eight hours; it's a bloody disgrace. Feral's your star player. What's Teddy like?'

Rupert produced a photograph:

'I'm not mad about babies, but he's really sweet.'

Marcus then put his knife and fork together and, saying he'd just got to ring his agent, joined the stuffed bear in the foyer, so Rupert rang Louisie to check on tomorrow's runners at Epsom.

Alexei was filling up his and Marcus's glasses with wine as deep red as Vermelho's colours.

'I ought to switch to water,' protested Elijah. 'I must have a clear head tomorrow.'

'I vouldn't,' said Alexei. 'Tchaikovsky died of cholera after drinking infected water in this very restaurant. You steek to vine. Vill Rupert keep team if you lose tomorrow?'

'I don't know,' said Elijah, 'he's put such a fortune into the club, been so generous. Some of the older players would find it hard to find other clubs.'

Elijah couldn't manage more than half his stroganoff. Alexei was forking up the rest.

'What about leetle Dolphy?' He looked at Elijah speculatively. 'He's going to be a great player when he stops being so unselfish. What's his background?'

'He's an orphan. Came from a children's home.'

'Marcus and I saw heem at press conference after crash, and he was so upset when he thought you'd been keeled.'

'He's a sweet boy.' Elijah felt himself blushing.

'And mad about you.'

'I have a wife and children,' snapped Elijah, 'and I'm twenty years older than him.'

'I more than twenty years older than Marcus. Too old, I thought. True artists can never belong to each other, only the world, I told him, and went back to Moscow. Then I realised I was wrong. I couldn't live without him.'

Oh, the beauty of Alexei's deep, deep voice.

'You only have one life, Elijah, and if you have the chance of happiness, follow your heart.'

'This red is delicious,' said Elijah, trying to normalise the conversation. 'What is it?'

Alexei examined the label and laughed. 'Appropriately, it's called Gai-Kodzor Malbec.'

They were interrupted by a returning Rupert and Marcus. Over more Gai-Kodzor and a delicious chocolate-covered soufflé, they drank Searston's health and talked about music.

As they came out into the broadest daylight, Rupert, determined to keep his intellectual end up, quoted from *The Tempest*, pointing out 'the cloud-capp'd towers, the gorgeous palaces, the solemn temples'.

'Good luck tomorrow,' Alexei murmured to Elijah. 'Remember to follow your heart.'

Back at the hotel, Rupert rang Taggie:

'Just had a great dinner with Marcus and Alexei and Elijah. They all send huge love and wish you were here. How are Bianca and Teddy?'

'They're fine. Feral's a bit quiet. The Wags will be with you tomorrow morning. Dora's bringing Tember.'

'That's good, but Christ, I wish Feral was on that plane. And you. God, I miss you, and the boeuf stroganoff this evening wasn't a patch on yours.'

The moment he rang off, his phone rang back again.

'Heaven, heaven, heaven,' squealed Dora. 'Sir Craig and Jarred have been arrested! It seems they did orchestrate the sabotage of your car, screwing up the brakes and the steering and puncturing the fuel tank, and were responsible for the unnecessary crash-landing of the Galloper as well. Several policemen, Gablecross's boys, rolled up at Lady Grace's soiree waving badges and arrested Sir Craig when he tried to fight them off. There was a bit of a battle. I think Sir Craig will probably end up in a loony bin rather than prison. They've arrested

Jarred, too. I've put out a massive press release saying you and Elijah weren't avaricious and only interested in financial gain when you flew the players back from Turkey.'

'Fucking hell,' said Rupert. 'Tell me more.'

And Dora did, ending up: 'The poor Battery Ram was no longer needed to whisk Sir Craig and co. to Birmingham airport.'

'He can join the sheep on the hill opposite Searston, ensuring us more victories next year, and we'll have our own electric plane to help combat climate change.'

Switching off, Rupert turned to Elijah.

'Sir Craig and Jarred have been arrested. We'd better have another drink.'

Much later, Elijah fell into bed, alcohol slightly easing his trepidation about tomorrow's match. Outside in the white night, the sun was blazing, the streets full of happy tourists. Marcus was right: you couldn't have a Sabbath without sunsets. He'd been so moved to see Marcus and Alexei so clearly in love after so many years. Trying to calm the turmoil in his heart, he picked up his copy of the Old Testament, which fell open at the Book of Tobit in the Apocrypha:

'So they went forth both,' he read, 'and the young man's dog with them.'

Oh Dolphy, oh Grandkid, he thought in anguish.

68

Feral didn't read social media, but Eamonn had gloom-
ily told him everyone was saying Searston didn't have a
dog's chance. In the double bed with Bianca in his arms
and tiny Teddy in his cradle beside them, Feral was so
wracked with guilt about letting the team down that he
didn't fall asleep until dawn, only to be woken, it seemed,
a few minutes later by Bianca.

'Feral, babe, I think you should go to St Petersburg.
You're the best player in the side, and Dad desperately
needs you and could make more than two hundred million pounds if they win. And think how proud Teddy'll
be when he grows up that his daddy played in the biggest match on the planet. Teddy and I have got Shelagh
and Mum to look after us. I want you to catch a plane
now. You'll be in Russia by this evening.'

'Are you sure, babe?'

'Quite, quite sure. Eamonn's going to fly you to
Heathrow. There's a plane at ten, so you'll be in St
Petersburg about three thirty Russian time. Now hurry
up and get dressed.'

'And you worked all this out yourself?' asked an

amazed and touched Feral. Bianca had never expressed such interest in his career before.

'Of course I did,' said Bianca. She was jolly well not going to let her stepbrother Marcus call her a selfish bitch.

The plane bearing Dora, Tember and the Wags was nearing St Petersburg.

'Bastian's really excited about going to Russia,' said Daffodil. 'He'll be too busy writing his *Hauteur Biography* to play much football.'

'He should use a ghost, like everyone else,' reproved Rosalie Parkinson.

'No, he's determined to write it hisself. But, talking of ghosts, the night before last, he went upstairs to pack. Suddenly, I heard him screaming his head off and fort perhaps we have a ghost after all. But it was because the moffs had got at his cashmore jumpers.'

'Cashmere, Daffodil,' snapped Rosalie.

'No, cashmore – they cost more cash than other jumpers.'

Rosalie had already excelled herself in lack of tact, by expressing amazement that Tember was also on the plane.

'We weren't expecting you, but it'll be very gratifying for Griffy to have both ladies in his life cheering him on.'

Seeing Inez looking murderous, Dora had hastily drawn Tember forward to travel in the little cabin behind the pilot, advising her to 'ignore both the silly bitches'.

Dora was wearing dark glasses and a lot of concealer to hide the black eye and bruises given her by Sir Craig, and proceeded to give Tember all the gossip about his arrest.

Twenty minutes away from St Petersburg, she emerged from the little cabin:

'Come on, Wags, get your things together.'

'We are women in our own right, with our own careers,' snorted Rosalie. ' "Wag" is an outmoded term.'

'Buddyguard doesn't think so,' giggled Dora, 'nor does Grandkid or Banquo or Gilchrist or Cuthbert or Mildred the mongrel.'

'Why do you trivialise everything, Dora?'

Sensing tension, Charm gazed down at the ocean and the city with its gold turrets and crisscross of canals.

'There's St Petersburg,' she cried. 'I am so excayted about seeing the Whayte Naytes.'

News of Sir Craig's and Jarred's arrests and the Chief Constable's possible contrivance in diverting the Galloper and sabotaging Rupert's car rocketed round the world, coupled with awareness that Searston, with four of their best players taken out, and no Feral, were Davids facing up to mighty Vermelho's Goliaths this evening.

So, in one of those U-turns so typical of football, a great tidal wave of love and support descended on Searston in St Petersburg.

They therefore woke from fairly disturbed sleep to find themselves heroes of the world and, on a wander round the glorious city after breakfast, were mobbed with crowds, selfie-seekers and pretty girl tourists.

This was followed by a gentle training session in a nearby park, with fans, media and several Vermelho spies rolling up to watch.

Earlier, Elijah had taken the opportunity to draw Parks aside at the hotel and tell him, very regretfully, he had been replaced as captain by Griffy.

'You'll be on the bench, Parks, so we may well call on you. But I think that your torn calf muscle has slowed you up as well as giving you a lot of pain, and distracted you as captain.'

Did he almost detect a glimmer of relief on Parks's face when he replied: 'Griffy's a good choice. But can we tell people, particularly Rosalie, that I'm only on the bench because I've been injured?'

Elijah was relieved the players seemed delighted by this decision. During a lunch of chicken and pasta, which they were all too nervous to eat, he had raised his glass and said:

'Let's drink a toast to our new Captain Iron Man.'

And everyone cheered, and a grinning Griffy was no longer upset by the cruel nickname.

After a brief sleep, they all went down to the hotel lobby to join Rupert watching The Story So Far in the Derby, and were thrilled to encounter a newly arrived Dora, Tember and the Wags.

To their additional delight, there was Taggie in the paddock at Epsom, looking stunning in a Prussian-blue trouser suit and a blue-and-green-striped scarf. Normally so shy, she was telling ITV's Ed Chamberlin in her soft, gruff Irish accent:

'This lovely filly, The Story So Far, is the daughter of the late leading sire Love Rat. Story belongs to Searston Rovers football team. As I'm sure you know, they're in Russia playing in the Champions League final this evening. My husband, Rupert Campbell-Black, Story's trainer and also their chairman, is out there with them. I longed to go too but felt Story needed me to hold her hoof as she's the only filly in this race, and a filly hasn't won the Derby since 1916 – that's over a hundred years ago – and she's being ridden by a wonderful jockey, Rupert's grandson Eddie Alderton, so we're keeping it in the family.'

Then, as Louisie led up a gleaming chestnut Story, Taggie added:

'This is lovely Louisie, who looks after Story and is going to marry Josef Droza, one of Searston's best players.'

'Christ, you're a lucky sod,' called out Barry Pitt to a grinning Josef.

'So can we take this opportunity,' ended Taggie, 'of wishing Searston huge luck in St Petersburg tonight.'

And the players cheered their heads off, even more so when little Story, ridden by Eddie Alderton in blue and green Searston colours, romped home in first place.

'I had twenty grand each way,' boasted Midas. 'That'll keep me going for a few months if Rupert has to sell us after tonight.'

'Shut up,' hissed Griffy, then shouted out, 'if Story can trounce the boys, we can beat Vermelho.'

An ecstatic Rupert had immediately rung Taggie.

'That was fucking marvellous. Brilliant little Story and Eddie, and you were brilliant on the box. You'll be taking over from Matt Chapman next. Thank you for boosting Searston – the boys are knocked out. And how did you get to Epsom? Are Bianca and Teddy OK?'

'Fine. It was Bianca who insisted I went. Eamonn flew me in the chopper, and Louisie and I are going to fly straight home to watch the match. All the luck in the world, my darling.'

'Oh God, I wish you were here. I'd better go and stop the players ordering champagne on room service.'

An even more wonderful surprise greeted them a minute later as Feral, the playmaker, sauntered in wearing a 'Dad of the Year' sweatshirt, and his overjoyed teammates fell on him as if he'd scored a hat-trick.

Dolphy was especially touched when Feral later gave him a photograph of Grandkid asleep beside Forester and Rupert's dogs in the giant red-curtained four-poster. In the corner, Taggie had scribbled: 'Good lick Dollfi.'

69

Although the players were buoyed up by the arrival of
Feral, they were still very jittery. There was nearly a
punch-up in the dressing room before the match
because Midas, having nicked Barry Pitt's *Daily Mail* in
order to fill in Barry's beloved crossword, pretended he
had only chucked the paper away to hide a bitchy piece
about Feral.

'Feral can't fucking read,' Barry had snarled.

Whereupon Elijah had yelled, 'Fight the fucking
opposition, not each other,' which shocked the entire
dressing room into silence. So Elijah gave them a last-
minute briefing, reminding them who were the chief
danger men, who was short-fused and could be wound
up, who had pace or power and who had better left or
right feet.

'Try to read passes and intercept them, look around
the whole time to see who's on offer. Think before you
kick, particularly into goal. Let's win for Rupert and to
honour our comrades who died. "We few, we happy
few" ' – Elijah's voice deepened as he smiled round at all

his players – ' "we band of brothers. For he today that sheds his blood with me shall be my brother." '

Glancing at his watch, he realised it was nearly ten o' clock – not the Sabbath any more, so a perfectly OK time to play football.

Over in the Vermelho dressing room, no one was in any doubt that victory would be confirmed by midnight, so they could party until dawn.

Zeus, echoing his players in a dark-red velvet suit and wafting Dior Sauvage, emphasised the fact that not much defending would be needed. Although not match-fit, Feral Jackson was Searston's best player, so they'd better put two men on to him.

'What matters,' continued Zeus, 'is pressing forward, steeking close together and scoring an avalanche of goals. We have the chance of going into the heestory books weeth the beegest ween ever in Champions League, so wheech of my star strikers weel score most? I hope Beeg Ben, best of men' – he smiled at Bruiser Martin – 'weel strike ten.'

Then he turned lovingly to his beautiful ash-blond goalkeeper, Alan Bordesco, known as Alan of Troy.

'And you, dear boy, weel have so leetle to do, you might as well take the afternoon off.'

And the players roared with laughter.

The packed-out Krestovsky Stadium totally excluded any blazing sunshine from outside. Inside, it was a blue heaven, with azure seats and tall darker blue boards, covered not with ads but with powder-blue squiggles, to separate the crowd from the players. High above the top seats were more powder-blue squiggles, meant to illustrate the tops of footballs but resembling greyhounds following in single file round the stadium, which seemed a great omen.

Among the pundits, filmed round their shiny blue table like the only diners in a restaurant, Ludo had been warned once again by Rio Ferdinand and Owen Hargreaves not to be too partisan.

The photographers, all massed behind Searston's goal in anticipation of Armageddon, were also trying to get pictures of musical superstars Alexei Nemerovsky and Marcus Campbell-Black sitting in the main stand with the Gallopers' handsome blond chairman. Directly below them was the Searston technical area, where a pacing Elijah had added a blue-and-green-striped tie to last night's dark suit.

'We adore your Elijah,' Marcus told Rupert. 'And we're praying he's going to take the smug smile off the face of that wanker Zeus Martinez.'

As the teams came out, leading excited little boys by the hand, Searston, in black armbands, caught sight of their travelling army of blue-and-green fans unfurling a huge banner showing photos of Angus, Orion, Downing and Wilfie, captioned 'In Loving Memory', which was replicated for several seconds on the stadium's big screen.

As the two teams lined up, divided by three refs in buttercup yellow, it could be seen how much taller and massively hunkier were Vermelho.

'Those Vermin Hellos are huge,' muttered Dolphy to Bastian.

'"Vermin Hello",' grinned Bastian. 'Great title for my next chapter.'

During the one minute's silence round the centre circle, Captain Griffy put an arm round Ahmed, who was wiping his eyes on his shirt as he remembered Angus.

Griffy's wife, Inez, in a wildly expensive new emerald-green skirt suit with a sapphire-blue shirt, although reeking of Facundo's Fracas, was thoroughly enjoying herself upstaging Rosalie as Searston's new captain's lady.

'I bet poor old Parks'd like a minute's silence from Rosalie's yakking,' reflected Midas, as he waved discreetly up at Charm surrounded by the rest of the Galloper Wags, who yelled, 'Good luck, boys, you can do it,' as the team took up their positions.

The official match ball, with interlocking red and yellow stars over a white background, was placed on the centre spot and Galgo kicked off. But alas, the Gallopers were off to their usual disastrous start and, as Vermelho pressed ruthlessly upfield, kept missing passes out of nerves, or passing straight to the opposition.

'Are they fucking colour-blind?' raged Rupert. Why the hell had he listened to Elijah and not given them a roasting before the game?

Within ten minutes, a vengeful Facundo, embodying the Curse of the Ex, had blasted the ball into the net, then, to show off his golden body, whipped off his dark-red shirt, whirling it round before sliding on his knees to soak up the adulation.

The whole stadium seemed to be blushing as Vermelho fans leapt up in excitement, brandishing dark-red flags and scarves in the air.

'Were not you crazy to sack me?' Facundo shouted across at Elijah. 'All I needed was a decent manager.'

None of Facundo's team seemed to be hugging him.

'They don't like him any more than we did,' observed Bastian.

Inez, however, forgetting her new role as captain's lady, was screaming from the Wags' stand: 'Brilliant play, Facundo, well done. Isn't he fantastic?'

'Silly bitch,' shouted Dora, who was sitting with Tember on the edge of the same stand.

'Facundo's knocking off Jean Jacques's wife,' Tember whispered back, 'and it's when the other woman finds about the other other woman that the shit really hits the fan, so there should be fireworks by midnight.'

As huge Bruiser Martin, spurred on by Facundo scoring the first goal, pounded down the field, sending Midas flying, Barry Pitt howled at his quaking defence to get off their fucking arses. He then stopped the ball, which Bruiser had clouted towards the goal, only for it to fly out of his hands, enabling Bruiser to pound it back in.

'Two–nil.'

'Butterfingers,' sighed Tember. 'But isn't Griffy stunning?'

Although still very thin, she had washed her lovely Titian hair, concealed the dark circles under her eyes and was wearing a blue-and-green Searston shirt.

'You look gorgeous too,' reassured Dora, who had a headache and was still hiding her black eye and bruises with heavy make-up and dark glasses.

As well as the travelling army of Searston supporters, thousands of wildly excited fans from Sierra Leone and Nigeria had turned up to cheer on Ahmed and Ezra. The Russians in the crowd seemed hardly to react to either side. 'Dead Panski,' scribbled Dora.

*

Back in England, at Penscombe, night had fallen, and much wine was being consumed by a big party round the kitchen table to ward off gloom about the score.

Entering the house, seeing the Stubbs missing from Rupert's office and faded squares on the walls in the drawing room where a Gainsborough, a Lely and a Romney had once hung, they were aware that this might be Searston's last match. Taggie and Louisie were back from the Derby, brandishing the trophy, which now glittered on the dresser. The Story So Far, after a heroine's welcome, had been tucked up in her box.

Louisie was gazing at her Theo Fennell emerald engagement ring and praying Josef might score soon. Shelagh and Taggie were toasting cheese sandwiches for everyone and making hot chocolate for Sapphire and Timon, who was surreptitiously knocking back mugs of white wine.

Little Teddy was beaming on Bianca's knee. But taking it in turns to cuddle him were Wilfie's mother, Mary, and Mimi, who'd rolled up with Hughie Winston.

Kind Shelagh and Eamonn had also taken in Tilly and Minnie, who were so excited to see Daddy Griffy playing. While Mildred the mongrel had joined the other dogs stretched out on sofas and, like Banquo, Buddyguard, the Jack Russells and Grandkid, was missing her master and continually glancing at the door, listening out for his return. Everyone was laughing at the picture on the *Cotchester Times* website of gallant Buddyguard in Sir Craig's red sombrero and saying how brave he and Dora had been.

'There's your daddy,' Bianca told little Teddy, as a shot from Feral hit the bar and bounced over.

Feral hadn't played for a month. Despite training every

day, after sleepless nights kept awake by Bianca, and a long flight, he was finding it difficult to get stuck in.

'Oh Feral, you must do better,' wailed Bianca, particularly as the Vermelho striker, not to be outdone by Bruiser and Facundo, who'd hit on his wife, scored from a free kick, taking the score to 3–0.

The Vermelho supporters were roaring themselves hoarse. One of their midfielders, Ruben Carlos, Elijah's little weasel, however, was waiting for treatment, rolling on the grass, groaning, screaming and clutching his knee as the medics ran on, so the camera switched to the pundits.

'That is not a penalty,' insisted a boot-faced Ludo. 'Ruben Carlos dived. He's wasted on football, should be in Hollywood.'

'Steady, Ludo,' muttered the other pundits.

'Isn't Ludo marvellous?' sighed Mary. 'He won't suck up to anyone.'

On cue, at Penscombe, there was a bang on the kitchen door. The dogs barked, wagged and looked up in excitement, until Mary's husband, Dougie, sauntered in, very smart in a blazer and Searston striped shirt.

'Good evening, especially to you, Taggie,' he smirked. 'I thought you ladies might enjoy some male company and we should all raise a glass in memory of my and Mary's beloved son Wilfie.'

To everyone's amazement, little Mary jumped to her feet.

'Just bugger off,' she cried, 'you're not welcome here, you horrible man,' and everyone cheered.

'We've got Hughie,' giggled Mimi, 'and Teddy's male company too.'

'This is a private party,' raged Mary. 'Go away. I never want to see you again. Get out of my life for ever.'

'And Hughie will handle your divorce,' called out Mimi, then, as everyone howled with laughter, 'and this *is* a private party.'

'I'm afraid it is,' apologised Taggie, sending a furious Dougie off into the night, which was filled with much brighter stars than those playing for Searston in St Petersburg.

Everyone congratulated Mary for dispatching her gatecrashing husband, but no one minded when Safety Car wandered into the kitchen and Louisie gave him a bowl of red wine.

'There's your master, darling,' cried Taggie as the camera panned on to Rupert, yelling at his players as both sides battled to score.

Dolphy was running everywhere – 'Come on, we've got to win for Elijah' – and the next moment, Josef dodged past massive, bullying Bruiser Martin and belted it in. 3–1.

And the stadium went crazy, the fifteen thousand Searston fans making more noise than the rest of the crowd put together. There was a slight lull in the din as the players reassembled for kick-off. Marcus had been busy earlier in the day, finding a tenor from the opera house.

'Campbell-Black Beauty,' the most beautiful voice echoed round the stadium.

> We thought you were snooty,
> Now we think you're a cutie.
> A generous and fair man,
> Thank God you're our chairman.

This was followed by roars of laughter and applause.

'You're actually blushing, Dad,' laughed Marcus.

451

'Kind of them,' said Rupert, trying not to look flattered.

But as the umpteenth spectator from a nearby stand tapped him on his shoulder – 'Could you possibly ask Marcus Campbell-Black to sign my programme?' – Rupert reverted to type and told him to eff off.

Half-time and still 3–1. The Searston players, already shattered from running and battling, had collapsed on the dressing-room floor, many of them taking their shirts off.

'Well done,' said Elijah, 'bloody good defending, and that was a great goal, Josef. I know they're brutes, and a lot of you are having to play through pain, but go out and try to enjoy yourselves.' Regrettably, Elijah told them, Midas, having been sent flying by Bruiser, was coming off because he didn't want to wreck his back completely, so young Rollo would be making his debut.

'Nothing like starting at the top, in the biggest game on earth,' said Elijah.

'I might earn enough for a Lamborghini,' crowed Rollo.

Next moment, Rupert had strolled in.

Oh hell, thought Elijah, but Rupert smiled round at them. 'That was just the warm-up; now it's time for the real thing.'

70

Avid for goals, £3 million each in bonuses and everlasting fame, Vermelho pressed even further forwards, leaving a great gap of pitch behind them, whereupon Galgo streaked down the sideline into the gap, lashing in a beautiful goal over the blond head of a dozing Alan of Troy.

'Three–two, marvellous finish, totally against the run of play,' said the commentators.

Then Feral finally caught fire, passing to Josef, who passed well ahead of him back to an accelerating Feral, who unleashed another Exocet, making it 3–3. As an example of Searston's camaraderie, his ecstatic teammates fell on him, even Barry Pitt running halfway down the field yelling: 'Welcome back, Jackson.'

'Searston have got their tails up,' said the surprised commentators.

'Oh, shut up,' chorused the party at Penscombe. 'Don't count our chickens.'

And predictably, shortly afterwards, Facundo swollen-headed the ball into goal.

'Well done, darling, well done, Facundo,' screamed Inez.

'Wrong side, Inez,' yelled Dora.

Even worse, Jean Jacques scored five minutes later, taking the score to 5–3.

Searston proceeded to defend their hearts out, Ahmed and Ezra blocking shot after shot, a frustrated Vermelho getting rougher and rougher.

At eighty minutes, Alan of Troy lofted the ball upfield and Griffy, who had been directing the players with his back to his own goal, leapt four feet in the air, miraculously stopping the ball and powering it back into Vermelho's goal, to reduce their lead to 5–4.

'Christ, he ought to take up ballet,' said Alexei.

'Don't hug me too hard,' pleaded Griffy, as his teammates fell on him.

'Well done, Griffy, well done, darling,' screamed Tember, leaping to her feet. 'That was the greatest goal ever. Well done, oh well done, darling.'

Along the row, Inez raised a plucked eyebrow.

'You do realise it's my husband you're yelling about?'

Although utterly preoccupied with the game, Rupert was increasingly aware of a tall man with dark-grey hair and a beard, shouting his head off in the stand to the right. Elijah was too obsessed with his players to notice.

The score was still 5–4 to Vermelho, with only three minutes left of injury time, bringing an end to the Gallopers' hopes. Then Ahmed dribbled the ball down, placed a beautiful assist between the goalposts, and a hovering Ezra headed it in – only his second goal for Searston – it was now 5–5 and the game went into extra time.

'Ezra Time,' Dora scribbled joyfully in her notebook.

*

Back in Searston, fans from all over the Cotswolds, for whom there hadn't been enough tickets allotted in St Petersburg, had crowded on to the Deep Woods pitch to watch the match on the big screen, raided the bar and were now engaged in a huge celebration, waving flags and scarves and holding up posters.

Zeus, on the other hand, was having a hissy fit rather than a history-book fit that Vermelho weren't further ahead and wouldn't produce the greatest Champions League victory. After he had unleashed more thunder-bolts in the dressing room, the Argentinian captain and Ruben Carlos, the Weasel, both scored, putting Vermelho 7–5 up. So they eased off a little. Having stopped a shot from Josef, Alan of Troy fell on the ball, kissing it lingeringly, then spent ages getting back on to his feet and repositioning himself before kicking the ball back into play. Whereupon Jean Jacques scooped it up and mockingly kicked it back and forth to his team-mates round the pitch to waste more time, until an exasperated Griffy gently tried to take the ball off Ruben Carlos and was yellow-carded as Ruben fell to the ground, writhing in much pretended agony.

'Vermelho ought to be bloody shot,' raged Ludo, as Zeus wasted yet more time subbing players, and any cheering was drowned by the Cotswold Travelling Army booing their heads off. Even the Russians in the crowd were getting less dead-panski.

With five minutes to go, Bruiser Martin, seeing Galgo and Josef descending on him, kicked the ball miles out of play. It was then picked up by a Vermelho supporter, who shoved it under his red T-shirt, pretending to be pregnant, reducing his fellow fans to howls of laughter and only relinquishing it when the ref yelled at him.

Griffy then chose Ezra, who'd endlessly practised throw-ins, to take over. Bravely ignoring a fearsome ring of advancing red shirts, Ezra chucked the ball over their heads to young Rollo, who shouted with joy as he scored his debut goal for Searston, making it 7–6.

Three minutes of injury time were left, the stands roaring their heads off. But as Zeus held up his hand for another substitution, Feral lost it. Snatching up a pass intended for Facundo, he hurtled down the pitch, feigning a pass to a surrounded Galgo, then flicking it instead to a racing-past Dolphy, who paused for a second – 'Left foot, right foot, fink before you kick' – and, gathering all his strength, lashed the ball 30 yards into goal with his left foot.

'Fucking hell, what a worldie!' cried the ref in wonder, then remembered to blow his whistle so the game went into penalties.

As overjoyed teammates buried him, Dolphy caught sight of an ecstatic Elijah. Thrilled at the prospect of more thrills to come, the crowd were yelling their heads off, with the Cotswold Travelling Army making even more din, clapping and thrusting, their big green-and-blue flags waving back and forth like a regatta on a choppy blue ocean.

Each team would now have five kicks and the team which scored the most penalties from these five would win. As Searston, who'd played their hearts out, collapsed on the ground, Elijah walked up and down, wondering which of his team should take them. If only Orion and Downing were alive. When he saw who was taking Vermelho's kicks, he was able to wise up Barry Pitt on the shooting pro-clivities of each player. 'But trust your instincts, Barry.'

From his own team, he chose Galgo, Feral, Josef, Dolphy and Griffy to start. If the sides were level after five penalties each, they would go into Sudden Death, and the first team to let in a goal would be the loser.

Barry Pitt was suddenly panic-stricken. Normally, he had ten players to defend him. Now he was totally alone. The stadium seethed with excitement, prayers rising like fountains.

'Let Griffy's strike go in,' begged Tember.

Rupert was touched to see Alexei and Marcus, whose cheers had been louder than anyone's, clutching each other's hands. Ludo had also abandoned any attempt at impartiality. He was fed up with being a pundit; he was going to train as a manager and have vast crowds dependent on him for their happiness each week.

Searston went into a team huddle, arms around each other's shoulders, as Elijah gave them last instructions:

'Now, remember: walk, don't run. On the one hand, choose where you're going to kick and stick to it, but if they move before you kick, then make a lightning swivel in the other direction.' Noticing Dolphy was trembling with nerves, he had to fight the temptation to stroke the back of his neck. Aware that he hadn't been on top form earlier, Feral was determined to score for little Teddy.

'The sun still blazing outside must be desperate to gatecrash the stadium and witness such a thrilling ending,' scribbled Dora in her notebook.

As Vermelho won the toss and would go first in the shoot-out, the teams lined up with linked arms on either side of the goal. The ball was placed on the penalty spot. Barry was the first goalie to defend.

Bruiser Ben Martin strode out, six foot six of arrogance, placed the ball on the penalty spot and went insane with rage when his shot flew over the bar. The tumultuous Searston cheers faded, however, when he had to go again because Barry had strayed forward off his goal line, which was not allowed. At a second attempt, Bruiser blasted it in and sauntered off looking smug.

'Sorry, boss,' Barry muttered to Elijah as he was replaced in goal by the Vermelho keeper, Alan of Troy, who was finding his evening more taxing than expected – particularly when Galgo hit the back of the net, falling to his knees, joyfully crossing himself and taking the score to 1–1.

Goal machine Jean Jacques and Feral then both scored, making it 2–2, with Feral holding up his shirt to display the words 'I love Teddy' on his T-shirt underneath. Everyone at Penscombe screamed with delight.

Facundo sauntered out next, theatrically raising his arms and smiling round at the cheering crowd, before kissing the ball and placing it on the spot.

'Isn't he gorgeous?' shouted Inez. 'Come on, Facundo.'

'Shut up,' yelled Dora, noticing Jean Jacques's voluptuous wife, also reeking of Fracas, scowling at Inez from the Vermelho Wags' side of the stand.

Facundo's smile faded as he turned towards Barry, then paused for a long ten seconds before smiting the ball goal-wards, whereupon Barry flew through the air and miraculously stopped it, keeping the score still 2–2. Sand Pitt's scream of joy was drowned by an explosion of cheering.

Glancing up, Elijah made a thumbs-up sign to Rupert as Josef strolled forward, crossed himself and powered the ball towards the top left-hand corner.

Alas, Alan of Troy, determined to outshine Barry Pitt, somehow managed to bat it away. As Josef fell to his knees in despair, Louisie's wail, 'Oh, my poor, poor darling,' must have been heard in St Petersburg.

The handsome Vermelho captain then came out and unleashed an Exocet into the back of the goal, to the ecstasy of his red-velvet-suited manager.

3–2 to Vermelho.

Dolphy followed him, knees knocking, quaking with terror.

'Take time to fink,' he was telling himself. 'Choose where you're going to kick and stick wiv it. Our Farver which art in Heaven.' He was about to kick to the right, then, seeing Alan of Troy take off to his left, Dolphy made a lightning switch to his own left and walloped it in. 3–3.

As he returned grinning with relief, the cheers nearly took the roof off the stadium. Even Vermelho's supporters admired quick thinking.

Barry Pitt was back in goal facing Vermelho's fifth contestant, the Brazilian world-class finisher, and trying to remember what Elijah had said about him. Next moment, he'd lofted a shot past Barry's ear, but the net didn't shiver. Still 3–3.

As Captain Griffy walked out, he was aware that everything depended on him. If he missed, each side would be level after their five goes, and Sudden Death would follow. The stadium fell silent. Just for a second, Griffy's thoughts flickered to Tember – the only other thing that mattered was to spend the rest of his life with her. Alan of Troy bounced on his goal line. Behind him, Vermelho fans hurled missiles into the back of the net, even shining laser pens into Griffy's eyes to confuse him.

Bloody unsporting, fumed Griffy. Ignoring them, he closed his eyes, pondering for a good ten seconds.

Tember couldn't bear to look, covering her face with her hands, pleading: 'Please, please God.'

Luckily, God had his hearing aids in. Griffy opened his eyes, composed himself, then lashed the ball between the left-hand post and the goalie's flying fingers, so it slid deep into the net.

4–3 and victory to Searston.

There was a long, incredulous silence. Then, because Vermelho had been so unsporting and the win so totally unexpected, the crowd went berserk. The Cotswold Travelling Army was holding up Searston Rovers streamers and swirling their scarves around, still bellowing louder than the rest of the stadium put together.

'Fucking, fucking marvellous,' howled Ludo to the horror of his fellow pundits. Rupert was hugging Alexei and Marcus. Midas, in the players' area of the stand, was shouting:

'My auntie Ruth had twelve grand on at thirty to one; I can buy effing Searston Rovers myself now.'

'Ow, ow, bloody ow.'. A wincing Griffy shook off the pack of players jumping on him and, running towards the touchline, for the first time in his life showed off his lean and beautiful body by whipping off his shirt and chucking it over the dark-blue perimeter board to an ecstatic fan.

'Look, look, Tember,' cried Dora, because, through Griffy's growing chest hair, which Inez had always made him wax off, could clearly be seen his first-ever tattoo, proclaiming in large letters:

'I Love Tember West For Ever.' And he smiled up as

Tember screamed with joy and leapt from the Wags' stand down into his arms for a kiss that went into extra time.

'And I love you too,' Tember gasped when she finally came up for air. 'You played so fantastically and captained so brilliantly. When did you get that tattoo done?'

'Yesterday,' panted Griffy. 'They nearly inked it in Russian, and the tattooist said I mustn't play for at least three days, so it's a bit sore. You'll have to treat me gently in bed tonight.'

A furious Inez was intent on separating them, when Fracas appropriately met Fracas, and a vicious shove from Facundo's latest squeeze, Jean Jacques's wife, sent Inez flying.

Down on the pitch, Alan of Troy, who'd seen better daisies, was kneeling with his head and arms on the grass, sobbing his heart out.

'Better luck next time, you poor fing.' A passing Dolphy patted him on the shoulder.

Zeus was so outraged to have lost that he vanished down the tunnel, refusing to talk to anyone.

Elijah and Rupert were going round congratulating their players and shaking hands with the rest of the opposition, when Elijah and Dolphy met face to face. Not caring what anyone thought, they fell into each other's arms, passionately kissing.

'I love you always,' cried Dolphy.

'I'm never going to let you go again,' gasped Elijah.

Then, over Dolphy's shoulder, he saw a familiar figure approaching, and paused in terror because it was Rabbi Abner Cohen, his father – but he was smiling broadly. Walking up to Elijah, Abner held out his hand, embraced him, then, in a voice hoarse from yelling, said:

'Well done, son. I'm so proud of you. What a victory, absolutely marvellous.'

Still holding Dolphy's hand, Elijah stammered his thanks and then said:

'And this is Dolphy.'

'I know it is,' said Abner, shaking Dolphy's other hand with his other hand. 'What brilliant goals. Well done, Dolphy.'

Next moment, a tearful smiling Ruth had joined them, hugging Elijah.

'I'm so sorry, son. Please forgive us.' Then, turning and hugging Dolphy: 'Hello, Dolphy. We hope you're going to be part of our family.'

She was followed by Elijah's wildly excited children, whose friends had all been messaging them to praise their father.

'Congrats, Dad, you was brilliant,' said Isaiah. Then, turning to Dolphy: 'So were you. We can't believe you beat Vermelho.'

'You've come all the way from London?' asked an incredulous Elijah. 'How did you all get together?'

'We decided to introduce ourselves to our Grandpa and Granny Cohen,' said Naomi, taking Ruth's hand, 'and they're so lovely, we all decided to come and cheer you on.'

'Isaiah and Naomi convinced us how bigoted we'd been and how incredibly proud we should be of you,' confessed Abner, 'and how good it would be if we were all together again as a family.'

'And we've got a coat for Grandkid,' said Isaiah. 'We hope he's going to join our family as well as you, Dolphy.'

And Dolphy screamed with joy: 'I've got a family, I've got a family.'

'And they're not wild about Mum,' Naomi whispered to Elijah. 'They're so pleased you've shacked up with Dolphy.'

At that moment, a grinning Rupert came up, nodded at the Cohens and said:

'Come on, Dolphy, we've got to go and lift the trophy and get your medal.'

In front of a huge blue circle inscribed with the word 'Winners', Griffy was holding up a vast three-foot-high silver cup, now trailing green and blue ribbons, as he and his players, already drenched in champagne, disappeared in a snowstorm of white paper snowflakes.

'Well done,' Rupert said to Elijah, as the players took it in turns to be photographed hoisting the trophy. 'We're kings of European football.'

A beaming Dolphy was being interviewed by Sky as Man of the Match.

'As soon as the ball left my foot, I knew it was going in. I fort, wow, there is a God, and he's on my side and Searston's too. It's a dream come true.'

Back at Penscombe, as another joyous party unfolded, Grandkid, hearing his master's voice and seeing him on the screen, jumped up and put his head on one side, wagging his tail.

'It's your lovely master, darling,' cried Taggie. 'He looks very happy. He'll be home tomorrow.'

Next moment, there was a knock on the door, and a very thin but pretty Black woman walked in.

'Omigod,' gasped Bianca.

'Please forgive me,' quavered the woman, 'but I have

been watching my son Feral scoring a goal for his son, Teddy, and as Teddy's my grandson, I hope you don't mind me dropping in to see him?'

'But that's wonderful,' cried Bianca, tears spilling down her cheeks. 'This is Feral's mum, everyone, and Teddy's granny.'

Lifting a sleeping Teddy from his carrycot, she held him out to Nancy, and Teddy, when Nancy cradled him in her arms, woke up, opened his eyes and beamed up at her.

'Oh, you little angel.' Nancy's voice broke. 'He's more beautiful than the Christ child.'

'It's so lovely you're here,' said Taggie. 'Let's have a huge glass of champagne to celebrate.'

In the corner, celebrating their individual masters' victory, Grandkid was joyfully humping Mildred.

71

Back in Russia, jubilation, coupled with incredulity at such an unexpected victory, led to a glorious midnight party on the lawn outside Team Searston's hotel. Here the sun, shut out of the Krestovsky Stadium, took great delight in blazing on the players as they lined up for a White Knights photograph, cheered on by Marcus, Alexei and a bursting-with-pride Rabbi, Ruth and grandchildren Isaiah and Naomi.

Too nervous to eat before the game, in between enjoying rave reviews on their iPhones, the team were stuffing themselves with chicken Kiev, truffles, dumplings, meatballs, blinis filled with caviar and smoked salmon, plus every kind of ice cream, washed down with beetroot soup, champagne and full-bodied Russian wines.

'At this rate, we'll need a throw-up coach rather than a throw-in one,' Rupert murmured to Marcus, before clapping his hands for silence. 'I don't want to waste party time making speeches, but I'd just like to say well done to all the team. To do what you did today after the great loss of your teammates takes real guts. You've done them proud. And I'm so proud of all of you.'

'Is that all, boss?' piped up Dolphy, who'd been at the champagne and was now sitting on Elijah's knee. 'Aren't you *fucking* proud of us?'

'No.' Rupert paused. 'I'm fucking fucking fucking proud of you,' and even the Rabbi roared with laughter.

'Briefly,' continued Rupert, 'you all played brilliantly. Elijah is a great manager and watches all your backs.'

'I want him to *wash* my back.'

'Shut up, Dolphy. A great manager, and it's great to see his family here in St Petersburg.' Rupert smiled at Rabbi Abner and Ruth. 'And Griffy has proved a miraculous captain, keeping his nerve, nailing the final penalty and, as only the brave deserve the fair, he's got his reward' – Rupert raised his glass – 'with lovely Tember.'

Griffy, who'd been gazing into Tember's eyes and stroking her freckled face in wonder, looked round and smiled, saying, 'Two miracles in one evening is pretty cool,' and everyone cheered.

'Three miracles, if we count The Story So Far winning the Derby,' shouted Midas.

'And you've done great, boss,' added Dolphy, 'staying wiv us when it looked as though everyfing was lost, and I'm so frilled to be a family member, and meet your son Marcus, and his husband, Alexei.'

'OK, Dolphy, that's quite enough speeches,' said Rupert. 'Story's tucked up in bed at Penscombe. Taggie sends buckets of love. Don't stay up too late – our plane's leaving tomorrow at ten a.m. Russian time. Eamonn's going to meet us at the other end and pop into Deep Woods so we can have a bit of a celebration to thank the ground staff.'

*

Everyone was having a ball. Josef had cheered up when so many people told him his opening goal had been crucial. Daffodil, Charm and Sand Pitt were dancing with Ezra and Ahmed, Bastian was writing his *Hauteur Biography*, Rupert was touched to get a congratulatory text from Valent, and Feral was showing everyone pictures of baby Teddy, when Dolphy's mobile rang. After listening briefly, he said:

'You're very kind, but I'm perfectly happy where I am.'

'Who was that?' asked Elijah, as Dolphy switched it off.

'Alan Garcia, ordering me to have lunch wiv him on Monday because lots of top clubs are after me, but I told him I was sorted.'

Then, putting his arm round Elijah's shoulder, fingering his black locks, he murmured:

'Barry Pitt advised me not to indulge in public displays of affection in Russia, but could we go upstairs and indulge in some private ones?'

Elijah took his hand. 'We certainly can.'

Tember and Griffy were already in bed, not drawing the curtains because Tember wanted to admire Griffy's tattoo.

'It's the loveliest bedside reading I've ever had. Did it hurt dreadfully?'

'Not nearly as much as losing you. I had to do something to convince you I loved you. I was so devastated getting home and finding you'd gone.'

'Didn't you get the note I left?'

'What note? Bloody Inez must have torn it up.'

'Are you sure it won't hurt too much if I go down on

467

you?' murmured Tember, her lovely hair spilling over his belly and thighs.

'Nothing hurts now you're here. But you excite me so much, I'll come in a second.'

'No, you won't. I've got a song for the fans to sing.' And, bursting into song herself: 'Griffy's too squiffy to come in a jiffy, Griffy's so clever, keeps going for ever.'

Seeing the sun on her laughing, loving face, Griffy pulled her down beside him.

'Tember, darling, could you possibly bear to spend the rest of your life with me?'

'Oh, Griffy, I couldn't possibly bear not to.'

Dora, meanwhile, was on an endless call to Jackie Carslake, overjoyed to learn that the Chief Constable had been arrested and would appear in court with Sir Craig and Jarred next week.

She was irritated that Ryan Edwards was taking all the credit for exposing them – 'Bloody man' – but she was enchanted that Buddyguard would be awarded a canine VC for bravery.

'It's so exciting here too,' went on Dora, 'not just winning the match. We're going to have to have a wedding supplement. Everyone's getting off with everyone. Rupert's already promised Lou-Easy and Josef a June wedding, and Tember and Griffy have just gone off to bed together. I think Inez got knocked out cold by Jean Jacques's wife, and Elijah and Dolphy have gone up too. Yes, I promise you, Dolphy keeps referring to Elijah as his future husband – very Males and Boon – so that's a loser's medal for Madison. And Feral's such a huge star, now he'll feel worthy enough to marry Bianca and legitimise little Ted.'

'My God,' said Jackie. 'What about you and Paris?'

'We're fine. I'll see him tomorrow and it's a great party here. The manager keeps coming in and telling us to shut up because no one can get any sleep. So we all keep singing "Nessun Dorma".'

72

Euphoria somehow dispelled hangover next morning, when the team were waved off in their private jet by a mass of media and fans, including Marcus and Alexei as well as the Rabbi, Ruth and the grandchildren, who'd decided to stay on a few days longer exploring St Petersburg. Also in the private jet were Tember, who couldn't bear to be parted for a second from Griffy, and Dora, who was needed for media duties and was desperate to get back to Paris and Buddyguard and Mew-Too. The Wags were having a lie-in and coming home on a later plane.

In the private jet, the players who weren't catching up on sleep were enjoying more rave reviews on their iPhones. Bastian was wondering whether to rename his *Hauteur Biography* the *Naughty Biography*, to describe the goings-on. Across the aisle, Dolphy had fallen asleep, his head on Elijah's shoulder. Rupert was talking to Taggie, who said the party at Penscombe had only just finished.

'We were all so excited you won, Banquo wagged like mad when he saw you on telly, and Grandkid went crazy when he heard Dolphy talking. Wonderful Paris went and kidnapped Mildred the mongrel, who horrible Inez had left locked in the house. And I'm over the moon Griffy's got together with darling Tember. Someone should send Inez a loser's medal, as well as Madison. And best of all, you'll never guess what – Feral's mother, Nancy, turned up! She was so overexcited seeing Feral on television showing off his "I love Teddy" shirt that she couldn't resist coming over and she absolutely adored Teddy. We all had champagne and Bianca insisted she stayed the night. Don't tell Feral; Bianca wants to surprise him.'

'Blimey,' said Rupert, 'you seem to be having more excitement at Penscombe.' Then, sending up a prayer: 'Darling, you haven't had your test results back yet?'

'Not yet.'

'Promise to ring me the moment you have.'

The private jet dropped Team Searston off at Rutshire airfield, where they were met by a beaming Eamonn, another huge crowd of fans in blue and green stripes, and press trying to interview every player.

'I just want to pop into Deep Woods to raise a glass to the ground staff there,' said Rupert as he took the front seat just behind Eamonn on the blue-and-green Searston coach, 'then I want to go straight home to Taggie. Is she OK?'

'Enchanted by your winning. They had a great party. Safety had so many bowls of wine, he's more hungover than Timon.'

'Taggie mustn't get overtired.'

'Shelagh'll keep an eye on her.'

The players were knocked out to find the twenty-mile

road to Cotchester teeming with more cheering fans, people hanging out of cottage windows waving flags, calling out players' names and singing 'Campbell-Black Beauty'. The sun looked pretty good in England too.

Ludo, back in the Cotswolds, had dropped in on the Griefyard, where he found little Mary tending and crying over Wilfie's grave.

'I've just received a text from Rosalie Parkinson,' she told Ludo, 'telling me to go and clean her house and boutique and fill them with flowers, because she and Parks are expecting a mass of press.'

'Tell her to eff off,' said Ludo. 'For ever.'

'And I don't know what to put on Wilfie's headstone.'

' "Fastest, sweetest boy", for a start,' laughed Ludo, then, drawing her into his arms: 'I'm giving up being a pundit. How would you like to abandon shit Dougie and move in with a manager who truly loves you and would like to sign you up for the next thousand years? Let's go and welcome home Searston.'

'Oh, yes please,' gasped Mary.

73

As the coach travelled along the top road, Deep Woods could be seen in the valley below.

'Look,' shouted Bastian, 'the whole pitch is covered in placards and posters.'

'Saying "Fanks Rupert, fanks Feral",' cried Dolphy, '"fanks Elijah, fanks Griffy" and, goodness, one saying "Fanks Dolphy" – that's nice.'

'Bloody isn't,' exploded Rupert. 'Those posters are merely covering the fact that the pitch has been dug up.'

'Thousands of fans who couldn't get to St Petersburg rolled up there,' explained Eamonn, 'to watch the match on the big screen. The result was a great party – great for bar takings.'

'Good thing we've got until pre-season to get the pitch sorted,' said Rupert. 'Any news of Madison? Her children are still in St Petersburg with Elijah's parents.'

'She's left,' Eamonn told Rupert.

'Left-wing or left home?'

'Both. Although she'll probably come rushing home now Elijah's such a star.'

'He'll need all your bouncer skills to chuck her out.'

Rupert was seriously worried. Since they'd landed, he'd repeatedly tried calling Taggie, but she wasn't picking up. Perhaps she'd been so devastated by her test results that she couldn't bear to tell him. Nor could he get any answer from anyone at Penscombe.

'Where the hell are we going?' he demanded as the coach entered the outskirts of Cotchester, with even more crowds lining the route, hanging from scaffolding, shouting from the windows of ancient houses. 'I said I wanted to go to Deep Woods, then back to the yard. I need to find Taggie. Turn the coach around.'

'Just want to show you something in the Market Square first,' said Eamonn.

'I hate the Market Square. They hung me from a gibbet there the other day.'

'I know, I pulled it down.'

'I'd rather be hungover than hung up.'

To the right soared Cotchester cathedral, its great bell striking five o'clock, the shadow of its spire lying across the town and the water meadows beyond, which now were also covered by cheering crowds.

'Taggie and I got married there. Where the fuck is she? She's still not picking up. If you don't take me home, you can look for another job. We've still got to thank the ground staff.'

But, to the amusement of the players behind them, Eamonn ignored Rupert and swung the coach right towards the Market Square, making even slower progress as green-and-blue-clad crowds spilled on to the pavement, pointing out favourites: 'There's Ahmed, there's Josef, there's Ezra.'

A huge banner lay across the road, saying 'Champions League Winners', as they entered a packed Market

Square, and there, rising out of the crowd, was the sculpture of Charles I, who'd been dressed in a green-and-blue Searston shirt, astride his horse, who was wearing a green-and-blue rug.

'Look, look,' cried Dora, 'there's Taggie and Banquo and the Jack Russells.'

Next moment, Josef had leapt out of the still-moving coach into Louisie's arms, followed by Dora hurtling towards Paris and Buddyguard, and Ahmed towards Harmony. Then Tilly and Minnie and Mildred the mongrel, who'd been staying with Shelagh and Eamonn, rushed joyfully up to Griffy and Tember, saying: 'Gabby and Ally so wanted to come but they're revising for exams tomorrow.'

They were followed by Feral, jumping out to embrace Bianca, then catching sight of his mother and hugging her joyfully but gently, because she was proudly cradling baby Teddy in her arms.

'Mum,' he yelled, 'how did you get here? You look fantastic.'

'She gatecrashed our party last night,' giggled Bianca.

'And discovered the loveliest grandkid in the world,' cried Nancy, dropping a kiss on Teddy's dark head.

Meanwhile, another Grandkid, held on a lead by Shelagh, slipped his collar and shot forward, flashing his silly toothy grin at Dolphy, nudging him, whimpering with joy.

'Hello, young man's dog,' said Elijah, crouching down to stroke him.

Rupert, patting his own dogs, was also reeling with relief to see Taggie in a blue-and-green-striped Searston shirt, looking so well and happy. Drawing her trembling body into his arms, he stammered: 'Any test results yet?'

'I have.' Taggie beamed up at him. 'They said I'm doing amazingly well. They'll have to do the occasional future test just to check, but I've been given the all-clear. I'm cancer-free.'

'Oh my God.' Rupert shut his eyes in ecstasy. 'Oh my angel, thank God.' Then, trying to make himself heard over the uproar: 'I've been trying to get you all day.'

He was about to kiss her, when he was interrupted by Sapphire grabbing his hand:

'Put Granny down, Grandpa, we've got a lovely surprise for you.'

'Look, Rupert.' Taggie's voice broke as she pointed to some blue and green screens, 30 yards away on the other side of the square. Triggering gasps of amazement as they were drawn back, they revealed a second sculpture of a man, in showjumping kit, his cap tipped over his nose, astride a beautiful stallion with a long flowing mane and tail.

'Christ, it's Love Rat.' Rupert had fought his way across the square in a trice, stroking the horse, fingering his mane and tail, walking joyfully around him, touching his powerful neck. 'It IS Love Rat.' Rupert was fighting back the tears. 'It's the most incredible likeness, even his huge dark eyes. It is *so* beautiful.'

'So's the bloke on top,' shouted Ludo.

'It's you, darling,' cried Taggie.

'Christ, so it is,' said Rupert.

'Hi Rupert.' Jupiter Belvedon, Dora's smooth, grey-haired brother, had joined them. 'Glad you like it.'

'It's stunning. Who the hell did it?'

'Dora's and my sister, Emerald. She's been working on it on and off for some months.'

'Love Rat is incredible.'

'She's captured you pretty well, too.'

'Safety's wildly jealous,' confided Taggie. 'He so wanted to be the horse carrying you, but with his one ear and straggly mane, we all felt Love Rat was the better bet, more heroic.'

'I'm sure that's why Safety drank so much red wine last night,' Sapphire told the surging-round crowd. 'He was sulking. My brother Timon's got a hangover too. Love Rat was such a kind horse. Timon and I used to sleep in his box, and I used to ride my trike through his legs.'

'Who organised this?' asked Rupert, who was still stroking Love Rat.

'It was a group effort.' Jupiter Belvedon had grabbed a microphone. 'Ladies and gentlemen and dogs, welcome to Cotchester. This beautiful sculpture has been sculpted by my sister Emerald Belvedon, whose work is admired all over the world. On its plinth will be engraved the words: "In honour of Rupert Campbell-Black: Olympic showjumper, Minister for Sport, owner, breeder and trainer of great racehorses, chairman of Champions League-winning football club Searston Rovers, astride his global leading sire Love Rat. This statue has been erected by admirers in gratitude for the glory Rupert has brought to the Cotswolds."

'As we had to wait until late last night to learn of Searston's epic Champions League victory in St Petersburg,' went on Jupiter, in his deep, plummy voice, 'that event has been added temporarily to the other words on a laser-engraved plaque' – he pointed to the base of the sculpture – 'but will shortly be engraved in stone on the plinth. Well done, Rupert, this is a colossal achievement.' And the square and far beyond erupted in overjoyed applause.

When this died down, Rupert took the microphone.

'Thank you, I am incredibly honoured. I'm sure Love Rat is whickering with delight in heaven.' Then, joking to stop himself breaking down: 'And it's certainly the first time one of my erections has had its own plaque.'

'Rupert, hush,' giggled Taggie.

'But please reserve your gratitude,' Rupert went on, 'for Searston's marvellous manager, Elijah Cohen, and all the Searston players and club and ground staff, who brought even more glory to the Cotswolds with yesterday's match of the century. And I'd particularly like to thank Tember West, Searston's amazing club secretary, who holds the place together and makes everyone feel special, and also to thank my fantastic press officer, Dora Belvedon, who both protects me and spreads the word about the wonder of our club.

'Finally' – Rupert took a deep breath – 'I'd like to raise a toast in loving memory to our boys Angus, Downing, Orion and Wilfie, as well as Marketa and Cadenza, who were tragically assassinated because Craig Eynsham and Jarred Moreland sabotaged my car, thinking I, not them, was travelling in it. May they rest in peace for always.' And, after a long pause, everyone cheered and shouted, 'Hear, hear.'

'Don't cry, Grandpa,' called out Sapphire, taking the mic. 'It's a shame we can't take Love Rat home to Penscombe, but he won't be lonely here, because he's got that king's horse as a husband just across the square.'

'I'm not sure Charles I would fork out Love Rat's hundred-and-fifty-grand stud fee so his horse can have a bit of rumpy-pumpy,' quipped Rupert. And that was why he hadn't been able to get any answer from Penscombe – because most of his yard and stud staff, not to mention

Searston's ground staff, seemed to be present and cheering in the square. He was also delighted to see Ludo locked in an ecstatic embrace with Wilfie's mother, Mary.

'By the way, Rupert' – Jupiter took him aside – 'I haven't sold on your Stubbs of Rupert Black. Your many admirers thought you deserved to keep it. I'll drop it back to you tomorrow.'

Pleased to see how happy this made Rupert, Elijah was stroking Grandkid.

'Such a lovely dog,' he said to Dolphy. 'Shall we walk him home to Buttercup Cottage?'

'Oh yes, please.'

As they set off, hand in hand, across the water meadows, Grandkid took off galloping round and round in a big circle, as though he was still on the racetrack, then returning, wagging ecstatically, he gently took Elijah's other hand in his mouth.

'"So they went forth both, and the young man's dog with them,"' repeated Elijah. 'We're in the Bible.'

'And,' sighed Dolphy, 'wasn't it nice Rupert calling it the match of the century?'

'Lovely,' said Elijah, taking Dolphy in his arms, 'but you and I are the love match of the century.'

74

Despite being reluctant to leave such joyous celebrations in Cotchester, Rupert was glad to get home. He had insisted Dora and Paris drop in for a quick drink on their way back to Pear Tree Cottage, but before they arrived, he had time to pop down to the yard and hug little The Story So Far, whose box was festooned outside with banners celebrating her miraculous victory as the first filly to win the Derby since 1916. Unable to rouse Safety Car, still out cold from a hangover in his box, he nipped down to the animals' graveyard to share his delight with Love Rat.

'You'd be knocked out by your sculpture in the Market Square, old boy.'

Back on the terrace, Rupert rejoiced in the beauty of his valley. The birds, enjoying a warm evening, were singing their heads off. The sun, sinking behind his beech woods on the right, was still gilding the trees opposite in their pale-green summer glory. Many of them were horse chestnuts, flaunting their white candles, as they had done four years ago when he'd come home devastated by the news of Taggie's cancer. Now she looked so radiant as she joined him, carrying glasses and a bottle of champagne.

She was followed by Dora, Paris and Buddyguard, who, ecstatic at having his mistress home, was glued to her side and refused to romp with any of the Penscombe dogs.

'Gossip, gossip, *rivettato*,' cried Dora, waving her iPhone. 'Ryan's been pursuing Lady Emma again, and Hooray Harry was so petrified of having Ryan as a step-father that he arranged for Lady E to have dinner on her birthday with her estranged husband and Harry's father, Sir Ralph, and they ended up in bed together, and, deciding he wanted his land and his house, albeit with a crumbling roof, back again, Ralph's moved back in. So Lady E needn't relinquish her title.'

'So it's back to Squire One,' quipped Paris.

Rupert laughed. 'OK, that's enough about Lady Emma.' He filled up everyone's glasses, then, getting out a sheet of paper, he told them, 'Just sit down and listen for a few minutes. I didn't praise you nearly enough ear-lier, Dora. But I want to thank you for all your flair and hard work, and for supporting me and Searston Rovers through very thick and thin. You fought off the trolls and defended and praised us whenever we looked like going under, and you brought in the crowds by launch-ing Safety Car, Cuthbert and Gilchrist's football demos.'

Rupert patted Gilchrist and, looking down at his notes, continued: 'And you took the piss out of Sir Craig, galvanising the boars so they dug up his pitch at Deansgate, painted "Eynshambolic" all over the stands, filmed Craig shagging Janey Lloyd-Foxe and rescued Buddyguard from dying of heat in a boiling car.'

'I did,' beamed Dora, hugging a wagging Buddyguard.

'If you hadn't tracked down Jarred and discovered he'd sabotaged my car, and then wised up Gablecross so he arrested Sir Craig and the Chief C-word in time, getting yourself horribly beaten up by Sir Craig in the process, before brave Buddy rescued you, they'd certainly have assassinated me by now. And I know you're working to help Alphonso the pilot to bring his family over from South America.

'I've also spoken to Jackie Carslake,' added Rupert, 'and I know how you've revved up the *Cotchester Times*. And I bet you had more than a hand in the sculpture of me and Love Rat in the Market Square, and me getting the Stubbs back. *In toto*' – he smiled at her fondly – 'you are an utterly brilliant press officer.'

'Gosh,' stammered Dora. 'I cannot believe this.'

'We can,' cried Taggie.

'And I've witnessed it,' said Paris.

'Also, ginger pussy Mew-Too and Buddyguard are both "rescues",' added Rupert, 'to use a nauseating phrase.'

'So am I,' grinned Paris, putting a hand on Dora's shaking shoulders. 'Dora rescued me.'

'And rescues need the security of their own home,' went on Rupert, 'so, as a reward for you guarding us all, I want to give you and Paris Pear Tree Cottage, and an acre or three around it, as a present.'

'You can't,' stuttered Dora. 'I've got the best job in the world and I wake up excited every morning and you've let me bury darling Cadbury in your graveyard, and you've let us live rent-free in Pear Tree Cottage.'

'And now it's your very own home.' Taggie went over and hugged Dora. 'We love you and Paris, and we want you to always live near us.'

Dora shook her head and wiped her eyes with her sleeve.

'I just don't know what to say.'

'That'll be a first,' said Rupert, and everyone laughed.

'I can't begin to thank you,' went on Dora, 'but you mustn't give us so much. Even with the Champions League dosh and Story's win, you've still forked out millions for all the dependants of the people who died in the crash.'

'Maybe not.' Rupert produced another sheet of paper. 'I've had an interesting email from Lady Grace:

' "Dear Rupert – may I?" ' he read out, adding, 'No, you bloody mayn't.' Then, putting on a very refined voice: ' "Congratulations on winnin' the Champions League with a tragically reduced team. I want to sincerely apologise for so many players passin' away because of hubby Sir Craig interferin' in your vehicle. I'm aware that you've graciously compensated their familees. But whatever the results of the court case, I will still be a wealthee laydee." '

'You really should take up acting, Rupert,' said Paris, wiping away tears of laughter.

'Don't interrupt,' ordered Rupert and continued, ' "And I would like to take over all these debts from you. So when you return to Britain, why not pop over to Deansgate Manor for a few noggins and a spot of luncheon, and we can discuss things. Yours very sincerelee, Lady Grace." '

'Wow,' gasped Dora. 'She's always had the hots for you. Let's bleed her white.'

'I've already forked out for the dependants,' said Rupert, taking a slug of champagne, 'except for little

Wilfie's bastard father, Dougie, who never stops nagging the office for his own share.'

'I've got the answer.' Dora clapped her hands in ecstasy. 'Send Dougie Bradford over to Lady Grace. They're made for each other. They can enjoy snoggin' over endless noggins and the BBC can record it as *Mis-Match of the Day*.'

'We must go,' said Paris, taking her hand. 'Neither Dora nor I have any idea how to thank you for giving us Pear Tree Cottage. We're just so lucky.'

'We must go back and break the incredible news to Mew-Too,' cried Dora, hugging Taggie then Rupert. 'And catch *Hudson & Rex* in time for Buddyguard. All I can say is I'm a very, very im-pressed officer.'

After they'd gone, Taggie hugged Rupert.

'That was one of the loveliest things you've ever done, darling.'

'No, the loveliest thing I ever did was marrying you,' said Rupert, adding, after a long and loving kiss, 'and could you possibly find some Alka-Seltzer for Safety Car?'

Acknowledgements

Having finished my last novel on flat racing in 2016, I was casting around for a new subject. I then had a lovely lunch sitting next to the mighty former Manchester United manager Sir Alex Ferguson, who I found so charming, modest, witty, wise and inspirational that I decided to set the novel in the world of football and call it *Tackle!*

As a football ignoramus who still can't recognise offside, I then had a lot to learn. Sir Alex apart, other megastars who helped and inspired me included Alan Curbishley, former great player and manager of Charlton and West Ham, and author of brilliant books *Game Changers* and *Valley of Dreams*.

Oli Christie, entrepreneur and founder of Neon Play, then introduced me to Rupert Lowe, ex-chairman of Southampton FC, and Chris Wright CBE, co-founder of Chrysalis Records, lifelong sports fanatic and former owner of Queens Park Rangers FC, who were both electrifying on the travails of masterminding a football club. More stories of football politics were provided by the former QPR chairman Nick Blackburn, and super solicitor Steven Barker.

It was also a great thrill to meet Richard Scudamore, former executive chairman of Premier League football, and to become friends with my wonderful neighbour Tony Adams, Arsenal and England legend, author and now dancer, and his adorable wife, Poppy.

I am incredibly lucky that my dear son-in-law, Adam Tarrant, works for the League Managers Association and took me up to St George's Park, the national football centre in Staffordshire, to meet Howard Wilkinson, the last English manager to win the former top English league, the First Division, in the 1991–2 season with Leeds United. Now chairman of the League Managers Association, Howard spent the day showing me around and, as a thrill, introduced me to England manager Gareth Southgate, who many years later incredibly kindly sent me a framed, signed England shirt, wishing me happy birthday and congratulating me on finishing *Tackle!*

The list goes on – another treat was my delightful friend, former home secretary Michael Howard, the Rt Hon. Lord Howard of Lympne CH KC, taking me to a great match at Liverpool, where I met the revered Steven Gerrard. I must also thank lovely, larky Lord Johnny Astor of Hever for introducing me to another megastar, Sir Hugh Robertson KCMG DL, former Minister for Sport and for the Olympics.

I was also incredibly touched that John and Carolyn Radford invited me to a super lunch and match at Mansfield Town FC, when the Stags were playing at home, and sent a helicopter to collect me.

On my travels, I also met the great Sir Kenny Dalglish and his gorgeous wife, Marina.

Most of these luminaries were incredibly busy and nobly answered my endless questions, but, as *Tackle!* is fiction, I only followed their advice where it suited my plot and the end product is in no way a reflection of their expertise.

I am incredibly fortunate, too, that my local football club in Gloucestershire, Forest Green Rovers, is one of the most beautiful in the country. Ravishingly rural, it is surrounded by woods, rolling hills and meadows full of grazing sheep. Owned by eco warrior, climate change campaigner and founder of Ecotricity, Dale Vince OBE, it is the only vegan club in the world, with a pitch kept emerald green by rainwater and a solar-powered robot lawnmower.

Way back in 2016, I started going to matches there, watching training sessions, enjoying delectable vegan food, getting to know players and their wives and the ground staff. I also travelled up to Wembley to witness two nail-biting play-off finals, experiencing delirious happiness after the second trip ended in victory against Tranmere Rovers FC.

People I have particularly to thank at Forest Green Rovers are former CEOs Henry Staelens and Helen Taylor, former press officer and pitch announcer Richard Joyce, former club secretary James Mooney, managers Scott Bartlett, Mark Cooper and Rob Edwards, commercial manager Paula Brown and her team, and Richard and Tracey Burge, who masterminded the Directors' Lounge, ensuring visitors were made very welcome. Here I met ex-FGR director and Stroud's much-loved ex-MP David Drew and his wife, Ann, who knits amazing striped socks.

As I live locally, I got to know many of the players, James Norwood, Sam Russell and later captain Joseph Mills and his sweet wife, Amy.

Three of the star players who particularly inspired me were the dazzlingly fleet-footed Keanu Marsh-Brown, handsome Aarran Racine, whose seventeenth-century ancestor was France's greatest playwright, and glorious, gladiatorial Jon Parkin, nicknamed 'The Beast' and favourite of the fans, who used to chant, 'Feed the Beast and he will score.'

This led to a huge share of my gratitude going to David Clayton, marvellous senior news reporter and journalist at Manchester City and author of countless wonderful books. David also helped Jon Parkin write his autobiography, *Feed the Beast*, to which I was honoured to write the foreword. David consequently has become a great friend, always available to answer questions, reading *Tackle!* and pointing out factual errors, and bringing his lovely family down from Cheshire to visit me.

Back in 2016, I was also honoured to be asked to write another foreword, to *The Rise of Forest Green Rovers: The Road to Wembley*, by club supporter Chris Gardner.

People in football tend to change their jobs so often that if I had included their CVs, these acknowledgements would be longer than the Bible, so I've tended just to add the position they were holding when I met them.

Besides Forest Green Rovers and Manchester City, another favourite club was Reading FC; I enjoyed another trip to Wembley, to see them play against Huddersfield, with their charming co-chairman Sir John Madejski, OBE, DL, who has become another great friend. Devoted to Reading FC, he hosts the most riotous and delectable lunch parties in the boardroom before matches. I was also privileged to be shown at length around the club by the stadium manager, Ray Booth, and advised on background detail by their brilliant club secretary, Sue Hewett.

Another great chunk of gratitude must go to the divine, dazzlingly glamorous sports journalist Hayley Mortimer, who previously worked at the *Stroud News & Journal* and *The Citizen* before moving on to make documentaries for the BBC. Hayley regaled me with endless stories of behind-the-scenes football shenanigans and naughty behaviour.

The writing of *Tackle!* was rolling merrily along with the end in sight. Then, in March 2020, Covid and the pandemic lockdown struck. As a writer, I find it crucial to witness events that I'm writing about, which was impossible as everywhere closed down and my world became my own house, with no matches to watch or football people to chat to.

As a result, *Tackle!* only covers the years from 2016 to late spring 2020, and therefore doesn't include Covid or the tragic invasion of Ukraine by Russia, VAR or women's football. But again, because it's fiction, events that occurred later may have slipped into the story.

Covid, however, did give me the time to read some marvellous football books – *One Way or Another* by the aforementioned Chris Wright, *Broken Dreams* by Tom Bower, *The Deal* by Jon Smith, *Sober* by Tony Adams, *Manchester Stories* by David Clayton, *Quiet Genius* by Ian Herbert, everything by the hilarious Secret Footballer, and especially the utterly brilliant *Does Your Rabbi Know You're Here?* by Anthony Clavane, about Jewish involvement in football, which helped me hugely with creating my Jewish hero, Elijah.

The beautiful game produces beautiful writers. Journalists do not automatically expect kindness from their own profession, but no one could have been more helpful than titans Oliver Holt and Ian Herbert from the *Mail* and Jonathan Northcroft and David Walsh from the *Sunday Times*. Local journalists who supported me include Ashley Loveridge, Ben Falconer, Vicky Temple, Rachel Wyse of Sky Sports, Jenny Ashwood, Sue Smith and Rob Iles.

I'd also like to thank The Ivy in both London and Cheltenham, the Wheatsheaf at Northleach and my own local, the Bear Inn at Bisley, for providing such glorious food and drink when so many of my meetings with people in football took place there.

Thanks are also due to Phil Bradley, Paul Groves, Wonky's Wheels – led by Wonky and his super team – and my own son, Felix, for driving me miles to matches and interviews and beguiling me with football gossip.

Thanks, in addition, to my football-loving friends David Wintle and his cousin Chris Wintle, Rollo Chad, Freddie Miles and Harry Luard.

Meanwhile, my dear friend Brigadier Andrew Parker Bowles OBE was epic on racing, which forms a large part of the plot, and another friend, Simon McMurtrie, gave me inspired intellectual support with my story. Mark Richards helped me on explosives; sports massage therapist Sarah Clatworthy, my hairdresser, Jill Reay, and my bookkeeper, Mandy Williams, all advised me wisely on cancer; while Lady Annabel Goldsmith, Dr Mary Jane Fox and Judy Zatonski provided me with magical tales about dogs and comforted me when my darling greyhound, Bluebell, died in 2021.

Tackle! took a very long time to write and, in the fourteen months after it was delivered in 2022, to massively rewrite. I'd therefore like to thank my publishers, Transworld, and particularly managing director Larry Finlay and chief editor Sally Williamson for their help and perseverance in coping with my sulks as I tried to meet their requests to hugely change the story. I'm particularly grateful to publicity director Patsy Irwin and her ace department for keeping in touch, and to my former editor, Linda Evans, and former agent, Vivienne Schuster, for their advice after reading the synopsis.

In addition, I am blessed to have a marvellous and charismatic literary agent, Felicity Blunt at Curtis Brown, who is also a best friend, who inspires and protects me and curbs my cross-patchery!

I would also like to thank Felicity's assistants, Rosie Pierce and Flo Sandelson, for their very helpful comments on the manuscript and overall kindness throughout.

I am also extremely lucky to have the wise and wonderful team at Weatherbys Bank to safeguard my finances.

This must be the longest thank-you letter I've ever written but, to my shame, I additionally took down the telephone numbers of so many people and never followed them up – for this I apologise, and even more to anyone who has helped me whom I haven't acknowledged. Thank you all.

Tackle! is a long book, so consequently another lioness's debt of gratitude must go to heroine Celia Mackie, for deciphering my horrendous handwriting, typing the manuscript, and saying kind things when I desperately needed them.

I also have a miraculous home team. I cannot exaggerate how much my life is enhanced and protected by the huge industry, flair, wisdom, sweetness and incredible memory of Amanda Butler, who spreads happiness wherever she goes. In Amanda's case, PA stands for Perennially Adorable.

Amanda also has an enchanting husband, Phil Butler, who produces magical musical CDs to cheer and personally inspire me, one of which consisted entirely of football anthems.

Nor could my books ever be written without my lovely housekeeper of forty years, Ann Mills, and sweet Judith Ford, who joined me more recently, who stoically muck out my house and restore it to order and beauty.

Huge thanks to dear Julie Laws and Carol Forbes-Boulter, who stay overnight on alternate fortnights, provide me with suppers worthy of Escoffier, and stoically endure watching football matches on television instead of *Lewis* and *The Good Wife*.

More thanks must go to Bryn Jones, David Apps and Mick Mills for tending my garden and preventing it from disappearing under tidal waves of wild garlic.

My own family have been beyond reproach. They include my stepdaughter, Laura Cooper, and her Chelsea-mad supporter son, Kit.

While down in Gloucestershire, my son, Felix Cooper, his wife, Edwina, and their daughters, Scarlett and Sienna, my daughter, Emily, her husband, Adam Tarrant, and their three sons, Jago, Lysander and Acer, have once again provided their essential mixture of huge love, fantastic copy and good cheer.

Finally, I'd like to thank footballers everywhere. People continually moan that they are paid too much, but I think they deserve every penny for the pleasure and excitement they bring to the world. A bad defeat may cast their fans into a week's black gloom, but this will be transformed into a week's euphoria after a good win. God bless them all.

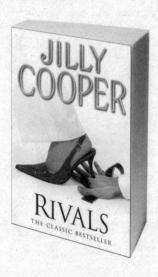

Into the cut-throat world of Corinium television comes Declan O'Hara, a mega-star of great glamour and integrity with a radiant feckless wife, a handsome son and two ravishing teenage daughters. Living rather too closely across the valley is Rupert Campbell-Black, divorced and as dissolute as ever, and now the Tory Minister for Sport.

Declan needs only a few days at Corinium to realize that the Managing Director, Lord Baddingham, is a crook who has recruited him merely to help retain the franchise for Corinium. Baddingham has also enticed Cameron Cook, a gorgeous but domineering woman executive, to produce Declan's programme. Declan and Cameron detest each other, provoking a storm of controversy into which Rupert plunges with his usual abandon.

As a rival group emerges to pitch for the franchise, reputations ripen and decline, true love blossoms and burns, marriages are made and shattered, and sex raises its (delicious) head at almost every throw as, in bed and boardroom, the race is on to capture the Cotswold Crown.

Soon to be an exciting new original series, streaming exclusively on Disney+

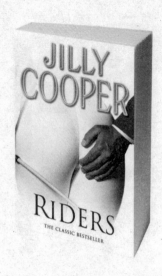

Brooding hero Jake Lovell, under whose magic hands even the most difficult horse or woman is charmed, is driven by his loathing of the dashing darling of the show ring, Rupert Campbell-Black. Having pinched each other's horses and drunk their way around the capitals of Europe, the feud between the two men finally erupts with devastating consequences at the Los Angeles Olympics . . .

A classic bestseller, Riders *takes the lid off international show jumping, a sport where the brave horses are almost human, but the humans behave like animals.*

'Sex and horses: who could ask for more?'
Sunday Telegraph

'Blockbusting fiction at its best'
Mail on Sunday

'A delight from start to finish'
Daily Mail

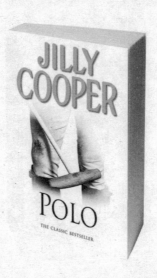

Ricky France-Lynch is moody, macho, and magnificent. He had a large crumbling estate, a nine-goal polo handicap, and a beautiful wife who was fair game for anyone with a cheque book. He also had the adoration of fourteen-year-old Perdita MacLeod. Perdita couldn't wait to leave her dreary school and become a polo player. The polo set were ritzy, wild, and gloriously promiscuous. Perdita thought she'd get along with them very well.

But before she had time to grow up, Ricky's life exploded into tragedy, and Perdita turned into a brat who loved only her horses – and Ricky France-Lynch.

Ricky's obsession to win back his wife, and Perdita's to win both Ricky and a place as a top class polo player, take the reader on a wildly exciting journey – to the estancias of Argentina, to Palm Beach and Deauville, and on to the royal polo fields of England and the glamorous pitches of California where the most heroic battle of all is destined to be fought – a match that is about far more than just the winning of a huge silver cup . . .

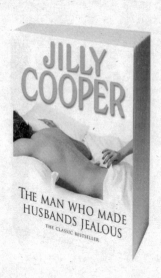

Lysander Hawkley combined breathtaking good looks with
the kindest of hearts. He couldn't pass a stray dog, an
ill-treated horse or a neglected wife without rushing to the
rescue. And with neglected wives the rescue invariably led to
ecstatic bonking, which didn't please their erring husbands
one bit.

Lysander's mid-life crisis had begun at twenty-two. Reeling
from the death of his beautiful mother, he was out of work,
drinking too much and desperately in debt. The solution
came from Ferdie, his fat, fast-operating friend: if Lysander
was so good at making husbands jealous, why shouldn't he
get paid for it?

Let loose among the neglected wives of the ritzy county
of Rutshire, Lysander causes absolute havoc. But it is
only when he meets Rannaldini, Rutshire's King Rat and
a temperamental, fiendishly promiscuous international
conductor, that the trouble really starts. The only
unglamorous woman around Rannaldini is Kitty, his plump
young wife who runs his life like clockwork. Soon Lysander
is convinced that Kitty must be rescued from Rannaldini at
all costs, even if it means enlisting the help of the old
blue-eyed havoc maker: Rupert Campbell-Black.

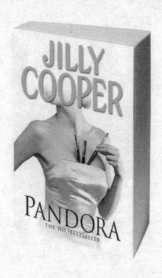

No picture ever came more beautiful than Raphael's Pandora. Discovered by a dashing young lieutenant, Raymond Kelvedon in a Normandy Chateau in 1944, she had cast her spell over his family – all artists and dealers – for fifty years. Hanging in a turret of their lovely Cotswold house, Pandora witnessed Raymond's tempestuous wife Galena both entertaining a string of lovers, and giving birth to her four children: Jupiter, Alizarin, Jonathan and superbrat Sienna. Then an exquisite stranger rolls up, claiming to be a long-lost daughter of the family, setting the three Belvedon brothers at each other's throats. Accompanying her is her fatally glamorous boyfriend, whose very different agenda includes an unhealthy interest in the Raphael.

During a fireworks party, the painting is stolen. The hunt to retrieve it takes the reader on a thrilling journey to Vienna, Geneva, Paris, New York and London. After a nail-biting court case and a record-smashing Old Masters sale at Sotheby's, passionate love triumphs and Pandora is restored to her rightful home.

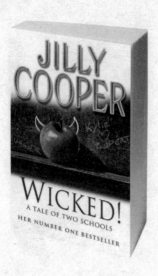

At Bagley Hall, a notoriously wild, but increasingly academic, independent, crammed with the children of the famous, trouble is afoot. The ambitious and fatally attractive headmaster, Hengist Brett-Taylor, hatches a plan to share the facilities of his school with Larkminster Comprehensive – known locally, as 'Larks'.

His reasons for doing so are purely financial, but he is encouraged by the opportunities the scheme gives him for frequent meetings with Janna Curtis, the dynamic new head of Larks, who has been drafted in to save what is a fast-sinking school from closure. Janna is young, pretty, enthusiastic and vastly brave – and she will do anything to rescue her demoralised, run-down and cash-strapped school.

Neither parents nor staff of either school are too keen on this radical move, although some can see the possible financial advantages. For the students, however, it offers great opportunities to get up to even more mayhem than usual.

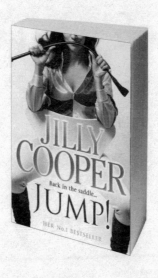

Etta Bancroft – sweet, kind, still beautiful – adores racing and harbours a crush on one of its stars, the handsome high-handed owner-trainer Rupert Campbell-Black. When her bullying husband dies, Etta's selfish, ambitious children drag her from her lovely Dorset house to live in a hideous modern bungalow in the Cotswold village of Willowwood.

Etta's life is transformed when she finds a horribly mutilated filly wandering in the woods. She names her Mrs Wilkinson and nurses her back to health. The filly charms everyone in the village, and when tests reveal her to be a spectacularly well-bred racehorse a village syndicate is formed to put the filly into training.

Captivating vast crowds as she progresses from point-to-point to major races, she brings fame and fortune to the syndicate, until, at last, she is entered in the greatest jump race of them all. Can Mrs Wilkinson win the Grand National? And can Etta gain her heart's desire?

Rupert Campbell-Black is back...

Mount!

The Sunday Times No.1 bestseller

Jilly Cooper

Rupert is consumed by one obsession: that Love Rat, his adored grey horse, be proclaimed champion stallion. He longs to trounce Roberto's Revenge, the stallion owned by his detested rival Cosmo Rannaldini, which means abandoning his racing empire at Penscombe and his darling wife Taggie, and chasing winners in the richest races worldwide, from Dubai to Los Angeles to Melbourne.

Luckily, the fort at home is held by Rupert's assistant Gav, a genius with horses, fancied by every stable lass, but damaged by alcoholism and a vile wife. When Gala, a grieving but ravishing Zimbabwean widow moves to Penscombe as carer for Rupert's wayward father, it is not just Gav who is attracted to her: a returning Rupert finds himself dangerously tempted.

Gala adores horses, and when she switches to working in the yard, her carer's job is taken by a devastatingly handsome South African man who claims to be gay but seems far keener on caring for the angelic Taggie. And as increasingly sinister acts of sabotage strike at Penscombe, the game of musical loose boxes gathers apace . . .